Microchip
The Agenda is Now

Chey Barnes

Day Owl Press Corp Publishers

Copyright © 2015 by Chey Barnes

Cover Illustration Copyright © 2015 by Day Owl Press Corp. Cover design by Day Owl Press Corp.

For permission requests, write to the publisher, addressed "Attention: Permissions Coordinator," at office@dayowl.net

Printed in the United States of America
First Printing, 2015

Cataloging Information:

Barnes, Chey.

    Microchip - The Agenda is Now / by Chey Barnes.
    413 pages cm
    Includes bibliographical references.
    ISBN 978-1-940401-68-3
    ISBN 978-1-940401-63-8
    ISBN 978-1-940401-67-6
    ISBN 978-1-940401-66-9
    ISBN 978-1-940401-64-5

    1. Dystopias--Fiction. 2. Computer science--Fiction.
    3. Integrated circuits--Fiction. 4. Science fiction.
    5. Suspense fiction. I. Title.

PS3602.A775635M53   2013   813'.6
              QBI13-600154

Ordering Information:

Quantity sales: Special discounts are available on quantity purchases by corporations, associations, and others. For details, contact the publisher at the address above.

Orders by U.S. trade bookstores and wholesalers visit www.dayowl.net

"All that is necessary for the triumph of evil is that good men do nothing."

Edmund Burke

Prologue

Winthrop Shaw called for a meeting that was out of the ordinary. It was to be at the Bohemian Grove and include only the highest-ranking members of the Trilateral Commission, the Pinay Circle and the Bilderberg Group. This was a private affair, not meant for the eyes of the other top decision-making committees. The secret session was to take place two weeks before the Global Union's annual assembly and was to be discussed by no one prior to the meeting. At that time, Shaw would unveil his master plan to the general assembly. In the meantime, he wanted to make arrangements and strategize with his closest confidants.

He prepared by directing his personal assistant, Nelson Thurn, to draw up a summary outlining the points of the covert meeting. Notifications were hand-delivered to a few select individuals by a vetted courier, and the paper notifications were destroyed once the recipients received their message. Soon the meeting would take place, and everything would go precisely as planned.

Chapter *1*

A Secret Gathering

The evening of the furtive gathering, the guests were admitted by Nelson Thurn, who guided them through a majestic marble rotunda into the den, where a toasty fire was crackling in the fireplace. Fine art and Renaissance tapestries from Old World masters covered the walls, and antique Oriental rugs gave the dark room a slightly musty smell. An unused billiards table and a mahogany bar consumed a large portion of the room.

As the men arrived, each was offered cognac or sherry in crystal decanters held by a waiter dressed in white tails. Shaw greeted each by his first name and positioned himself at the head of the room; seated next to him in a high-backed, red leather chair was the Czar of the Global Union, Devin Rothfeller.

Most of the 15 influential men had come from very far away to be there, and each present was among the most powerful in the world. These were the men who determined all world policy; they decided when and where wars would break out and their outcomes, who would lend the money to support each war, and who would lend the money to rebuild the destroyed countries. They owned the central banks and controlled the Federal Reserve, determining discount rates, prime rates and money supply; and dictated which countries would receive loans to be guaranteed by their taxpayers. They regulated wages and salaries all over the world, shipping production to the cheapest countries and importing the best technicians from depressed countries.

These were the men who determined which candidates would be allowed to run for such offices as president, prime minister and chancellor and also whom they would appoint to be simple dictators. They manipulated the financial markets, running exchanges either up or down, and most recently declared martial law after initiating a worldwide stock, currency and banking collapse in order to institute new measures to their liking.

"Thank you, gentlemen, for coming on such short notice," began Shaw to the intimate gathering. "As you know, the annual Global Union Assembly will be on the 15th of this month. I am going to share with you in advance some of the edicts that will be issued at that meeting and also address some very dramatic adjustments that we will not be sharing with the general assembly."

Shaw produced his notes and cleared his throat. "The time has come, my friends, for drastic change." His blue eyes blazed in the dimly lit room. "The stage is now finally set to implement our grand plan. Last year's international banking collapse is quickly leading us to our goal of one world standardized bank and the New Global Union.

"Each one of you here already is well aware of the progress we have made in the grouping of nations into one centralized governing entity. Many years of hard work have led us to the successful integration of 18 European countries into the European Economic Community; the convergence of African nations and the Middle East into the African Council; the merge of 16 sovereign Pacific Rim nations into the Asia Pacific Economic Cooperation; and the Slavic nations' combination from 32 countries which have been absorbed into the European Union. All that is left to finish now is the Council of the Americas. We will expand the North American Free Trade Agreement this year to include the Caribbean, Central and South American countries, and our vision of the New World Order will be complete in approximately 18 months." The 15 power brokers murmured softly among themselves at this disclosure.

"Now on to centralized banking: We have successfully integrated the European Central Bank, the World Bank, the Fed, the International Monetary Fund, and the BIS into one entity that has seized the assets of all the remaining individual banks worldwide. The amalgamated banks are converging into one as we speak, and the one new global bank is now officially known as the World Central Reserve."

This was what they had all been waiting for. The anticipated news was met with looks of satisfaction, and congratulations were passed throughout the room as Thurn distributed the banking prospectus to the room of finance magnates.

"This is the perfect time to obliterate the outdated paper, checking, credit card and NFC reader systems and launch the new WCR Microchip; Nelson, if you would, please." Thurn left the room momentarily and reentered with a shiny aluminum box, which he handed to Shaw. He theatrically opened the box and presented a tiny metallic appendage, shaped like a grain of rice but smaller, sitting on a blue velvet display pad. Shaw handed the box with its contents to the first plutocrat to his right. The man examined the tiny chip, and then passed it on to the man seated next to him.

"This chip, gentlemen, is the first prototype of the one that we will be introducing to the populace beginning next month. It's a passive biochip transponder so it requires no battery, nor are there parts to wear out. It has a 160-year life span and requires no maintenance.

A simple device, really, the bio chip transponder itself consists of just four parts: a capacitor, an antenna coil, the capsule and, of course, the IC chip. The chip is actually the smallest component of the overall design, about the size of a grain of sand; the antenna and capacitor take up most of the space. You'll notice that each end of the chip has a white tip; this is an anti-migration coating. It encourages tissue growth so the chip won't move around inside the recipient's body." Shaw kept a close eye on the chip as it was passed from hand to hand. He continued on.

"This particular model is vastly improved over the previous ones and holds 30,000 gigabytes more information in a tinier amount of space. It not only contains the recipient's entire profile but also his or her DNA genotype, human leukocyte antigen and a clone image of an iris scan of the eye. He lifted a new paper and began reading off a list.

"It contains every detail about the subject's life, including his date of birth, Social Security number, current address, physical description, fingerprints, banking information, photo, prior residences, criminal record, credit rating, credit report, military record, recent purchases, Internet surfing history, marital status, and information on children, family genealogy, siblings and parents. It list all assets and debts, mortgages, deeds, club registries and memberships, medical records, meetings records such as Alcoholics Anonymous, library records, favorite subjects, hobbies, vehicle registration, driving record, insurance information, profession, salary, tax records and purchasing patterns.

"Virtually any information available about a person can be hardcoded on this single chip but the chip also transmits to a series of databanks in our cloud that have the ability to store unlimited amounts of data. And ..." Shaw looked up from his paper, amusement in his eyes ... "the chip also sends coordinates to our Global Positioning System that can track any person's location at any time and from anywhere on the entire planet." One of the bankers let out a low whistle of respect for the range of information held in such a tiny chip. "As you know," he continued, "a compulsory micro-chipping program has been in the in developmental stages for quite some time; we may now do away with the voluntary bio-chipping program of the past several years and begin enforcement of a new mandatory policy. With this chip in place, we will be able to monitor every financial transaction taking place in the entire world, billions of transactions per second. Nothing will escape our notice – nothing! Further, there will be no need to worry about political dissent or uprisings; for the masses will be held firmly under our control."

The men in the room buzzed with excitement at the range of possibilities the future held in store.

"The chip is easily injected into the body just under the skin," he explained while unwrapping a plastic injector. "It is a relatively painless procedure. Would anyone here like to see a demonstration?" Several hands in the room went up.

"I will need a volunteer." All hands went down.

"Nelson, I need you to come here and show these fine gentlemen how easy this is," Shaw ordered his assistant Thurn. He came forward and extended his arm to Shaw, who took his wrist, turned it up and quickly injected the chip beneath the round, fleshy portion of his right hand, just below the thumb. The injection caused Thurn to wince slightly; he rubbed his wrist and examined the spot, then turned to the gathered members and held out his hand for them to have a look. There was little sign of trauma, no trace of bleeding; only a tiny welt had risen.

"The chip I injected into Nelson Thurn was a blank; there is no need for us to hold Nelson firmly under our control ... he already is," Shaw quipped. The men in the room guffawed at the wisecrack made at Thurn's expense, and Shaw took pleasure in watching from the corner of his eye as Thurn squirmed uncomfortably under the scrutiny.

"And now on to a controversial subject," he continued. "As you know, the world's population is quickly approaching the 10 billion mark; it is estimated that we will reach that figure this upcoming year. It has long been the view of this consortium that the Earth simply cannot sustain such a massive encumbrance and efforts must be made to contain the problem. The chip will help us in our endeavors to segregate the masses into suitable groupings so we may determine the best course of action at a later date. This subject will be discussed further at our next meeting, which is scheduled six months from today." He turned and looked at Rothfeller, who acknowledged his approval with a nod.

Shaw wrapped up his discourse by inviting his comrades' comments and questions, after which he and his associates conversed well into the night.

After the meeting wrapped up and each man was escorted from Bohemian Grove, Thurn met with Shaw in the emptied den.

"I'm at a bit of a loss as to how we are going to get the public to accept this chip without revolts springing up left and right," Thurn warned his superior.

"That's all taken care of, Nelson; don't worry yourself about it."

"Well, sir, it seems unlikely that they will just line up for an injection without some sort of insurgency," Thurn argued.

This remark was met with stony silence.

"Sir, have you thought about this problem?"

It would be entirely too easy to drive all of America to its knees, thought Shaw to himself. *A well-placed electromagnetic pulse bomb would temporarily paralyze the national power grid, sending the masses into widespread panic. Just a few days without communications or electricity ... when the lights finally do come on, they'll collapse all over themselves. And this is just one of many different methods. Yes, just one small method indeed.*

"Sir? Can you hear me, sir?"

Shaw glared at Thurn. "OK, Nelson, if you must know, the public will be more than delighted to be receiving their chip."

"Really? Why is that?"

Shaw carefully considered the information he was about to reveal to his close assistant and replied with a question.

"Have you ever heard of the septum pellucidum?"

Chapter 2

Ten Billion

The year's annual Global Union Assembly was hosted in Frankfurt, Germany, by the heads of the European Central Bank. Invitees were the usual representatives for the Royal Institute of International Affairs, the International Monetary Fund, the Carlyle Group, the Bilderbergs, the Council on Foreign Relations and of course, the Trilateral Commission. This was an exclusory, private event for delegates only; the press was absolutely barred. Attendees were checked at the door for recording devices.

The general assembly was called to order, and CFR spokesman Sir Chandler Van Duyn made several brief announcements and introduced Devin Rothfeller. To a ripple of cordial applause, Rothfeller stood and greeted the small audience with a quick wave, then quietly sat down; at 84, his days of giving speeches were long over.

Nelson Thurn distributed the conspectus to the assembly, and a projector was turned on to highlight each point. Winthrop Shaw quickly took the podium and cleared his throat.

"Thank you, gentlemen," he began. "I would like to commend each of you for attending this year's event, which is of exceptional significance.

"On today's docket, we will go first go over the results from last year's summit meeting and the progress we have made toward achieving our goals. Then we will then present our five-year plan, which institutes many changes, and then finally we will focus on one of the more important subjects of our discussion today, the global population explosion and the approaching 10 billion mark. Now, if you would, please refer in your conspectus to line order number one."

Papers rustled and the scent of cigar smoke wafted throughout the room as the gathered members glanced over the docket. Shaw heard the expected mumblings of amazement and disbelief when the elect group saw the items on the agenda, and a faint smile played on his lips.

Chapter 3

Toni

"Toni, would you please pay attention and listen closely to the assignment?"

"Huh? Oh yes, Mrs. Baxter, could you just repeat the question?"

Mrs. Baxter regarded Toni coolly. "I was asking for the sum when converting this fraction to a decimal." The teacher turned to the blackboard and revealed a large, scaly, dinosaur-like tail, which swished and knocked over a pencil holder.

"Oh, not again!" exclaimed Mrs. Baxter. "This thing really does get in the way at times."

Toni Vickery began to make a comment about the fraction, but a small pack of wild dogs came running into the classroom. They started barking and chasing Mrs. Baxter around the room, nipping at her very grand tail. The children in the classroom squealed with delight to see the regimental Mrs. Baxter in such an undignified position. They pounded their fists on their desks and began chanting, "Kill the pig, kill the pig," their little faces distorting into monkey masks. Somewhere in the distance, someone was playing an old Beach Boys tune.

"Awwww," Toni groaned, slapping the snooze button on her alarm clock radio, but the Boys kept right on singing, she decided the best course of action was to throw it against the wall.

"Oh, gaawd. I feel just awful," she moaned, untangling herself from the sheets. That's the last time I go boating with those guys on a Sunday. How many margaritas was that? Four, five ... she counted on her fingers. No, six! Ugh, and that bottle of wine, now that was the killer. "Oh no! I have a tutoring to do tonight!" She sighed out loud. "Good Lord, never again."

Toni sat up on the edge of the bed and watched the room spin. She made her way to the shower and turned the water on, as hot as she could stand it, then reversed, turning up the cold to the maximum in attempted hangover relief. She stepped from the shower and observed herself in the full-length mirror. Her raccoon eyes looked back at her pathetically. *Boy, I've really packed on the pounds,* she thought to herself. *I need to lose 10 or 12, and soon. Perhaps I should join a gym?*

OK, she thought while reaching for her toothbrush. *Time now for a miraculous transformation.*

After 30 minutes, the transformation was almost complete. Toni looked every bit the young professional fifth-grade teacher. Her clothes were neat and clean. She appeared slightly tired but ready to face a Monday morning classroom full of rowdy children.

She brushed her dark, wavy hair that revealed her Jewish-Italian heritage. Her petite, 5-foot-2 frame, large nose and big, deep-set eyes with extraordinarily long lashes combined for an overall effect that was quite cute. She made her way downstairs and was almost knocked over by her young son Joey and the dog Bowser in a race to the kitchen.

"Joey, don't try my patience today!" she barked.

"Sorry," he mumbled while rummaging through the refrigerator looking for milk for his Captain Crunch.

She poured a cup of coffee and resisted the urge to spike it with a shot of Kahlua; then, glancing at the clock, she noticed the time. "Shit! It's almost 7:15. You ready to go, Joey?"

Toni and Joey made small talk in the car while sitting in the early-morning fumes on the Jacksonville, Florida, highway.

Joey reminded her so much of her ex-husband Mitchell, such a sports-minded kid into playing with any kind of ball he could throw. The way his hair flopped in front of his face made him look like a cute little puppy dog; Toni had kept trying to get him to the barber, but he wouldn't hear of it.

Miss Vickery arrived at Greenview Elementary School at 7:35 and stacked her papers on the side of her desk. Her son Joey took his seat in her fifth-grade class next to two chattering girls. It was nice to have Joey in the same classroom that she was teaching, but it sometimes reminded her of couples who work together, live together and do everything else together – too much familiarity.

Oh, well. Joey was as close to any male company as Toni had had in a long time. The dating scene was dismal. When she did meet an interesting guy, as soon as he found out she was a single mother of an 11-year-old boy, they usually politely and promptly lost interest. *I do hope that Jack guy is with Rick and Cathy again next weekend; he's awfully cute for a bald guy,* she thought as she looked out the window at the flawless blue sky.

The beginning of the school year always ushered in new policies and brought announcements. She glanced at several memos that had been placed on her desk before she arrived. *Let's see,* she read each memo. *Special education updates, OK; school advisory council, student handbook, reduced lunch program, gifted and talented program boundaries, OK; immunization schedules, OK. What's this? 'Duval County Public Schools has scheduled a series of town meetings beginning this Thursday, the 16th of September, at 6:30 p.m. in City Hall Room 238 with a very important announcement from the school board. Attendance is mandatory for all teachers.'*

"Oh, that's just great," she mumbled, "no karaoke this Thursday."

Chapter 4

Glick

"Young man, are you overcharging me?" the old hag croaked.

"Naw, lady, look here" said the scary-looking attendant. "The oil change is $27.95 for premium grade oil, and the service charge of $4.95 plus $1.97 tax equals $44.68."

"What?!!" cackled the antique mother hen. "You must think I'm just plain stupid. I never asked for premium grade! Now give me a refund for the difference between low grade and premium. I'm surviving on Social Security, and I can't be wasting money unnecessarily."

"Sure, lady" replied Glick. "The customer is always right. Here, I'll back out $2.95. Now that will come out to $42.97."

Glick watched the frugal oldster hobble out of the oil-change establishment and he quickly drew up a duplicate receipt with the correct figures. He lit a cigarette and fingered the extra pocketed cash that didn't make it into the register when suddenly the store manager appeared behind him from nowhere.

"Mr. Glick! You cannot smoke in here! This is a smoke-free workplace. Please extinguish your butt immediately!" The spectacled manager was standing dangerously close to the monstrous and menacing-looking biker.

"What did you say about my butt?" snarled Glick, towering over the baby-faced manager.

"Um, I ... er ... said I ... you need to put out your cigarette."

"Fuck you!" Glick calmly sneered in a deep baritone.

"Mr. Glick, we really need to talk," the manager stammered. "I just don't think this is working out. I'm going to have to ask you to punch your time card and clean out your things. We really don't need your kind here at The Oil Rig."

Glick blew a stream of smoke at the manager's glasses. "What was that squirt? You want me to punch something?"

The manager stared incredulously at Glick, who suddenly laughed out loud. "Haw! Just kiddin', I'll be by Friday to pick up my check."

Glick dropped his cigarette to the shiny-clean floor of the reception area and crushed it under his boot. He sauntered out to the parking lot of The Oil Rig and took a moment to admire his prized possession, a 1975 Shovelhead Harley.

He had long ago altered her appearance, giving her a radical profile. Her suspension had been removed, and the front forks had been extended. Her handlebars had been modified with chubby ape hangers, and the stock exhaust he had swapped out for homemade, straight, un-muffled pipes, giving his bike one of the loudest growls around. He also had a custom paint job – shiny jet-black background on the tank, covered in silver, grinning skulls. Although Glick loved his bike and the attention his loud pipes drew, he also found himself attracting the unwanted attention of many local police officers, who by now knew him all too well.

He spit-polished a spot of grime on one of the grinning skulls and jauntily sat on her black, custom leather seat. In a good mood, he clucked to himself, *I've got too many one-dollar bills in my pocket, and I know just the place to unload a few.* Then he kick-started her up and peeled off down the road.

Glick pulled into the lot of the Mermaid Lounge, home of the coldest beer in Daytona Beach, Florida, and parked next to two other hogs. He strolled into the dank dive that reeked of sweat, smoke, stale beer and stale women. He squinted as he strolled in, his eyes adjusting from the bright Florida sun to the darkness and burst of flashing lights inside. Even in the dark, he could still see the looks of fear and dread in the faces

13

of the other men frequenting the strip club as they watched him approach the bar. Glick relished the reaction; he enjoyed the feeling of power that his gargantuan bulk evoked. With several trips in and out of the joint, he had developed his forearms to massive proportions. He had also recently developed an equally massive beer gut. At 6-foot-7 and 365 pounds, he was one horrifically intimidating character. His scruffy beard, chains, tattoos, biker gear and overall dirty appearance only heightened the impression.

He took his favorite seat next to the stage, and two of the girls came up to him right away.

"Heeay, Glick," they teased in harmony, "you in need of a little fun today?"

"Where's Jade?" Glick snorted.

"Oh, she had to take her cat to the vet," replied one of the strippers. "It almost died choking on a hairball."

Aw piss, thought Glick. *She's the only reason to come to this dump in the middle of the day. The music sucks, and the rest of the girls are just a bunch of heroined-out junkies.* Glick motioned for the cocktail waitress. "I'll take one of those $14 beers," he ordered.

"You got it, baby," she winked. Glick watched her fat ass jiggle in the G-string as she trolloped up to the bar.

Christ, what a cow, he thought to himself. When she returned, he let her know that her eyes were as blue as the water in his toilet bowl.

The two strippers sat next to Glick and whined about how slow it was, but Glick wasn't paying attention. His mind was elsewhere, daydreaming about how he was going to get Jade to go on a date with him. If she'd agree, then he would take her to some nice place where they have those real cloth napkins, and some fancy-assed waiter would serve you some shit you couldn't pronounce. Then he'd get her real drunk and take her to his trailer. There, he'd fuck her on the kitchen table doggie-style. *She'd like that. Bet she ain't never had it that damn good.*

"Hey Glick, you ole sumbitch." Glick heard a familiar voice behind him. He turned to see his longtime buddy Bulldog stepping up to his table. The two enthusiastically exchanged a back pat and a handshake from their old gang days together.

"Where you been, man?" Bulldog asked with a bright smile. "I haven't seen you around the shop in a long time."

"Oh, I got into it with Jay. That asshole tried to say I took some dough out of his drawer. Can you believe that shit, man?"

Bulldog grunted in reply. "We're goin' to Sturgis next summer! Got ourselves a nice cabin booked, you should join us. You can see some of the family and get out of this fucking heat."

"Sure, that sounds real good."

"Hey, you think you could help me out with my bike, man?" asked Bulldog. "My punk nephew laid her down last week, she needs some major bodywork, and I need to replace the tailpipe. You're still the best mechanic and body man around, mate. Think you can squeeze her in?"

"Sure, no problem," Glick replied. "I'm between jobs right now."

"That's great. I need to get her on the road as soon as possible."

The two watched some older gal slither about on stage, wrapping her spidery legs around the pole and back again. *Yuck,* Glick thought to himself. He turned to his old buddy and announced, "Let's get the hell out of here!"

The pair progressed to barhopping and partying all that day and the rest of the night. By 5 a.m., they had exhausted every after-hours club to be found in the vicinity. Glick was ready to call it quits and head home to his trailer, but his buddy was reluctant to go.

"C'mon, mate, just one more drink," Bulldog slurred as they walked out into the empty parking lot of the vacated nightclub in the dingy warehouse district. "We can go over to Boopsies and visit my favorite chica."

"Naw, man, I gotta be getting my shit together. I need some sleep," Glick grumbled. He sat on his Harley and started her up, turned and waved goodbye to his buddy just in time to see him stumble over a curb and fall flat on his face. Glick just kept on going.

Turning onto his street on his way home, he saw a paperboy tossing the morning paper in front of his neighbor's trailer. He reached down, scooped it up and stuffed it into his denim jacket. After parking his Harley, he trudged up the stairs to the front entrance of his tin can of a home and fumbled with the house keys, dropping them and cursing all the while. Upon entering, he tossed the newspaper onto his rank couch, cracked a beer and glanced at the front-page headline:

"Governor Announces Enforced Statewide Micro-chipping Program."

I wonder what that means, he thought.

Chapter 5

Winthrop Shaw

Winthrop Shaw awoke at 8:30 a.m. and had his slippers delivered by his factotum. He meditated and performed his morning rituals to the soft music piped over the speakers concealed in the vaulted, 40-foot ceilings of his luxurious oceanfront mansion. In his robe and slippered feet, he strolled through the palatial house on thick Oriental rugs spread over Macassar Ebony floors throughout.

He stepped outside and assessed the dazzling morning view of the beach and ocean that was particular to this region of the Hamptons. He breathed in the salt air and, observing some fluffy clouds gathering in the east, announced to his butler Jenkins, "Looks like there may be some rain today."

"Yes, sir," answered Jenkins, pulling out a heavy chair for Shaw at the beautifully arranged breakfast table, complete with rare Asian orchids, exotic fruits and an assortment of fine English teas.

Shaw enjoyed a leisurely poolside breakfast of poached eggs, potatoes, bacon and fresh-squeezed orange juice delivered by the Hungarian maid on an antique silver serving tray. She buttered his croissant just the way he liked it and served it to him on fine china. She poured him aromatic coffee from a sterling silver pot and stood by respectfully until dismissed.

Shaw ate his eggs and had his daily reports delivered to him, which he briefed after breakfast, lingering in the foyer.

His razor-sharp eyes quickly scanned the documents momentarily, focusing on labor production in the Philippines and the financial markets. He finished by looking for reported news leaks or deviations from the expected. Such leaks were rare. The mainstream media was mostly under tight control, and maverick reporters generally saw their reports quashed long before they'd reach the attention of someone at the level of Winthrop Shaw. Any obvious leaks had been carefully orchestrated well in advance to generate the appearance of a free press or, sometimes, to disgrace a nihilistic affiliate. For Shaw, it was all too easy to give the public what they wanted to hear and deny them the information he didn't want them to know as long as he held controlling interest in every major media outlet in the entire world.

Once satisfied with the reports, he stepped into his study to pick up his daily schedule, which had been arranged for him by his secretarial staff. He placed a call to his office and announced that he was heading out. Climbing the circular staircase, which swept to a landing leading to the upper wings of the house, he ascended into an upstairs chamber to dress for the day ahead.

A custom handmade silk suit with matching tie had been laid out for him. When he noticed a slight fray on the right French cuff of his shirt, he grimaced in disgust and threw the shirt into the garbage can. He went to call for his chamber maid but then decided just to do it himself.

Stepping into his 600-square-foot walk-in closet, he gazed upon the abundant array of row upon row of designer clothing, all organized by style from formal wear to casual. A copious display of European handmade shoes, belts, hats, ascots and scarves covered an entire wall. Shaw picked a particularly beautiful linen shirt with a colorful tie; he then turned to the hermetically sealed compartment that held his finest smoking jackets and evening wear. The refrigerated compartment made a hissing sound when he opened it. He flipped on its interior light switch and saw what he wanted. Shaw reached for one of his old favorites, an Italian jacket he had inherited from his father when he died. Shaw had disposed of most all the clothing his parents had possessed, but this one jacket had always been held in high esteem. Shaw held the jacket in his hands for a moment and an unpleasant memory of himself as a small child filtered through his mind's eye.

"No, Mommy don't go. Please, Daddy come back. Come back." The boy ran barefoot across the cool marble floor and a nanny quickly scooped him up. As she carried him to his room, Winthrop Shaw watched through tears as his parents walked out the front door to leave for the entire summer, their servants following closely behind carrying dozens of sets of Louis Vuitton luggage. Such exhibitions were commonplace in the Shaw household of his youth. Shaw had grown up in a cold, un-loving environment. He had been shuffled off first to boarding school and then to military academy. For as long as he could remember his frequent request for attention from his parents had always fallen upon deaf ears.

They got theirs in the end Shaw thought, recalling his reaction when first informed of the unfortunate accident that had taken both parents lives. Shaw had reacted with the same cold aloofness that his parents had displayed his entire life.

He put this jacket on and it was still a perfect fit. Shaw now felt himself smartly dressed and he studied himself carefully in the full-length mirror to confirm. Tall and chiseled, the bird like features on his tight face revealed a certain cruelty that he could not hide. He smoothed his combed-back hair, nodded to his reflection and then headed out the front door, where his chauffeured limousine sat waiting.

Shaw's private valet with white gloves and spotless uniform held the door for him as he slid into the buttery leather rear seat of the luxurious automobile. "Have a good day, Mr. Shaw," he said. Shaw ignored the greeting and ordered his chauffeur to deliver him to his private helipad. From there, his pilot proceeded to deliver him to a series of board, government and banking meetings.

Shaw had been born to an opulent life of privilege, which he took for granted. His Hamptons house was just one of many voluptuously magnificent mansions established throughout the world, some of which he had never even been to. Others he flew to by private jet when the weather was most favorable and when he allowed himself the time, which was seldom.

Despite the lavish lifestyle that his great wealth allowed, Shaw rarely relieved himself of his work long enough to enjoy his princely surroundings. His ambitions exceeded even those of the world's most extraordinary men.

Invitations to polo with a Windsor or to share aquavit with the king of Sweden went largely ignored. Shaw considered himself to be too much an intellectual to waste time on such frivolities. Even his incomparable 500-foot yacht, the Suzerain, he barely used. His few recreational hours were spent in the evenings with his colleagues smoking fine Cuban cigars and playing billiards while discussing policy, which Shaw predominantly dictated. His cold, calculating and dominant personality yielded him few true friends, only associates and yes-men. He occasionally took on a sponsored prostitute. Although Shaw was still legally married, he had been separated from his wife for the past 17 years, he had no children.

Shaw hailed from a long genealogy of the elite ruling class. He could trace his lineage all the way back to ancient Sumerian kings on up through the current rulers of the modern-day world. These did not include such men as senators, presidents and prime ministers; instead, these were the men who worked behind the scenes determining who the candidates for such office would be. Indeed, a position such as president would be a huge step down for someone of the caliber of Winthrop Shaw.

Under his control were not just presidents and their cabinets, statesmen and ambassadors but also virtually all branches of the U.S. government and its financial institutions. He held controlling interest in most of the Fortune 100 companies and monopolized huge media conglomerates, including newspapers, magazines, TV networks, public radio and publishing houses. He oversaw labor unions, law firms, think tanks and various foundations. He also had a hand in a majority of black-market arms and narcotics distribution networks worldwide.

He answered to no one other than the Czar of the Global Union himself, Devin Rothfeller, and his sights were set on that seat as well.

Yes, thought Shaw to himself, admiring the sunset view from his helicopter, *if all goes as planned; my days of answering to anyone are soon to be over.*

Chapter 6

Just Think of the Children

Thursday evening arrived, and Toni Vickery ate a TV dinner and took Bowser outside so he could do his business. She gathered her keys, announced she was headed to a meeting at city hall and hollered to Joey, who was watching MTV:

"Joey, did you finish your homework?"

No answer.

"Well, there's a TV dinner in the microwave for you. I'll be back around 8:30." She then reluctantly headed out the door to the dreaded town meeting.

As she pulled into the city hall parking lot, she noticed a large crowd had gathered by some booths with personnel distributing information pamphlets. Toni entered the building to the buzz of heated conversation. She took a seat on a metal fold-up chair with the rest of the audience and waited for the superintendent of schools to begin.

"Thank you, ladies and gentlemen, parents and teachers; we have something of great importance to announce tonight," began the superintendent. "We have received notice from the school board that all children enrolled in Duval County public schools this year will, in addition to their regular vaccinations, be required to receive a WCR identification microchip. It is to be inserted into the lower right quadrant of their right hand in the fleshy portion just below the thumb."

The crown murmured in wonder at this bit of news.

"In addition, all public school teachers, as government employees, will also be required to receive the microchip in order to receive to receive their pay. If you need more detailed information on the WCR banking requirements, a pamphlet is available at one of the booths set up outside and also at your school's main office. These requirements are in anticipation of a nationwide ruling that will require all citizens of the United States to receive the new microchip. So please be advised that you will likely at some point in the near future be required to do so yourselves.

"We welcome all parents wishing to receive your microchip at the same time as their student children to avoid an additional trip. There will be a representative for the World Central Reserve Bank at each chipping location who will be happy to assist you."

At this, several people in the room stood and walked out while others shouted their questions to the superintendent. He fielded questions for a short time and ended the meeting with a reminder that, beginning the next morning, chipping stations would be set up at all public schools.

Toni left the meeting in a state of mild shock. She wasn't sure how she was going to bring herself to do this to her son or how much time she had before she had to take it herself. She resolved to find out all she could about this chip business before she just blindly accepted it.

The next morning on the way to school, Toni wondered what the day ahead held. She had seen voluntary chipping stations in the school for the past several years, usually at the beginning of the year, but she had never really paid much attention. Now, with it being a mandatory requirement, she felt violated. When she arrived, she saw a station at the entrance with a small crowd of children gathered. Most were watching injections in progress, while a few others were lined up. Toni told Joey to go ahead of her into class and that she'd be along shortly. She found another station in the auditorium with a larger group of children; some had their parents with them. One woman behind the counter, she recognized as being in charge of the voluntary micro-chipping stations in the past.

Toni approached the booth and looked at the apparatus being used. A nurse was pricking the fingertips of the child seated in front of her for a blood sample while a second nurse opened a sterile prefilled syringe. The children were instructed to look into an iris imaging camera and then fingerprinted while a third assistant scanned the information and entered it into a computer.

This was new. Toni didn't remember any eye cameras or blood work in years past. She ventured as close as she could get to the computer screen and saw that it displayed a photo of the boy being processed. There was additional data to the right of his picture. Toni could make out his name and Social Security number but had a hard time seeing the rest.

She made her way through to the front of the booth and peered over to witness an injection firsthand, watching as the nurse applied alcohol and nimbly administered the injection. The nurse then waved a reading wand over the boy's wrist, an audible beep came from the computer. Toni craned her head to get a good look. She saw pages and pages of data quickly filling the screen. The nurse, satisfied with the result, smiled at the boy, handed him a lollipop and sat the next student in the vacated chair.

Toni approached the woman she'd seen in past years and introduced herself as one of the teachers. The woman pumped her hand enthusiastically and, with a huge, toothy smile, greeted Toni radiantly.

"Hi there! So very nice to meet you! My name is Cindy," she said, pointing to her name tag. "It's so great to meet the faculty members; I have so much respect for the job you teachers do and the ..."

"Hold on there a minute," Toni interrupted. "Can you tell me why do they need our blood, for Christ's sake?"

With great joy, Cindy described in detail the work they were performing on behalf of the students. She continued for several minutes, fully describing all the wonderful benefits and perks associated with the microchip. Then she gave an animated grin to Toni, who shook her head and quizzed her. "So let me get this straight – you think this is a good thing?"

"Oh yes, absolutely! Yes indeed! It eliminates all sorts of problems: Terrorists will be quickly identified; fraud will be a thing of the past. But most importantly, think of the children. Do you know that every year, over 800,000 children are reported missing and just 2 percent of the abducted children were fingerprinted or had any personal information recorded before they went missing? Imagine how many could have been recovered sooner if their information had been made available to the officials. Plus, the chip contains the child's entire medical record: their blood type, Rh factor, known allergies. Many parents can't be reached when their child requires medical attention, you know."

"Mmmm." Toni mulled this information over in her mind.

"Also, think of the convenience factor. You won't have to carry your wallet ever again! Just run your hand over this scanner, and all your information is right there." She once again gave Toni that gigantic, toothy smile.

"What if I make an Internet purchase?" Toni asked.

"That's no problem at all" the young woman replied. "This is a home scanner." She directed her to a small rectangular plate with a flat metallic surface. "You run your wrist over it like so, and voilà! It forwards you from the shopping cart directly to your account information. You'll have to purchase one, of course, but you can get one at any participating office supply; there are many models to choose from."

"I see," said Toni, looking at her watch. "Thank you for your time, but I have to be getting to class now." She turned to hurry, for she was now officially late.

Well, she certainly was happy about the whole thing, thought Toni as she walked down the hall toward her fifth-graders, *like she took too much Prozac or something.*

Chapter 7

Where You Gonna Go?

Glick awoke with a pounding headache. The neighbors were building something and had been hammering and making noise for hours. *What the hell's wrong with these people, making all this racket so early in the morning?* Rolling over, he looked at the clock. It was 4:23 in the afternoon.

He opened the trailer window and threw an empty beer bottle at the noisy neighbor. It missed and hit his mailbox.

"A man can't get any sleep around here," he grunted. "Guess I'd better get up." Scratching his hairy belly, he slogged his way into the bathroom.

He then stumbled over to the kitchen and drank a huge glass of water. He groaned when he remembered he needed to go find a job, he lifted the newspaper from the couch and went straight for the classifieds. He would need a job and fast; the lot rent was already past due. He scanned, looking for mechanic or body shop work, but unfortunately all that he saw were places where he'd already worked and couldn't go back to. Then he saw something that looked interesting – boatyard mechanic to work on diesel engines. Glick picked up the phone and scheduled an interview for the following morning.

The next day, Glick put on his best jeans and went for the interview. A nasally voiced receptionist with big hair and a short skirt handed him an application to fill out, then proceeded to file her nails. Glick dropped his pen on purpose so that he could get a closer look at her legs, and then dutifully filled out the application, listing all his experience and credentials. The second page of the form, however, featured something new that he had never seen before. It was a direct deposit form for the World Central Reserve Bank; with it was a questionnaire for the WCR banking information microchip and a list of local chipping stations.

Huh? This must have something to do with what I saw on the front page yesterday, thought Glick; wish I had read the whole article. He carefully looked over the questionnaire. It was asking for some very personal information, the kind he wasn't sure he was willing to share with some boatyard employer.

"Uh, excuse me there, Missy."

"Yes?" she said, looking up from her nails.

Glick placed the application on her desktop. "About this application," he said, "I'm not real familiar with some of what they're asking for. Can you please explain it to me?"

"Sure thing," said the Jersey girl. She removed a piece of gum from her mouth and stuck it on some paper. "This here is a form that sends all your money to the new World Central Reserve Bank, and this here is a questionnaire, and this here is a list of chipping stations. Got it now?"

"No" he replied. *Jeeez, this chick's a real brainiac.*

"Well," said the receptionist, "here's how it goes: There aren't any little banks anymore or even any big banks; there's only one giant bank that's out of Hamburger or Frankfurter or somewhere like that. They process all the paychecks now. We don't even send out checks like we used to – they take care of all of it. Our money goes directly to them, and they take it out of our accounts and deposit the money directly into our employees' accounts. It's great, really! We don't even have to do payroll anymore, it's all handled automatically for us. We just receive a ledger at the end of every month. I like it much better than before."

"What about this microchip?" he asked. "What's that?"

"Oh, that's the really cool part. See, I have one!" She displayed her arm for Glick to look at, but he saw nothing.

"Just what am I supposed to be looking at?"

"It's in here above my wrist," she said, pointing to the mound below the thumb of her right hand. They put it in and I'm all good to go. I don't need a credit card, a debit card, a cellphone reader or anything! And if there's ever an emergency, all my medical records are in it. There's other stuff, too. My gym membership is in here so I don't have to carry my gym ID anymore; it unlocks my car door and my house when I walk up to them. It even turns on the front door light. And when I buy groceries or clothes, I don't have to do anything but swipe my wrist, just like I got my own barcode built in! It's so awesome."

That's just great, thought Glick; *now we're all just like a head of broccoli.* "How long have you had that thing in you?" he asked.

"About a month, right after they sent out notifications. I got mine the very next day, it was real easy, there weren't any lines, and it didn't hurt much."

"All right," he said. "What if I don't want to get chipped like some kennel dog? Can I get this job without it?"

"Honey ..." replied the secretary, "let me tell ya, you won't be able to get anything without this chip. Don't you know? All the banks have been rolled into one, and this bank is doing away with paper money, checks, debit cards, credit cards – all that stuff. They just won't work anymore after the first of next month."

"The first of next month!? Today's the 23rd, that's just nine days from now!"

"Yeah, honey, you better go and do's what you gotta do. I'll hold the application for you. If you go get your injection I'll bet you can be back before lunch, and I'll schedule you an interview for this afternoon."

"OK, thanks. You were real helpful."

"Sure thing," said the receptionist, putting the gum back into her mouth.

Glick wasn't sure what to do. He looked at the list of chipping stations and crumpled it and threw it on the ground outside the door. *I ain't doing that shit!* he thought as he fished in his pocket for his cellphone and the business card that his buddy Bulldog had given him the other night. He dialed the number and scheduled a lunch meeting at the Rusty Nail.

Glick pulled into the parking lot of The Rusty Nail at 11:45, went and sat at the bar and ordered a beer while he waited for Bulldog. The Rusty Nail was a landmark in Daytona; it hosted a dirt floor and all sorts of junk hanging on the walls. They also served a half-pound burger, which was sounding pretty good to Glick, who hadn't eaten all day.

His burger arrived just as Bulldog walked in, the two friends exchanged some hand jive, and Bulldog sat down on a rickety chair and ordered the same thing as Glick. "Buddy," Glick inquired, "I gotta get some kind of work; the park's already up my ass for last month's lot rent. Do you know where I can get something under the table?"

Bulldog thought on this a moment and responded: "I think I might know somewhere that you can get some work, but I don't really think it'll do you much good. Without the almighty chip you won't be able to get paid. Cash isn't going to do a damn thing for you; might as well wallpaper your trailer with it. Why don't you just go and get the chip? Do it and get it over with?"

"No way! I ain't doin' that," Glick snarled with his mouth full of food. "They're not gonna tag me like some mutt! Next thing they'll be controlling where you're allowed to eat, sleep, shit – you name it."

"Well, I don't really see any other way. These guys are setting themselves up so they can see everything we do. There sure won't be any more black market goings-on. You better bury your stash of guns, too; they're going from house to house confiscating them. Things are going to be radically different from now on, that's for sure." Glick caught the look of distress on Bulldog; the years were really starting to show in his craggy, wrinkled face, and his long, braided hair had turned mostly grey.

"Is it like this all over?"

"Nope, so far it's mostly states in the East and California, but it's just a matter of time before it goes federal. I imagine the whole world will be going this route soon. I haven't really been following what's going on in Europe or anywhere like that. I'll have to watch CNN tonight and see if they talk about it. You know," continued Bulldog, "this has been going on for longer than most people know. Do you remember Mudeater?"

"Yeah," Glick nodded, "I remember that asshole."

"Well, right now he's serving 15 in the Coleman Federal Prison. He wrote me over two years ago and told me they had microchipped him and all the other inmates. They put the chip right into their heads at the base of the skull."

"No shit?" Glick replied. "I was doing time around then. How come they didn't chip us?"

"You were in a state pen. He's doing federal time, remember?"

"Oh yeah."

"He seemed to be OK with it," said Bulldog. "He said he was expecting a riot, but everyone just took it real cool, and he said he felt fine afterward."

"Who gives a shit how that douchebag felt," Glick said, recalling a coke deal with Mudeater gone bad. Mudeater had taken Glick's money and left him sitting on some hooker's couch for hours before he finally gave up and left without the coke. Mudeater had took the money and run. That was almost five years ago; Glick hadn't seen or heard of Mudeater since.

Glick got a look in his eye that Bulldog recognized; it usually meant he was about to do something crazy. "What are you thinking?" asked Bulldog.

"I'm thinking it's a good time for a road trip out west, maybe Montana or something."

"Mmmm," replied Bulldog.

"What are you gonna do?" Glick asked. "Where you gonna go?"

Bulldog chuckled. "I'm not going anywhere, kiddo. I'm staying right here; I'm going to get my chip and go about my life like nothing's happened. It's not worth running over."

Glick sat silent for a moment "I'm gonna miss your mangy old carcass," he muttered, feeling somewhat nostalgic.

"Yeah, sure, just don't forget about my tailpipe before you go and haul ass on me, man."

Chapter 8

Emma

Emma Jackson had some nice, fluffy pancakes on the griddle with some bacon and sausage for the boy she so dearly loved. *I'm wishin' he'd wake up. I sure hate waking the poor darlin' when he's so doggone tired.*

The TV announced that they were looking for the next contestant on The Price is Right. *Oooh, I gots to see this dining room set,* thought Emma, distracted from the pancakes momentarily.

T.J., her 6-year-old great-grandson, came into the living room of the flat that the two shared. Sleepy and rubbing his eyes, he held out his arms for Grammy to pick him up. Emma reached down to lift the growing boy and felt a jab of pain in her low back, which she ignored. "Oh yes, here we go, big boy," cooed Emma as she picked him up and gave him a lengthy hug.

"Oh my goodness, the pancakes!" she quickly put T.J down and went to the scorched cakes. "Looks like it's going to be oatmeal today, T.J."

"We has to hurry up an' eat, honey; Grammy gots to be at work here shortly," she told T.J. as she emptied an instant oatmeal package into a bowl that she put into the microwave.

"Why you gotta go to work, Grammy?" asked little T.J. while sitting down to his bacon.

"That's a real good question, young-un" answered Emma. *Hell, a woman my age shouldn't have to work so damn hard just to have a whole heap o' nothin,* thought Emma, feeling all of her 74 years. *I've been wiping these geriatrics' asses so long that I'm damn near now a geriatric myself. I wonder who's gonna wipe my ass here soon?*

"I sure wish your momma would call. I'm awful worried about her," Emma voiced a thought. She immediately regretted speaking out loud. She didn't want to upset the boy; he'd already had a hard life for such a young child.

"What's wrong with my momma?" asked T.J.

"Nothing, boy, she's jes' fine, never you mind." *Nothing wrong with her but the usual bullshit,* she thought. T.J.'s momma, Tianna, was a Class A crackhead who had dumped baby T.J. off on Emma when he was just 5 months old. It was a miracle that the baby was even alive. He looked like he hadn't been fed the whole time, and was every bit as skinny as his momma. *"Looks like one of those Ethiopian babies they always showin' on TV,"* she thought the first time she saw him, all wrinkled and emaciated when he should have been plump and precious at 5 months.

Emma was delighted to take the baby from her granddaughter's care even though it would be very hard to get by on so little money. So Emma took on more hours at the nursing agency, and they did manage to get by. She provided as much loving care for T.J. as she could; and with lots of attention and mashed potatoes, the boy thrived and grew. That is, until he was 3 years old and Tianna made her triumphant return. She pronounced herself off crack once and for all and wanted her baby back. For Emma, giving T.J. to Tianna was the hardest thing she ever had to do. She had very little confidence in the girl's ability to stay clean for any length of time.

Her fears were well-grounded, for it wasn't long before she received a phone call from the police. They had found T.J. abandoned and wandering loose in the streets of Detroit. They couldn't find his mother or guardian, so he had stayed several days in a shelter before they were able to track Emma down and deliver him to her. Skinny as a rail, he ran into his Grammy's arms when he saw her. Emma swore she would never let Tianna have him, ever again, as she kissed his face over and over.

And so it went that over the years Tianna would come back and Emma would do everything in her power to keep T.J. from her, including hiding him at her neighbors' apartment. Then Tianna would arrive with the police and court orders, again demanding the right to take back her little baby, whom by now wasn't so little. She would tire of him after a few days and bring him back or she would just get lost and drift around aimlessly, carting little T.J. behind her; sometimes bringing him with her into various crack houses.

Just pathetic, really. She wondered sometimes whether, if Tianna's own mother had lived, things would have been different. Maybe Tianna wouldn't have taken up that damn pipe if she hadn't been so despondent about losing her own momma; dead of breast cancer at the age of 34. *If we'd just had some decent insurance for that poor girl I knows she would have lived,* Emma lamented thinking of her long-dead daughter.

She hadn't seen or heard from Tianna for a very long time now, which both relieved her and disturbed her at the same time. Her instincts were very good about these sorts of things, and she didn't have a good feeling about the missing girl. Emma had a sixth sense that had helped her greatly in life – she had learned over the years to trust her feelings totally – and as long as she paid attention to them, they never failed her. She wasn't sure what to do about Tianna, however; she had already checked the local jails and she wasn't locked up, so perhaps she should file a missing person report. She took out a paper and wrote herself a note to do so if she didn't hear from her very soon.

T.J. tugged on the pant leg of his great-grandmother's nursing uniform. "Grammy, can I get a puppy for my birthday?" he asked a slight whine in his voice.

"Well, baby," she replied "they don't allow dogs in the complex. How about a nice little kitten?"

T.J. thought on this a moment and beamed. "Sure, a kitten yeah!"

Emma was thinking about the price of cat food and vet visits when she heard a special news brief.

"Michigan Senate leaders are in discussions this very moment about the compulsory microchip program being instituted by the U.S. federal government. State and federal legislators are expected to vote on an emergency moratorium later this week."

An odd feeling overcame Emma upon hearing the news, but she wasn't quite sure what it was or why. She turned off the TV and gathered her keys and purse.

"Come on baby, we needs to go now," said Emma, pinching T.J.'s butt as she scooted him out the door. He giggled as they headed into the hallway.

Chapter 9

Tim Connor

Tim Connor barely slept all night. His back was bothering him again, but he was just too stubborn to get up and take an aspirin, so he just lay there most of the night watching the ceiling fan spin around slowly while his wife, Beth, made little snoring noises in her sleep. He rose before the alarm went off and shut the buzzer off so as not to disturb her; he stumbled in the dark, tripping over their son's size 12 sneaker that the dog had carried into their bedroom earlier that evening. "Damn dog," said Tim, kicking the shoe into the corner.

Thank God it's Friday. Tim put on his work clothes and headed out the door. It was still dark out and the misty September morning air held a refreshing chill. *Better enjoy it now,* he thought, *won't be long now till the snows fall. Looks like we're in for an early winter – the leaves are already starting to change.*

He stepped into his city truck and headed to work at the Fairfax, Virginia, Electrical Utility Plant, where he worked as an electrical distribution mechanic. Tim mostly worked on street-light lines and occasionally did some underground cabling, but most of his work days were spent driving around, killing time. The day's work schedule was usually completed by noon, so the rest of the day was pretty easy. Despite Tim's undemanding job, he still counted down the days to retirement. After 18 years of doing the same thing every day, he was growing seriously restless.

Yep, thought Tim pulling into McDonald's for an Egg McMuffin, *just seven more years and I'll get me a house on a lake with a little bass boat. I'll do nothing but fish and hunt all day long. That's the life.*

Tim's wife had a dream of owning a small café that served breakfast and lunch so she could put her cooking skills to the test. By then, their two kids Jason and Kelly would be in college and he and Beth could enjoy the simple life with no cares and plenty of fresh air.

"Hey, Connor, you read me?" came a voice over the two-way radio. It was Tim's co-worker, Frank Farney. "I copy, come back," responded Tim.

"Try to get in a little early if you can. There's a ruckus going on here."

"Oh yeah? What kind of ruckus?"

"The city managers are here distributing some new requirements, and everyone's having a fit."

"10-4, I'll be there in a few minutes." Tim backed out of the long McDonald's line and headed east toward the office.

When he arrived, there was indeed a ruckus going on. "This just isn't right!!" Tim heard his boss exclaiming to the city official from behind the closed glass doors.

"What the hell's going on?" Tim asked Farney.

"Here, get a load of this," he said as he handed a paper to Tim.

It was an official announcement bearing the seal of the County of Fairfax, Virginia. It stated as follows:

```
In accordance with the policies of the
World Central Reserve Bank, effective
immediately, all government employees are
to receive the WCR banking identification
microchip in the lower right quadrant of
the right hand. Salaries will not be
issued to any city employees not bearing
the WCR microchip.

Furthermore, paper paychecks will cease
to be issued by the city of Fairfax.
Weekly pay will henceforth be disbursed
only by direct deposit into the World
Central Reserve Bank. If you have not
already set up a direct deposit account,
please fill out the enclosed form and one
will be set up for you before the next
pay cycle. Enclosed is a list of chipping
stations, their addresses and hours of
operation. The County of Fairfax Virginia
apologizes for any inconvenience that the
new policy may cause.
```

"You have got to be kidding me!!" exclaimed Tim to Farney with a dumbfounded look on his face.

"Tell me about it," replied Farney dryly. "Jesus, today's Friday; I need to get my paycheck! Let me see that list again," he said, grabbing the paper out of Tim's hands.

Chapter *10*

Marlene Carson

"Mrs. Carson, here are the results you asked for." Marlene Carson took the paper from her secretary. "Thank you, Kim," she replied. "I need one more thing. Please get me the complete data from last night's newscast and from the public opinion poll we ran on Friday."

"Yes, ma'am," responded Kim as she spun around to fetch the most recent figures.

Marlene looked at the latest polls and frowned. They were showing that her once-significant lead over her opponent Jim Spencer in the Ohio Senate race was now narrowing. With just two months left before the election, she was starting to get a bit nervous. *Just relax*, she told herself, *I still have him by a huge margin. This one's a slam-dunk.*

Marlene as the incumbent obviously stood a greater chance of winning the election than Spencer, who had little actual political experience; but, with his tremendous charisma and his growing grass-roots campaign, the voters were starting to listen. The citizens really had had it very bad over the last two years with the banking collapse and the ensuing depression; it was very difficult for most families to survive. *But things are like that all over the world right now, not just in Ohio, and I can hardly be blamed for the mess they got us into,* thought Marlene, turning in her swivel chair to look out the window of her high-rise office to the Ohio River below.

Marlene had come a long way from her humble beginnings in the southern Ohio Valley, from which hailed only the poorest people. She had put herself through college, working two jobs and going to school full-time, and had clawed her way through the ranks to the top in politics. She began as a clerk in the district attorney's office and quickly ascended to a county commissioner's seat, and after two terms there ran a hugely successful bid for governor of Ohio. After four years in that office, she ran for the U.S. Senate and won. Marlene was currently in her second term as a member of the U.S. Senate.

Marlene's life had been a series of victories, one after another; but it wasn't just dumb luck. Marlene had accomplished a tremendous amount in her career. From her commissioner's seat, she had made great strides in developing the Ohio region where she had grown up.

Through clever negotiations and with state economic development aid, she helped change that part of the Ohio landscape from poverty-stricken slums and abandoned industrial areas into booming metropolises full of industry, culture, housing and shops, propelling her into the governor's seat. There, she created a special task force to address unemployment and gave employers huge tax incentives to keep auto industry jobs in the state, resulting in plenty of work. She reduced classroom size while increasing the number of schools and helped divert traffic from Ohio's big-city downtown areas by implementing a high-speed rail system that ran through the suburbs into the cities.

She took a cutting-edge approach, increasing the state's holdings by expanding into areas that many considered private enterprise and implementing bond issues for state-owned commercial properties. She also proposed tax incentives to encourage green building practices and attract green industries to the area.

When the current economic crisis hit and she found her state in severe need of cash, she auctioned off portions of the state's infrastructure to the public sector, selling bridges, toll roads, airports and even the state lottery to the highest bidder. While the ensuing toll increases may have strained the citizens in the region, the decision was still a wise one in the end, for Ohio was one of the few states to avoid complete bankruptcy and place additional tax burdens upon its people.

Marlene's good instincts, coupled with powerful allies, had helped her cut through red tape to get the kind of results that the voters appreciated. Marlene took comfort in her accomplishments to get her through this election. *I've seen the Jim Spencers of this world come and go. I should have no worries.*

Kim returned with the figures, and Marlene decided to go over them at lunch with Robert Albright, her press secretary. Marlene's schedule was very tight for the next few weeks, and she would barely have a chance to talk to him, so she had better get as much time in with him as possible. There also was that matter of the emergency moratorium vote tomorrow afternoon at 4:00 on the anticipated World Central Reserve microchip.

Marlene hadn't yet had time to look at the bill that was distributed late yesterday afternoon and was expected to be voted on less in less than 24 hours –563 pages that had to be reviewed.

She sighed knowing the vast majority of the House and Senate would never take the time to read it thoroughly; they hardly ever did when this type of legislation was put in front of them and they were pressured into voting in such short period of time.

It wasn't unusual for this sort of thing, though. It was becoming more and more prevalent all the time. Marlene hadn't failed to notice that the bills they were under the most pressure to act on quickly, with little to no time to review, were the ones that had the most lasting repercussions, and usually not for the better – a bad trend indeed. It was odd, though, for one with such ramifications to be passed this quickly. *I'll read it thoroughly right before the 4 p.m. vote, she told herself.*

Chapter *11*

Bread Anyone?

Emma Jackson was listening to talk radio on her way home from work. It was a program surrounding the contentious subject of the upcoming mandatory microchip program being instituted by the WCR and the U.S. federal government. Emma had received notice from the nursing agency about the new policy a few weeks back. Now suddenly it was being talked about everywhere; it was all over the news, TV channels and radio stations. There were posters and billboards popping up urging the citizens to "get your chip", and fliers were being distributed by workers standing on many street corners. Emma wondered where all the organization was coming from.

She lent her attention to a heated argument going on over the radio waves. The two differing parties were a spokesman for the WCR and a representative for the Civil Liberties Union. The WCR spokesman was giving a very convincing argument about why the new microchip was so important to help stabilize the worldwide economy after the recent currency collapse that created the depression and also to the safety and security of the United States. He contended the chip was necessary to dramatically deter terrorist activity both in the U.S. and abroad. He claimed the proposed change would stop money-laundering and other criminal activity, criminals would be unmasked, there'd be no cash to smuggle, the sale of illegal drugs would cease, and the spread of AIDS would be curtailed as drug abuse ended. Stolen items could no longer be sold without a trace, and personal security would be assured. Tax evasion and cash payments in order to avoid sales tax would end. Most importantly, he stressed that the cost of government would be reduced, as well as the cost of conducting private business. The national debt would be reduced and the world financial markets would finally come into balance as the new, monolithic system was established.

"The people want and need stability," he argued. "It is our multi-currency system that caused the price differential among goods and services to begin with. We can fix that problem by moving to a single global credit system, which will provide what the people of the world want – durability and permanence. This will eliminate current account imbalances and the need for foreign exchange reserves, and bring other benefits worth trillions. This will reduce the impact of the global financial turmoil such as we are now experiencing."

He added further weight to his side of the debate by touting the logic of a uniform national identification system, and closed his appeal by urging citizens to act quickly. Time was running out. Cash would very soon be a thing of the past– like it or not.

My gracious, this sure did come about suddenly, thought Emma, turning off the radio. *I guess I better go get an appointment to get one of these things before I can't buy a loaf of bread.*

She turned into a parking lot and stepped out of her car to retrieve a flier being handed to her by a teenage girl. The flier listed all the micro-chipping stations in the county and their hours. Emma took a pen out of her purse and circled the location nearest her, then headed south to pick up T.J. from kindergarten.

Emma pulled into the Kinder Care Children's Day Center and studied the faces of the children in the crowd, seeking her precious little boy. She spotted him and waved. T.J. came running to the car with a big stack of construction paper and a bag of colored markers. He excitedly jabbered to Emma about a fight he'd witnessed in the playground and how two boys were in big trouble.

"Here you go, Grammy. This is for you," he said, thrusting a paper into Emma's hand. It was a notification from the school board announcing the new mandatory micro-chipping program being instituted by the public school system.

"Grammy already knows about this, honey. We's goin' down this afternoon to go get it taken care of, but first let's go get some ice cream, all right?"

"Yummy!!" yelled T.J. "Can I get marshmallow man mash?"

"What on earth is that?"

"It's got marshmallow superheroes mixed in with caramel and asteroid zinger bombs."

"I suppose so," replied Emma. "I'm not sure what ever happened to vanilla."

Emma and T.J. sat down in the corner ice cream shop and shared a bowl of marshmallow man mash. Emma noticed that some of the customers were paying for their ice cream by sweeping their wrist over a sensor; others were simply paying with cash.

"You see that, T.J.?" Emma pointed to a man waving his arm over the sensor. "It looks like that's how we gonna have to pay for our goods now."

"Yeah, I know," said T.J. "Jamal got one. He said it hurt like hell."

"You watch your language, boy! I ain't putting up with that kinda talk from you, not this young."

"Will it hurt, Grammy?"

"I don't know; we's gonna find out here in just a few minutes. Here you go child, finish this ice cream off. That's the nastiest stuff I ever tasted."

Emma and T.J. took off for the chipping station. They searched for a parking spot but had to park across the street. The stations were starting to get very crowded. Emma took T.J.'s hand and led him across the parking lot toward the booths, looking for the one with the shortest line. She spotted one that looked good and strolled toward it. She then glanced around and noticed something that struck her as very peculiar; there were clearly different groupings of people, and they appeared to be segregated by race. Emma observed a large crowd of Caucasians in line for one booth, while another booth had only blacks in line. Yet another booth appeared to be all Hispanics. She then looked to the line she had originally chosen and noticed all the people appeared to be Asian. A queasy feeling came over Emma. She stepped back and took some time to observe the process. She watched as people approaching the booths were herded into the appropriate line by representatives for the WCR and the local police department. One of the reps for the WCR spotted Emma and T.J. and, with a smile, waved them closer.

"I don't like the looks of this, boy," she said, looking down at T.J. "I think we need to go home."

"Why, Grammy? What's wrong?"

"Nothin', child, jes' you never mind," Emma said as she turned and ushered T.J. back to their car. Disturbed and confused by what she had just witnessed, she wondered on the ride home what they would do now.

Chapter *12*

1984

Tim Connor walked in the front door to greet his family later than usual; the sun had already gone down and his dinner had grown cold. His afternoon and early evening had been spent with fellow co-workers after hours at the local pub discussing the latest news and how it affected their lives. Most of the fellows at the plant were of the opinion that the chip wouldn't affect them in any way and it was just a necessary evil like vaccinations or pesticides. Others, like Tim, weren't so sure. It left him with an uncomfortable feeling clinging to the pit of his stomach; he wasn't one bit happy about the whole thing.

"Hi sweetheart," Tim greeted his wife, Beth, with a kiss and a very prolonged hug.

"What's up, Tim?" Beth asked, pushing him away. "Why are you acting so weird, and what are you doing coming home at 8:30? I made lasagna. The kids and I have already eaten. I get no phone call from you and you wouldn't answer your phone. It's really inconsiderate."

Tim stopped her. "Honey, I've got something important to talk to you about. I'd prefer not to discuss it in front of the kids. Here, come into the bedroom," he said, taking her arm.

They went into the bedroom and sat on the edge of their bed. Beth focused on Tim, concern in her pale green eyes.

"Sweetheart, there is a new policy at work, and it's going to be affecting you and the kids." Tim paused a moment to gather his thoughts. "They want us to take a microchip inside our hand just so they can give us our paycheck."

"What? What kind of microchip?"

"Well I'm not really sure," replied Tim. "They're making it a simple process so it looks like it may not that big a deal, but since the kids are in a public school, they will have to get one. You might even have to eventually. If what everyone is saying is true, then all U.S. citizens will be required to get one within the next few weeks in order to buy or sell anything."

"Why would you need this just to get your paycheck? What's wrong with the way we've been doing it over the past 25 years?"

"I don't know. It has something to do with the new World Central Bank; they're the ones demanding it, and the City of Fairfax is enforcing it. We absolutely will not get our pay if we don't do as they say."

"Good god!" exclaimed Beth. "You know, Tim, we read about this sort of thing happening years ago when I was in school. It's just like that book by George Orwell, "1984"; that they made us read in the ninth grade."

"Yeah, I know. We talked about that tonight at O'Hara's. Seems like the end of the world, huh?" he laughed.

"I don't think it's very funny. Tim, you can't keep working there if that's what they're going to make you do."

"Well, let's not be hasty," replied Tim. "We'll have to think on that one."

"This is something that we probably should be discussing with the kids since it affects their schooling," said Beth. "We need to let them know what's going on now. Come on."

Tim and Beth went to the kitchen table and asked the kids to join them. Their two children, Jason and Kelly, were bundled up on the floor with pillows playing a video game.

"Hold on a minute 'til the game's over," Jason yelled from across the room.

"No, you come over here right now," Tim ordered. "We have something important to talk about."

Jason ignored Tim, but his older sister Kelly stood up and kicked her brother in the ribs; he reluctantly got up off the carpeted floor, sulking to the dining-room table.

"Your mother and I have called this family meeting because there are some things going on at my work that you need to know about. They are requiring me to do something that your mother and I don't necessarily agree with."

"You're going to have to start going to a private school," Beth blurted out.

"What, are you kidding me?" Kelly cried. "Mom, you can't do this to me! I just made the cheerleading squad, and all my friends are going to Fairfax High! Please, Mom, don't make me go to some private school where they have to wear uniforms. I wouldn't know anybody. I would just hate it – hate it!"

"Hold on a minute there," said Tim, holding his arms up. "Who said anything about a private school? Just how do you think we are going to be able to afford that?" he asked, glaring at Beth. "Times are really tough right now."

Beth thought a moment. "I'm not sure how we're going to do it, but that's exactly what's going to happen, and your dad's going to get a different job."

"Wait a minute! Change jobs, are you kidding me? In case you haven't noticed, we are in the middle of a very serious depression right now. I'm damn lucky to have a job at all. Have you seen the lines at the local unemployment office? You have no idea what's it's like out there. People are losing their homes and walking the streets holding up signs. It's awful."

"I don't care, Tim, this is something more critical than a paycheck or losing a house – it's about all those things that I never thought I would see in my lifetime or even the kids' lifetime. I just can't believe they want to microchip us." Beth sobbed as she placed her face in her hands, despairing over the situation. Tim walked over to his wife and picked her up to her feet; he lifted her chin and gazed into her beautiful eyes. His heart felt like it was being torn out of his chest.

"Everything will be all right," he soothed, stroking her blonde hair. "Don't worry."

Chapter *13*

The Messenger

Marlene Carson approached the Bellagio Restaurant and looked at the huge line. *Wow, this place has really become popular,* she thought, remembering when the area was just a slum. Now it had been transformed into a cosmopolitan polestar, and Bellagio was its centerfold, the place to see and be seen. The maître d' immediately recognized the senator and escorted her past the line inside to the best table in the house.

"Thank you," she said as she graciously accepted the comfy chair he pulled out for her. "My lunch companion, Robert Albright, should be here any moment. Please show him to the table when he arrives."

"Of course, madam," replied the maître d' as he presented her with the menu.

Marlene examined the huge menu carefully. It featured a fine array of French cuisine with subtle Italian influence. *Hmmm, I think caille aux framboises for an hors d'oeuvre, then just a salad.* Marlene heard the chair across the table move and felt someone sit down.

"It's about time. You're twenty minutes late," she lambasted, her face still buried in the menu. "I have a lot to go over with you and very little time," she said, reaching down for her briefcase. "Just wait 'til you see these figures." She put down her menu and was shocked to see the face of a man she had never seen before staring at her from across the table.

"Excuse me, who are you?"

The oily-looking man lifted his finger to his lips in a "shhhh" gesture. Marlene looked around for some wait staff to escort the oddity from her table when the man spoke.

"Ms. Carson," he began, his voice as slithery as his looks. "We are terribly sorry to interrupt your fine repast, but we have a matter to discuss with you that's of an urgent nature."

"'We'? Who are 'we'? I only see a 'you'," she addressed the man in the Armani suit. He reminded her of some of the types she used to encounter in her travels to South America, particularly Colombia. Sharks were what they used to call them, killer sharks.

"There is a moratorium to be voted on tomorrow afternoon, Ms. Carson. We highly recommend that if you value your post as a United States senator and wish to maintain that position, you will vote to reject the moratorium having to do with a microchip."

"I don't know what you're talking about. I haven't read all the details on the matter, and it's doubtful I'll be making any decisions based upon the recommendations of whatever lobbyist group you represent. What group did you say you represent?"

The mystery man continued: "I think you know, Ms. Carson, that there are certain factions that have a large vested interest in seeing this matter ratified quickly. These same individuals can 'arrange' to have you taken care of, either in a good way or perhaps in ways you might find unpleasant. I believe in your position, and with the election so close, it is to everyone's benefit to let this one pass."

Marlene's eyes met the messenger's, and she understood. She was up against a powerful force, a force so omnipotent that even a senator and all of her strongest allies couldn't stand against it. She knew who these people were and what they stood for. She had a lot of thinking to do.

Marlene saw the waiter approaching the table and waved him off.

"I must be leaving now," hissed the enigmatic figure. He then put on dark sunglasses and stood up. "For your sake, I hope you do the right thing."

Marlene watched the man as he quickly exited the restaurant, observing him carefully until he disappeared into the crowd. As she was still looking out the window, she saw her press secretary, Robert Albright, jogging toward the maître d'. He was shown to the table, where he sat panting.

"You wouldn't believe what just happened to me," he said, reaching for her water.

"I'll bet I would," Marlene replied, rubbing her eyes.

"On my way here, four cars got on all sides of me and wouldn't let me get around them or pass; they blocked me in for over a half an hour. I called the cops, and they never even showed up. Finally just got out and ran up the road because I knew you'd kill me if I was late again. I just left my car sitting there. Can you believe it?"

"Oh, yes, I can totally believe it," said Marlene calmly even though she was still flabbergasted at the audacity.

"Well, do you want to go over your numbers now, or do you think I should try to get a lift back to my car?"

"I think you can go get your car," said Marlene. "I believe it will be clear by now."

Albright gave her a quizzical look and asked, "What about the polls?"

"I have a feeling the polls aren't going to matter much this year," Marlene replied. "Here," she said, "why don't you call a cab to drop you at your car?" She handed Albright a hundred-dollar bill. "I'll have Kim call you to reschedule our appointment sometime next week. Something has come up, and I have a lot of work to do right now."

Albright gave her an additional confused look, and took another sip of water before he headed out the door to hail a cab.

Marlene pondered the situation a moment. In a last ditch effort in a war probably already lost, she picked up her phone and dialed her secretary. "Kim, I need you to pull all the available information on the moratorium vote on the WCR chip. I'm also going to need you to cancel all my appointments this afternoon." Marlene stood and left the table, disregarding her lunch.

Chapter *14*

Nuts

The dismissal bell at Greenview Elementary School went off at 3:15, and most of the children poured out of their classrooms into parking lots or buses or headed toward their after-school activities; some went to stand in line for their microchip. Toni Vickery gathered her items and headed into the halls, anxious about what may lay ahead. She noticed some teenagers were handing out fliers for the program, and some were stapling announcements to the walls and posting notices on the bulletin boards.

She saw her best friend, Dina Patterson, the guidance counselor, in the hall and quickened her steps to join her. "Hey Dina, wait up," she yelled. Toni caught up, and the two women chatted while walking down the hall.

Toni and Dina had been friends since early childhood. Their mothers had started as neighbors and grew quite close, resulting in the two girls growing up like sisters. Toni remembered Dina as a freckled, eternally sunburnt, buck-toothed little girl with extra short bangs and knobby knees that grew into a graceful swan of a young woman by high school. The two had spent their early years playing with tea sets, making mud pies and playing with Barbie dolls, which inevitably wound up with the same bad haircut as Dina. They planted gardens of colorful flowers that would bloom beautifully in the warm Florida winters but would quickly die by late April in the harsh Florida sun, and spent countless hours in the muggy tropical evenings trying to spot the constellations in the indigo, star-filled skies.

Toni's photo album was filled with pictures of her and Dina from the time they were just small, hunting for Easter eggs in their matching pale pink taffeta dresses, birthday parties, proms and graduation ceremonies. Her mind was filled with memories of those early years together. They used to play dress-up, raiding the closet of Toni's mother, pulling out silk scarves, jewelry, heels and any clothing they deemed exotic-looking. They would cover their little arms in silver bangles and pretend to be gypsies, can-can dancers or members of a rock band, shaking their tambourines and banging a tiny drum as they walked around the block of their quiet residential neighborhood.

As they evolved into pre-adolescence they spent their every free moment together, often going the skating rink at the mall after school or horseback riding on the weekends. In junior high, they cut out pictures from Teen Beat magazine, which they taped all over their bedroom walls, and would spend hours at the cosmetic counter at the mall, spritzing themselves with perfume and testing makeup that they could not afford to buy.

Their teen years were spent at the beach, where they discovered cheap strawberry-flavored wine and boys; the boys preferring Dina with her elegant features over the dark, chubby girl with the big nose. Both Toni and Dina wanted to be child psychologists when they grew up, and eventually discovered that the only careers available with that degree were preschool teacher or guidance counselor.

The two had only been apart one time in their entire lives. When Dina was 15, her parents announced they were moving away from Florida to find better work and hopefully a better, more affordable college for Dina. The two girls cried and cried when her parents made the announcement. They locked themselves in their room together, refusing to come out for nearly 40 hours until hunger and fatigue finally forced them to. But like most transients who say they're leaving Florida never to come back, the Patterson's did just exactly that. After a two-year absence, the family returned and Dina and Toni had a joyous reunion, quickly picking up where they'd left off as if they had never been apart, eventually going to Florida State University together and growing up to be on their own. They even wound up sharing similar teaching careers at the same elementary school.

"So, what's been going on with you, Toni?" Dina asked while munching on an apple as they walked down the hall.

"Well, to be honest with you, I'm not sure. This whole thing with the microchip has come up so quickly. F frankly I'm not really comfortable with the whole thing. What do you think?"

"Yeah, I know what you mean," agreed Dina. "I've heard some crazy talk about it."

"Oh, yeah? Like what?"

"Well, you know Carrie, right – that girl that works at St. Ann Hospital in Pensacola? She said that all the newborn babies there have been routinely getting these identification chips now for the past six months. There were never any announcements made about it. They just take them and chip them when they do their PKU test right after they're born; no consent forms are offered or anything. And get this: She's seen people coming into the ER that have tried to remove their own chip themselves. It's really creepy. I guess if you try to remove it yourself, it sends some kind of shock that temporally paralyzes you and creates all kinds of neurological problems later."

"What!? You have got to be kidding me!" exclaimed Toni.

"No, and that's not all. She said these people that tried to take their chip out did it 'cause they claimed they were hearing things."

"Hearing things? What kind of things?"

"Like a high-pitched squeal, but some of them said they were hearing voices, too."

Toni took a moment to digest this information. "That's the craziest thing I've ever heard in my life."

"I know, and what do you think about that new rule?"

"Huh? What new rule?"

"They're now requiring the chip to be inserted into the head as well as the hand. Didn't you hear about that?"

"What!!?"

"You'd better start keeping up with the news, girl. I saw it myself on FOX last night. Anyone getting a chip after the first of the month will be required to take two, one in the wrist and one under the scalp in the flat part by the front of the head. What do you think about that?"

"That's just nuts. I'm moving to Siberia."

"Yeah," laughed Dina. "I'll join you. Hey, I have to run. I've got to get my niece to gymnastics class before 4 o'clock; call me later. OK?" Toni waved goodbye.

Toni walked through the halls punchy from shock, feeling as if someone had knocked the wind out of her. As she passed by the first chipping station, she found herself wanting to shout out to the people in line, "Stop! Don't do it!!" She wanted to come through with a baseball bat and destroy all their computers and their damned equipment and throw it all in the dumpster. How she wished she could just run away from all this mess.

When she got home, she plopped on the couch, exhausted from mental anguish. Joey walked in the front door with his friend Jared and asked, "What's for dinner?"

"I'm not really in a cooking mood tonight, Joey. Why don't you order some Chinese food or something?"

"Yuck, no thanks. How about pizza?"

"Whatever!!" Toni snapped.

"What's wrong with her?" she heard Jared remark to Joey as they walked into his bedroom.

"I dunno. She's been a real bitch lately."

Toni opened a bottle of red wine and turned on the TV. The president of the United States was on, making a speech about the importance of complying with the new laws.

"Today," his oration began, "marks a great new beginning for the United States and the rest of the world, a new age of peace and safety, a brave new world of prosperity and security. The rest of this small planet looks to us this day as shining examples of what to do for the good of humanity. We owe it to ourselves as citizens to set the standard for the rest of mankind to follow. I urge all citizens to closely follow the instructions given them by their community leaders in these trying times. Our American government applauds your participation in this global effort to root out terrorist and criminal activity. Let it be known this day that the republic reigns forever in the hearts of all Americans, and comfort and security will be given to all its citizens who abide by its laws. God bless America and all that it stands for ..."

The rhetoric was giving her a headache. She turned the TV off and picked up the phone to call her aging mother in Miami.

"Hello, Mom," she sighed into the phone.

"What is it, honey?" asked her mother. "Are you all right? You sound just awful. What's wrong?"

"Well, Mom, there's so much on my mind right now, all these changes; I guess I'm just not ready for them yet. I simply can't get used to the idea of our government invading our bodies by injecting some foreign object into it. I've made a decision about the microchip: I've decided I'm not going to take it, and I'm not going to let Joey take it, either."

"Toni, now you listen to me." Her mom said "you need to put all those thoughts out of your mind and go get your chip. It's all perfectly fine. Your father and I have already done it."

"Well, Mom, I've heard some really outrageous things about the chip – that it messes with your mind."

"Oh, that's utter nonsense. Vito and I have never felt better. He's certainly been in better spirits than I've seen him in a long time."

"Well, how does it make you feel? Do you feel different? Have you been hearing any voices?"

"Voices? Toni, have you been drinking again?"

"No, Mom," she lied, reaching for her glass.

"Toni, you need to think about that young son of yours. You're not going to be able to survive without doing what has to be done. Just how do you think you would manage? You couldn't buy food or clothes or pay your mortgage. You need to ignore all those silly rumors; this is just another part of life. If you want to live, you will have to do as they say. Why don't you send Joey up here for a few days if you need a break? We'll make sure he is taken good care of."

"Sure, Mom," said Toni, hanging up the phone without saying goodbye. Her normally feisty mother sure seemed to be mellowing out lately; she and Dad must be getting old. Toni felt spent. She closed her eyes and listened to the drone of the neighbors' lawnmower. Soon she felt herself dozing off. She was quickly awakened however; she jumped with a start at the sound of someone knocking at the front door.

"Joey, come get the door please," she shouted.

"It's probably Suzi," said Jared as he came down the stairs. Joey followed his friend down to see. It was indeed Suzi, Jared's little sister. She was a sweet girl with freckles and a cute little gap in her teeth. Toni was very fond of her and always happy to see her.

"Jared, Mom says you need to come home soon."

"OK," he answered, "but we just put together a marble run. I want to see a couple of runs first, then we'll go, OK?"

"All right, but hurry up. Mom made meatloaf, and I'm starving."

Jared and Joey ran back upstairs, taking two steps at a time. Suzi sat on the couch next to Toni.

"How are you, Mrs. Vickery?"

"I'm just fine, thank you. And how about you, what have you been up to at school these days?"

"I got this today, see?" Suzi stuck out her arm for Toni to take a look. "I got a chip today; they put it right here under this Band-Aid. Can you see it?" asked Suzi, lifting the bandage.

Toni took the child's wrist and examined where Suzi pointed. "No, I don't really see much of anything, just a little red spot." Her heart ached at the thought of pretty little Suzi getting a chip. *I swear if this baby gets hurt in any way I'm going to start raising hell.*

"Jared got one today, too."

"Oh really? Hey, Joey," Toni hollered up to her boy. "Can you send Jared down? I'd like to talk to him."

Joey and Jared came and sat across from Toni. "What's up, Mom? We're kind of busy right now."

"I hear you got a chip today, Jared. Can I see?"

"Sure," he said rolling up his sleeve. "You can't see much, though."

She looked for the spot, but it was even less pronounced than Suzie's red mark.

"Did it hurt?"

"Nope, not a bit."

"Did so!" yelped Suzi.

"Shut up, Suzi; she wasn't talking to you." Jared turned to Toni. "No, really, I thought it would hurt, but it wasn't bad at all. Most of the kids in school got theirs today. I don't think there are too many left that haven't done it yet."

"How come we haven't done it yet, Mom?" asked Joey.

"I'm still thinking about it," she mumbled. "How are you feeling, by the way, Jared?"

"Oh, I feel great. Thanks," he responded with a blank look. "I think I should be heading home now, though."

Toni nodded. "You two take care of yourselves, and tell your mom I said hi."

"OK, bye."

Toni sat on the couch and thought long and hard. After some time, she picked up the phone to call her ex-husband Mitch. She dialed and the paused a moment; she really didn't want to have to make small talk with that stupid bimbo Jeannette. *I hope she doesn't answer the phone*, thought Toni as she resumed dialing.

Jeannette was a real sore spot for Toni. Mitch had married her immediately after the divorce and was taking Joey over to her house even before their divorce was final. Toni never did know for sure if they weren't having an affair while she and Mitch were still together, but it didn't matter anyway; their marriage had fallen apart long before she ever heard the name Jeannette. Toni just couldn't see the attraction, though; the only thing the woman ever seemed to talk about was shopping and getting her nails done. *I guess that's all she's interested in.*

Jeannette answered the phone. "Hello, Jeannette. How is everything with you?" Toni made the obligatory gesture toward friendliness.

"Oh, we're fine, thanks. Mitch is out right now, he's at the Lexus dealer having the car looked at. I did tell you we just got a new Lexus last Thursday, didn't I?"

"No. It's at the shop already? Is it a lemon or something?"

"Oh, heavens no," tittered Jeannette, "we're just putting in some upgrades. If you need to talk to Mitch, call him on his cellphone, OK?"

"Will do, thanks." Toni grimaced. She hated calling him on his cell almost as much as calling his house. He was always blowing her off, telling her he was in a meeting or basically just trying to get her off the phone as quickly as possible, but she dialed anyway.

"Mitch here."

Toni heard his deep, sexy voice and responded with heaviness in her gut. "Hey, Mitch; long time no hear."

"What can I do for you, Toni? You obviously need something."

"I do. Mitch, I have something very important to tell you." There was a prolonged silence on the other end of the phone.

"Well? Spit it out Toni. I haven't got all day."

Toni's voice quavered "Mitch, I'm leaving the country and I'm taking Joey with me."

"What?! Are you kidding me? Why? Why on earth would you do such a thing? And where do you think you're going?"

Toni sighed, "Canada I think. I'm not sure yet."

"Over my dead body! You are *not* taking Joey anywhere, do you understand? It's bad enough you fought me so hard for sole custody and – now you want to take him halfway across the continent. I must remind you that per our divorce decree, the conditions clearly state that you and I must remain within...."

Toni hurriedly hung up the phone and put her hand to her mouth. The room began to spin. She took a deep breath and exhaled hard. Then the phone rang; one- two-three-four rings. She reluctantly picked it up.

"Toni" Mitch spoke quietly now "if you violate the terms of our divorce, I *will* sue you for custody and I *will* win."

"Mitch, please, please be understanding – this is an emergency."

"What kind of emergency?"

"I can't tell you."

"Then you can forget it! You have some harebrained idea that you clearly haven't thought through, and you're not dragging our son through it." Mitch was now yelling "I'm going to fight you every step of the way if you do this Toni do you hear me!!? Do you??!! Don't you dare go anywhere!!! Hello? Hello?" There was mute stillness on the other end, she had already hung up.

Toni cradled the phone in her hands a moment before unplugging it at the jack. She rose and went to the kitchen for a paper and pencil and she began to compile a list. She would need an assortment of supplies for her trip to Canada. As soon as she found a place that she considered safe and comfortable, she would let Mitch know where they were and he could come visit Joey as often as he liked. Then she and Joey would live happily ever after in this new unknown place. She would even be willing to bring Joey down herself to visit with his father. *This situation will work out just fine* she thought. Money would be a problem, though; she had virtually no savings to speak of, her meager teaching salary even combined with child support and alimony barely afforded her to pay her mortgage payment.

Traveling takes money and lots of it. Who can I borrow from? she thought she plugged the phone back in and started to call on her list of friends and family.

Chapter *15*

Hit the Road

Glick had been holed up in his trailer for the past two weeks. Unable to find work or anyone willing to hire him without the dreaded microchip, he remained hidden inside his tin box of a trailer, ignoring the persistent phone calls and knocks on the door from the landlord. The statewide chip mandate had been in effect for five days now, and his refrigerator had long stood empty. Soon they would turn off the electricity, and then he would really be screwed. It was time to get out of Dodge.

He went to his closet and picked out only the barest essentials that he would need for light travel. He grabbed blankets and warm clothes and shoes; because where he was headed it would be very cold. He grabbed a sleeping bag, toilet paper, shampoo, toothpaste, a road map of the United States. He took his Beretta 92FS off the shelf, opened her up and gave her a once-over, then he took some extra rounds and wrapped them in a sock. Finally, he took down a picture of his parents off the wall, removed the old photo from its frame, folded it and tucked it into his wallet. Glancing around one final time at the messy trailer, he went outside and put the items in his saddle bags. He took one last look at his rusting trailer and blew it a kiss goodbye. He then peeled out of the trailer park doing 50. Glick quickly slowed down, however, realizing he needed to conserve gas; he already stood at less than a half-tank and had no way of buying more.

He looked to the sky. The day was beautiful and the air smelled so clean. He would miss Florida. He wondered what Montana would be like; he had never spent any time there. Then his stomach rumbled, and he wondered how he was going to get there without any food or gas.

Several hours on the road and Glick approached Interstate 75 heading north; he looked and saw the on-ramp in the distance but had to pull over out of weakness. He needed food before jumping on. He pulled over into a residential neighborhood and scoured for orange trees. He spotted a beauty in a back yard, loaded down with fruit. He pulled his bike over about a block away from the yard that held the fine tree and stepped carefully behind the chain-link fence. He looked around for dogs and, seeing none, he ran for the tree and gorged himself on oranges, their sweet stickiness like ambrosia to the starving biker. He picked several more fruit for his pockets but soon felt eyes watching him from behind. He turned and saw a portly woman staring at him from inside her screened-in patio door. He carefully backed away from the tree and then bolted from her yard. Dropping an orange behind him, he turned and scooped it up as quickly as possible before running down the road toward his bike. Panting, he thought to himself, *that was the most exercise I've had in quite a while.*

The oranges were good, but Glick needed more. He pulled away from the residential neighborhood and into the street, saw a Popeye's Chicken and drooled. He scoured the parking lot for scraps that someone may have left behind. Seeing nothing, he lifted the lid to the dumpster and peered inside. Nothing.

He decided to hit the road, thinking he could get all the food he needed once he reached Montana, but there was a big problem; he was already needing to fill his tank. He drove up the road looking for an easy mark. He spotted a thin, pale man with a toupee filling his tank. Glick pulled up next to him and stepped off his Harley. He effortlessly yanked the gas nozzle out of the man's hands and gave him a hard shove backward. The man stumbled in reverse and fell onto the curb with a look of horror on his face. His toupee fell to the side of his head.

"Sorry," Glick said, looking over his shoulder at the poor man. The thin fellow scrambled for his car and took off, leaving him to fill the tank of his motorcycle. After he finished fueling, he went inside the gas station to pee. On his way out he shoplifted some Twinkies and a bag of Fritos, which he devoured in the parking lot. *I wish I could have snagged a beer,* he thought, wiping his face on his sleeve.

Glick traveled on his tank until dark. He had already made it past the Tennessee border and was making pretty good time, but he was getting tired; he was also getting tired of the constant growling in his stomach. He pulled off the interstate and looked for a place to sleep. Spotting a nice spot along a canal behind a warehouse district where no one would bother him, he rolled out his sleeping bag and lit his last cigarette. He listened to sirens off in the distance and felt a smug satisfaction that he hadn't been nabbed after the gas station episode.

He smoked half his cigarette and saved the rest for an emergency, which would be in the morning. He wasn't looking forward to a long full day on the road with no food, no cigarettes and no gas. "No hope," he sighed as he drifted off to sleep.

The morning sun rose and relieved Glick of some of the chill that he had experienced most of the night. Birds were chirping, and it looked like another good day for weather. *That helps. At least it's not raining; that would really suck.*

Glick was already having nicotine fit. *If I could just get something to eat, that would help get rid of the cravings.* He fired up his bike and cruised the streets looking for an opportunity. He noticed the sign on a Days Inn announcing a free continental breakfast. *Sounds good to me.*

He parked his bike in the back and strolled inside the cozy lobby. He was greeted by the smells of hot coffee and pastries. Glick salivated in anticipation of a grand feast. He hung his jacket on an empty table and loaded up on steaming waffles with butter and syrup, hard-boiled eggs, bagels, apples, Danish and orange juice. He shoveled the food in like a madman, ignoring the looks of disgust from the other patrons. He went for seconds and then thirds, finally letting out a huge burp when he had finished. He then put his feet on the table and picked his teeth with a matchbook. He was about to go back to the buffet and fill his pockets with more food, but the hotel manager came into the dining room and was giving Glick a funny look, so he decided he had better not push it. He left the Days Inn empty-handed, but at least his stomach was full.

He cruised for seven hours and was getting ready to merge onto I-70 toward Kansas City, but it was getting to be time to fill his tank again. He was also starting to feeling hungry, too. He had long ago smoked his half-cigarette and thought he would go out of his mind with cravings.

What a miserable experience, thought Glick … and then it started to rain.

"Thanks!! Thanks a lot!!" he yelled at the sky. Now soaked, he pulled into a gas station and saw a well-dressed young woman in her early 20s filling her tank. He pulled up next to her.

"Give me your gas!" he growled.

"Excuse me?" She looked at the beastly, bug-eyed man with rain dripping from his beard.

"I said *give* it to me!!" He yanked the nozzle away and inserted it into his tank. She reached in her purse and retrieved her cellphone to call 911. Glick grabbed her wrist and plucked the phone out of her fingers.

"Thanks. I could use this, too," he said as he crammed the phone into his pocket.

The young woman made a hasty retreat into the gas station, and Glick resumed filling his tank. He took off quickly before the cops could get there and quickly jumped on I-70.

He tossed the cellphone into the bushes and gunned the engine. He drove three more hours; the rain let up, but it had now been 10 hours since he'd last eaten. He pulled over at a rest area and spotted a black teenager eating a submarine sandwich at a picnic table. Glick approached the boy and demanded his sub.

"What?! You nuts!!?" The teen replied.

Glick grabbed it out of his hands and wolfed it down in front of him. "Give me that Mountain Dew!" he commanded the bewildered boy.

"No. I don't think so. I'm thirsty, too ... bitch!"

Glick gave the boy a shove off the bench. He lay on the ground and stared at Glick with his big brown eyes.

"Don't look at me like that!" barked Glick while licking his fingers.

"Crazy cracker motha fucka," responded the boy.

Glick downed the soda, tossed the empty can at the boy's head and turned and walked away. He mounted his ride and took off down the road.

He was now on I-29 headed toward Iowa. He drove a few more hours in and out of torrential rainstorms that were moving throughout the Midwest. It was now past dark, and he would soon need to find another spot to rest for the evening. He was thinking of how nice it would be if he could strong-arm his way into some old fart's house and borrow their shower and bed for the night. *Wishful thinking*, he told himself. *I'll be lucky to find a dry overpass I can crash under.*

Glick was passing through a particularly desolate area when he spotted something up ahead in the middle of the road. He squinted through raindrops to see if his eyes were deceiving him, but no, there was definitely a figure up in the middle of the road ahead waving his arms over his head. He slowed down to take a close look and came upon a man in a wet raincoat.

"Please stop!" yelled the man. "I need help!"

Glick came to a stop just short of the distressed fellow. He shut off his engine and asked what the problem was.

"My car broke down," said the man. "I could really use some help."

He looked over to the man's old Toyota Camry sitting on the side of the road and thought about the situation a moment. The guy really didn't look like he had anything that he could use.

"Got anything to eat?" asked Glick.

"Some cookies and a pear in a brown bag, that's about it."

"OK, I'll be needing those," Glick replied as he walked over to the man's car. Despite its age, it appeared inviting and dry inside the automobile. He turned to the man. "I'll give you a lift in the morning if I can sleep in your car tonight."

The man quickly agreed, and the fatigued biker climbed into the front passenger seat and immediately collapsed into a deep, dreamless sleep.

Glick awoke in a fog of exhaustion. His eyeball was just an inch away from the open mouth of a snoring man that he didn't recognize, and his clothes were still damp from the night before. It took him a full minute to remember where he was and what he was doing there. He sat up in the cramped Toyota and bumped his head on the interior light. Arrrg!! He went to punch the roof of the auto but then remembered his manners and opened the car door instead.

The rain had let up, and the resulting morning was cool, misty and beautiful. There was a grove of trees next to the highway where they were parked. Glick tromped over in his soggy boots and pissed against a tree, steam filling the air. When he returned, his unknown companion was just waking up.

"Got a cigarette?" he asked while rooting through the man's ashtray.

"No sir, I don't smoke," the man said with a slight Southern accent. It was true; the ashtray was as clean as a whistle.

"Fuck," said Glick, removing his waterlogged boots. He wrung his socks out the door and looked at his pruned feet. "So what did you say is wrong with this car?" he asked.

"Not sure. It was raining too hard to get a good look at the engine."

"Let's check it out." He popped the hood, wiggled wires and tightened screws with his fingers. "Got any tools?"

"Sorry, no."

"I don't see anything obvious."

"The gas gauge isn't working. It's possible I just ran out of gas."

"Did you run out of money, too?" asked Glick.

"No, I have plenty on me if I can just get to somewhere where they will take it."

"Oh yeah?" Glick looked the man up and down. He was a tall fellow with a magnificent head of wavy, white hair, somewhere in his late 60s. He looked like he might have been pretty strong in his day, but Glick felt confident that it would be easy to grab his cash and split. He had, however, made a promise to give the poor bastard a lift.

"Where you headed?" asked Glick.

"Utah, how about you?"

"Montana, I guess, maybe South Dakota, I got friends there; I haven't seen them in a long time, though."

"I see."

"You got a gas can? We're gonna need one."

"No, I'm afraid I don't."

"Well, you'll have to get on the back of my hog then. I'll get you to a gas station, but then you're on your own after that."

"That's fair enough. I appreciate the lift, thank you."

"Yep, here, hop on; you'll need this," said Glick, handing the man a German-style half helmet complete with spike on top and an iron cross on the backside, and they were off. Glick cruised till he came to the next gas station. He figured he might as well fill his tank again, but he didn't see anyone else filling up at the empty station, so he circled around the parking lot several times waiting for his next victim. Soon, a heavy woman pulled up in a minivan full of kids. He watched her closely as she struggled to squeeze out of her Dodge Caravan and plodded toward the pumps. She swiped her wrist on the reader and began fueling.

"I need you to get off the bike for a sec," said Glick, turning to the curious man seated behind him. He left the man standing in the parking lot with the silly helmet; pulled up next to the fat woman and stepped off his Shovelhead.

"Hey dumpster! Gimme me that nozzle!" The woman looked up, befuddled; Glick jerked the nozzle from her hand and inserted it into his own gas tank.

She went ballistic, clawing, scratching and screaming. Glick covered his eyes with his arm, and she bit him in the armpit. Her two sons, spotting the action, ran out of the Caravan and jumped on Glick's back, pounding him with Tonka toys. Her two daughters, not to be outdone, hopped out and started kicking him in the shins and biting his knees.

"Christ!! Get them off me!" begged Glick to the man stationed behind him. The white-haired man ran to Glick's assistance and tore the boys from his back. The fat woman clobbered him with her purse.

"Let's get the hell out of here," yelled Glick, shaking a pigtailed girl with braces off his leg. They both jumped on the bike and peeled off. After a while, the shook-up biker spotted a rest area and pulled over.

"Thanks for having my back, old man. I owe you one," said Glick, taking off his helmet. He lifted his arm to examine the bite mark and winced. "Good god, did you see that shit? I just can't believe they would do that to me!"

The white-haired man said nothing.

"Whew, I need to sit down after that," said Glick, walking toward a picnic bench. "Here, old man, have a seat," he said, patting the bench. "Boy, I could really use a beer," he said, turning to his companion. "Don't that sound good?"

"No. I don't drink."

"Well, I suppose you have your reasons," he said, rubbing his fingers through his greasy hair. "Name's Glick," he said, extending his gigantic, calloused hand to the gentleman.

"Mine is Vernon Bloom," said the man, taking his hand. "Pastor Vernon Bloom."

"Oh," said Glick, fairly embarrassed. "So you're some kind of priest or something, huh?"

"Minister for the Calvary Baptist Church of Pickens, South Carolina," said the man, shaking Glick's hand. "Nice to make your acquaintance, although I must say I think you could certainly spend a little time brushing up on your Bible study."

"Yeah, I had plenty of that crap when I was growing up," replied Glick. "Don't try converting me, Preacher. I've heard it all before."

"Well, I'm glad to hear you've had some fundamental background while growing up. The lessons do stick with you your whole life, even if you choose *not* use them."

"Yeah, right. You think I *want* to steal fucking gas? I can't get anywhere without doing it, and I heard you say you wish you could use your cash, too. That means you don't have a chip, either, do you?" He grabbed Pastor Bloom's wrist and examined it closely for evidence of an impression.

"No, I don't, thank you very much," he said, pulling his hand back sharply.

"See, we're not so different after all!" laughed Glick.

Bloom just shook his head.

"What are you planning on doing once you get to Utah?" asked Glick.

"I'm going to rendezvous with a group of Christian non-conformists. I'm gathering information to bring back to my congregation. We're hoping to relocate to a new area, one that doesn't require us to be micro-chipped. I'm told Utah has one of the biggest groups of Americans migrating to avoid taking it."

"Really? That sounds like just the thing. I'm headed anywhere I don't have to be chipped myself. I'm just guessing Montana. I don't know a soul there. Like I said, I know a bunch of people in the Sturgis area. I suppose I could go there. But right now ... I'm just drifting."

Glick sat silent for a moment, then added: "You know, I could probably use some company on the road. How you feel about tagging along? I'll get you to Utah, then I'll move on up to where I'm headed after I drop you off."

"I'll have to think about that one."

"You better think quick, 'cause I'm hitting the road here again in a few minutes."

Pastor Bloom meditated on this a moment. He wasn't sure how he was going to get his car fixed or what was even wrong with it. Time was running out back home. His flock had been doing without for weeks, and he would need to get back to them before they broke down and went for the chip just to survive. He looked at the disgusting man sitting next to him; Glick was busy picking at his black fingernails. Then he picked his nose.

The Lord certainly works in mysterious ways. "OK, Mr. Glick. I'll take you up on that kind offer, and thank you."

"Sure thing, Preach, just hold on tight. I don't want your ass falling off the back."

Glick and Pastor Bloom were soon back on the road, headed west toward Utah. A few hours on the road and they found themselves in need of supplies. Glick pulled into a Piggly Wiggly grocery store and told Bloom to wait for him outside.

"Hold on a minute there," said Bloom, "what are you planning on doing here?"

"Mind your own business, Preach," said Glick as he turned toward the entrance.

Pastor Bloom hollered behind him, "I won't eat stolen food, Mr. Glick!!"

Glick strolled into the store pushing a cart and snatched a stack of plastic grocery bags from a cashier whose back was turned. He weaved through the aisles filling his bags with meats, bread, Sterno, matches and, of course, beer. He picked up some fried chicken from the deli and munched on that as he made his way through the store. He stopped a moment and regarded some pre-made sushi.

Hmmm, I wonder what that tastes like. He opened the plastic container and popped a tuna roll into his mouth.

"Ugh!! Gross!!" He gagged, spraying rice on a display stack of canned Hormel chili. He finished the chicken and pitched the empty box into the garbage. He then pushed the cart with the bagged groceries out the door, his head held high. As he approached Pastor Bloom, he was amazed to see him sitting on the back of his bike happily eating a steaming hot, extra-large pizza seated on his lap.

"Where did you get that?!"

"Someone gave it to me."

"Why?"

"She said she didn't like mushrooms. They're *my* favorite."

"Hrmph," grunted Glick as he pulled a Budweiser out from one of the bags. He drooled as he stared at the pizza.

"Want some?" Pastor Bloom extended the box toward Glick.

"Does a bear shit in the woods? I haven't had pizza in a coon's age!"

Glick beamed as he crammed a whole slice into his massive mouth and gobbled it in one bite. Then he took another four slices and piled them on his knee. The two laughed and joked while eating their lunch. They enjoyed it as much as any meal either had ever had.

Glick and Pastor Bloom resumed their road trip and cruised several more hours on I-80 as they passed through Nebraska. They stopped only in order to pee and for Glick to drink the occasional beer. Though they had plenty of food, they soon found themselves in need of gas again. Glick turned in to a BP and turned off his ignition. Pastor Bloom got off the bike to stretch his legs. He did some toe touches while Glick sat on the edge of the curb.

"What do you suggest here, Preach? I know you ain't into watching me smash some poor fool for his lunch money or his gas."

"The Lord will provide," responded Pastor Bloom.

It didn't take long; no sooner were the words were out of his mouth than two college students came pulling into the gas station in an antique VW Beetle bus, smoke pouring out of its engine.

"Oh great, what now?" groaned the young driver as he exited the van and went toward the back to where the engine was housed. "I bet it's a water pump or something."

"Check out that dumb ass there, Preach," said Glick, elbowing Pastor Bloom. "He don't know that thing is air-cooled; it don't have a water pump."

"That's quite impressive, Mr. Glick. What year is that antique, anyway?" asked Pastor Bloom.

"Probably the late1960's, long before our time."

"I think you should put that knowledge to good use and help the young men out."

"It would be easier just to bash them in the head and take their ..." Glick stopped himself short. "Maybe I could just cut off his arm and wave it under the scanner," Glick laughed out loud to the pastor, who gave him the expected open-mouthed look of shock.

"All right, all right." Glick lifted himself from the curb and walked toward the two baffled young men. They appeared to be trying to recapture the glory of the 1960s. They sported crumpled tie-dyed shirts and long hair. Glick looked them over closely as he approached. He could tell they were just a couple of middle-class kids playing dress-up. The one boy had nails that were clean and manicured. He had an expensive pair of shoes and a cute little turned-up nose that made Glick wonder if he'd had some kind of plastic surgery.

"You two on your way to visit the graves of the Grateful Dead or something?" came his great booming voice from behind. The two turned and looked up at a hideous, grinning monster standing behind them. They weren't sure whether to laugh or cry. "Here, let me help you," he said, pushing the boy aside. "I know a thing or two about these engines."

"You do? Oh my god, that's so awesome. I can never find parts or anything for her. It's been tough."

"Yeah, big surprise," said Glick with his head stuck in the back. "Gimme a wrench."

"Hold on." The kid produced a toolbox.

"You need your carburetor rebuilt," he said, "cause there's excessive fuel coming in right here; see it?" he said, pointing at the carb. "I can't do it here, but I can make an adjustment that can get you to the nearest shop. You might want to look for one that specializes in these old wrecks. Looks to me like you need a valve adjustment, too."

"Wow, thanks," said the grateful boy.

Glick worked on the bus for about an hour and got some problems taken care of. He gave the boys a list of things that were wrong with the vehicle. Before he sent them on their way, he advised them to either dump it or be prepared to put some serious money into it. The appreciative fellows happily filled Glick's tank and waved goodbye to the odd couple on the Harley.

"Good luck," called out Glick to the two as he and the pastor departed. "You need it."

"Now, how did that feel?" Pastor Bloom asked the biker seated in front of him.

"Nowhere near as satisfying as a good ass-stomping," replied Glick.

The pastor just shook his head.

Glick and Pastor Bloom traveled many more hours until dark. The grizzled biker began to grow weary, his eyes scanning the environment for a place to set up a camp for the night.

They were now in the heart of western Kansas, and the vast emptiness made Glick feel depressed. There were, however, plenty of places that looked hospitable to rest for the night. Conditions were also quite good; the sky was clear and it was not too cold, only in the mid-50s. Glick pulled off the interstate and took a dirt road that ran along a cow pasture. From there, he spotted a hiking trail amid a row of birch trees that ran along a pretty stream. He turned in and cut his engine.

"This is it, Preach. I can't go on another minute; my ass is numb," said the tired biker as he strained to remove himself from the leather seat.

The two quickly set up camp in the peaceful, secluded spot. They collected firewood, and Glick patted himself on the back for remembering to get matches even though they reminded him of how much he needed a smoke. Pastor Bloom collected some large rocks to surround the pile of wood, and soon they had a blazing fire.

This ain't so bad, thought Glick as he wrapped himself in a fuzzy blanket and sat on the ground against a sycamore tree. *Hell, I even got a couple of beers left.* He cracked a warm brew and leaned back into the small tree. He drained it in one long gulp and crushed the can flat between his thumb and forefinger. Then he burped as he tossed the can into the fire.

"That's quite a talent you have there, Mr. Glick."

"Would you please quit calling me 'Mr. Glick'?"

"I could do that, if you would please quit calling me 'Preach.' What do you prefer I call you?"

"Glick, just plain old Glick."

"Do you have a first name?"

"Nope."

"Surely your parents didn't name you just Glick. I'm certain they gave you a first name to go with it."

"Nope."

"I see."

The two sat in silence, listening to the sounds of the wind in the sycamore trees, watching nothing go by. The stars were so bright in the countryside evening; one could see millions of them.

"You don't get to see too many nights like this in the city," said Glick to Pastor Bloom. "I forgot how beautiful it was to actually see the stars; you can barely see that big one there when you're in Daytona. What's it called again?"

"That's Venus. It's not a star, it's a planet."

"Oh. Say...you wouldn't happen to have a joint on you, would you, Preach?"

"What kind of man do you take me for, Mr. Glick?"

"Then I guess some crank's out of the question, huh? Har! Har! Har!" Glick laughed so hard at his own joke that he nearly choked, and then his mood turned more serious. "How many people are there in that group that you're heading to? And what is it about the microchip that someone like you won't take it? It seems to me you got nothing to run from. And all those other people that you're meeting, what's up with them?"

"Well, I'm glad you brought that up, Mr. Glick. It gives me a chance to explain some of the more arcane chapters of verse." Pastor Bloom went into his belongings and pulled out a worn Bible. He leafed through the pages until he came to the passages he was looking for. He set his Bible down for a moment.

"You see, what is happening today was foretold thousands of years ago by a man named John who wrote down a vision he had of the future while he was languishing in prison. Some people think he was one of the 12 apostles John, and others believe he may have been John the Baptist. No one is really sure, but what we do know, is he wrote down some things that seemed very far-fetched when he originally wrote them down. As time unfolded, the things he prophesied started to seem not so unlikely anymore. In fact, they are starting to happen right before our very eyes."

The pastor then opened his Bible to the passage once again. "It says it all right here in Revelation Chapter 13, Verse 16: 'He causeth all, both small and great, rich and poor, free and bond to receive a mark in their right hand or in their foreheads. And that no man might buy or sell, save he that had the mark, or the name of the beast, or the number of his name.'" Pastor Bloom looked up to Glick and said, "Without the mark, no one will be able to buy or sell anything."

"Yeah," Glick answered, "I heard of that before. Sounds like today, I suppose. I always thought they were talking about some kind of tattoo, though."

"Well, there is something quite significant here in this one little word. It says that he causes all men to receive a mark *in* their hand, not a mark *on* their hand."

"A microchip," whispered Glick. "No shit. Let me see that."

"Sure, here it is, right here in black and white, written over 2,000 years ago. There are other things you should know, too, things you need to be on the lookout for. But first, I would like to answer your other question. You asked me how many people I'm meeting in the Christian dissenters group. Well, there are already tens of thousands that have migrated to Utah right at this very moment, and more are pouring in every day. The governor has announced that Utah will never participate in the federally mandated microchip program, and he himself has refused to take the microchip. He says he never will. We may actually have a safe haven there in that one place."

"Hmmm," said Glick. "That's sounding better all the time; but I ain't hanging out with a bunch of holy-rollers."

"You may not have much to fear there, Mr. Glick. The community I'm a part of is by invitation and application only, and each application must be reviewed by the board members before approval is granted."

"Man, I asked you to stop calling me 'Mr. Glick.'"

"I'll make you a deal. I'll stop calling you Mr. Glick if you'll tell me your first name."

Glick stewed angrily. "OK, you stubborn old coot, my first name is Richard ... and if you call me Dick Glick, I'll kick your fucking ass."

"No need to worry, Richard."

"Oh, great," mumbled Glick.

Chapter *16*

Beggars Can't Be Choosers

Emma Jackson looked at the clock beside her bed. She counted down the minutes she had left before the Michigan mandate took place that would require her to take a microchip into her body. The clock struck midnight, and it was now official; she would no longer be able to buy or sell anything from this point forward. She struggled inside. Sleep had been a rare commodity since the exhibition at the chipping station, and she knew tonight would be no different. She got up to go to the kitchen and take another inventory of the canned goods and food that she had stocked up on over the past week. She figured she could survive for about three weeks, but then after that, she wasn't sure what she would do for food.

Emma weighed the circumstances and thought about what life might be like with the chip. On the surface, all seemed well. Everyone she knew had already taken the chip and seemed to be faring just fine, but she still couldn't shake the feeling that something was very fundamentally wrong. She thought back to the crowds herded into specific racial groupings and recalled Hitler's concentration camps. She really didn't want to unload her concerns on T.J. and did her best to keep her mouth shut around him, but he knew instinctively that something was up, and he would constantly ask his "Grammy" what was wrong. All she could do to hush the little boy was rock him in her favorite chair. Those moments helped comfort Emma as well.

She went to her medicine cabinet and took out a Valium to help her get to sleep. She had been taking so many lately, they were starting to lose their strength. She doubled the usual dose and went back to bed for the night.

Over the next several weeks, Emma repeated her normal daily routine. She continued working for the nursing agency but was unable to receive payment for her toils without a chip, so the money simply accumulated in the agency's account. She spoke to her supervisor about the situation, and although they were sympathetic to her concerns, they were of very little help. They simply couldn't understand why she would want to put herself through such hardship and urged Emma to go get a chip like all their other nursing staff. She occasionally wondered if she wasn't just being overly cautious and felt tempted to break down and receive the chip, but something inside told her no. She stopped herself short every time. She eventually had to notify the agency she had worked at for the past 15 years that she would no longer be able to work for them. She had to find another way to get by.

More time passed. Emma squeezed a last bit of ketchup on a stale saltine cracker and handed it to T.J. By now his little ribs were starting to show. If she had ever gotten T.J. that kitten, she would have gladly eaten the cat's food, or maybe even the cat itself. Poor T.J. couldn't even get fed at school. Without the microchip, they would no longer even let him attend his class.

It had now been four weeks since the mandate had passed, and Emma had reached the end of her rope. She never realized just how difficult it would be. Everything in the world revolved around commerce and the buying and selling of goods and services. She sat on her couch and cried for a very long time. When she reached the point where she had cried out all her tears, she stood and steeled herself for a painful decision.

Emma couldn't believe what she was about to do. Stepping into her great-grandson's room, she searched for a black marker pen and some poster board. She was going to go out and beg.

She found poster board and wrote in big letters "Will work for food". On the backside, she wrote "Starving, please help!" Then she knocked on her neighbor's door to see if they would watch T.J. for the day; they did not seem enthused but they agreed. Once situated, she stepped outside into the cold October morning on the streets of Detroit and looked for a good place with a lot of traffic to stand. A cold breeze blew straight through her bones, the sky above was ominous and gray, and it appeared that it could snow at any moment. She quickly found a good spot, but there were so many other people now begging on the street, it was very hard getting anyone to notice her.

A whole day went by, and Emma hadn't had a single response to her sign. Since people could no longer donate cash to the beggars, they had to instead offer them food or other such sundries. As soon as some kind soul would gift one of the destitute, all the other panhandlers would take notice and engulf the humanitarian like a flock of birds, clinging and pleading for mercy. Most people who offered help once were reluctant to do so again after experiencing such an ordeal. Darkness began to fall, and Emma, disheartened, went home to T.J., who was watching TV.

"Where'd you go, Grammy?"

"I had to work, honey."

"You got a job now?"

"Sort of."

The next day, Emma decided to change her tactic; she took out a pen and wrote a new sign:

"Will Clean Houses for Food and Board."

Then she pondered what to do with T.J. She couldn't leave him at the neighbors' place again, so she resigned herself to taking him with her. She bundled him up in his warmest clothes and packed some water bottles, it could be a long day.

"Come on, baby. We gots something to do today."

"OK, Grammy."

Emma held T.J.'s mittened hand and scoped out the area, looking for the best place to set up camp. She decided on a corner that was fairly sheltered from the wind, surrounded by two high-rise brick buildings. She told T.J. to stand behind her, and she stood and held up her sign.

"What do you think you're doing?" She heard a voice behind her. Emma turned to look and saw a haggard-looking woman standing behind her.

"I'm looking for some help for me and my grandbaby."

"Not on this corner, you're not! This is my spot. You got that?"

"Yeah, I got it."

Emma set out to find another spot, but most of the good ones were already taken. Almost every corner had someone already there holding some sort of sign. She finally settled on an area that didn't have as much traffic, but it appeared relatively warm and safe. She and T.J. stood for several hours without a single person stopping to accept her offer of cleaning. She grew tired and despondent and sat against the wall. There she propped her sign up next to her and sat down. While she waited, she prayed. Eventually, a woman stopped and questioned Emma about her credentials. The woman was well-dressed and in her mid-40s. Emma quickly stood to greet the woman. She explained that she was a visiting nurse by trade and would prefer that line of work to cleaning but would take whatever she could get. She also explained that she would soon be out of a place to live and needed a place to stay. When the woman questioned the appearance of the boy, Emma answered, "He comes with me wherever I go."

"I'm sorry," the woman replied. "I'm really not even looking for a live-in maid. I'd much prefer a not live-in situation, and with the boy it would just be too much." And off she went; the only bite she'd had after standing all day. Emma hung her head as she walked over to the wall that T.J. was standing against. She picked up the sign to go another round, and T.J. said to her, "Let me try it, Grammy."

"Sure, honey – what have we got to lose?"

She handed him the sign and went and sat back down against the wall. She pulled in her legs against the cold wind that was picking up speed. She looked up and noticed flecks of snow were starting to fall; soon they would be forced to go home for the day.

T.J. took the sign to the corner and held it up high into the air. He stood like that for a very long time. Emma watched him as he sought out every face, imploring for help from some kind stranger, but hardly anyone noticed the little boy holding the sign that was every bit as big as he was. In Emma's mind, she was trying to figure a course of action but couldn't see any way out of her desperate situation. She couldn't continue like this; she would have to find another way. Her train of thought was soon interrupted. A short, older man wearing a fedora had stopped to read T.J.'s sign.

"You're going to clean houses, are you? Shouldn't you be in school instead?" he asked T.J., all the while looking at Emma. She rose and stepped cautiously toward the gentleman. She was wary of him, fearing that he may report her to the authorities for keeping the boy out of school in order to beg on the street; but he had a kind face, and when he smiled at Emma, she grew more courageous.

"It's me doing the cleaning, sir," said Emma to the man with the sweet smile.

"Yes, I figured as much," said the man. He had a slightly formal air about him for someone who was walking about in one of the worst parts of the city. His clothes appeared older but were of good quality, and his shoes had been buffed to a high shine.

"Why don't you go to the local shelter?" asked the man. "There's a good one on 42nd Street."

"Yes, we been there already," she replied. "They wouldn't let us in without proper identification."

"And ...why don't you have that?"

"We never took a microchip," said Emma, looking down at her feet.

"I see," said the man. "You know, you're not alone in your predicament. What exactly is your particular aversion to the new technology the powers that be had decided to bestow upon us?"

"I didn't like the looks of the whole thing. They was lining everybody up by they color. I jes' couldn't do that to my poor baby here; but I may not have much choice, the way it's goin'. We starvin' now. Ain't had nothin' but peanut butter for the last week, and now it's gone, too. I gots to get back to work. You got any for me?"

"No, I don't have work, but I have something better. Here is my card. I want you to call me in the morning."

"Not work? What's this about, then?"

"There is a community of dissenters that you should be made aware of. These are people like you and I that hold similar beliefs and are distrustful of the current Establishment's modus operandi."

"Where they at? Can I go there right now? I'd sure like to hear what they has to say."

"This isn't a local community, and it requires several days' travel to get to them. It is imperative that you hold the information that I give you very close to yourself. The very survival of the community hinges upon its members keeping tight lips."

"I don't got no money to get nowhere."

"Don't worry. We will take care of all that. Like I said, you are not alone; there will be a bus and some meals provided. That is, of course, if you are interested."

"Oh, yes, I'm interested, all right. That's the best offer I had in a long time."

"Good, then. Call me in the morning and we will talk further." With that, the man left, disappearing into the cluster of people pouring into the street. It was shortly after 5 p.m., and people were just getting off work. Emma turned to T.J. and weighed the decision whether to stay and try to get lucky with their sign or go home. She decided that they had already had their lucky break for the day. She left her homemade sign on the sidewalk behind her. Never looking back, she and T.J. made their way through the crowd toward home with a renewed spirit.

"Tomorrow's a new day, baby," said Emma to T.J. while walking down the street.

"OK, Grammy."

Emma and T.J. both went to bed hungry that night, but Emma didn't care, she wished she could call the man right that very minute. She took out his card and gazed at the name for the tenth time-Joel Brandenburg Esquire. *This man's an attorney*, she said to herself. *I wonder why he's being so nice. They don't exactly got a reputation for being charitable.*

The next morning, she awoke at the crack of dawn and went to turn on the TV, but the screen was black. The cable bill hadn't been paid for over two months, and they had shut off service. She had been anticipating the shutoff for some time now and was surprised that it hadn't come sooner.

"Oh, well," sighed Emma. *None of that much matters anymore.*

She pondered if it was too early to call Mr. Brandenburg. It was only 6:35, so she sat in the kitchen staring at the clock until 7 o'clock, and then she dialed.

"Hello?"

"Mr. Brandenburg, this here is Emma Jackson. We met yesterday."

"Oh yes, Mrs. Jackson; a pleasure to hear from you."

"I didn't wake you, did I, sir?"

"No, not at all. Can you please be at my office at 9 a.m. sharp? The address is on the card I gave you. Do you need directions?"

"No, sir, I knows the area well."

"Very well, then, see you at 9:00."

Emma arrived at Mr. Brandenburg's office and looked about. The office was already packed with people. Emma counted: 36 other people were already crammed into his office, and more were coming in by the minute. There were no chairs left to sit on, so she stood by some other people who were also standing and waiting. I could be here an awful long time waiting for them to call my name.

She didn't wait as long as she thought she might. Mr. Brandenburg entered the room at 9:15 and greeted the waiting congregation.

"Hello, everyone. I'm glad all of you could make it here today," he began.

"Each one of you is here today because you have been hand-selected as members of our great American society who have been placed in a difficult situation that you would not be in were it not for interference from the World Central Bank in conjunction with the United States government. All of you here have one thing in common; like myself, not a single person in this room has taken a WCR bank microchip."

The gathered throng looked about at each other. An instant camaraderie was felt by each person in the room. Brandenburg strolled through the space and met the eyes of every person there. There were all sorts of different types in the room. There were clean-cut-looking college kids, ordinary housewives, Asians, blacks, whites, Hispanics, crying babies, middle-aged and elderly men and women like Emma. Some were wearing suits, and others were in rags, but they all shared one common characteristic: Each had a look of desperation and fear in their eyes.

"I am going to present an opportunity to the people gathered here this morning. There is a large community located in Utah where the members have resolved never to take a WCR microchip. They live their days in relative peace and comfort even while working outside the standard commerce system."

The listeners were amazed at this good news. Their smiles lit up the room.

"Members of the community are expected to do their share. There is a great deal of hard work involved, and there will be no room for anyone that doesn't participate fully and to the best of their ability. Membership in the community is by invitation only. It is considered a privilege to be there, and anyone who doesn't do their part will be asked to leave."

The people nodded their heads, and some raised their hands with questions. Brandenburg addressed each of their concerns, explaining how the community members depended upon bartering for goods and services and how they grew their own food and made their own clothes and more, much more. Everyone was excited by the hope of a fresh new start and asked how long until they could arrive at the wonderful-sounding place.

"We will be scheduling staggered bus trips over the next several weeks. Gather your loved ones and prepare them for the long trip. Seating is limited, so sign the registry now and let us know how many will be in your party, and please limit your belongings to only items that you can carry with you. We simply do not have room for anything over what is absolutely necessary."

A hand went up in the room, and a mousy-looking woman asked: "Are you well enough supplied? Do you have enough food, and how are you getting the gas for these bus rides?"

"That's a good question," answered Brandenburg. "We have been anticipating and preparing for these events for a long time now. We have been stockpiling food and water and warehousing gasoline and generators over the past year; that's when we first started seeing the warning signs of what was to come. You will get to see firsthand the high degree of organization once we arrive there. Much thought and careful planning has gone into the development of our sovereign community. We are quite proud of what we have accomplished."

"What happens if the federal government raids us? What if we all wind up shot for treason?" asked a young man in his early 20s.

"At this time, there are no legislated penal codes for not receiving a microchip nor are there any against bartering. They have simply done their best to make it impossible for you to survive without it. Everything our community does is completely legal. Believe me; I know the laws regarding this subject explicitly. I am an attorney, you know."

"What will we do when we get there?" asked a sharp-looking young woman. "I'm a stockbroker. I don't really have sewing skills or know how to run a plow."

"We will give an evaluation and run some tests on where your aptitudes lie. Some of you may have to find some new skills. Don't worry. We will be patient and will also provide training. As members of the community, we stick together and support each other."

Another woman raised her hand. "Why are you doing this for us?"

"Another excellent question," replied Brandenburg. "Each of you here were hand-selected because you stood out. It was obvious that you were not micro-chipped and were opposed to the concept or you would have taken the chip long ago. Our community needs members of a like mind. We also believe that there is strength in numbers, and frankly, we need people from different walks of life to afford us the wide range of skills and diversity that we will need to make us successful. Personally, I'm doing this because of the joy I get from saving the lives of those with whom I share ideological similarities."

Emma raised her hand. "Where do I sign up?" she asked.

"Right here." Brandenburg picked up the top paper from a stack of applications on his desk and held it in the air. We will need all your information. Please be aware that we will perform background checks, and we will check your references."

Almost everyone signed the register and made application. Emma was the first to put her name on the list. "I can't wait to tell my grandbaby," she said excitedly to the woman standing next to her.

"The bus schedule is posted on the bulletin board behind me," announced Brandenburg, motioning behind his head. "You will see that buses are leaving twice daily Monday through Saturday for the next several weeks, or until further notice. We hope to see everyone there."

Emma went home with a happy heart. It felt so good to know she wasn't alone. She packed her belongings and retrieved T.J. from the neighbors' house.

"I have good news, baby – we gonna go on a trip to Utah," Emma said excitedly to T.J.

"What's Utah, Grammy?"

"It's a wonderful place where all your dreams can come true."

"What's there, Grammy?"

"Honestly, I don't know," said Emma. Thinking of Utah brought to mind sand dunes, canyons and blazing hot desert. Not exactly heaven, but better than freezing to death in the streets of Detroit.

"Maybe we'll see some cactus and some lizards," said Emma, packing T.J.s belongings into duffel bags.

"And cowboys?" asked T.J.

"Sure, baby. I bet there's lots of cowboys there."

Emma had her items packed and ready to go in just under two hours; she wanted to catch the 4 p.m. bus that very afternoon. She felt a stab in her heart when she thought of Tianna. If the girl did come around, there would be no way for her to track Emma down. Emma left the phone number for Mr. Brandenburg with the neighbors in the event of an emergency and left the key for the landlord in their care as well. She left her apartment and the majority of its contents behind and towed her baggage in a red wagon with T.J. sitting on top.

She reached the address of the industrial district and found the designated place where the buses were leaving from. There she saw several old school buses sitting off to the side of a large repository. She was early, so she took a seat on a curb and waited along with some other excited people. She recognized several of their faces from the meeting earlier that same morning. As 4 o'clock approached, a large crowd had begun to gather. *I wonder how we all gonna fit on this bus*, thought Emma.

Mr. Brandenburg and two assistants made an appearance and began a head count. "We can only fit 28 people on each bus," he announced through a loudspeaker. "If you have small children, put them on your lap; we have a very limited number of rear-facing child safety seats. If you do not want to put your child in your lap, you may have to wait for the next bus, and we cannot guarantee that you will receive a child safety seat. There should be no unbelted passengers seated behind seats with child safety restraint systems. Please place your items under your seat and strap them in place with the provided bungee cords. We have some additional room on the top of each bus, but again, space is limited, so please – only one item per person. We have three buses leaving this afternoon, so there should be room for everyone; no need for crowding. Please watch your step as you take your seat."

Emma took a seat and put T.J. next to her. He was too big to put in her lap. The bus quickly filled, and soon the small convoy of three school buses was on its way to the destination. The bus was crowded and smelly, the passengers were visibly nervous, and one fellow appeared to be drunk. Emma didn't care; this was a chance of a lifetime. She had never lived outside of Detroit her whole life, and her travels had only consisted of visiting relatives in Midland County. That's as far as she had ever been; to go somewhere as strange as Utah was as exhilarating as a trip to some exotic foreign land.

Three full days' travel it would take to arrive. They would all be sleeping on the bus, and sandwiches and sodas were to be provided by the organizers. There wasn't much to do and boredom was rampant, but the three days soon passed, and everyone cheered when they saw the roadside sign that beaconed, "Welcome to Utah."

Several more hours passed with the crowded bus maneuvering through some very rugged canyons and mountainous terrain, mostly over dirt roads. Emma thought she would be sick several times but held on, they were fast approaching their final destination. The bus driver announced their arrival to the weary passengers. Emma peered out the bus window to see a large gated property in a ranch-type setting. The community was surrounded by high fencing that went as far as the eye could see. There must have been thousands of acres of land.

Emma noticed two men guarding the entrance to the facility. They were holding semiautomatic weapons around their necks. She also noticed two towers on each side of the entrance gate. These also held guards. The driver got out and met with the other organizers in the buses behind them. They unlocked a large sliding gate and, after a brief exchange of words with the guards, resumed driving down the dirt road, kicking up a large cloud of dust behind them as they worked their way closer to the retreat.

Finally, the bus came to a stop. It was now time to survey their new home. The fatigued groups disembarked, gathered up their personal effects and were ushered toward a barnlike structure. Emma squinted in the bright daylight to see the faces of some people standing nearby; it was a welcoming committee. They greeted each new member with friendly smiles and hellos.

"Welcome to Hidden Village," said a tall man with an elegantly groomed brown beard as he shook the hand of each person. He wore sandals and loose clothing, reminding Emma of some sort of monk. "My name is John Reese, and I am the head coordinator for your group; just think of me as your guidance counselor. Follow me, please – I will help you get settled in to your new surroundings."

Reese turned and led the group of 28 people plus children through the barn and storage areas to a wide walkway, which opened up into a valley that held a camp. There were all sorts of activity, and the racket of blasting generators was deafening. Hundreds of people were busy building small houses out of logs. Travel trailers, campers and tents were scattered throughout. To the north, there were more people building what appeared to be the commercial district; a town. More were to the east erecting rows of windmills. The whole thing reminded Emma of the Wild West gold rush days.

"This way, please," said Reese, stepping over a log. "Your quarters are over here." Reese led them to a plywood structure that held enough cots for each member of the small group. A curtain separating each cot offered little privacy. Emma looked for a bathroom or kitchen and saw nothing that resembled any such thing; only cots.

"I'm afraid it isn't much at the moment," Reese said to the group. "We have a community gathering area with a large kitchen and a banquet hall/dining room. There's a small recreation center with a television and a pool table. There are several showering facilities set up in the western end. It may be a bit crowded occasionally. I suggest you schedule yourselves at different times in order to avoid running into long waits. Also, you are advised to begin plans on the design and building of your own living quarters as quickly as you can."

This advice was met with several dumbfounded looks. "Don't worry, we provide a great amount of support to accomplish this. Remember, everyone is expected to do their part and work very hard. I must warn you the Utah summers get very hot and the winters are very cold, so keep this in mind in your design. There won't be any central heat and air conditioning available in these quarters I'm afraid, but there is a nice lake on the property for cooling off in the summer. I'll have my assistant Cassandra show you the parameters and the boundaries later on this week. We have over 24,000 acres of property here at Hidden Village. We grow our own food and are completely self-sufficient. There is enough room, we believe, for a good-sized community to have a decent, fairly normal life. We have already made some outstanding progress in producing our own power, and we maintain an enviable septic and water distribution system. Hopefully, we will be able to live unmolested by the government for many years to come. Does anyone have any questions?"

"When can we see some more of the place?" asked a husky young man.

"There will be the first of a series of three different guided tours beginning on Friday at 8 a.m. We will have you very busy over the next few weeks with orientation classes, filling out paperwork and questionnaires, then taking trade classes. We are lacking in certain areas of expertise and are looking for skilled people to fill certain positions in the community."

Another hand went up, and a Hindu man in his early 40s asked, "Where did all this property come from?"

"Good question; some of it was donated by a wealthy industrialist who prefers to remain anonymous. This has been anticipated for many years now, and the preparations you see today were made well in advance. We have community round-table meetings every Thursday evening where you can voice your questions and concerns, so have them written down before the next meeting and we will answer them to the best of our ability. Any other questions?" Reese looked around.

"Yes," said a young Asian in a baseball hat. "What are those arched structures running the perimeter of the property?"

"Ah, yes," responded Reese. "Does everyone see these structures he's talking about? That's an above-ground aqueduct system; we also have one running underground that you don't see. It distributes water from the mountain springs and wells spread throughout the property right to where we need it, a very sophisticated system. Does anyone else have any questions?" When no one responded, Reese quickly withdrew.

"I'm going to leave you in the care of my assistant Cassandra for now. She will show you around to the showers and so forth. I'm sure everyone would like to get cleaned up. Please enjoy your stay. I will see you on Thursday."

Cassandra gave the group a quick tour of their immediate surroundings. The children squealed with delight upon seeing a playground, and most ran to play, leaving their confused parents wondering whether to chase them down or let them go. Cassandra encouraged the parents to let them play and seated the group on the grass under a tree. She gave some general directions, including locations of coordinators' cabins, maps of the facility and instructions for where and when they were to next meet and left the group to familiarize themselves on their own. Emma, exhausted from the long drive and the stress of the move, decided to forgo a shower and stake a claim to a cot so that she could rest the remainder of the afternoon. She had to pull the reluctant T.J. from the playground; he loudly protested kicking dirt into the air while tagging behind his aging great-grandmother.

Once Emma and T.J. settled into the sheets, they both fell into blissful slumber for the rest of the afternoon. Despite the paltry living conditions, Emma felt confident she had found the one place they could now call home.

Chapter *17*

Looking for a Loophole

Marlene Carson yawned and rubbed her eyes. She looked up to the clock on the wall of her corner office. It was approaching 2 a.m. and the documents in front of her were starting to blur. *Just another night at the office*, thought Marlene; *not much unlike so many others, especially in the early years.*

Marlene had earned her reputation as a hard-nosed, dedicated congresswoman long before reaching the floor of the Senate. She couldn't even count all the many long nights that had been spent sleeping on the fold-up mattress in her office after spending the evening putting together various reports and writing bills. That, coupled with her near-perfect voting attendance record, left little time for anything but work. Marriage and family had been postponed indefinitely until she could realize most of her goals, and by the time she finally had gotten married, at the age of 46, it was long past time to think of having children; the price one pays for a lifetime career devoted to perfect service.

Marlene considered driving home, then went to a corner closet and pulled out a fold-up mattress. The hearings on the moratorium vote would be at 9:30 the following morning, and she wanted to be sure not to miss them.

The next morning, Marlene headed into the Senate hearings on the issue at hand. There were speakers from both sides, and the debate continued until well in the afternoon.

Marlene carefully listened to both sides of the argument. The pro-microchip delegate primarily stressed the importance of retaining data that would allow the government to track down and prosecute perpetrators of all sorts: terrorist, pedophiles, kidnappers, extortionists, ID thieves and drug dealers. Representatives for the Libertarian Party and outraged members of the Senate gave heartfelt hours of long appeals, pleading for the other Senate members not go down the totalitarian road.

It was 4:15 when the senators finally cast their votes.

Marlene watched the eyes of her fellow senators to try to guess which direction they would go. Their faces were not difficult to read and she wasn't surprised at the direction the voting went. Marlene wondered how many of them had received the same message she had from the mystery man in the dark sunglasses. When it came her turn in the roll call she cast her vote in opposition of mandatory chipping. She knew deep down inside that she had sealed her fate, but she had never once in her life regretted standing for what she believed in. In this case it was no different. Despite being on the losing side of the argument, she still left feeling she had done the right thing. When the final votes were tallied, the Senate had voted in favor of the mandatory micro-chipping measure.

Marlene couldn't control herself. She stormed from the Senate floor, tears streaming down her face. Once outside the doors, she threw her copy of the mandate documents into the air, scattering them all over the entrance to the Capitol building. She choked back tears as she watched the brisk wind carry the papers all over Capitol Hill, some flitting up toward its famous dome, others landing in fountains and some under the wheels of passing cars. She knew that life for all U.S. citizens would never be the same.

Time passed and November arrived. The masses herded in to cast their votes for the public servant of their choice. The balloting was no longer secret; the new electronic system now required a swipe of the wrist and each American's vote was clearly noted and tallied. By now Marlene felt much more confident that she truly had the support of her constituents. All the public opinion polls showed her clearly in the lead, and she was considered by most to be a shoo-in for reelection. The vote count continued well into the night while Marlene waited in her office with her support staff, drinking coffee and nervously watching the television. Her staff busied themselves blowing up balloons and setting up for the victory party that would soon follow.

When the results came in for the state of Ohio, however, the office of the incumbent senator went silent. A look of disbelief came over every face in the room. Jim Spencer had been declared victorious in the election. Marlene Carson had lost the race; she and her 36 employees were officially now out of jobs.

She assessed her situation on the drive home that evening, feeling disillusioned and thoroughly disgusted. Marlene had been around the block a few times in her day, she knew how easy it was for the well-financed to hack into black box voting systems, coding to switch every 10th vote or so to the opponent. She'd thought she would never see it happen to her. She pulled into the driveway of her detached garage, and her loving husband, Curt, greeted her at the entrance. He put his arm around her and told her how sorry he was to witness such an outrageous miscarriage of justice. Together they walked into the house and sat at the dining room table, where she began to cry.

"This is so wrong," she burst out between sobs. "I've worked so hard my entire life just to have it come to this. Now what am I going to do?"

Curt wasn't apathetic to the situation, he took her hand and let her weep, knowing it was better to just let her get it all out. His mourning wife was ever grateful. She looked at him with her reddened, tear-stained face and asked out loud: "What did I do to deserve you, Curt? You're the best thing in my life."

Marlene thought back to the first time she had laid eyes on Curt Ludington at the yacht club in Cape Cod some eight years ago. Cocksure and so young, he had that jaunty, carefree air possessed only by those who come from old wealth, his family being one of the great aristocratic ones that settled in the Northeast in the late 1700s. Curt had flirted with Marlene mercilessly that day at brunch, right in front of his appalled family. Marlene was glad for the diversion as she found the rest of the Ludington clan to be rather insipid, but this young man was so very different, and quite the charmer with his mop of blond hair and sassy talk. He asked her on a date that day and she wasn't quite sure what to say; Curt had to be at least 15 years her junior, but he had needled her mercilessly until she finally agreed.

At the time, Marlene had been just another conquest for Curt. After a succession of gorgeous but empty headed model types, Curt was now keen on sampling this fascinating woman that stimulated him mentally as well as physically; plus he had never before bedded a U.S. senator and the challenge intrigued him. It wasn't that Marlene wasn't superlatively attractive for her age, she certainly was still quite the looker – but Curt's intentions were simply another notch on the bedpost. He had no idea that the simple tryst he had in mind would turn into a bonding with the great love of his life.

Marlene, it turned out, was quite the charmer herself – witty, smart and a great cook, too. They soon found that they shared many common interests, everything from architecture to literature and their political views were also in tune; but first and foremost, there was simply no denying the physical attraction between the two. They dated for an entire year before Marlene finally succumbed to Curt's advances. By then, Curt was hopelessly in love with the beautiful senator, and he surprised her with a marriage proposal on bended knee the following morning. They had been an inseparable couple ever since, balancing her career in the Senate and Curt's work at his architectural firm with romantic weekend getaways and quiet, stay-home weekdays.

The years passed and they still were going strong. Curt sold his business and spent the majority of his days sailing off the Cape and traveling to visit friends and relatives. He took up poker and baccarat as hobbies and spent a lot of time just waiting for Marlene to come home. Marlene, ever the consummate worker, remained at her Senate post, never once considering any other way of life. She enjoyed her work, being center stage in the events of the day and the respect and privileges that came with it. She wouldn't have traded her life for anything in the world.

But all that was coming to an end now, and Marlene couldn't even bear the thought. She had been in the political arena her entire life and had no idea where to go or what she was going to do with herself. She also had a lingering dread over the prospect of her and Curt taking a microchip; that very same issue that had cost her lofty career would soon be coming home, taking from them their precious liberty. It wouldn't be long now, and shortly they would be forced into the same boat as the rest of the nation – micro-chipped. Her golden retriever, Sammy, sensing her anxiety, came and rested his head on her lap. He looked up at her empathetically with his tender brown eyes while she stroked the tawny hair on his head. He let out a soft little whine.

"Where do I go from here, Curt?" she wailed to her patient husband.

"Maybe you could work a foundation," he offered, "or perhaps take up lecturing at colleges. I hear there's good money in that."

"Money isn't the issue, darling; you know I still have my annuities along with my state, congressional and Senate pensions, plus with *your* portfolio we'll never suffer financially," she sighed. "I just don't know what I'm ever going to do with my time." Her petting Sammy became more therapeutic. The dog pulled away and lay down at Curt's feet.

"You could do what I do," Curt offered. "Do nothing."

"Nothing? Hmmm, I wonder if I could."

"It's easy once you get used to it." He stretched his arms out over his head lazily like a cat waiting for a good scratch.

"No," Marlene shook her head. "I just can't picture myself retired. I have too many good years left."

"You certainly do, hot stuff." Curt put both his hands on her hips and gave them a little shake.

"Stop!" She giggled like a little girl, pushing Curt away. He responded by tickling her ribs while holding her wrist.

"Oh, you're impossible." She broke free and stood with a smile. "Thanks for trying to cheer me up, honey. I really do need that sometimes."

"Think nothing of it," he replied with his typical devil may care attitude. "Don't sweat the small stuff, babe. Trying to find something to occupy your time is an enviable position to be in."

"I already know of something that I can do right now, research. I need to find out if any protocols were violated in the passing of this bill. I'll be in the den for a while if you need me for anything."

"Fine, dear, good luck. I'll be right here, having a deep conversation with the dog."

Marlene went to her den, sat at her computer and turned on the power button. *Surely this thing can be repealed. All I need is a loophole, a screw up on someone's part and we'll have a case.*

She logged into the Congressional Research Service, using her still-active pass codes to get into records not accessible to the general public. She spent the majority of the day scouring the electronic records for something, *anything* that would substantiate a claim. She started with the considerations that preceded the bill's drafting and found nothing. Then she looked for transcripts of the committee hearings and floor debate. Nothing. This was very surprising. It was as if the records hadn't been entered yet, even though almost two months had already passed. The minutes of the moratorium vote were still unrecorded – no briefings, no congressional testimony, nothing. She turned next to the Legislative Information System. Again nothing; in fact, there was nothing under all known sources of federal legislative information; very strange indeed. Her hopes were to find enacted laws' oversight, but without the necessary recordings she had very little to go on. Finally she turned to outside agency activities and still, nothing. She wrapped up her day of research with frustratingly little luck. She sat in her chair and stared at the ceiling. What would she do? What should she do?

Marlene turned off the computer. It was time to go in person. She decided that a visit to the Library of Congress in Washington would be the next step in her search for answers.

She left the den and went to the bedroom, where she packed her small overnight bag. She gazed at Curt who was tranquilly lying on the bed taking a late-afternoon nap. She scribbled a quick note, kissed him on the forehead and scooted out the door quietly before he could wake up. She grabbed a box of strawberries from the fridge, got inside her car, and soon she was headed to Washington, D.C.

It didn't take Marlene long to travel from Columbus to D.C. She typically drove too fast and was there in just under seven hours. During normal circumstances, all she had to do was give ample notice and a jet would have been provided for her courtesy of the U.S. taxpayers, but times were different now. Those sorts of conveniences would have to wait until a new position could be established for her. And you can bet Marlene Carson was nowhere near giving up on politics. She would make a strong comeback. Everyone would see it for themselves. She would run again against Jim Spencer in the following election, and this time she would be ready for him. There were just some preparations to be made. She had to make sure her guns were fully loaded this time. No more mistakes.

It was dark and Marlene was tired. She checked herself into the best suite at the Ambassador Hotel in the heart of Capitol Square but still suffered a restless sleep. When she did fall off, Marlene dreamt of giant computers that came to life, strangling their owners to death. She woke at 3 a.m. with her suitcase on top of her head. She had no idea how it got there.

Marlene couldn't fall back asleep, so she turned on the TV and waited until a decent hour arrived that she could get to the Library of Congress just two blocks from the hotel. Soon enough 8:45 arrived, and Marlene walked out the door into the chilly northern air. She was the first to enter the library at 9 a.m. sharp. She immediately went to the library's computer records to see if there was anything there that were not in the Internet cloud. But she saw exactly the same thing that she found at home, nothing. She then turned to the Law Library of Congress, the largest legal collection in the world, 2.65 million volumes of primary legal sources. She spent over six hours poring over the records and found very little. Finally, in desperation she turned to the law librarian's research assistance team for help. A congenial woman directed her to the Thomas Records and sat down and assisted her personally in her research. Together, they pulled up microfilm from the day that the congressional hearings had taken place. What they found was disturbing.

The minutes of the hearing, it turned out, actually had been recorded but they were blacked out. Someone had taken a black magic marker and crossed through the words, making it impossible to read the contents of the microfilm. Page upon page of minutes were crossed out entirely. Marlene turned to the law librarian in disbelief. The librarian just shook her head; she had seen this sort of thing before.

Marlene demanded that the originals be produced. The librarian informed her that the originals had been warehoused and it would take weeks to produce them, but she assured Marlene that she would make it her number one priority to see that they were retrieved for her even if she had to dig through the records herself.

Marlene was very grateful to the librarian for her assistance and thanked her repeatedly. They closed with an exchange of business cards. Marlene could really do nothing more than just wait and see. She already knew, however, that even when the records were produced she was going to find the exact same thing. Originals with black magic marker crossed through. If they would allow her to take copies, perhaps she could find an expert that could read through the marker. Only time would tell for sure.

Marlene knew she could do no more. It was time to get back home. She skipped lunch and headed straight to her car for the drive home. Curt would be disappointed to hear her quest had been for naught. On the way home, Marlene had plenty of time to think. She thought long and hard about what she'd discovered; the time had come to contact friends and allies.

I need a federal magistrate, the top dog, she thought as she retrieved her phone from her purse and began dialing. She contacted some of her fellow senators and some old friends from Congress. She had no real contacts herself within the federal judiciary system but she knew plenty of people who did. She started with her colleague Cathleen Cramer, a congresswoman out of Pennsylvania. Her husband was an associate judge at the Commonwealth Appellate Court in Harrisburg Pa. He might be able to get her an audience with her main goal, the chief justice of the United States.

She got Cathleen's voice mail and left a message. She then dialed Rudy Sanborg, a senator in the Rhode Island General Assembly. He was close friends with Rhode Island Lt. Gov. Richard Brighton. Marlene remembered that Brighton had once mentioned that he vacationed with Rhode Island Chief Justice Paul Suffolk regularly. This would be even better than Carol's husband, a mere associate judge. Surely he would know the U.S. chief personally. She needed to reach out to someone who knew him right away.

Again, she got a voice mail. "Hi Rudy, it's Marlene. Long time no hear. Listen, I need you to please help me with a project I've taken on and I think I could use the assistance of Rich Brighton. Could you please get in touch with me and get his me contact info as soon as you can? Thanks, I appreciate it."

"Damn," Marlene cursed out loud as she hung up. Impatient by nature, she hit her hand against the steering wheel. "Where *is* everybody today?!"

She tried one more person, but it was a long shot. The U.S. attorney in Indiana had been an acquaintance for several years, but Marlene couldn't say she was particularly fond of the woman. She found her a tad rude, always interrupting, and she just generally rubbed Marlene the wrong way, but she decided to give her a try anyway. She dialed the woman's cellphone but it had been disconnected. Great. She then dialed 411information and got the number to her office, and the secretary answered.

"U.S. attorney's office."

"Hello, this is Senator Marlene Carson calling. Is Patricia available?"

"What is this regarding, ma'am?"

"I'm a U.S. senator. Isn't that enough for you?"

"One moment please, I'll transfer you."

The phone call was transferred and Marlene sat on hold for about five minutes, and then she hung up.

Hmmm, the chances weren't too good of her being able to help anyway. I need someone a little higher up the food chain than a U.S. attorney. Marlene exhaled. She had exhausted her options for the moment. She still remained on the phone, however, the rest of the drive home reaching out to the people in the contacts folder of her Blackberry. Someone would come through for her eventually; those members of her inner circle didn't let their own down.

There wasn't much she could do now, though, except wait. Wait and cross her fingers.

Chapter *18*

Let's go Shopping

Toni Vickery gathered the last of her belongings that she would need for her trip to Canada. She was really hoping it wouldn't take long to find a good place for her and Joey to settle; somewhere suitable near a good school. She already had her car tuned up for the long road trip and had put in for a leave of absence at Greenview - just in case she had to come back. Hopefully all would go well and it would be permanent. She was also hopeful that she would land another teaching job in the same school that Joey would go to. She picked up the phone and called her mother and told her that she was leaving for a few weeks, then quickly hung up before the questions could begin. She didn't want too many people to know she was leaving town, but on a whim dialed Dina Paterson, her old friend, to say goodbye.

"Hey Dina, how are you?"

"Toni? Where have you been? I heard you quit working at Greenview. Is everything all right?"

"No, I didn't quit, I just took a leave of absence, but it may turn out to be permanent. Dina, I'm doing my best to get out of here, or at least I'm trying. I want to go to Canada to start a new life. I'm leaving first thing in the morning to scope out the area to hopefully find a new place to settle down."

"What about Joey? Are you taking him out of school?"

"Yes" she sighed "I don't see any other way. He is giving me a fit about it though. He likes old school and doesn't want to go. I don't blame him, he's been here his entire life. All his friends are here."

"What about all your furniture and stuff? Are you renting a U-Haul?"

"No, I'm leaving everything behind. I'm driving my car"

"Everything? What about your townhouse? Are you going to sell it?"

"I don't know, Dina," said Toni, wiping her brow with a tissue "I haven't even thought that far ahead. I just know I have to get out of here while I still can. In just seven days we won't be able to buy anything, and I'll never be able to get out of here. I have to leave now."

"Hold on, Toni, don't leave just yet. I want to come with you."

Dina Patterson was given just two days to prepare. Toni had mixed emotions about having a tag-along. On one hand she was happy to have her best friend and comrade to help, and on the other she feared Dina would only slow her down. She weighed the options in her mind and decided that regardless of how she felt, she couldn't leave a friend or anyone else behind that wanted out of this situation as badly as she did.

Two days passed and it was moving day. Toni had been prodding Joey for two days to pack his things but he still hadn't done it. It was now almost 6:00 am and he just refused to budge; they fought about the move that entire morning. Exasperated, she finally grabbed a duffle bag and crammed it full of his clothes along with his favorite football and placed them in the trunk along with the rest of her own things. She then went back inside her townhouse to retrieve her boy.

Joey was sitting on the floor of his bedroom with his arms folded in front of him, he was clearly very upset. "C'mon son" Toni stood over him extending her hand. "It's time to go."

"Please mom, can't I just stay with Dad? I don't want to go."

"We're leaving now and that's final! You will understand later. I'm very sorry but this is the way it has to be." Toni nudged Joey out the door to the waiting car. He plopped into the back seat and pouted.

Toni pulled into Dina's driveway at 6:45, Dina was packed and ready. They started on the road to face whatever challenges were headed their way.

Toni thrust a map in the lap of her friend and pointed toward the red pencil outline she had made marking their route. "Were going up I-95 until we reach North Carolina then we'll jump on the 77 into Pennsylvania, then 90 to 75. We will enter Canada at the Lewiston Bridge around Buffalo, New York. It looks like about 18 hours of driving; we should be able to drive straight through. You OK with that?" Toni smiled. Dina nodded and pulled her pillow over her eyes, it would be a long day.

The girls had packed a cooler full of food so they would not waste much valuable time stopping to eat. They drove straight through without stopping when fatigue finally forced a pit stop on them. Toni already felt road beat to death, her back ached and she hadn't changed her contact lenses in days. She placed her open palm over her eyes and squinted. She feared she might start hallucinating soon if she didn't get some rest.

The three stopped to grab a quick dinner at a Denny's in Pittsburgh and freshen up. The two women chatted over coffee while waiting for their food to arrive, Joey sulked in his booth. The boy hadn't spoken a single word the entire trip.

"So," Dina asked to Toni, "once we're in Canada, what's the first thing you want to do?"

"Relax in my hotel room with the TV and a bottle of wine."

"No, I mean a little longer-term."

"Oh you know the plan. I think we should just look for the best, fastest place to settle in and get an apartment. We need to make sure there is plenty of available work, too. Hopefully we can pick up good teaching jobs; it's still early enough in the school year. We should be able to find something."

"Does any particular area interest you?"

"No, I don't know the first thing about Canada." Toni frowned. "I've never been there, even once. Somewhere just outside of Ontario, I'm guessing. I'll bet the winters are damn cold. This is going to take some getting used to." Toni's mind drifted to sunny Jacksonville beaches and seagulls.

"We will need to pool our funds for a while, too. After we get on our feet, I'll help you apartment hunt and you can get your own place." Toni wasn't thrilled about the prospect of having a roommate, but money was awfully tight, she wasn't quite sure how she was going to make it. The three stood to leave. Toni felt bad about leaving just a 10 percent tip, but it was time to start tightening the belt. *I might as well get used to it now.*

Toni sat in the driver's seat and reached for the map. *I wonder what TV is like in Canada? Am I going to have to learn to speak French?*

They resumed driving until almost 2:00 in the morning, reaching Lewiston. They arrived as close as they could get to the border crossing and took a look at the incredibly long line of cars; rows upon rows. Despite the early hour, there were tens of thousands of cars all stopped in their tracks. Many people were simply standing outside of their cars or sitting on their hoods, waiting for the monumental lines to move. Hundreds of thousands people, all looking to cross over into Canada.

"Looks like we weren't the only ones with this idea," commented Dina.

"Holy shit," replied Toni. "Would you just look at all of this? This could take forever. I don't think I can handle this line Dina. Why don't we go back to that motel back there and get some rest? We can get in line first thing in the morning and hopefully it won't be as long."

Dina had to agree. After almost 20 hours of driving the last thing she wanted to do was sit in line for another 20 more. "Alright Toni, I'm all for that." The trio checked in to the rundown roadside motel, pulled the curtains tightly shut and crashed out hard in the small dingy room.

Around 5:15 in the morning Toni woke up. She poured herself some water from the tap and sat on the edge of the bed. *I hope there's no bedbugs in here* she thought patting about the edge of the bed for evidence of infestation. When she got to Joeys side of the bed she noted his lumpy form under the heavy blanket; but something seemed wrong. She patted the lump and pulled back the covers. All that was there were three pillows lined up in a row, Joey was gone.

"Oh my god no!" Toni screeched as she turned on the light. Panicking she rushed into the bathroom and looked behind the shower curtain. Nothing. She ran outside and looked down over the balcony rail to the street below hollering his name. "Joe-y! Joe-y!"

"Please say this isn't so." Toni picked up the phone and dialed Joey's cell phone, it went straight to voice mail. She then dialed the front office.

"What's going on?" Dina asked while lifting her head off her pillow.

"Shhhh" Toni waved her off. "Hello front desk? This is room 17. My son, he is 11 years old. He's missing, he's not here. No, I just woke up and he was gone. Oh my God please no. Please call the police right away!"

Toni and Dina spent the next several hours answering questions and showing pictures of Joey for the local police department, the FBI was called in and an APB was put out on Joey, but there were no sightings of him anywhere.

The FBI officer scolded Toni for not having her son microchipped. He informed her that this entire situation could have been easily avoided as the chips communicate to a Global Positioning Satellite and Joey could have been recovered in a matter of minutes. Instead they were left wondering.

She wanted to go out and search for her son but the police ordered the women to stay put in the motel until there was news; so they did just that, staying put in the hotel for the next agonizing 19 hours waiting. Waiting and pacing and praying.

Toni dreaded the phone call she was going to have to put into Mitch, but when she finally gathered the resolve to call him she discovered that the FBI had already long since been in touch with him. The blistering punishment she received from Mitch on the other end of the phone made her feel sick to her stomach but she just took it all in, listening, absorbing every last word.

Six more hours passed without a peep. It was now 9:15 am, when suddenly the phone rang. Joey had been found! He was back in Jacksonville walking on the side of the road headed to his father's house. He had hitched a ride on a semi-truck all the way to an Atlanta truck stop and then he had picked up another ride south into downtown Jacksonville.

When Toni heard the news she cried for joy. She had never been so relieved in her life. But now she had to further face the wrath of the ex-husband.

"He hitchhiked Toni! Hitchhiked!!! Do you have any idea what could have happened to him!!?" Mitch roared into the phone from 1,300 miles away Toni held the phone a full foot away from her head and could still hear the yelling "you're an unfit mother and clearly mentally unstable, I'm filing an emergency injunction to prevent you from making contact with Joey again until you've had a full psychological evaluation. If you ever try...."

Toni hung up the phone and turned to Dina. She quietly spoke "I have to go back for him."

"Think about what you're saying Toni." Dina placed her hand on top of Toni's "Mitch is a man of means honey, and his lawyers are a whole lot bigger than yours. He would tie you up in court forever and what good would that accomplish?"

"I can't just leave Joey."

"Toni we are running out of time, and another entire day has now passed. Let's go find a place to settle and we will go back for him. I promise to help you."

"You will?"

"Yes, you can count on me. As soon as we find the right place to settle in, I'll help you come back for him."

Toni threw her arms around her dearest friend and cried on her shoulder. She finally broke down and admitted to herself that it was for the best. If she couldn't get into Canada right away her chances of ever being able to help Joey were nil.

The two women loaded up without even bothering to shower. Toni took the wheel and headed straight to the closest convenience store leaving Dina to wait in the car. She emerged with a bag of ice and three bottles of cheap pink wine which she crammed into her cooler. A bag of corn chips completed her breakfast meal.

"Good heavens, Toni, let's get good and drunk, that will make this trip go extra smooth." Toni ignored the remark and backed out into the street.

Once again they approached the border. The scene that awaited them was no different than before; with thousands of cars stopped dead in their tracks waiting for movement. The U.S. - Canadian border crossing more closely resembled a parking lot.

"Well, I guess we'll just have to wait," said Toni. She reached into her cooler and took out a bottle of zinfandel and poured some into a plastic cup. "Want some?" she offered to Dina.

"No thanks. Maybe I should drive."

"OK, suit yourself."

The two women swapped seats and sat and waited. Hours passed with the line barely moving, Dina changed her mind about the zin. She poured a big mouthful, which was all that Toni had left of the three bottles; she looked over to see her napping. Many more hours passed, and the girls were finally nearing the border.

"Toni, wake up, we're almost to the checkpoint!" Dina nudged Toni awake. She sat up groggily and looked at the clock. "Oh my God, I've been asleep for six hours and we're still not in yet?"

"We've been at a standstill for the most part. Each car's taking forever to get through. Just two more and we'll be next, so it won't be long now."

Dina and Toni watched the cars ahead of them. The border patrol agents had each person step from their car and administered a thorough frisking while their counterparts briefly searched the interior of each car waving scanners. Meanwhile, contraband-sniffing dogs strolled the perimeter.

"What are they looking for? I've never seen security this tight at the borders."

Toni frowned. "Looks like they're really tightening things up. I'm not surprised." She saw in addition to Immigration and Customs Enforcement agents the presence of several different U.S. governmental departments: Homeland Security, FEMA and the National Security Agency. She also saw several Canadian departments as well, the Communications Security Establishment, the Canadian Security Intelligence Service and one she had never heard of, the Northern Command. The women observed as a World Central Reserve representative made his way to the drivers of a red Chevy pickup truck two cars ahead of them. They seemed to be in a heated discussion that lasted for several minutes; then the WCR officer handed the driver a piece of paper and pointed in an easterly direction. Finally the Chevy turned off the main entry onto a service road over to the right side and then drove off into the distance.

"That didn't look too good." The two women looked at each other. The car ahead of them pulled in for its inspection. This one moved a tad quicker. The driver stepped out, was given a quick scan and granted access to the entrance; the driver returned to his car and drove through.

Dina pulled up to the border patrol agent and smiled. "Hi there."

"Please state your business in Canada."

Toni leaned over and spoke directly to the officer. "We're just visiting."

"How long will you be here?"

"Two weeks."

"Please exit the vehicle."

The two women nervously got out of their car. Toni walked to the driver's side. "Please, ma'am," the officer pointed. "Go back to the passenger's side."

"OK." Toni timidly walked back over to her side.

"License, registration and passport please."

Dina fumbled in her purse for her passport. She asked Toni for the registration and handed it over to the border officer.

"Are you carrying any firearms or explosives? Has anyone asked you to carry any items over for them?"

"No."

"Are you bringing anything with you that you intend to leave behind?"

"No."

"Are you traveling with any animals?"

"No."

"Are you carrying any meat or dairy products?"

"We have a cooler full of food, if you would like to take a look."

Toni moved over to allow a man to inspect her car, and then a woman gave her a quick frisk.

The WCR officer made his way toward Toni. "Please extend your right arm, palm up, ma'am." Toni extended her arm suspiciously.

"You're not going to try and stick something in there, are you?"

He waved a scanner over her arm. "No reading over here," he called over to his fellow officer.

"None on this one, either," the other replied, letting go of Dina's wrist.

"Do you not have an implant, ma'am?" he asked Toni.

"No, I don't."

"Sorry, ma'am, no admittance unless you have a WCR biochip." The officer handed Toni and Dina a piece of paper with a map drawn on it. "You can get one at a chipping station located just off the service road you see here to the right. Its only about two miles away, and the road will circle you back around to the end of the line to get into Canada."

"I'm not getting any microchip, and don't even try putting me in back in that line again." Toni fumed at the officer. "When did this become policy? Who the hell do you think ...?"

"Toni! Get in the car! We're leaving!" Dina bore at Toni, a pleading look on her face. Toni stopped herself and returned quietly to her seat in the passenger's side.

"What now??" she wailed out loud as they made their way down the service road.

"All I know is I wanted to get out of there as soon as possible," Dina replied. "Those guys gave me the creeps."

The two drove on until they saw the chipping station that the WCR had told them about. They pulled into the parking lot, stopped the car and looked at each other. "What do we do now, Toni? Do you want to do this?"

Toni sat thinking for what seemed like a very long time. "Well, let's see," she finally responded while attempting to pour a few last drops from a bottle of zinfandel. "Here are our options. One, we can't get into Canada. Two, we can't stay here. Three, we can't go anywhere, and I'm definitely not getting chipped. So that leaves just one thing left. It's the only thing we can do."

"What's that?"

"Go shopping!!"

"Shopping? What, are you crazy? We were just talking about how we need to conserve money! How is shopping supposed to help anything?"

"I figure we're going to need to buy some things to get us through. These credit cards are going to be worthless in just a couple of days, and we won't be able to buy anything ever again, so we're going to need to stock up on some items that we can trade. And since the world is coming to an end anyway, we need to load up on all kinds of essentials. I think we should drive to the nearest shopping mall right away and shop till we drop."

"You're a genius. How many credit cards do you have?"

"I have three, and I brought them all with me; how about you?"

"I just have two, but they each have close to an $8,000 limit on them."

"Oh, that's good. I have a line of credit on the townhouse too. I can get another ten out of that. So this is what we can do; we can go back to Jacksonville, stay until we get officially thrown out on the street, and then we'll trade the things we buy for a place to stay. Maybe something will change in that space of time and things will be back to normal. At the very least, it will buy us some time so we can work on Plan B."

They turned south and headed back to Buffalo, along the way they stopped to re-fill their cooler full of cheap pink wine. They then drove around downtown until they came upon a magnificent, brand new mall.

"Oh, this looks like just the thing," said Dina, pulling in. "Oh goody, I see both a Sachs and a Bloomingdale's. I think we should head straight for the jewelry department."

"Oh yes, most certainly," said Toni, holding up her glass. "And to think I used to care about useless nonsense like my credit rating."

The two made a big party of the day while they shopped the entire afternoon; they found many beautiful items. Dina picked several pieces of fine jewelry, designer luggage and handbags. Toni did the same and also found a great portable wine cooler and two bottles of Perrier-Jouet Champagne. After just three and a half hours, the two had quickly blasted through over $47,000.

"That was the most fun I've had since being a five-year-old at Christmas," said Toni heading back to her car, her arms loaded up with bags and bags of purchases.

"Oh my God, I don't want to stop. What can we do next?"

"I think we should pop this Dom while it's cold," answered Toni.

"Ooh, let's."

She uncorked the bottle inside the car and sent the cork flying out the window. The two drank straight from the bottle, passing it back and forth between them like they used to in high school.

"Hey, look." Toni spotted something interesting. "Let's go to that tavern over there. It looks like a nice place, and I see a couple of cute guys out front, too."

"Hmmm, very GQ. I think we should."

Toni and Dina preened themselves in the car mirror while applying the latest new fashion colors. They looked both smashing and slightly smashed when they entered the crowded neighborhood pub. It was late Friday afternoon, and the place was standing room only. The girls looked around the busy room and their eyes grew big. It was filled with handsome executive types sporting expensive suits and fresh haircuts; the tantalizing smell of fine cologne lingered in the air. The girls wandered around a few moments and nabbed a recently vacated high top, the only available spot in the bar.

"Jackpot!!" The two beamed and slapped high fives. They ordered the first of many Tom Collins's and proceeded to get very drunk.

"Oh gosh, it's hot in here," said Toni, waving her skirt up and down and then her blouse. "They really should turn down the heat."

"Here, let me cool you off," said Dina, pouring a remaining glass of ice cubes down Toni's shirt.

"Aaaaagh!! I'm going to get you for that!" Toni leapt from the table and chased Dina across the room clutching a handful of ice. Dina fell to her knees and crawled under a patron's table, grabbed the ankles of the married couple seated there and pleaded, "Hide me, hide me."

"Haaaa!!!" Toni caught Dina by the foot and pulled her out, knocking over the woman's chair and spilling her drink. Toni fell on top of the woman. "Oh, I'm soooo sorry," she burbled, straightening out the table cloth and picking up the startled woman's glass. She picked an ice cube off the floor and stuck it down Dina's pants and broke out giggling.

She wandered off to the bar and stood next to a large group of men ordering a round of drinks. She added a Tom Collins to their order and smiled sweetly at the man placing the order, then she slapped him on the rear and remarked, "lookin' good, baby."

She rooted in her purse looking for her lipstick, which when applied, missed her mouth completely, mostly hitting her teeth. She then scooted back to the two top with drink in hand, where Dina waited, laughing her head off.

"Let's play truth or dare" said Toni.

"Oooh, fun."

"You go first."

"Truth or dare?" Asked Dina.

"Truth."

"What was the most embarrassing thing that ever happened to you?" she asked.

"Oh Lord," said Toni. "I was trying to make a good impression on Mitch's parents the first time I met them. We got all dressed up and went to some lavish dinner at their club. This was serious; black tie, string quartet, the whole nine yards. Well, I went to the ladies' room, and when I came out I must have had a whole roll of toilet paper stuck to the bottom of my shoe. I walked from the bathroom and strung it out the whole way across the marble floor all the way to our table. The whole club was laughing at me, and I had no idea until Mitch's father pointed it out to me. I was so young and just livid."

"Oh, that's a good one. It's your turn now."

"OK, truth or dare?

"Dare."

"Hmmm, I want you to stand on the table and sing 'I'm a little teapot.'"

"Oh, hell no."

"You said dare."

"All right, all right." Dina teetered on the tiny two top table while Toni held it steady. "I'm a little teapot short and stout; here is my handle, here is my spout ..." she sang with exaggerated motions. "I don't remember the rest," she protested with hands on hips.

"Bull."

"Tip me over and pour me out!" She smiled and took a bow.

"Whooo hooo, congratulations!" Toni clapped.

"OK, my turn now," said Dina. "Truth or dare?"

"Truth."

"What is your deepest, darkest secret?"

"Oh no you don't. I'll take a dare instead."

"OK, but it's going to have to be an extra tough one for you backing out of a perfectly good truth."

"Yeah, yeah, lay it on me."

"Let's see ... I want you to ... wear your bra on top of your head and walk around the room asking everyone, 'Have you seen my brassiere?'"

"You're too much, girl." Toni went to the bathroom and removed her bra. She wished it was one of the pretty lacy ones considering she was going to have to wear it on top of her head.

Oh god, here goes, she thought as she exited the stall and headed out to the overflowing bar.

She approached a table with four smartly dressed men.

"Have you seen my brassiere?" she asked.

"Yeah, it's on top of your head," pointed an observant fellow.

"What's your name?" asked another.

"No time for chit-chat," Toni replied, flitting to the next table. "I'm on a mission."

"I'll bet it's Victoria!!" they laughed.

"You're close, it's Antonia," she replied looking over her shoulder.

She went to the next table where two men and two women were seated. "Pardon me, have you seen my brassiere?" The two women scowled at Toni, so she stumbled over to the next table. *This is kind of like trick-or-treating.*

"Have you seen my brassiere?" she asked two young men.

"You mean this one?" The blond young man grabbed the bra off the top of Toni's head. The other one, darker, snatched it from his partner and began waving it around in circles above his head. "Yee haw, I caught me a bra," he whooped. Just then the manager approached the table.

"I'm sorry, ma'am, but I'm going to have to ask you and your friends to leave."

"But we're not even with them," the two young men complained.

"Out! Out! All of you, now, before we call the police!"

"Awwww," Toni draped herself on the manager, "and I was having so much fun. Wait!! Let me grab Dina."

Toni and Dina had to be escorted from the premises. On the way out they broke out in verse, singing loudly as they stumbled out the door with the two young men following closely behind. One of the men asked the girls, "Where are we going now?"

"How should I know?" replied Toni, fumbling for her keys. "We're not from around here."

"Whoa, ladies," responded the dark one. "You're way too drunk to drive."

"Naw, we're just fine," Dina slurred.

"No, really, you should let us give you a lift. Where are you heading?"

Toni ignored his offer "Now where did I put those keys?"

"You mean these ones?" The dark chap dangled her keys up in the air.

"Gimme those," Toni lurched forward, tripped and fell forward, landing face down. She lay on the pavement like that for a while, not moving. Everyone gathered around her.

"Toni, you OK?"

"Ha, I'm fine," she lifted her head, "but I think you're right, I'm waaay too drunk to drive, and can I have my bra back please?"

Dina and Toni really didn't remember much about the rest of the evening. They did, however, wake up in the morning in a nice comfortable Holiday Inn, fully intact. Toni even had her bra. She was the first to wake, and she stumbled around looking for the bathroom. Then she peered out the hotel window to get her bearings. From her vantage point she could see the shopping mall where they were at yesterday. Suddenly a feeling of panic overtook her.

"Oh my god!! Dina wake up! We need to get to the car. All our stuff is in there!!"

"Huh? In where? Where are we?"

"In some hotel. Here, get it together," she said, tossing Dina's shoes at her. "We have to get to our stuff quick."

"Huh?" said Dina, still in a fog.

"All we bought yesterday! It's all still in the car; and I don't know where the car is!!"

"Oh no! I forgot totally about that." Dina stood and then quickly sat back down. "Do we have coffee?"

"C'mon, let's go." Toni pulled her arm and led her out the door.

"Oh lord, I'm never drinking again … I'm never drinking again … I'm never drinking again … " Toni repeated the mantra over and over as she and Dina walked up the street toward the shopping mall. They rounded a corner and reached the parking lot of the tavern they had partied at the night before, and behold, sitting all by itself, in plain view, was Toni's Honda. She ran up to it and looked in the windows and saw everything was still there.

"Oh, thank god!" She kissed the hood. "Am I glad to see you!" she cooed to her precious automobile. "Now I could use a drink."

"No, let's go get that coffee instead," said Dina, smiling. "I'm driving, I assume?"

"Yes, please. I don't think I could see the road right now."

Dina took the wheel and took the interstate back south again. They drove for quite some time, and Dina brightened at seeing an exit with a little café on the side of the road.

"I need to use the restroom," she said, pulling off the highway.

"Good," replied Toni, "I'm starving." The pair went inside and sat in a vacant booth. They ordered coffee while they looked over the menu. When Dina returned from the bathroom, there was a nice cup of steaming java waiting for her.

"Why did we do that?" she asked Toni.

"Do what?"

"Get so plowed. What on earth were we thinking?"

"Stress relief, obviously. Putting off today's problems until tomorrow; but now tomorrow has arrived and the problem hasn't gone away." Toni watched the customers of the greasy spoon as they paid at the register; most were using the new wrist swipe method. She had a terrible headache and as she rubbed her temples, she tried to visualize what it would be like living with her mother.

Mom, she pictured herself saying, *me and the kid are going to have to move in with you and daddy. Do you want me to take the couch or just sleep outside on the lawn furniture? Oh, and by the way, I have no job and probably never will again.*

A friendly waitress approached. "What can I get for you girls?"

"Eggs and bacon for me," said Dina.

"Pancakes and sausage, please, and a glass of milk."

"OK, be right back," she said, collecting the menus.

"What are we going to do, Toni? Do you think we can go to another country besides Canada? How about Mexico? Do you think we can get in there?"

"I doubt it. If we can't get into Canada, we won't be able to go there, either. I think we may have to go somewhere extremely remote, but if we don't do it in the next two days, we'll never be able to get anywhere. I'm afraid time is running out, Dina. We waited too long. I really just don't know," she said, shaking her head.

It hurt Dina to see Toni looking so depressed when she was typically so upbeat. She placed her hand over Toni's and gave it a squeeze. "I think we should hold out as long as I can to see if the barter system will work. Let's give it our best shot." Toni appreciated her words of encouragement but inside, knew it was just a matter of time before they, too, would have to take the dreaded chip under their skin; bartering would only buy them a little time.

"OK, I'm with you on that," she replied. "Let's head on back home and see how long we can make it."

Just then the two were approached by a short man in a fedora hat. "Hello, ladies." he began. "I couldn't help but overhear your conversation. May I please sit down?"

"Yes, of course." Toni scooted over for the short man to sit with them.

He handed two business cards to Toni and Dina. "My name is Joel Brandenburg, Esquire."

Chapter *19*

Priorities

Winthrop Shaw was conducting business as usual, this time from the cockpit of his Falcon 900 EX jet. Shaw was barking orders into his satellite phone, which was greatly annoying the pilot, but he was far too prudent to utter a word in protest.

Shaw rarely flew his own planes despite being an experienced pilot, but he did enjoy occasionally sitting in the front and taking the controls to do a few maneuvers. The thrill would usually quickly wear off and he would retire to the back of the plane; there a staff of 11 awaited his every request. Shaw always traveled with his entire entourage, even on the smallest jaunts. Included were his chef, executive secretary, personal trainer, masseuse, finance adiminstrator, aesthetician, valet and three former Green Beret security guards; lastly, his trusted assistant Nelson Thurn would always be in attendance. The pilot right now was getting impatient, he couldn't wait for Shaw to get out of the cockpit and go get his damn facial or massage or whatever it was that he did back there. He turned and smiled at his employer, who failed to notice. Shaw was engaged in berating the man on the other end of the phone.

"Get them over there right now," Shaw bellowed, "and they had better be waiting for me when I arrive. I don't want another incident like last week with the prime minister. I'll be arriving in about one and a half hours." Shaw looked at his watch. "I'll check up with you when I land."

Shaw turned off the phone and exited the cockpit to the relief of the pilot. He went to his bedroom to lie on the bed and have a quick snooze until they landed. Shaw's schedule was tight today. He would be in meetings until late in the evening, when he had an audience with Devin Rothfeller. Everything was coming together perfectly, and tonight he would get Rothfeller to agree to accelerate their agreed-upon timeline. Shaw laid his head on a feather pillow, closed his eyes and drifted off into peaceful slumber.

He was awakened by a beautiful young woman in a pixie haircut. "Sir, we'll be landing in a few minutes," she whispered into his ear.

"Thank you, Selena." Shaw sat up. He considered ordering Selena to sit next to him for a moment and then glanced at the clock. Not enough time.

"Selena, get me a cappuccino."

"Yes, sir." She backed out of the bedroom.

The plane taxied into a private landing strip near Tirana, capital of the tiny nation of Albania, one of the few remaining sovereign Slavic nations left unincorporated into the Indo-European Union. A chauffeur sat waiting for him there. He retrieved luggage and held the car door open for Shaw. Thurn opened his own door while hastily making phone calls. The two sat alone in the back of the chauffeured vehicle.

"Is everyone assembled?" asked Thurn to the person on the phone. "Are the translators in? We'll pick them up in about 40 minutes."

"They're ready, sir." He reported to his superior seated next to him.

"Good." Shaw replied as he lowered his window and appraised the charming landscape. As they drove past the capital into the beautiful Albanian countryside, Shaw took in images of sheep eating lush green grasses surrounded by ancient ruins.

"What a peaceful place," he remarked to Thurn. "If they want it to remain peaceful, they had better divest today. I've just about run out of patience with Topi." He loosened his tie, removed his eel-skin shoes and spoke out loud to the driver. "Did you know that in just a matter of a few short hours, this country, too, shall be swept into our illustrious global union?" The driver had no idea what Shaw was talking about.

Shaw and his men met with the president's Cabinet along with the chairman of the Council of Ministers of Albania for many long hours. When the meeting was over, the Albanians were the newest reluctant members of the recently formed Indo-European Union. *One more down,* thought Shaw as he left the meeting, *only three more to go.* It was now getting late and approaching the time to meet with Rothfeller. Shaw once again boarded his Falcon EX and headed to Luxembourg to eat dinner with the aging Czar of the Global Union.

Shaw and Rothfeller met at their usual restaurant, the Le Cigalon. Shaw would have preferred to eat somewhere else, but it was at the insistence of Rothfeller, who also insisted upon sitting in the same chair, receiving the same waiter and ordering the exact same meal every single time. The two dined on artichoke and black truffle soup with a warm mushroom brioche and a wild salmon entrée while they discussed the day's events. After the meal, they withdrew to Rothfeller's villa to finish their talks. They were escorted to their car by Rothfeller's bodyguards, who followed closely behind in a nondescript sedan until they arrived at Rothfeller's estate safely.

Once settled in, the pair sat in a cavernous den, adorned with ancient artifacts stolen by German Nazis that dated back tens of thousands of years, including pre-Columbian and ancient Oriental art, pottery and textiles. There were Mesopotamian scrolls over 4,000 years old, Egyptian statues and a mummy still resting in its sarcophagus. There were some more recent acquisitions as well: priceless items looted from Iraqi museums during the gulf wars; the sacred vase of Warka said to be over 5,000 years old; Assyrian statuary of their ancient gods and the famous black obelisk of

Shalmaneser III. There were even sacred books thought burned in the fires of the Library of Alexandria in 48 B.C., containing arcane knowledge of subjects such as alchemy and transmutation, some of the most sagacious works ever written in the history of man. There were in this den rarities and conversation pieces such as Charlemagne's own sword, Roman coins, original mathematical computations by Copernicus, sketches and paintings by Michelangelo, primeval clockworks and prototypes for flying machines designed by Leonardo Da Vinci, Galileo's original telescope and an entire collection of the crowns and scepters of early Saxon kings. A plethora of archaic, venerated treasures filled every corner and every wall within.

Shaw casually went to the humidor to retrieve two cigars. "Which do you prefer," he asked Rothfeller, "a Flor de Farach or a Ramón Allones?"

"The Ramón."

"All right, then; two Ramóns." Shaw clipped the ends off the cigars and handed one to Rothfeller.

Rothfeller waved it off. "Light it for me."

He lit the cigar, and his hand brushed against Rothfeller's cool, papery skin as he passed it over to him, causing Shaw to cringe with revulsion.

"Now pour me a drink."

Shaw poured an obligatory cognac into an extra-large snifter and gingerly pressed it into Rothfeller's slightly trembling hand.

"Tell me about your progress in the Balkans," queried Rothfeller.

"Just three more countries left to finish the Indo-European Union." Shaw leaned back in his chair. "We should have it one hundred percent wrapped up by the end of the quarter; then we will move on to finish the Council of the Americas. That one will take a little longer. The Americans are still harboring some romantic, John Wayne notions of being a sovereign world superpower, but we will manage to correct this error in their thinking. I believe we will finish well ahead of schedule."

"Good. Are there any remaining banks left to deal with?"

"Just two major players; we've further tightened funds so we expect to see them default any day now."

"Good. No more delays. I want you to look through the rosters. I need two new men. I need a new propaganda minister and new man to replace Buckley; he's taking his retirement this spring. Make sure his replacement has a good financial background."

"Yes, of course."

"But don't even consider running Harrison by me."

"Really?" Shaw's face went stony taut. "Why is that? He would have been my first choice."

"The family. His nephew dined with us over the holidays. He actually had the nerve to compliment my dining room chairs. Damn cheek."

Shaw nodded in agreement as he drew on his cigar.

"Now tell me, Shaw" Rothfeller changed the subject "how is your project progressing? Have you cleared up your line of sight issues?"

Shaw's ears perked up at the mention of his favorite subject.

"Yes. HAARP can bounce the signals off the ionosphere, and we've set up a network of receivers, repeaters and transponders for remote locations and dead spots. The major cities were easy; we simply lit up the dark fiber running underground. Rural locations have been a little trickier but certainly doable. And a high-direction satellite transmission will take care of those living in the sticks. Right now we can transmit a sound wave frequency that can induce anything from euphoria to pain so extreme one could only wish they were dead. We can produce sleep, transmit suggestions, and interfere with memory. Our subjects can be made aggressive or lethargic, and through temporal lobe stimulation, we can activate images stored in the subject's memories, such as monsters or other nightmares. We can through just a simple electromagnetic pulse, manipulate and control every bodily function."

Shaw smiled, revealing his shiny white teeth. "Can you image an insurgence breaking out where suddenly everyone felt the urge to run home and sit on the toilet?" He and Rothfeller enjoyed a good snigger at that visualization. "No we won't be seeing any more "demonstrations" like the ones of recent years. Crowd control is from here on the least of our concerns."

"Good work," nodded Rothfeller. "It sounds as though you have done an exceptional job in a short period of time. You've proven yourself a truly worthy successor."

Shaw took a long pull on his cigar. "I have something I would like to show you," he said to Rothfeller. He went on his jacket and retrieved an envelope, which he handed to the czar.

"I know that you wanted to wait until we reached the 10 billion mark before we started making these preparations," began Shaw, "but since we are so well ahead of schedule, I've taken the liberty of producing a summary outlining the steps we will take to assure that the remaining dissenters will be forced to take the chip as an inoculation against our own engineered biological agent."

Shaw leaned back in his chair. "Once this virus is released into the world's **water** supplies, the WCR microchip will be the only known source for the desperately needed vaccine. This will serve us well by accomplishing two goals; first it will bring the world's population to a more manageable level of around 2 billion, and secondly the World Health Organization will assist us in forcing inoculations as the resolution to a public health epidemic.

"Also in the outline are the measures we will take to protect ourselves and our loved ones during the process. We will, of course, not be bringing up the subject at the next Global Assembly, but the procedure will move forward regardless.

"Our efforts will help preserve the planet and the most gifted specimens will ..."

Rothfeller held up his free hand. "I'm well aware of your noble intentions here," he said as he handed the envelope back to Shaw, "but we simply aren't ready for these measures. Not yet."

"What?!" Shaw stared at Rothfeller in indignation. "You haven't even looked at my proposal!" he protested. "At least read it first, then make your decision!"

"I have already made my decision, Winthrop. I don't need to read it first. We will stick to the timeline that we established long ago. There is still far too much work ahead for us to begin this massive undertaking. We may not even get to see it fulfilled in our own lifetimes."

Shaw's face turned red. He seethed inside with anger and frustration. He stood and turned his back to Rothfeller so that the czar couldn't see his fury; then he poured himself a large shot of cognac and downed it in one gulp. *When is this decrepit old bastard going to die?* He spun on his heels, took three steps and bore down over the seated czar, fixating on the tiny blue veins that crisscrossed over the translucent skin on his bald head. He imagined himself wrapping his fingers around that frail, thin neck and snapping it in two like the wishbone off some Thanksgiving turkey.

"Shaw! Sit down!!"

Shaw regained his composure and sat in his chair.

"I believe it is time for you to be leaving now." Rothfeller buzzed his intercom, and a valet showed at the door. "Please escort Mr. Shaw to his plane." He turned and looked at Shaw. "I will be seeing you again in exactly one month from tonight at the same time and place. Battenberg will be with us at the next meeting. Please try and have your priorities straightened out by then."

Oh yes, thought Shaw as he exited the chateau, *my priorities will be straightened out all right. You can rest assured of that.*

Chapter *20*
Survival Mode

Pastor Bloom awoke at the crack of dawn. He tiptoed so as not to wake the still-sleeping monster of a man on the ground tightly bundled in blankets. *He looks cold,* thought Bloom as he hunted for another blanket to throw on Glick. The small fire from the night before appeared to have been dead for many hours; this morning had to be in the mid-20s or perhaps even colder. *Seems colder today; a front must have moved in,* observed the pastor. He breathed warm air into his hands and rubbed them together, and then he rummaged some more through their possessions. Bloom couldn't locate another blanket, so he searched for a place to do his morning prayers before Glick awoke.

He knelt in a nice, soft spot with young underbrush and plenty of dead, fallen leaves. He silently prayed for protection and blessings. When he was done, he turned and saw that Glick was now sitting up.

"What time is it?" asked Glick, yawning and rubbing his scraggly beard.

"6:32. Feel like getting back on the road?"

"Shit no, not really; but I guess we can't just sit here like a bump on a log. Let's get her rounded up."

The two rolled up their meager belongings and crammed them into the saddlebags. "You need to pick up those beer cans, Richard," Pastor Bloom said to Glick.

"Yeah sure, go ahead, do-gooder."

Bloom shook his head once more as he picked up the two beer cans left over from the night before. He wedged them into the already tight bags and hopped on the back of the bike. Glick kicked the ignition over, but it didn't start. "Don't worry," he said, "she don't like cold weather; neither do I." He kicked her again, and the Harley sputtered, then sluggishly started.

"See, I told you we got nothing to worry about. I think we're low on gas, though." Glick removed the cap and peered into the tank. He jiggled the bike to see the fluid level. "Looks like we got about two hours if we're lucky."

"I'm sure we will be fine," said Pastor Bloom. "Remember, the Lord will provide."

"Right," grunted Glick, as they headed off the dirt road. Glick turned onto the highway, then merged on to Interstate 70 heading into Colorado. The landscape was so different in Colorado. Panoramic views of white-capped mountains suddenly filled the horizon, and even the jaded Glick was left in complete and total awe of their majesty and beauty. The autumn leaves were now at the height of their splendor, and the crisp fall air invigorated the two as the winding road they traveled on led them past pumpkin patches, haystacks and scarecrows along the climbing interstate. After two hours, they had worked their way past Denver but were now in desperate need of gas. Glick's engine started to sputter again. He switched over to the reserve tank.

"We need to pull over here, Preach." Glick turned into a shopping center parking lot.

"What's going on?"

"Nothin'," replied Glick. "Just need to stretch a little. You need to use the bathroom?"

"Yes, as a matter of fact, I think I should," said Bloom as he touched his toes. "Where can I go?"

"Well, I like to piss on a bush, but you might prefer to go inside that drugstore there," said Glick, pointing at a busy pharmacy.

"OK, I'll out in be a few minutes."

"Okee-dokey. I'll be right here."

Pastor Bloom returned several minutes later to find Glick lying on the ground next to a Chevy Tahoe, a piece of rubber hose hanging out of his mouth.

Pastor Bloom approached Glick, who looked like he was about to be sick. "What on earth are you doing?!"

"Oh God!!! Blaaaagggghh," Glick puked on the ground at Bloom's feet. He jumped backward to get out of the way.

"Good heavens, is this really necessary??!!" Bloom angrily picked up the rubber hose and shook it at Glick. "You were trying to siphon gas, weren't you?!!"

"Nuuuuggg. Leave me alone!!" Glick rolled over and held his belly. He retched once again but nothing came out. Then he sat up and wiped his chin. "Ugh, I must have swallowed a quart of gas."

"Do you think you deserved it?"

"Shut up you pathetic old fossil! I don't deserve any of this shit!!" Glick stood up and kicked the Chevy full force with his boot. It left a lasting impression.

Bloom stood quietly for a moment. "Richard, I think it's time we parted ways."

"Suits me fine; you're nothing but a pain in my ass anyhow."

"I'll need to get my things," said Bloom as he rooted through the saddlebags. He retrieved his clothes and his Bible; there wasn't much else. He turned and began to walk away.

"Hold on a minute there Preach," said Glick in a muffled voice. "I'm sorry. You really haven't been bad company at all; it's just me. Please don't go."

"Quite all right, Richard," said Pastor Bloom, turning back; "we all have to find our own way. Right now I need to go my own way. But I'll tell you what, I'm going to write down a phone number of the location I'm going to be at over the next few days."

Bloom tore a corner of a page from his Bible to write on. "I have a lot of work to do once I get there, a lot of coordinating. I must make arrival preparations for almost 700 people, and I also have to arrange safe passage for them as well." Bloom wrote down the phone number to the group he would be rendezvousing with. "Call me if you have an emergency or even just to let me know how you've made out." He handed the tiny scrap of paper to Glick. "I really would like to hear from you. Please, don't forget to call."

"All right," said Glick. Once more he outstretched his gigantic hand to the minister for a handshake. "No hard feelings, old man. I promise I'll call. Uh ... and before you go, do you think I could maybe borrow some cash?"

Bloom fished in his wallet and pressed a fifty into Glick's hand.

"Wow, thanks, man!!" Glick then watched Pastor Bloom walk to the edge of the parking lot and cross the street. He extended his thumb to the westbound traffic and was immediately picked up by a blue-haired woman in a Buick Skylark. *Good*, thought Glick. *She looks perfect for him, maybe he'll get him a little tail*, and then they were off.

Glick sighed. He suddenly felt very alone in the world. *I don't know a soul out here. What the hell am I doing?* He pictured himself knocking on Jimbo's door in South Dakota and getting it slammed in his face. *That's not going to happen.* He tried to put the thought out of his mind, *I hope.* He thought it would be a good time to test whether his cash would work. He wheeled over to a local BP and went inside. He laid the fifty on the counter and said to a man in a turban, "fill 'er up."

The man gave him a blank stare. "I'm sorry, sir, but we no longer accept cash. Would you like to put this purchase on your WCR account?"

Glick's heart sank. *Oh shit, now what? Colorado's out, I'd better get over to Jimbo's place quick. I need help.* He went back to the Chevy Tahoe and resumed the business of stealing gas, then turned and headed northbound for the journey to South Dakota. He traveled until the sun set in the west, passing through the soaring canyons of Wyoming into Pierre, S.D. He stopped little and made good time. By sundown he had reached his destination. Glick cruised the city he barely remembered, trying to recall the name of the street where his buddy lived, but he was drawing a blank.

Crap, it's got to be around here somewhere, he said to himself in frustration while cruising around in circles. *Wish I had his damn phone number.* He finally threw in the towel and pulled up to a local biker bar that he had frequented last time he was in town. He sat in the parking lot and stared at the entrance. *I wonder if they'll take this fifty. I wonder if I should spend it here. That really would be a terrible waste of money. But it could be fun.* He argued back and forth with himself for several minutes, then finally said, "Oh, fuck it!" and went inside. Once inside, he smiled broadly. "This is more like it." The place had everything a biker could hope for. Old rock tunes were blaring on the jukebox, scantily clad female bartenders were serving beer in gigantic mugs, and two men were hunched over a pool table.

"Ahhhh, home sweet home," said Glick as he sat on a stool and ordered a beer. He figured he would deal with the cash issue later when it came up. He swallowed the whole beer in one big gulp and ordered another, then another and then another. Feeling better now, he stepped over to the pool table. The two men playing took one look at the gargantuan, half-drunk Glick and immediately stopped their game. They sheepishly offered the table to Glick, who just laughed out loud.

"Yeah, and give me your sticks, too," he growled to the two cowed men. They handed them over and quickly exited the building. Glick just threw the cues on the table and walked away disgusted with the chicken shits. Then he sat back on his barstool and ogled the two barmaids.

"Have you seen Jimbo?" he asked an easy-looking blonde in cutoff shorts sitting next to him.

"Huh? Jimbo who?"

"Never mind" Glick sighed. "Do you have a raisin?"

"What? Raisins? No."

"Then how about a date?"

"Ugh. No thanks."

"Look, I know this ain't no grocery store but I can tell you're checking me out."

"Honestly, I wasn't even ..."

"C'mon toots, I'm just like chocolate pudding. I might look like crap, but I'm as sweet as can be."

The blonde got up and moved to another stool. Undaunted, Glick ordered a shot of Jack and another beer. He asked the bartender if she knew where Jimbo lived. She just looked at him like he was nuts.

"Do you mean Jimbo from Gorilla Automotive?" Glick heard a man's voice a few stools away.

"Yeah, that's him!!" Glick happily turned to address a man who had no teeth.

"They're living out at the cabbage patch. He lost his house, and his old lady left him. He's got some new little momma now, and they're camped out in the dunes. At least till the food holds up."

"The cabbage patch ... got it," winked Glick. He had been there before, that's where they used to do drag racing and sometimes demolition derby. It was really nothing more than a big cleared field with an open fire pit where the guys could hang out and party without being harassed by the cops. There was a sandlot for racing with some bleachers set up. It was always good times there, even though the place was sometimes hot and dusty. One thing's for sure, it wouldn't be hot this time of year.

"Think you could buy me a beer?" asked no teeth.

"Yeah, no problem," replied Glick, "put it on my tab. Let's buy everyone a beer," said Glick, raising his glass. "Drinks are on me!"

Glick was suddenly a popular guy. He stayed at the bar surrounded by friendly strangers until last call, eating chicken wings, smoking cigarettes and drinking shots. When the check arrived, he retreated to the bathroom, crawled out an unlocked window and fled to his Harley.

As he pulled away, he saw in his rearview mirror the bartender chasing after him. She threw an ashtray and screeched, "Come back here, you jerk-off!!!"

Glick crowed to himself. "Sure, that's right on top of my list, go back and pay bill."

It was now around 1:45 a.m., and Glick made his way in a drunken stupor to the cabbage patch. Everything seemed familiar and foreign at the same time, and in the dark it was hard to see. He tried closing one eye so the road would quit moving around so much, but it didn't help. He finally left it to his instincts to get where he was going and then he drove right to it: the gates of the cabbage patch, fabled biker hangout. He pulled inside, laid his bike down beside a stack of used truck tires and promptly passed out.

The morning sun felt like God's flashlight beaming down right between the eyes of the parched biker. He sat up and smacked his dehydrated mouth open and closed. *Did something crawl in my mouth and die last night?* Desperate for water, he stumbled around the barren backdrop looking for a faucet, a stream, anything. He found an empty wheelbarrow half-full of rainwater. He regarded the rusty old thing and wondered whether he might die if he drank from it. He decided he would soon be dead of thirst anyway, so what the hell. He dunked his entire head in the murky-looking mess and drank deep. It wasn't so bad, but it did remind Glick that it had now been four days since he last showered.

"Yuck," he thought as he removed his shirt and splashed water on his armpits; the water stung the forgotten bite on his pit. "Shit, I really need a place to lay my head at night," Glick grumbled out loud. "I can't wait for things to be back to normal. Just give me a job and a trailer. I never asked for much, I don't need much."

He wandered around the makeshift campground looking for signs of life. It turned out there were plenty of people living there, probably more than he had ever seen at the cabbage patch all at the same time. He passed row upon row of parked Harley Davidsons, stopping periodically to admire some of the more eye-catching ones. Tents, campers and sleeping bags littered the desolate parcel as far as the eye could see, but there were also other items littering up the scenery as well, junk and clutter everywhere. He worked his way around old abandoned cars, garbage bags full of refuse, a washing machine, empty paint cans and an abandoned shopping cart awaiting further employment.

He peeked inside tents and various campgrounds looking for Jimbo and received more than a few dirty looks from aggravated occupants. "Have you seen Jimbo?" He stuck his head around a hanging rug.

"Get the hell out of here!!" yelled back a naked man, his back covered with hair.

"Oh god! My eyes, they're burning!!" Glick laughed, covering his face as he stepped away.

Unable to locate his friend, he walked over to the dirt track. He saw a few vagrants hanging around, sipping moonshine from a crude, homemade still; but he saw no sign of Jimbo. Glick walked up to the still to observe its inner machinery. He watched hot steam bubbling up from the bottom and the condensed vapors as they dripped from the winding, soft copper tubing into a tin bucket that held the clear liquid.

"Want to try some shine?" asked a wrinkled man.

"Uh, no thanks. I'm already hung over, I'd better not."

"Hair o' the dog," replied the old stiff, "nothing better." Glick simply walked away and approached a younger group of boys at the dirt track.

"Why's nobody racing?" He asked one of the loiterers.

"Got no gas," responded a lanky kid of about 20.

Mmmm, thought Glick, *sounds familiar.* He turned to face the young lad.

"You seen Jimbo around?"

"Yep, he's camped over there." The boy pointed to a shady area off in the distance.

"Really? Thanks."

Glick stepped lively to greet his pal from years ago. He hoped Jimbo hadn't forgotten him. It had been so many long years ago. They were just kids back then, not much older than that lanky boy back over at the sandlot. Rowdy and foolhardy; no one could tell them where to go or what to do. *Hell, I didn't even know he went and got married, and now he's got him a new one. Time sure flies.* He made his way over felled trees and sleeping bodies toward the area the kid had pointed to. From a distance he spotted a tall, thin, hunched-over fellow with long brown hair. Even from the distance he recognized Jimbo right away. He was sitting on a log with a blanket spread out in front of a teepee. Several little children were playing at his feet, and he had a young woman at his side.

Looks like he shaved his beard, Glick noticed. He couldn't believe his good luck finding him out here of all places.

"Hey," yelled Glick waving his arms up in the air. He saw Jimbo retreat into the teepee and come out with a rifle.

Oh, shit said Glick to himself, *he doesn't know who I am.* "Hey, Jimbo it's me, Glick!! Don't shoot me, man!"

"Who?" replied Jimbo. "Do I know you?"

"It's me, Glick, you dumb ass," he said with a big grin as he walked up to the couple. The apprehensive young woman was now standing behind Jimbo. She peeked her head out to get a look at the menacing mountain of a man coming at them. Frightened, she grabbed the arm of one of the children and stood back behind the wary Jimbo.

"She's a little young for you, ain't she? You old wolf," winked Glick as he approached.

"No, it can't be. Is that you, Glick?" asked Jimbo, lowering his gun. "I thought you were supposed to be dead!"

"Well, there was a rumor that I was there for a while; but as you can see, I'm very alive," said Glick, beating his chest like Tarzan.

"Yeah, I guess so," replied the confused Jimbo, a slight frown on his face. He didn't exactly look thrilled to see his old buddy from his wild younger days. "What are you doing here?"

"I came to see you, man. I just couldn't live without you another minute," Glick poked Jimbo in the ribs.

Jimbo smiled and let out a little guffaw at that remark. He seemed to be loosening up a little. He gave Glick a light punch on the arm. "It's good to see a familiar face, amigo. Sorry about the gun. Things have been so tense lately; you never know whose out to get you for something or other."

"I hear that," responded Glick, "It's been a real bummer trip for me, too; this world's falling apart at the seams."

"You can say that again. My god, how long has it been? Must be going on 15 years since I last saw you; 14, 16 years, something like that," said Jimbo, scratching his head.

"Yeah, it's been around 15, I think. Those were the days, huh?! Did we party or what?!"

"Oh, yeah!" Jimbo stopped talking, and there was an awkward silence for a moment. "Glick, I'd like you to meet my girlfriend, Amy," Jimbo said proudly. He turned, and Amy stepped out to be seen.

"Hi," she said, "nice to meet ya." She was a cute, girlish-looking young woman with freckles and strawberry blonde hair. She was holding a baby and smoking a cigarette.

"Oh god, can I please have one of those?" begged Glick, pointing at the smoldering cig.

"What? You want a baby?" Amy looked amused.

"No. One of those cigarettes. Please!"

"I don't have too many left," she sighed as she dished him one out.

"Thanks, got a light?" Amy produced a lighter.

"These you guys' kids?" asked Glick.

"No, they all belong to Amy. I had a daughter with Tonia. She stayed with her mom. She's a good kid, 8 years old now. It would be nice to see her."

Glick counted heads: four children all together, two toddlers, a baby and what looked like a boy around 5. "You've been busy," he cracked to Amy.

"You can't even imagine how busy," she replied.

"Yeah, they keep us on our toes," Jimbo smiled. "This one here is Billy," said Jimbo, placing his hand on top of the head of the oldest boy, who squirmed out from under his hand and ran off. "The two twins are Pablo and Petra; their daddy was Spanish; and the baby's name is Amanda," said Jimbo, picking up the redheaded infant that greatly resembled her mother.

"How long have you been out here?" asked Glick.

"Longer than I thought possible already. I never dreamed my life would come to this. I got so much to tell you, man ... you wouldn't believe it. This place sucks. We got to get out of here, but we don't know where else to go. I think most everyone living out here has lost everything either from the depression or just not wanting to be micro-chipped. You chipped, man?"

"No! Hell, no!" answered Glick angrily, holding up his arm. "I'll never do that; they'd have to kill me first. That's not happening to me."

"Same here. Me and Amy, we won't do it, either. That's why we're stuck out here in this hellhole. We know a bunch of people feel the same way; we're all gonna march on Washington when we get our act together. You know, get organized."

"Really?"

"Aw, I don't know," said Jimbo, sitting down on his log. "Even if we ever do get organized, we couldn't get there right now. How we supposed to get there? You can't jump on a plane, can't buy gas. We're screwed. They're going squeeze us hard 'til we finally give in."

Glick frowned. "Let me tell ya, you wouldn't believe what I had to go through to get out here. I cruised all the way from Florida because the Western states still hadn't made it the law yet. By the time I got out here ... well, it's looking like I'm too late; it's everywhere."

"Naw, I hear there are still a handful of states that haven't done it yet."

"Oh? Which ones?" asked Glick.

"I've heard Idaho and Oregon, but it's changing every day. We don't have electricity out here so I can't keep up with the news; no radio, either."

"I heard Utah is the place to go," said Glick. "There's supposed to be thousands of people heading out there right now. That's not too far from here; about an eight-hour ride or so." Glick's stomach let out an audible growl. He rubbed his belly and thought about the food remnants in his saddlebags.

Jimbo nodded. "We should talk about that later." He turned to Amy. "Do we have anything we can give Glick to eat?"

"Just got a couple cans o' tuna fish left. You want some?"

"No, you guys need it more than I do. I have some food at my hog. I might even be able to spare some. Walk me over to get my bike?" Glick asked Jimbo. "It's parked over at the gate."

"Oh man, you shouldn't have left your bike there unattended even for just a minute. Those scumbags will strip it bare in no time."

"Yeeps! I'd better hurry!!" Glick took off sprinting, and Jimbo followed close behind. Sure enough, when they arrived at the gate, four skinny, scruffy men were surrounding Glick's bike, rooting through his belongings. Two were cramming the last of Glick's food into their mouths at a furious pace, one was attempting to remove the tires, and yet another was trying on Glick's clothes.

"Hey!! Get away from there!!" Glick yelled. The four thieves scattered like the wind, toting their stolen articles. "You'd better run," he screamed. "You don't want me to catch your sorry asses!!" He shook his fist in the air.

Glick and Jimbo picked up the discarded saddlebags, now depleted of anything of value. Glick turned them upside down, an empty candy wrapper drifted to the ground.

"Nothing! Nothing is left in here. I can't believe the shitty luck! They took my blankets and my clothes, my fucking gun!! SHIT!! SHIT!! SHIT!!!" Glick kicked the ground over and over again.

"Oh, we can get you those back," said Jimbo somberly. "It's too bad about the food, though; can't get that back."

"Yeah, I had some good stuff in there, too, and to think I was rationing it to make it last. Humph, now I gotta go steal some more." The two looked at each other and laughed.

"Come on, man," Jimbo reached up and put his arm on Glick's shoulder, "I'll turn you on to some tuna fish straight out of the can."

"Yuck, I hate tuna fish."

"I know what you mean."

Glick wheeled his bike to the teepee and sat on the blanket. The day was crisp and cool with blue skies and big, fluffy clouds. Glick lay on his back and watched them roll by. He spent the reminder of the afternoon pointing out funny shapes in the clouds to the children and playing tag and hide and seek.

When the day progressed into early evening, they strolled over to where a big bonfire was raging in the middle of the cabbage patch. A small crowd was gathered there, and Glick quickly identified his own brown leather jacket on the back of a squirrelly-looking man that he recognized from stealing his clothes. The man saw Glick stepping toward him and took off running. Glick gave chase through the woods surrounding the makeshift campground, but the squirrelly man was too fast for him and quickly left Glick panting on the ground far behind.

"I'll get that son of a bitch, you watch," he gasped on his return to the laughing Jimbo. Glick turned to see Amy and her kids were laughing at him, too.

"Oh, fuck this!" he said, stomping off back to the teepee.

Glick made a small fire in front of the teepee and sat down all by himself. He hadn't eaten a bite all day and was starving but he wouldn't eat the remaining tuna – not so much because he didn't like it but because he wouldn't take what little food was left for Amy and her four children. *I'll get something tomorrow*, he thought, then he laid his head down and soon dozed off.

Glick woke up in the middle of the night to his stomach growling. He glanced at his watch, which said 2:30 a.m. *Damn it*, he thought to himself, *I fell asleep too early and now I'm wide awake*. His grumbling belly prompted him to get up and roam around the camp.

Maybe someone has some food lying around that I can borrow. He stood and wandered around sneaking peeks around the dying campfires of the sites closest to him, but he saw nothing.

Looks like it's time to take a cruise. He pushed his bike to the entrance of the camp, as he didn't want to wake anyone with his loud pipes. Except for a crying baby, the cabbage patch was pretty calm. Everyone was sleeping. He wheeled the bike outside the entrance and hopped on. Firing up his Harley, he did a wheelie down the road. Glick was starving, so he pulled into a gas station with a convenience store and walked up to the entrance, but it was locked. He stewed angrily, remembering his gun that had been in his saddlebag, when he noticed the clerk working behind a counter behind security glass. But then he had an idea. He stuck his finger up under his shirt and pointed it out; then he walked up to the window and pointed his finger at the clerk.

"Open the door!!" he demanded.

The clerk looked up from his porno rag and spoke from behind the glass partition. "Sorry, we keep the doors locked, just for bozos like you."

"Open up or I'll shoot!"

"With what? Your finger?"

"This ain't no joke," said Glick, "you open or I'll blow your head off!"

"Go ahead. This is finger-proof glass."

"Shit," said Glick gloomily, turning around to go back to his Harley but then he spotted a tall man in a cowboy hat approaching the attendant's window for some gas. Glick tried another tactic. He greeted the man in the hat. "Howdy there, partner. You think you could get me a bag of chips or something? I got some starving kids back at the ranch."

"Get away from me, you dirty hippie," snarled the man in the hat.

"Hippie? Humph," mumbled the dejected Glick as he walked back to his bike. He decided to drive a little farther to look for easier prospects. He soon came upon a 24-hour grocery store. He waited in the parking lot until he saw an elderly man come out carrying two bags full of groceries.

Perfect, thought Glick. He waited behind a parked van until the older gentleman opened his trunk, and just as he was about to put his groceries in Glick gunned his engine and shined his headlights on the startled senior, who froze like a deer. Glick easily snatched the bags right out of his hands and left the old-timer standing there wondering what just happened. Glick whooped as he took off out of the parking lot.

Success!! "There will be dinner tonight!" he yelled at the moon. He pulled off the road to get a look at what he had scored. Rooting through the bags, he discovered Geritol, dehydrated prunes, laxatives and… "Bingo, lunch meat. Yes!! And hot dogs too, and a can of creamed corn, oh yeah!" Glick tore into the lunch meat until it was all gone and then immediately felt a pang of regret for not saving some for Amy and her kids.

Oh well, there's plenty of food here, at least for a day anyway. He returned to the camp feeling somewhat proud for bringing all this good chow. He tiptoed back into the camp and fell asleep sitting up against a tree. The next morning arrived, and Glick awoke to two toddlers jumping on his belly.

"Hop, hop, hop, we like to hop on top of pop," they chanted in unison.

"Ugh! Get off me!!" Glick rolled over onto his belly, and they hopped on his back. "Hop, hop, hop."

"Amy!!" Glick called for the tots' mom.

"Come here, you two." Amy scooped them up, one under each arm.

"Morning, Glick, sleep good?"

"Yeah, not bad, thanks." Glick stretched his arms over his head. "I had to get up in the middle of the night, though, 'cause I was starving to death; but check it out, I got us some groceries."

"Really? Wow, that's great, where are they? What did you get? Hey Jimbo, Glick's got food. Wake up." Jimbo groggily exited the teepee.

"Food? Where?"

"I've got 'em right here" said Glick, patting the bags he was sitting next to. "I didn't trust anyone around here, so I sat with them on my lap all night long."

"Look," he said, emptying the contents of the bags. "I got dogs, buns, prunes, canned corn, jelly, toilet paper, a real smorgasbord."

"Excellent," said Jimbo, hastily opening the package of dehydrated prunes.

"What else is there?"

"Mmmm ... here's some pickled beets and some cottage cheese; that's about it, unless you want some Geritol."

"We may need that. Don't throw it out," said Amy, reaching for the iron supplement.

Glick and Jimbo's family were so busy with the grocery bags that they didn't notice the large gathering of refugees that were descending upon them.

"You have food?!?!" Glick heard a woman's voice behind him, and he turned to see some 15 people coming at them.

"Give me some!!" The woman and the rest were now running toward their camp.

"No! Give it to me!!" he heard another. Soon they were overwhelmed with hungry castaways tearing and clawing at their skimpy food supply. Jimbo ran into the teepee to retrieve his rifle, but it was too late. The food was all gone, except for the bag of prunes he had in his pocket; even the Geritol was gone.

"You have got to be kidding me!" Amy wailed, sitting on the ground.

Glick looked up, dumbfounded, and once again spotted his leather jacket on the back of the squirrelly man disappearing into the crowd. "AAAARGGHH!!! I'm gonna get him!!" Glick took off running, but once again, squirrelly was too fast and easily outran the overweight biker.

"Oh, man, I'm out of shape," Glick panted as he returned to camp. "Got a cigarette Amy?"

"No, we smoked the last one yesterday."

"What about some water?"

"There's a hose over by the Porto-potty. Here, fill up these bottles while you're there."

"All right," Glick grumped as he trekked over to the hose. He stood in line for some water, and when it was his turn, he drank long from the hose, realizing it had been a long time since he'd had some. *At least I can fill my belly with water. It's going to be a hard day.*

Glick returned to camp to find Jimbo's family finishing off the remainder of the prunes. "The baby needs formula," said Amy. "You think there's a chance of getting some?" she looked at Jimbo.

Jimbo turned to Glick. "We need to get out of here. Food just gets nabbed as fast as we can bring it in."

"Yeah, I see that." Glick said, wondering what he should do. The situation here was far worse than he had anticipated, and Jimbo really wasn't any help at all. Glick knew he would be much better off by himself but he just couldn't bring himself to abandon his old friend and his pitiful family. He determined to get more food and bring it back, but he would have to be much more careful next time. No one would know he was bringing food in. He would have to find a place to hide it.

"Where did you get the food last time, Glick?" asked Jimbo.

"Where do you think I got it? I stole it, right out of some old man's fingers. I gotta be careful – I don't want to wind up in jail over this, but at least they'd feed me there."

"Think we could go back today and get some more?" Jimbo shot back quickly.

"I do, but we need to switch off back and forth. I can't be going in every day and not buying anything, I'll get caught for sure. I'll show you where the supermarket is. You can go in today and I'll go in tomorrow. You can't take too much, either, just enough to hide in your clothes."

"Well, I need to get over there as soon as I can; baby needs milk right now."

"OK, let's saddle up and go."

Glick directed Jimbo in some of the finer points of shoplifting, and he came away with enough to get them through another day. When Glick met Jimbo around the corner for the ride home, he was happy to see that Jimbo had snagged several days' worth of formula but dismayed when he saw that all Jimbo had taken besides formula were a few pork chops.

"Oh, man, how are we gonna cook these without everyone smelling it? They're gonna come running and over and bombard us again. You need to nab stuff that people can't see, or smell."

"But they sounded so good, my mouth is watering."

"Yeah, get used to it. Oh, well, let's see what we can do about cooking them. I have an idea."

Glick went sailing at high speed down the highway. "Hey, man, why you going so fast," asked Jimbo, "you running from something?"

"Naw, I just need to get 'er warmed up."

Glick pulled off the side of the road onto an easement that led into a cow pasture. "Here, let me see those chops," he said.

Jimbo produced the pork, and Glick tossed them quickly onto his tailpipe. The chops sizzled.

"Ha! Would you look at that?" marveled Jimbo. "Pretty smart."

"Can't say I've ever done this before," said Glick, scraping the chops from the tailpipe with his pocket knife. "They seem to be done pretty good. Want a bite?" The two split a chop, and Jimbo tucked the rest in his pocket for the kids and Amy.

"Sure made a mess of my tailpipe," said Glick, glancing at the greasy residue the chops left behind.

"Yeah but it beats the alternative; from now on, it's Spam and ham, buddy. No more tailpipe barbecue, I promise."

Glick and Jimbo made their way back into the camp, and Jimbo quietly slipped the smuggled meat to the kids and Amy, which they quickly devoured. The meat was the best thing the children had eaten in weeks, but they still felt hungry afterward and whined and fussed that there wasn't more. Glick drooled with the knowledge that the children were inside the teepee eating juicy pork. He daydreamed of pork roast with baked apples and homemade mashed potatoes like his mom used to make when he was little.

I think I need to go hunt down some apple trees, he thought to himself, *or maybe I'll go hunting? We have a rifle.* Glick had never hunted before, but it seemed like a good idea considering the circumstances.

"C'mon, Jimbo, grab the rifle and some extra bullets. We're going hunting."

"Hunting? You? I didn't know you were such an outdoorsman," Jimbo laughed.

"Yeah, me, neither; let's give it a shot. Ha! I made a pun."

The two headed out down the dirt road on Glick's Harley with the rifle cradled in Jimbo's lap. Glick suddenly remembered the cow pasture they had stopped at earlier that morning. "Hey Jimbo, think we could kill one of those cows we saw back there?" Glick asked.

"You want to kill a cow?! How would we get it back to the cabbage patch?"

"Don't know. Let's go by there again and check it out."

The two drove up to the cow pasture, climbed the fence and walked through the tall grass toward the cows, which were at the far end of the field. The two bikers could see them off in the distance eating bales of hay, unaware of the menacing men creeping toward them, rifle in hand. They crept closer and closer, trying not to spook the animals into running away. As they made their approach, some of the cows walked away slowly, and others just stood there, curious. Glick spotted a nice small one, and he moved closer with deliberate motions until he was close enough to reach out and touch her. He felt the animal's rough hide, noting her long eyelashes. He petted her wet nose.

He turned to Jimbo and handed him the rifle. "Here, you do it."

"Me? I don't want to do it. You do it."

"Shit." Glick took back the rifle and raised it for aim, the cow started to wander off.

"Hold her still man, I need a clean shot right between the eyes."

Jimbo attempted to hold the cow still by wrapping his arms around her neck. This only made her start loping faster. Jimbo was now being dragged through the pasture with Glick ambling closely behind.

Just then, a shotgun blast rang into the air. Glick and Jimbo looked up and saw a pickup truck advancing on them. There was a man standing in the bed with a shotgun aimed at the two bikers, who took off running.

"Oh man, I thought that rifle sounded loud," puffed Jimbo while sprinting toward the Harley. The pair climbed over the fence and hopped on the waiting motorcycle. They took off as fast as they could.

"Man, we almost got an ass full of lead there," wheezed Glick, looking back to the men in the pickup. They had followed the bikers to the edge of the fence and were shouting profanities and waving their guns in the air.

"Got any more brilliant ideas?" asked Jimbo.

"Shut up, dummy. You think of something better?!"

"How about we go into the woods? Maybe we'll spot a deer. It's hunting season right now and we could get lucky."

"All right; show me the way and we'll go."

Jimbo led Glick to a wooded, mountainous region that looked perfect for hunting. The two slid off the Harley and combed the area looking for game. Soon they came across a deserted deer stand, they decided to climb up and try their luck. They sat for several hours without seeing a single deer.

"Oh, man, this is really boring," said Glick. "How can these guys just sit here all day like this?"

"Well, usually they have some feed on the ground to attract the deer and a 12-pack to keep them entertained."

"I'd eat some feed right now," grumbled Glick, "and don't even mention beer. It's been so long I've forgotten what it tastes like."

"I haven't," Jimbo countered.

The pair heard the noise of twigs breaking underfoot; something was headed their way. Glick held his index finger up to his lips. "Shhhh, something's coming."

Jimbo held the sights of the rifle up to his eyes in anticipation of spotting a great big 10-point buck. Instead what they got was the local game official.

"Hello, gentleman," he looked up and greeted the two startled bikers. "How's the hunting?"

"Not too good," answered Glick, "we've been here all day and haven't seen a thing."

"No, probably not, it's at the tail end of the season, I think most of the good game has already been bagged. Can you come down here, please? I'm going to need to give you a swipe to check the status of your hunting licenses."

The two bikers looked at each other and shrugged their shoulders. They climbed down and stood before the game warden, who produced a scanner from his holster. He waved the scanner over each of the bikers' arms and frowned.

"Well, I have no way of determining if your licenses are valid because neither one of you have the required biochip. Now, what are we going to do about that?" The two bikers just stood there without saying a word.

"I'm going to have to write you a ticket for hunting without a license," he said while writing a citation in his little book. "Another thing," said the game warden, looking the grubby bikers up and down. "What you're wearing isn't considered proper hunting attire. You need to be wearing an orange vest for safety, not whatever that vest that you're wearing is called."

Glick felt the rage boiling up inside him at the insult to his biker colors. Jimbo, sensing an outburst, pulled Glick aside. "Cool it, man, we'll be out of here in just a minute; and then you can go kick some trees or something."

"I'll probably get a ticket for that, too," grumbled Glick.

"I need both your names, please," stated the game warden.

"Mine's Jimmy Crackcorn," blurted Jimbo.

"Mine's Dick O' Toole," grinned Glick.

"Funny guys, huh? You two get out of here right now! I don't want to see you in these woods ever again. If I do, I'm taking you both in. You'll never get another break from me. Is that understood?"

"Yeah, we're going," said Glick. The two turned and made a hasty retreat toward the Harley. While walking, Glick elbowed Jimbo in the arm.

"So Jim, how do you tell the difference between a porcupine and a carload of cops?"

"I dunno, how?"

"The porcupine has the pricks on the outside."

"Hrmph."

"Hey, officer, want to see a trick? Go look at your wife!!"

"Oh, shit!" complained Jimbo. "You're going to get us busted. Walk faster."

"Hey, wasn't that one of the Village People?" cracked Glick in a fit of laughter.

"This ain't funny, asshole. What if he heard you?"

"Is that a 9 millimeter? That's nothing compared to this .44 Magnum!!

"Oh, my God, get me out of here!"

"Aw, he's just cranky 'cause his momma wouldn't let him play with his gun when he was little." Glick was now laughing so hard at his own stupid jokes that tears were running down his face. Jimbo, however, was not so amused.

"Jeez, man you really like to push it to the limits," fussed Jimbo as he climbed on the back. Both men took off down the road.

"I suppose we could try fishing," Jimbo hollered over the roar of the engine.

"Got any poles?" Glick bellowed back.

"No, but I'm sure we could make some. I have a couple of corks we can use as bobbers."

"That sounds pretty good," said Glick. "Hold on a minute, I see something." Glick stopped his bike in front of something dead in the road.

"What the??? ... Road kill? Are you out of your fucking mind??!!"

"But look, it's fresh," said Glick, kicking the dead possum. He found a stick on the side of the road and turned the vile thing over. Flies buzzed around. "I'll bet it isn't even but a few hours old."

"And what are we supposed to do with it? Skin it? Make possum soup? No thanks."

"Hey, it's better than nothing. I'll bet Amy can make it taste real good with some seasonings and such."

"Go ahead, scrape it off the road." Jimbo turned his back. "*I'm* not eating it!"

Glick picked the possum up and shoved it in his saddlebag. "Here we are, the great white hunters coming home with ... a flat possum."

Glick and Jimbo returned with the possum, which they threw on the ground.

"What? What is that thing?" Amy asked.

"It's a deer, can't you tell?" Glick joked.

"Looks disgusting."

"Naw, they're all right, a little greasy, though," said a voice behind her. Amy turned and saw a small crowd gathered to look at the esteemed road kill. "Oh no, here we go again," she said.

"I'll take that possum if you don't want it," said a skinny man.

"I don't know," said Amy, shaking her head. "What do you want to do, guys? You want this nasty thing?"

"We'll make you a deal," said Glick to the skinny man. "You can have it if you'll just save us a few bites, OK? But you've got to cook it and clean it."

"Deal," said the man. "There ain't gonna be too many bites, though. There ain't much meat on these things."

"That's all right. Just remember where you got it from," Glick smiled. The skinny man reached down and was off with the possum so fast he was practically a blur.

"You think we'll see him again?" asked Amy.

"I doubt it," Glick replied. "I bet he gets stampeded as soon as it's cooked. But if he does come through, when we're old and gray, we can look back and say we did everything. We even tried possum."

Glick and Jimbo decided to try their hand at fishing. They spent a couple of hours fashioning some handmade poles with string, sticks and safety pins for hooks, then the two men and Amy's oldest boy Billy took a walk until they came across a canal. They dropped the hooks in the water and waited. It took them a while to discover that fish don't care much for bits of dehydrated prune, so they and the children spent the next few hours looking under rocks for bugs that they could use for bait. They were successful at finding a few bugs but not so successful at catching fish; all they caught were two tiny brim, hardly enough to feed a large family. Later that evening, the men skewered the tiny fish with sharp sticks and roasted them over an open fire. They quickly fed them to the two toddlers and went to bed hungry once again.

And so it went that over time, the delicate days of fall were soon over. Each day was colder than the last until the beginning days of winter were finally upon them. The first season's snow came whispering one gray November afternoon. The men got to try their hand at ice fishing, and Glick instructed them not only on the fine art of dine and dash but also how to hang around outside of restaurants looking for kindly souls to pay for a meal or two. The ragtag bunch were always surprised at how generous the restaurant patrons were; but some of the owners did not take kindly to the stolen take out boxes and their constant begging outside of their eateries and quickly gave them the boot.

But pity the unlucky restaurateurs who would refuse them a spot to beg outside. The bikers would usually find creative methods of retaliation. After one particularly rude ejection from an exasperated owner, Jimbo held the doors of the restaurant open while Glick drove his Harley up three stair steps, to the inside, right next to the kitchen. He held his bike in place as he gunned the powerful machine, doing spins, leaving skid marks on the floor and filling the diner with exhaust fumes. He then lifted his front wheel and drove his bike up onto a table full of ladies who were having their Red Hat meeting, knocking over glasses of iced tea, coffee and salad. He howled with laughter as he watched the horrified patrons escape the foul fumes and the fearsome bikers that had suddenly taken over.

The wild pair crashed backyard BBQs and raided trash cans. They also perfected their shoplifting skills, dropping in on easy marks and avoiding centers with tight security. Despite their best efforts, however, the scanty tidbits that they were able to bring in still didn't amount to very much. There just simply wasn't enough food to go around. In a short while, even Glick, who was once so grossly overweight, began dropping pounds to the point where he wasn't so alarmingly huge anymore. The other people in the camp were faring far worse. Since the local food pantries and shelters were all overwhelmed, they were reduced to eating tree bark and mud. Some had already died from exposure, bad sanitation and the generally appalling living conditions. The only thing keeping the people alive was that the owner of the property was kind enough to keep a source of water turned on in the form of a hose. If the water supply was shut off, the rest would surely die as well.

Glick took a look around at the shivering, starving people, especially the children. Something had to give, and soon, or they were all going to die together. In desperation, he went inside his wallet and retrieved a phone number that was given to him almost two months earlier by Pastor Vernon Bloom. He stared intently at the scrap of paper that held the number and then stuck his head inside Jimbo's teepee.

"Hey, Jimbo, I need to talk to you."

"Yeah, what's up?" Jimbo had grown so weak he could barely leave the teepee anymore; a thin man to begin with, his ribs were now shockingly exaggerated under his clothing. His pale skin stretched tightly over his gaunt face, and his eyes were sunk deeply into his skull. He now far more resembled a walking skeleton than the robust man he once was. His malnourished frame shivered under his blanket as he came out from inside the relative warmth of the teepee to the cold, hard wind outside.

"I don't think we're going to be able to hold out here much longer," said Glick.

"Yeah, I knew it would come to this. They've won. They got us to the point where we have to take a microchip. I can't just let our kids die right in front of me, Glick. I've been thinking about this for some time now. Later on today I'm going to take the family downtown so we can all do it together. I know you won't take one, but if you think you could give us a lift to the station, I'd appreciate it."

"Hold on, man, don't do that," said Glick, holding up his hands. "I have something to tell you. I think I might know someone that can help us. On my way out to meet you here, I ran into an old man. He was a preacher, and he told me about a big group of people that were running to some refuge so they wouldn't have to be chipped. Do you remember when I said that I heard that Utah was the place to go?"

"Mmm, kinda."

"Well, that was the place that I was talking about. It sounded almost too good to be true. None of them are micro-chipped. They take care of themselves by trading stuff and growing their own food. They really got it together, and there's a shitload of them, too – tens of thousands, like its own little city."

"You knew about this place and you didn't tell me sooner? Why not?"

"It's not that easy getting in, Jim. It has to be by invite only, and honestly ... I'm not sure Preach even likes me, much less that he's gonna let someone like me just waltz in to live there with the rest of them soccer moms and churchgoers. I'm gonna try, though. I'm gonna call him."

Glick held up the scrap of paper. "I'll see if he'll let us in. What do you think of that?" he asked, smiling.

"I suppose." Jimbo didn't seem terribly excited.

"What's wrong, man?"

"Nothing, I just don't want to get my hopes up, that's all. Good luck Glick, I hope it works."

"Let you know," said Glick with a grin. Then he headed into town to find a telephone he could borrow, holding the scrap of paper firmly in his hand.

Finding someone to lend him a telephone wasn't as easy as he'd hoped; it was almost easier stealing food. Glick went from person to person asking if he could borrow their phone for an emergency call. He finally he found a genial man who agreed to let him use his. He nervously dialed the number Pastor Bloom had given him, and a woman answered.

"Is Preacher Bloom available, please?" asked Glick.

"Yes, I can get him for you. Hold on a moment."

Glick sat on hold for what seemed like a very long time. Finally he heard the familiar voice on the other end.

"Hello?"

"Preach!!! How are ya?"

"'Preach'?? This must be Richard Glick calling."

"It is me, Preach!"

"Are you all right, Richard? You've been on my mind a great deal, especially lately."

"Sure, I'm doing great, never better."

"Good, I'm so very glad to hear that. Were you able to locate your friends in the Dakotas? Were they able to help you?"

"Well, yes, I found them, but no, they weren't much help. To be honest, Preach, it's more like I've kinda been taking care of them. And no, we're not doing well at all. We're holed up in some place with no food, no toilets, we barely got water. The people here are dying off like flies. It's really bad. You gotta help us."

There was a prolonged silence at the other end of the phone. "You there, Preach?"

"Yes, I'm thinking."

"Can you let us in to that place you're at? The one you were trying to get your church to?"

"How many of you are there, Richard?"

"There's seven of us, and four are just little kids, 5 years old and under."

"Seven," Pastor Bloom muttered. "I'm not certain, Richard, we've been under a tremendous amount of pressure over the past few weeks. We have literally thousands of people a day trying to enter. Utah has given in to the micro-chipping mandates. There isn't a single state left in the Union that hasn't now. The entire nation is now under a federally mandated micro-chipping injunction. I'm afraid there are just too many people trying to get in to our little community."

"You can't leave us here like this!! We're going to die if we don't take a chip. Please, you've gotta help us!!"

"Richard, there is a waiting list; there are people that have been on the list for weeks now, and they still aren't in. I'm not certain how much I can do."

"You're gonna let us just stay here and die?"

"No, I didn't say that. I said I wasn't sure if I could get you in. I didn't say I wasn't going to try."

"Preach, you're the best!! Thank you!"

"Yes, quite all right, but as you know, I must present your request to the board. I'll say some words on your behalf at this afternoon's meeting. I should have an answer for you tomorrow around 4 p.m. Please call again at 4:30 tomorrow, and I'll tell you what they said."

"You got it, Preach! Hey, before you hang up, I have a question. How are you able to talk on a telephone? You have phone service out there?"

"It's a prepaid cellphone, the account has been paid in advance for the next three years, it's one of the only phones in the whole community. You're very lucky you were able to reach me, Richard. God must really be watching out for you."

Yikes! thought Glick. *I hope he's not watching too close.*

Glick hung up and went home. He and Jimbo's family spent the evening discussing the option of life in such a community and the possibilities. Then they patiently waited until the following afternoon for the news from Pastor Bloom.

When Glick returned at 5 p.m. the next day, they were already gathered together in front of the teepee anxiously waiting for the word on whether there was to be a new lease on life or not. When they heard the sound of his Harley as it approached the camp, everyone in the family came running in anticipation of the news.

Glick pulled up to the teepee with his head hung low. It didn't look good. "I got bad news, folks" he said.

Their expectant faces sunk.

"It looks like ... it looks like ... were gonna have to live with a whole bunch of HOLY ROLLERS!!!!" Glick threw his arms up in the air. "They said it was OK!!! They're gonna let us in!!!"

Amy came running up and jumped in Glick's arms. He tossed her high into the air in celebration. Jimbo high-fived Glick and slapped him on the back. Their small children, not really knowing what the adults were so happy about, danced and laughed and then threw themselves on the ground in typical toddler fashion.

"This calls for a celebration," said Glick. "I got us a big bottle of Dom Perignon, right here." He went inside his saddlebags and pulled out a 24-ounce bottle of Budweiser. "See? The finest vintage in the world," he laughed while pouring some for the three of them.

"Oh, I can't wait to get out of here," said Amy, taking a sip of the cool beer. "Imagine, three square meals a day, and oh, just to take a shower, alone, without an audience gawking at me."

"I can't wait to brush my teeth," said Jimbo.

"I can't wait to get my hands on an engine to work on," said Glick.

"Here," said Glick, pulling out a worn-out map. "He gave me directions on how to get there from here. It looks like it's gonna be about a 10-hour ride. See, we have to go around the Wind River mountain range." Glick traced his finger over the map. "It shouldn't be too hard. We're supposed to call when we get near, and he's going to meet us at the gate to let us in."

"There's an abandoned sidecar over on the west side of camp," stated Jimbo. "It needs a tire and some cleaning up, but I'm sure we can fit Amy and the babies in it. Me, you and Billy, we can all ride on the Harley."

"Mmmm, I guess that sounds all right. When should we take off?"

"Soon as possible. Today we need to stock up on supplies and get some gas, and we gotta get the sidecar ready to go, too; and then you can hit the road whenever you're ready."

"Tonight would be fine with me. Get Billy over here and let him know we're leaving town."

"I'm sure he'll be delighted to be leaving here," laughed Amy.

"I'll go to the store and load up," said Jimbo, mounting the Harley. "Hop on, Glick. I'll give you a lift to that sidecar. It's way over on the west side, buried under a pile of junk. You'll never find it unless I show you where it's at. Amy, you start packing the kids' clothes and get ready. I'll be back in no time," said Jimbo with a happy face. He was showing more enthusiasm than Glick had seen out of him in the whole three months he had been there.

Jimbo led Glick to the far west side of the camp, which fairly resembled a garbage dump. The two men waded through the piles of nasty trash. "It's over here somewhere," said Jimbo, stepping over a mattress. "There it is!" he pointed, "over by that bathtub."

"*That's* a sidecar? I think we'd have better luck driving the bathtub," said Glick as he approached the old rust bucket half-buried under some plywood. They lifted the heavy wood and Glick gave it a quick once-over. Then he and Jimbo pulled it out and hauled it out of the trash into the open area.

"Oh, boy," exclaimed Glick, "I hope this thing can hold us without the bottom falling out."

"We can put a piece of plywood in the bottom for reinforcement," said Jimbo, holding up a ¼-inch piece of moldy plywood.

"This seat's useless," said Glick, tugging the seat, the ancient leather crumbling in his hands as he pulled it out. "Let me see that wood."

Glick jammed the wood into place, and it was a surprisingly good fit. "They won't have a seat, unless we can rig up something for them to sit on. We gotta get a tire for it, too."

"Tires are all over the place, take your pick."

"Tell you what," said Glick, "you go for supplies, and I'll take care of getting a tire. Don't forget to fill 'er up."

Jimbo took off, and Glick resumed working on the sidecar. He looked high and low for a tire and rim that would suffice. It wasn't an easy task, for it required an odd lug bolt pattern, but he eventually came across a wheel that fit. There was, however, scarcely any tread left. Glick grimaced as he ran his fingers over the worn edges. He pricked his finger on a piece of steel belt thread and cussed out loud. *Oh, well, it's only for a few hours on the road. We'll have to cross our fingers and hope it makes it.*

He propped the sidecar against a stack of logs and struggled to get the wheel on by himself, then he tightened the nuts by hand. He would have to wait until Jimbo got back with tools before they could be tightened down further.

He wheeled the creaky sidecar out of the west side dumping grounds toward the teepee. On his way he passed a starving family with four emaciated children. Their mother was lying on the ground with a blanket wrapped around the stick-like figure of her youngest, trying to comfort her. It was of little use; without food, the child would soon die. Glick stopped pushing the sidecar and stood staring for a moment, they looked so much like Amy and her four children. He choked back a tear that had welled up in his eye and reached in his pocket for a tidbit to give to the little one, but he only came up with a lone peanut M&M, hardly enough to make a difference, but he went to the woman anyway and held the M&M out in his hand in offering. She looked confused and then reached for the candy. Her oldest son, however, beat her to it. He snatched it from Glick's hand and popped it in his mouth right in front of him. Glick glared at the tiny thief and then resumed pushing the sidecar 'til he at last reached the front of their teepee. Amy was already packed and ready to go.

They brushed off the pine needles, rust and grime that covered the relic from top to bottom, and then he carefully examined the retaining rod to make sure it wasn't going to collapse en route. He kicked the tire and pronounced her roadworthy.

"Jimbo should be getting back by now," said Glick to Amy as he sat on a log. "He's been gone a long time."

"Maybe he's having trouble," she replied, sewing some torn jeans.

"Could be." Glick stood and began pacing. He kept catching glimpses of the woman and her family he had passed on his way to the teepee. The boy who had taken the M&M was now crouched behind the teepee and kept looking expectantly at the giant biker. *Where the hell is Jimbo?*

He paced back and forth until Amy gave him a dirty look. He decided that it might be a good time to make his way over to the moonshine still. He walked the path to the dirt track where he had originally seen the group of moonshiners. The boy tagged behind at a small distance, hiding behind trees and bushes in an effort to conceal himself. When Glick approached the still, the same three men were standing around sipping the nasty-smelling booze.

"I don't know how you can drink that rotgut on an empty stomach," said Glick to one of the pallid-looking fellows.

"Oh, you get used to it," he slurred in response. "Here, try some," he said.

Glick sniffed the clear liquid and wrinkled his nose. "Smells like lighter fluid," he said, holding the bowl in his gargantuan paws.

"Yeah, but it's gooood."

"Sure it is," he said, handing the bowl back.

"No, go ahead take a li'l nip. It won't hurt ya, warm ya up."

Glick lifted the foul-smelling concoction, held his breath and took a sip. He gagged on the nasty brew but managed to swallow it down. He felt the liquid fumes burning as they made their way down his throat and into his stomach, which churned in protest.

"Uck, that's really awful," he said. Then he took another long gulp.

"Kinda kicks ya right in the kiester," laughed a man with a yellow pallor.

"Humph," snorted Glick as he took a third long draw, which hit him like a kick in the head.

"Oh, shit," he said leaning against a tree. "I wasn't expecting that."

"Naw, nobody does, specially the first time. You want some more?" asked the yellow man, topping the bowl off with some more of the potent, clear liquid.

"No, I can't," said Glick waving off the bowl. "I got to be prepared for our road trip."

"Road trip, huh? Where you headed?"

"Utah."

"Oh yeah? What's there?"

"Canyons," Glick said, laughing.

"Long way to go for some canyons," remarked the man next to him. He wore thick glasses and sported two weeks' worth of beard.

"Well, there is more than just canyons," he gloated. "We're getting out of this shithole, going somewhere real nice, somewhere where folks take care of each other; a regular Nirvana."

"Nirvana, huh? Don't think there's such a place, not anymore. Can't get nothing to eat, got nowhere to live. We're just gonna sit here and drink ourselves to death." The other two men murmured in agreement.

"No," Glick protested, "it's true! We won't need a microchip, no central bank, they've got plenty to eat, nice houses to live in, everything we need. We're leaving soon … tonight, just as soon as Jimbo gets back. Or it could be morning, I dunno." He reeled suddenly to his side and almost fell over.

"Easy there, big fella." The man with the Coke bottle glasses came to Glick's aid and steadied him back against the tree before he keeled over.

"Thanks," responded Glick. "Damn. That stuffs stronger than it looks. I think maybe I should have another taste, though, just to make sure."

"Sure. Here, have at it," said the yellow man, handing over the bowl." We got plenty." Glick looked at the yellow man and noticed something seemed odd about his eyes. Then it occurred to him that the whites of his eyes were every bit as yellow as his sickly-looking skin.

Good god, let's hope it don't kill me, thought Glick, taking three big mouthfuls. He slid down the tree, landing on the ground, where he sprawled out his long legs; holding the moonshine in his mouth, he allowed some to dribble out the side as he groaned in appreciation.

"Oh thass nice," he garbled, "iss been a long time. Hey you know what? You guys should come wit' us to Utah, I'll bet you'd like it there; lots of pretty girls in tight sweaters."

"You say there's a place to live there?" asked the yellow man.

"An' plenty to eat?" added the man with the Coke bottle glasses.

"Yep, that's right; dancing girls and a buffet.

"How we gonna pay for it?" asked the third man. He was the oldest of the three. The lines on his haggard face and the suspicious look in his eyes revealed a hard life with little rewards.

"Oh, it's all taken care of. All we has to do is just show up, and they'll roll out the red carpet. No need to pay for a thing!" Glick's eyes lolled about inside his head. He opened and closed them a few times quickly in a vain effort to keep his vision from blurring; then he attempted to stand up. He stumbled around a moment until he felt grounded and promptly sat back down again.

"I think I'll just sit here for a minute," he hiccuped.

"Hold on, buddy, there's someone I want you to meet." The yellow man took off in the direction of the campers and quickly disappeared into the background. He soon returned with his friends and family.

"This here is my mother," he said excitedly. "Her name's Matilda."

"Call me Millie." The ancient woman held up her wrinkled hand in greeting.

" ... and this here's my ol' lady Denise and my two sons, J.J. and Howard. This here's my cousin Eddie, his ol' lady and her sister. This is J.J.'s daughter Shelly and her boyfriend Sid. This is my niece on my sister's side, her name's Mandy, and these two here are her friends. I forget their names. Over there's my good buddy T-Bone and his ol' lady and their two daughters and their daughters' kids, too. This is Caveman and his two buddies Snake and Onion. Over there's Raunch and Stoneface. Behind Stoneface, that's Saint, Weasel, Crash, Toad and Mildew. Did I forget anybody? Oh yeah, here's Eddy's stepson George. They named him after George Washington."

The yellow man stood smiling. "Everybody's real happy to hear that we're getting out of here. They already told just about everybody at the cabbage patch the good news."

"Holy shit." Glick sat dumbfounded. "You told everybody?"

"Yeah, just about, word travels fast. Look, here they come now."

Glick looked up to see a herd of grungy, disheveled bikers heading his way. Descending upon him in great waves, they demanded information on the place they had been told of. He stood and attempted to walk away.

"Get the hell away from me," he waved off the wretched horde. "I was just kidding, there is no such place. It ain't real, go away!"

Moving quickly in an effort to get away from the eager mob, Glick weaved in and out of a thicket of scrub brush. It didn't work. The entire camp had worked its way into frenzy at the thought of free food. They closely trailed Glick all around the camp, to his teepee and back around again to the still. He soon became frantic, waving his arms over his head.

"Leave me alone! Quit following me around! Get lost!" Glick shoved and pushed a path through the crush. "I said get the fuck off me!! Are you stupid people deaf??"

"Who you calling stupid?" came a booming voice from behind. Glick had no time to react as he was shoved forward with huge force by someone in back of him. He tumbled forward, barely staying on his feet. He then turned and came face to face with one of the meanest, ugliest men he'd ever seen in his entire life. Glick squinted his eyes and gave the behemoth a quick once-over. The biker was muscular, big and broad; every bit as huge as Glick, maybe even bigger. Despite the cold, he was shirtless, and his entire body was covered in colorful tattoos. The tops of his hands, his shaved head and even his face were completely tattooed. His nose had been pierced, and spikes protruded from his flaring nostrils, braided strands of facial hair hung from his chin, and his earlobes, which had been bizarrely stretched in a tribal manner, were ornate with thick animal bones. Under the folds of skin on his stout neck clung a barbed-wire necklace, and on his wrist he boasted leather cuffs with 2-inch iron spikes. His beady eyes bore down on Glick, who shuddered at the sight of the atrocious monstrosity.

The crowd parted, stepping back for what they knew was soon to be a fight.

The two titans crouched; kicking dust up into the air, they circled each other like animals. The monster freak made the first move. Grabbing Glick by the neck, he deftly maneuvered behind, forcing him into a headlock. The inebriated Glick, realizing his life was in danger, responded quickly by flipping the giant over his head and stepping hard on his throat. The freak grabbed Glick's free ankle and twisted until he yelped in pain. He lifted Glick's leg, causing him to fall and land on his back. Seizing the opportunity, he pounced on Glick's chest and pounded him in the face over and over with his gigantic fist, raking his eyes with the spikes on his wrist cuffs.

Glick lifted the freak's hips with all his might and kneed him in the balls, causing him to fall off and curl into a fetal position. Glick stumbled to his feet and attempted to kick him in the head, but the freak quickly rolled over, and all Glick caught was the back of his shoulder. Glick staggered back 3 feet, blood gushing from his left eye. Wiping the blood off his brow, he scanned the ground for the freak but caught no sight of him. Glick held his hand over his eye and pivoted 360 degrees. "Where did he go?"

"Ugh!!" Glick felt a kick from behind in his lower lumbar. He fell to his knees as his body quaked in protest. He turned to try and face his assailant and received a stiff kick to his right ear. He held his ear in agony and then received a devastating blow to the left.

Now his ears were ringing *and* he couldn't see. Glick was starting to get seriously pissed off. Outraged, he stood his full 6 feet 7 inches and squared off against the freakish wonder who stood glaring, hands on his hips.

The two men stood sizing each other up. The cocky freak made a short taunting jump at Glick to see if he could make him flinch, but Glick was in no mood to play games. He charged with full force, knocking both of them to the ground. Landing on top, he wrapped his fingers around the barbed-wire necklace, tugging and twisting the wire, which dug into the tender folds of skin on the freak's neck. He responded by wrapping his hands around Glick's neck and shaking his head until his eyes bulged.

The two bikers were now in a stalemate, each attempting to choke the life out of the other. They tussled and squirmed, grunting and turning red in the face. Glick felt his field of vision starting to close, blackness slowly creeping from the outside in. In desperation, he looked about and spied a rock in the corner of his good eye. He scooted closer and stretched out his hand; straining to reach, he lost his vantage point and the freak rolled on top, pinning Glick to the ground on his belly. He sat on Glick's back and grabbed the backs of both ears. He began pounding his head into the dirt over and over while Glick inched closer and closer to the rock.

"You want that rock!? Here let me *give* it to you!" The freak easily reached over and plucked the rock off the ground, giving Glick such a blow to the back of the head he feared he might pass out. Glick bucked frantically, attempting to shake the freak off his back. It worked. He got him off balance just enough so that he was able to get on to his knees, and from there Glick was able to flip the monster face forward, where he landed confused on his back.

Glick stood and body-slammed the freak elbow out, catching him in the gut as he landed. Glick thought surely that would do it, but no, he simply brushed Glick off, rolled onto his knees and stood tall. He stepped toward Glick and popped a quick left jab that landed squarely to his chin, then a roundhouse right that caught him on the temple. Glick shook in torment, staggering backward. The freak stepped forward; again grabbing Glick by the ears, he delivered a quick head butt to the nose causing a terrific splatter of blood. He then quickly backed the woozy Glick up against a tree. He dealt a series of low punches to his abdomen 'til Glick's knees buckled. The crowd of bikers whooped and hollered in glee.

Sensing victory, the freak stepped back to behold the damage. Glick was hardly recognizable. His stringy hair was matted with blood, and his beard was wet with the blood that was pouring from his nose. His face was swollen beyond belief, and his eyes were almost sealed shut. He stood open-mouthed, gaping at his antagonist, drool spilling from his lips.

The freak smirked, revealing teeth that had been sharpened to fine points. He unclipped and gripped the Bowie knife that he had on the side of his belt, but then thought it would be more fun just to beat Glick to death. His beady eyes darted about, looking for something to finish the job. Off in the distance, he spotted a tree that had a low-hanging branch. He leisurely strolled over toward it and snapped off the stout branch as if it were a mere twig. He sniped off some rough edges, hefted it up and gave a practice swing. Feeling ready, he turned to face his prey, but what he saw caught him completely off guard. Instead of seeing a hopeless casualty, he foresaw the onslaught of a rabid gorilla gone berserk. Glick had lowered his head and was now charging full force like a wild, raging bull. The freak had little time to think. Dropping the branch, he held his arms out for protection, but it was too late. Glick, with the top of his head, slammed him with all his might, sending the freak flying 10 feet backward and knocking him unconscious.

Glick had never hit someone so hard in his life. He stumbled over to the unconscious monster and bent down, examining him closely.

"I can't see too good. Is he dead?"

"Naw, he's all right," said yellow man, coming to his side. "I don't think he'll be bothering you anytime soon though."

Glick's head spun with adrenalin and pain. "I need water. Give me some quick."

Yellow man ran to fetch water, and the rest of the squalid bikers gathered around Glick, cheering, slapping high-fives and patting Glick on the back. They again trailed him about as he made his way toward yellow man, who was returning with a large jug of water. Glick greedily drank deep from the jug. Blood mixed with water dripped down his scraggly beard.

Glick collapsed to the ground and just sat there. "Don't you *ever* let me drink that moonshine shit again, you hear?" he groaned, looking up at yellow man.

"When we leaving?" an agitated voice came from the back.

"Yeah, we want out of here and some food too, damn it!!" another demanded.

The turbulent group quickly worked themselves up again for another outburst. They gathered around Glick, inches from his face, shouting and waving their arms in total bedlam. "We're starving! Get us out of here!" they pleaded.

Glick stood enraged and yelled back at the melee. "I told you people already, leave me alone. I ain't taking you nowhere. Now beat it!!" He walked away while the dejected group stood disheartened.

Then Glick looked over and noticed hiding behind a bush the boy who had grabbed the single M&M from his hands, and he smiled over the irony. He walked up to the boy, who was crouched low to the ground, and he put his hand on his little head. He warmed inside remembering the boy's mother and her other children; the rest of these vagrants weren't much different than they were. Glick was silent a moment. His inebriated brain struggled to formulate a plan. He turned back to the expectant crowd.

"OK, listen up, assholes! You come to my camp first thing in the morning, and we'll go over how we're gonna get there. I'm gonna need some time to think."

Whoops and cheers went up from the decrepit bunch, and Glick shook his head wondering how he was going to pull this one off.

"We'll see you in the morning," said one of the old moonshiners as he made his way back to his favorite position by the still. The rest of the drove also began slowly thinning out, their voices buzzing in anticipation of the adventure that lay ahead.

Glick's head swam with pain, bad booze and the pressure to perform. He shuffled over to the boy sitting outside the bushes and plopped on the ground next to him.

"What's your name, kid?"

"Chucky," he said, backing away from the smelly, frightful-looking Glick.

"Chuck's a real good name, a good tough name. You're gonna need a tough name son, it's a tough world out there." The boy only backed away further.

"How old are you?"

"Seven."

"That's a good age, too." Glick reminisced back to the days when he was a little boy; playing stickball in the street, digging big holes that they called "forts," playing with little plastic soldiers and race cars doing loops on plastic tracks.

Shit, this poor kid don't have nothin' to play with except for some ants. Glick looked at Chucky's pencil-thin arms and legs. His belly was starting to swell from the first signs of starvation.

"Where's your momma?"

"Over there, watching Jessica."

"Where's your poppa"?

"He's out here somewhere. I saw him a minute ago."

"Hmm." Glick stood and walked Chucky back to his camp. It was starting to get late and the boy should be at home. He talked to his mom for a little while about the trip to Utah and excused himself to go back to his teepee and get cleaned up. He was anxious to see if Jimbo had returned.

Glick stumbled into camp and collapsed in front of the fire. Amy came out of her teepee in greeting. She saw Glick's condition, and her face froze in shock.

"My god, what happened?"

"Oh, I fell down and scratched my face."

"Dear lord, look at you." She came to his side and lifted his chin. "You've been fighting."

"Naw, its nothin', I'll be all right," Glick said, wincing.

Amy administered nursing to the best of her ability, as there were few first aid items available. She cleaned Glick's wounds with a wet rag and applied ointment.

"We don't have any Band-Aids, honey. You'll have to try and keep that eye clean." Amy frowned. "And the back of your head, too; it looks pretty bad."

"Yeah," Glick grunted, *where the hell is Jimbo?* He and Amy were starting to get concerned now. He had been gone for over six hours and should have been back long ago. Glick sat by the fire talking with Amy for a while. The weather was turning colder, and the warm flames felt good on his face; he was glad he had a beard to help keep it warm. He looked over at Amy and wondered what hers must feel like. *Cold, I bet. My, but don't she look soft and sweet with that pretty red hair and freckles. And she must like me a whole lot or she wouldn't have done such a good job doctoring me up. I betcha she wants it real bad.* But then he caught himself and shook his head. *Whoa, boy, better not start thinking those thoughts. I could get myself in some serious trouble.* Just then Glick thought he heard something. Yes, it was the unmistakable sound of a certain Harley-Davidson.

"I know that sound. That's my baby coming now. Jimbo's back!"

Jimbo pulled into the cabbage patch with saddlebags overflowing with supplies.

"Man, I'm so sorry it took so long," he gasped, "you wouldn't believe all the ... holy shit, look at your face!!"

Glick nodded and grinned, "Yeah, I been having fun."

"I guess so," Jimbo responded, dumbfounded. "You OK?"

"Yes, yes. I'm fine, just a little sore in the ribs," said Glick, rubbing his side. "I got interesting news, though."

"What?"

"We're gonna have some company with us on our way to Utah."

"Company? What kind of company?"

"Just a few friends ... and neighbors."

"Neighbors?"

"Yeah, friends and neighbors."

"Friends and neighbors, like who?"

"Uh, most everyone here at the cabbage patch."

Jimbo stood and paced around the fire. "Everyone?"

"For the most part, yeah."

"And how are we supposed to get them there? We can barely get ourselves up the road."

"I haven't thought that far yet."

Jimbo walked inside the teepee, and Glick heard him mumbling, "I think someone done kicked the brains out of you while I was gone."

Glick stuck his head inside to see Jimbo rummaging through some belongings. He produced a cigarette, which he promptly lit up.

"Damn man, where'd you get that?"

"I've been saving it."

"Gimme a drag."

"Hrmph," Jimbo snorted and grudgingly handed the cig to Glick, who inhaled all the way to his toes, sucking half a cigarette down in one big draw.

"Is that a cigarette?!" Amy squealed. "Give it to me!!"

Glick passed Amy the cigarette; she also dragged deep, handing it back to Glick, who took one more quick puff and then handed it back to Jimbo, burnt down to a nub. Jimbo scowled at the spent remains and tossed the filter out their fabric door.

"What were you thinking, telling all those scumbags about our place? They ain't never going to let us in now." Jimbo shook his head.

"I'm not any happier about it than you. They tricked me, man. Maybe we can sneak out tonight without them noticing."

"Look at you! You're in no shape to drive anything. Can you even *see*? What the hell happened to you, anyway?"

"Long story. Listen, word's out already for them to meet me in the morning, so you might as well expect everyone at this whole damn patch to be here first thing. We'll try and figure out a plan from there."

"Geeez, that must be close to 100 people."

"More, I think."

"Well, I hope you come up with something good, 'cause who knows what this bunch would do if you didn't come through. There might just be a riot, and they'd tear you to shreds."

Chapter *21*

Let's Take This Place

Morning came quickly at the cabbage patch, far quicker than Glick was happy about. The sound of rustling leaves and muffled voices rudely stirred him from his happy dream state, causing him to bolt upright to an array of eager faces peering over him.

"Oh Jesus, you people scared me half to death. What the ...? It's still dark out. It's not even dawn yet."

"Sure it is, look! The sun's just peeking over the mountains right now," said yellow man, pointing far to the east.

"Go away! Come back in three hours," Glick groaned. He rolled over and pulled his blanket over his head.

"Bullshit. You said first thing in the morning; now get up."

Glick refused to budge. It was bad enough that he was aching from head to toe from yesterday's fight, but he also had no idea what to do once he did get up.

How the hell did I become the babysitter for these derelicts? He wished he had snuck away in the middle of the night. He lay there motionless under his blanket waiting for the voices to fade away, but instead they only increased in volume. More people were arriving by the minute.

"Where is he?" he heard a woman's voice.

"Oh, he's right there under that blanket; thinks he's gonna sleep all day, I guess."

"Well, throw some more wood on that fire before it goes out," came a man's voice. "Damn, it's cold out this morning."

"I say throw some water on him," came another man's voice. "That'll wake him up."

Glick sat up and boomed, "You better not throw water on me!!" The group jumped back in alarm. "What's wrong with you people?!! You see, I'm sleeping good ... on the ground!!!"

He stood up and attempted to wake his sluggish self, grumbling and complaining all the while. "Oh man, I wish I had some coffee," he grumbled. The gang murmured in agreement. "With lots of cream and sugar."

Glick sat on a log and groggily reached for a cigarette and then remembered there weren't any to be had. He glanced around looking at the faces gathered there and dreaded what he was going to have to eventually tell them. Just then, Amy stuck her head out of the teepee. "What's going on? Why are all these people here?"

"You may as well get up, too, Amy. We're having a meeting."

Amy, Jimbo and the rest of their brood came outside the tent into the cold winter air. More and more people were gathering by the minute until a rather large crowd had swelled in front of Glick's camp. They stood bundled in their warmest hats and clothing, shivering and breathing into their cupped hands.

"Hey Jim, think we should start by counting how many people we have here?"

"Yeah, OK." Jimbo counted 32 heads. "Not bad; thank god the whole cabbage patch didn't show up."

"There should be more," said Glick, looking around. He didn't see the man with the Coke bottle glasses and his family nor the rest of the moonshiners.

"Here comes a big bunch now." Billy pointed to the west. Sure enough, the rest of the moonshiners were lolling their way over to the others. There must have been another 30 people coming, counting their families. Two of the moonshiners carried a big box, which they sat down on.

Hoo boy, thought Glick, *I figured as much. Preach ain't never gonna go for this. And with no gas, how would we get them there anyhow?*

Everyone was now assembled and anxious to hear what Glick had to say. He nervously cleared his throat and began to speak.

"Uh ... I guess by now most of you have heard that there's a private settlement out in Utah that has just about everything we need to live our lives without taking a microchip. They'll help out by feeding you and supporting you 'til you can get on your own feet. We'd have to help out and chip in, but if we do, there's plenty of food that you grow yourself, livestock and good houses that they help you build yourself. They've got electricity, water, everything. They're well-protected too, they got munitions and fences and everything."

"How'd they do it? We tried it here ourselves and couldn't make it," asked young man in the front.

"I hear, from what Preach told me, that they knew what was coming well ahead of time and started working on being self-sufficient many years ago. Now the times come and everyone wants to get in there, including us, but it's by invite only. Now, you folks gotta understand, I'm not sure I can get everyone in there. I had one hell of a time just getting them to agree to seven. Now there's over 60 of us. I wouldn't be a bit surprised if they tell us we can't come in." The cluster collectively moaned over the bad news.

"We got another problem too," added Jimbo. "This place we're talking about is at least a 10-hour drive from here. Unless you all are willing to hoof it, which would take weeks, I don't know how any of you are going to get there. Glick and me, we been stealing gas for weeks, but all of us pulling up on our hogs and ripping off some gas at the same time? I just don't see it."

"Maybe we could all go a few at a time?" remarked yellow man.

"I dunno. It's all too much for me to think about," said Glick, shaking his head, overwhelmed.

Yellow man stood from the heavy wooden box and removed the lid. He pulled out a jug of moonshine and poured it into a ceramic bowl. His partner held out an empty beer can, and yellow man poured some of the stiff concoction into the used can for him to drink. Glick could smell the vapors from 8 feet away.

Good grief, he thought. *I don't think it's even 6:30 in the morning, and they're already starting.* Then, suddenly, he had an idea.

"Let me see some of that moonshine stuff," he demanded to yellow man.

"Thought you didn't *want* no more ... said you didn't like it," needled yellow man as he poured Glick some into a glass jar.

"Oh, shut up. How much proof is this stuff?" he asked, sniffing the contents of the jar and stirring some of the oil that floated on top with his finger.

"You should know. It's close to 200 proof, damn near 100 percent alcohol."

"I wouldn't touch that stuff if I were you," remarked the young man in the front. "It's full of poisonous methanol and fusil oil. That shit'll make you go blind."

"Oh, my ass," remarked yellow man, "we run it through at least three times. It's clean."

"Yeah, and don't you just look the picture of health."

"How much of this do you have?" interrupted Glick, turning to yellow man.

"Cases upon cases, my friend. We used to have a real operation going before things turned ugly. Wish we still had all those customers."

Glick turned to Jimbo. "Man, are you thinking what I'm thinking?"

"I think I'm thinking what you're thinking. But you tell me, would it work? You're the mechanic."

"I don't see why not if we only use it to get from point A to point B. We'd have to tune the carburetors to run on alcohol.

It's gonna destroy the rubber components in the fuel systems, though. Even on just a 10-hour ride they'd be shot. I won't be putting any in *my* bike."

"Glick, if you weren't so stupid, you'd be a fucking genius," laughed Jimbo. "I can't wait to see this."

"OK, you knuckleheads," bellowed Glick to the expectant gang, "we're gonna experiment with this moonshine and see if we can't get to Utah on it. I gotta warn you, though, it's gonna destroy your vehicles. Your fuel lines are going to soften and break, some of the plastic parts might melt or the clamps might start to wiggle loose. Some of you may not even make it all the way, but we'll do the best we can. If we all stick together, we should be all right."

Whoops and cheers went up from the newly formed biker gang, and Glick felt like a hero for the first time in his life. The warm, fuzzy feeling was short-lived, however, for Glick suddenly glimpsed something ...the back of his prized leather jacket! For the first time in weeks, he finally spotted the squirrelly man who had stolen it from him. And there he was, just standing there, with his back to Glick, within easy grabbing distance. Glick took two steps to his side, snatched squirrelly by the hair and lifted him 5 feet off the ground. He snarled while squirrelly squirmed. Kicking and screaming, he tried to wiggle out, but it was no use, Glick had him held tightly in his grip, and he wasn't letting go.

"*Now* I got you!!" he growled, baring his teeth and shaking him by the hair. "You been enjoying my jacket?? Well now it's time to GIVE IT BACK!!"

Glick held his jacket by the collar and let squirrelly fall to the ground with a thud. He glowered over him and considered giving him a good, solid kick right in the ribs but instead put his jacket on, straightened his back and stuck his chest out.

"You're not worth getting my boot dirty." He eyed squirrel man suspiciously. "I suppose your sorry ass wants to tag along, too, huh?" Glick leaned down and squinted into the eyes of squirrelly, who scooted his butt backward in the dirt. "Better not let me catch you pulling any funny stuff, or your ass is mine! YOU GOT THAT?" Squirrelly nodded and then got up and took off running. Laughter erupted from the rest of the grungy bikers. They patted Glick on the back and slowly began thinning out to go and prepare.

Christ, now I know I must be getting soft, thought Glick while rubbing his head. *Ten years ago, I'd have planted that worm's head on a pole for touching my colors.*

Glick and Jimbo spent the remainder of the day preparing Harleys that volunteers delivered for the necessary adjustments, and soon they had the first moonshine-fueled motorcycles ready for action. The first few they tested spun wildly out of control then stalled, but with some additional modifications, they soon had a Harley that not only tested out perfectly but had even more horsepower than it did before. They spent the next few days modifying the remaining bikes and two pickup trucks; cases upon cases of moonshine were poured into each vehicle's fuel tank. The moonshiners mourned the loss of their favorite beverage, but soon the cabbage patch gang was ready to roll. Glick and Jimbo prepared the sidecar and packed their few belongings.

The last day at the cabbage patch, Glick gathered everyone around and advised them to travel light and not to worry about leaving items behind. Then, with everyone packed and prepared to go, each member of the gang rolled out into the sunset on the road to Utah.

They traveled together, entire families in the dark over the mountainous terrain, their newly charged Harleys rumbling in unison. Despite being so weak from hunger and hardship, they still had the strength to wreak havoc everywhere they traveled. They ran red lights together, threw moonshine bottles, raided convenience stores, urinated in public view and terrorized the citizens of every small town they passed through. Several pit stops were made on the way, slowing progress, but the long-lost thrill of the open road and the promise of a new beginning spurred them on. Once they were all on the road together pushing their choppers to the limits, they were all as one, bonded together in camaraderie. Their anticipation soared as high as the mountains with each state that they passed, and soon enough a "Welcome to Utah" sign was visible on the side of the desert highway.

At 10:30 the next morning, Glick and Jimbo were parked on the side of the road poring over their worn map, arguing about the best way to get to their destination. They had been traveling now for over 12 hours straight, and everyone in their troupe was exhausted and ornery.

"I say we take a right at the next street and then go left on Chilimi Way," said Glick.

"No, we already went that way, dumb ass! We've been driving in circles for the last 20 minutes."

"Don't call me dumb ass, you dumb ass. I know that's the way. It says so right here."

"Knock it off, you two," said Amy, "you're like a couple of little kids. Let me see that thing."

"Looks to me like we need to take the next left and then another left on Chilimi. Turn here."

The bikers turned down the desolate dirt road, and sure enough, they soon caught sight of an imposing compound surrounded by wire fence. There were two towers flanking each side of the entrance gate held armed guards brandishing automatic weapons. The weary biker gang could plainly see that the compound was buzzing with activity. Large trucks carrying supplies weaved in and out, and far beyond the fencing they could see the undertakings of many people engaged in a flurry of expeditious labor. They pulled their entourage several yards shy of the front gate.

"Well, I guess this is it," Glick said, stepping off the Harley. "You guys wait here. I'm gonna go talk to the guards."

Glick straightened his jacket and slicked back his grungy hair with a pocket comb. He gingerly approached the towers, where he was greeted by several machine guns pointing at his face. There were two armed guards on the ground level, one held up his hand. "Halt right there."

Glick stopped in his tracks and held his arms up in a surrender pose. "I don't got a gun," he said out loud.

The guard approached the gate and announced: "This is private property, sir. We're going to have to ask you to ..."

"Hold on," interrupted Glick. "We were invited. Preach ... I mean, Pastor Bloom is expecting us."

The two guards turned to each other and conversed privately for a moment. One retrieved a walkie-talkie and contacted someone.

"You say Pastor Bloom is expecting you? We're aware of a small group arriving sometime today, no more than seven. How many of you are there?"

"Uh, 64."

"Sixty-four?" The two guards turned to each other and snickered. "OK, we've reached the pastor's office, and they're sending him out to the front. He'll be with you shortly. You can go back to the rest of your group and wait. It shouldn't be too long."

Glick trudged back to the Harley and sat. Fifteen minutes passed and he was getting impatient. He stood, ready to ask the guards what was the hold up when he saw pastor Bloom with two others pull up on an electric utility vehicle. Glick watched the pastor speak to the guards for a moment and watched as he signed a paper that one of the guards passed to him on a clipboard. The guard led Pastor Bloom to the front gate and unlocked the heavy chains. The gate slid open, and Glick quickly embraced the pastor as he stepped outside.

"Preach, it's so good to see you!" Glick exclaimed, stepping back. He took Bloom's hand and pumped it hard several times. "Man, it's good to be here!"

"Yes, I couldn't agree more. It's wonderful to see you as well, Richard," said Pastor Bloom, smiling wide. "My, but you've changed. I'm afraid I can't say you look all that well at all. It appears as though you've been attacked by some wild animal, and you're almost half the size you were when we parted."

"It's been a tough road, Preach. I'm damn near starved to death."

"Hmm." Bloom nodded with a frown. "What have you been doing for food?"

"You don't wanna know."

"No, probably not. Are you hungry now?"

"Yeah, I'm always hungry. We had a few provisions with us, but some of them other folks over there, they're almost too weak to move they're so hungry."

"Yes, I see you have quite a large group here, don't you?" asked Bloom, walking toward the bedraggled bunch on their Harleys. "This is quite a bit more than we agreed upon, isn't it?"

"Uh, yeah," said Glick, looking at the ground, "but we'll be real good, I promise. We won't get in anyone's way, and we'll work real hard, honest. I wouldn't lie to you, Preach." *Not too much anyway.*

"We'll see to it that food is sent out to them, Richard, but I'm afraid I don't have very good news for you in regards to allowing them in."

Glick was dreading this. "You're not gonna let us in?"

"Richard, I must be frank with you. I used every bit of my influence on the board to get you in with just yourself and six others. No one gets in here without background checks and referrals; no one. For us to allow an unknown element inside these doors is absolutely unheard of." Bloom reached up and put his hand on Glick's shoulder; turning, he walked them back to the entrance gate.

"I must tell you my friend, this undertaking grew far larger and much faster than we ever anticipated. Right now, we are already fully to capacity and unable to take on any more people. I really wish you had arrived months ago. I might have been able to do something for them then."

Glick was dumbfounded. "What? You mean we came all this way and you're not going to let us in? You can't do that to us. Please just look at them, look at all the little kids. They're gonna die."

Bloom looked again at the failing bikers. The gravity of the situation was not lost on him. "I'll see what I can do," he said, looking up at Glick. "In the meanwhile, we'll see to it that they are fed. Cassandra will bring some loaves of bread and some chicken. You'll need water, too, I presume?"

"Oh, wow – chicken! That sounds great! When can we get it?"

"Go ahead and rest for a while. We'll get it out to you as soon as we can, all right?"

"OK, we'll be right here waiting."

Glick returned to his group, frustrated and forlorn. Jimbo could see from the look on his face that it did not go well. "What did he say, man? Are they going to let us in?"

"No."

"You're kidding."

"I'm not."

"Shit."

Glick sat on the ground under a tree with Amy and the kids. Most of the bikers followed suit and sat on the ground, too. Jimbo stood and paced.

"They're going to bring us some food here shortly," Glick said gloomily.

"Really? That's great."

"Yeah, I guess," said Glick, putting his head down between his knees. He sounded seriously depressed.

"What's going on?" asked one of the old moonshiners.

"We're screwed" responded Jimbo.

"Uh-oh."

"I warned you guys," Glick stated, "told you they might not let us in, especially when they saw how many of us there were." Glick lamented. He began tugging his hair and moaning "why me?"

Yellow man stuck his hand inside his mildewed shirt and produced a .25-caliber Browning handgun. "Think we could take this place?"

Glick squinted his eyes. "You must be nuts," he said. "Have you seen those machine guns? They're fortified, man."

"J.J., Eddie, and T-Bone – they all got heat, too. Raunch's got him a fully automatic Glock. We hid them good from the feds when they came looking for everyone's guns."

"No, thanks. I don't feel like committing suicide today."

"Might be better than dying slow."

"I'm gonna wait and see what Preach comes up with. No preacher's gonna just let us sit and die outside their door. Least I don't think so," said Glick while blankly eying a spider spinning its web in the branches of a bayberry bush. *I wonder what a spider tastes like?*

Forty minutes later, another utility vehicle pulled up to the entrance gate. An attractive woman, her long blonde hair pulled back into a ponytail, carried two garbage bags to the entrance. Another tall man with a brown beard carried two large aluminum containers that surely must be the promised food. The blonde woman spoke to the guards for a moment, and soon the gates were opened. She and the tall man carried the food to the starving bikers with the armed guards behind them vigilantly aiming their guns at the dreadful-looking gang. The starved bikers were on them in an instant; tearing the aluminum trays from the bearded man, they ravaged 12 whole chickens in just seconds. They tore open the garbage bags to many loaves of frozen bread and some tins of frozen corned beef hash. They crammed the bread into their mouths and used their pocket knives to chip at the frozen hash, which they sucked on like ice cubes. They moaned in ecstasy – it was the finest thing they had ever tasted in all their lives.

Cassandra delivered gallons of water and set the jugs at their feet. She then warily backed away from the hairy tribe, trying to move silently and quickly before they could notice that she had already backed inside the main gate and locked the door.

"Hey, where are you going?" yelled Glick with a mouthful. "Come back here!" But she and the tall, bearded man were soon gone.

"That's just great," said Jimbo, giving Glick the evil eye. "Look at this mess you got us in!"

"Oh shut up. You just ate chicken, didn't you? When's the last time you had any of that?"

Several hours passed and the morning faded into the afternoon. Some of the bikers napped, and others wandered around the outside perimeter of the fortress looking to get an estimate of its size. The fencing seemed to go on forever. There must have been thousands of acres. One of the curious bikers, a tall, hunched-over fellow, peeked through the barbed-wire fence and, perceiving an opportunity, attempted to cut the fence with wire cutters, but he was promptly met with a searing bolt of electricity coursing through his body. His cohorts dragged his semiconscious, twitching body to the front gate and presented him to Glick and Jimbo.

"What happened to him?"

"He got zapped by the electric fence."

"What?!" Jimbo stood and began beating on the front entrance gate. "We need help here, we have an injured man!"

The two front gate guards responded quickly, radioing for help to the other end. Soon, Pastor Bloom arrived with the same two men he had showed up with earlier that morning.

"Preach," said Glick, "look at this guy; he touched your fence and almost croaked." One of the men with Bloom bent down over the fallen biker, took his pulse and examined his pupils.

"He'll be fine," he announced, "his pulse is normal. Hopefully he won't be touching the fence again."

"Are you going to let him inside so you can take care of him?" asked Amy to the man.

"You need to talk to the pastor about that," he replied. "I think he's made some kind of bargain for you."

"Really?" All eyes turned expectantly to face Bloom.

"Yes, that is true," said Bloom.

"They're gonna let us in?"

"No, I'm sorry, that's not going to happen anytime soon."

"Well, what then?" demanded Jimbo, losing his patience.

"We're going to let you stay just outside the walls."

"What?! What the hell good is that?!!"

Glick turned to Jimbo and told him to calm down. "Cool it, man, I want to hear what he's saying, Jeez, usually I'm the hothead."

Pastor Bloom continued: "We're going to provide water, food and most importantly some electricity for you; it's only going to be a few extension cords, but that's better than nothing. If you're short on tents, we have a few we can spare also. You can stay as long as necessary, provided you don't create any problems for us. In the meanwhile, we will put each of you through the formal application process to become fellow members of our community; so there might just be some hope for you yet."

Glick and Jimbo looked at each other. A smile slowly began to creep over both their faces. Amy jumped up in Jimbo's arms, and she began to cry from joy. Soon, all the bikers were exuberantly cheering their good fortune.

Pastor Bloom directed the men with him to bring some supplies and help them get set up. Shortly, others arrived to assist as well. The clean-cut volunteers tried their best to overlook the slovenly appearance of the cabbage patch gang. They worked quickly and efficiently to provide a comfortable environment for the bikers to temporarily abide. They settled in the eastern corridor about a hundred yards from the development's walls. It was a nice spot with pretty trees and a stream of clean water that flowed through the middle, eventually winding its way into a small river downstream. It would be enough to keep them from dying of thirst.

The bikers were pleased with the living arrangements, although most had left their few possessions behind. They made do with what they had to work with, and their tents were pitched and campfires were stoked in anticipation of a grand feast. The drooling bikers watched as cases of hot dogs and canned goods were delivered to their doorsteps. The kindly humanitarians did as they promised, running several electrical cords to the camp, and brought some space heaters and electric blankets. They also provided basic utensils and distributed a few Bibles for the bikers' reading pleasure. Yellow man and another of the moonshiners pulled Cassandra aside and asked her if it was possible for her to bring some fresh corn.

"Corn? Why, yes, we have hundreds of acres of corn; it's one of our main crops. I'll be happy to bring as much as you want." The two moonshiners looked at each other and smiled.

That evening, Glick and Jimbo's family gorged themselves on hot dogs and canned green beans until they couldn't move. They then settled in for a good night's sleep, the first they'd had without any lingering hunger pangs in many long weeks. Glick used the Bible as a pillow for his weary head.

The next morning, Glick awoke early and took a long walk around to acquaint himself with the desolate area. On the lookout for signs of life, he walked up the banks of the stream for several hours until it finally widened into a river. Upon spotting a flat rock, he stripped his clothes and jumped into the icy waters, dunking his head and splashing himself all over. Despite the freezing temperature, it felt good to cleanse himself from the road, washing away the anxiety and hardship of his tortured existence. He pulled himself up onto the flat rock, marveling at how deftly his new frame maneuvered.

Six months ago, I never would have been able to just leap all the way up on here. "Hell, I'm practically a gymnast now," he said out loud, thumping his chest. He then lay naked on the rock basking in the sun until he completely dried out, then began the long walk back to what was now home. When he arrived, he found cereal in a bowl, no milk, but still highly welcome nonetheless. "Wow," said Glick, scarfing the Cheerios, "I could get used to this."

"The best part is it's almost lunchtime," laughed Amy.

"No kidding? What's on the menu?"

"Hot dogs and canned green beans."

"Heaven, pure heaven," said Glick with a smile.

"Have you seen Preach?" he asked.

"No, but Cassandra came by and brought some blankets and pillows."

That's amazing, thought Glick to himself. *These people treat me better than my own family ever did, and they don't even know me. I wonder what I can ever do to make it up.*

"She also brought these papers with her," said Jimbo, handing a stack of what looked like some sort of questionnaires to Glick. He looked at the papers and requested help from Amy for some of the bigger words. They spent some time examining the documents line by line.

She and Glick handed out the applications to all 64 of the hopeful occupants. Then they all passed around a single pencil. Most of the bikers were able to write fairly well, but there were a few who required assistance from Amy as they couldn't write at all. It took most of the day for her to collect an application from each biker and give each one a quick review before turning the stack over to Cassandra. The childish scrawl written on most of them gave Amy a sinking feeling, but all she could do was cross her fingers and hope for the best. That evening, Cassandra returned. Amy went to retrieve the stack of papers. She smiled sweetly as she handed the stack to Cassandra, hoping a little sugar would add some weight to their plea.

Cassandra was in the habit of bringing some sort of treat for the bikers when she dropped in. This time she brought some soap and a few washcloths to the grateful bunch, and the promised corn. She and Amy had a brief discussion on the possibility of all their crew being allowed admittance. Cassandra wasn't sure what to recommend for them, but from one look at the motley bunch, she knew they would never fully fit in even if they all were allowed entry. Additionally, she was quite certain most of them when checked would have extensive, and quite possibly violent, criminal records, which would most certainly prohibit their admittance. Inside her heart she really didn't harbor much hope for them and resigned herself to bringing occasional goodies and hoping they didn't start trouble. She and Amy soon parted with a wave. Amy didn't see or hear from her again for 10 days.

That night, the moonshiners set up their still and began the arduous task of producing more moonshine. They labored through the night and, by 8 p.m. the following evening, had their first batch of the new corn mash dripping into a metal basin. All the bikers, in a unanimous decision, thought it looked like a perfect time to have a massive celebration. They set up tables as fancy as possible and hooked an old boom box up to one of the electrical cords. Then they built a gigantic bonfire. Their bellies finally full, everyone partook in the merriment. Even the oldest grandmother, Millie, poured a big tall cup of the foul moonshine. They all listened patiently while Glick made a brief speech; then they toasted to their successful journey, choking down the foul brew. Most gagged and retched but promptly asked for seconds and even thirds. Soon the entire gang was in a shambles of insane revelry and mayhem. The boom box loudly blasted old-time biker favorites on its crackling speakers. Bikers were hunched over in every corner, behind trees and in bushes, puking up hot dogs and corn mash. Others danced loosely on the tabletops in a wild haze. Some stripped naked and streaked about like animals, while others openly fornicated on the snowy landscape.

Meanwhile, on the other side of the fence, the Christian inhabitants of the Hidden Oaks Village were holding Wednesday night church service. The lilting voices of their choir sounded in sharp contrast to the raucous music and wicked debauchery going on outside their walls.

"I can't conduct the choir to sing with all this racket going on," the head choirmaster complained to Pastor Bloom just as a fight broke out among the bikers.

"Yes, I know," Bloom said, pursing his lips while he looked out the window. From where he was standing, he could clearly see some bikers dancing nude around the fire and even worse. He shook his head and turned back toward the faces of his congregation. "Let's try Onward Christian Soldiers, shall we?"

Chapter 22

The Visitor

Toni Vickery rubbed her eyes as she awoke to the soft
pattering of slippered footsteps; a pot of tea had been placed
by her bedside. She shook her head and marveled at the good
luck that had placed her and Dina Patterson in such a
wonderful place. How fortuitous that, just when they were
speaking of where they should go and what to do, Joel
Brandenburg made his magical appearance, just like that. The
place was everything that he promised it would be; plenty of
housing, food in plentiful supply, intelligent life. The best part,
no tricks and no strings attached. Thank goodness teachers
had been in short supply, or she and Dina might not have had
the instant welcome that they so enjoyed. She felt very
privileged to be there, especially when she saw the many
people who were trying to get in every single day and how
many had to be turned away. Today, she would make
application once again and petition for her son Joey to gain
admittance. She missed him desperately. It would soon be
spring break, and perhaps she could squeeze in a visit.

Toni stepped outside her bungalow, teacup in hand, and
admired the production she saw there. She was very much
impressed that someone had the foresight to lay the
groundwork for such a place. So much work had already been
done. It was as if it had been custom-built just for them. An
initial series of guided tours were given in the first few weeks
and she and Dina had been shown the basics; after that, they
had been slowly introduced to some of the more "classified"

areas. She couldn't help but notice, however, that there were still plenty of off-limits areas to which she and Dina were not allowed admittance.

I wonder when they'll deem me worthy enough to see what goes on behind those walls, she thought while taking a sip of the strong, hot tea. She made a mental note to take a nonchalant stroll around the back entrances to see if she couldn't manage a sneak peek inside sometime in the near future.

She readied herself for a day of teaching her classes. Her predecessors had grouped the students together by approximate age. Her main class today would range in age from 7 to 10 years old, quite a deviation from what she was used to. And the books – well, they were hardly what she would call schoolbooks, old and worn, their content seriously outdated. She would have to make considerable effort to get these systems in better shape in order to have it resemble a real school.

What to do about the books? Toni was deep in concentration when Dina interrupted her train of thought.

"Did you hear that god-awful noise last night?"

"Yes, I think everyone did," replied Toni.

"When are they going to get rid of those nasty bikers? They look like they could attack the children at any moment. They're just gross, disgusting beyond words."

"Yes, of course," Toni replied absently. The bikers weren't really of a concern to her as long as they remained behind the fence. If anything, she was slightly curious.

"Well, I'm going to have to say something to Mr. Reese today. They've been here for months too long."

"That's a good idea," remarked Toni. "Let's start a protest movement."

"Come on, smartass, let's get going," chided Dina as they stepped out, heading to the old-fashioned schoolhouse.

After school was over, they went on an addendum tour of the grounds. Toni had to petition to get the supplemental tour, their "final" tour having been completed a few months prior.

She was never quite satisfied with her permissions level, and she obstinately and unceasingly pressed for clearance to go inside the off limits areas. Though her request was continually denied, the board reluctantly agreed to give her a supplemental tour, a tour that, when completed, only increased her level of dissatisfaction. She affirmed that she would just take care of the matter herself.

Later that evening, under cover of darkness, she snuck around the back of a Quonset hut to what appeared to be a hub of some covert activity. She lingered in the shadows for a while, observing a scientist or perhaps a doctor in a white lab coat flash a badge to a guard and go inside. She waited patiently for an opportunity. Hopefully, the guard would turn his back and she could slip inside unnoticed. She waited for what seemed like a very long time and quickly made her move. She was just about to slip inside when was stopped in her tracks by two armed guards.

"Sorry, ma'am," they barked. "No one is allowed in without an admittance badge."

"Damn." Toni grumped as she trudged her way back to her bungalow.

Time passed and the bikers remained camped outside despite numerous complaints from the other members of the community. They had been on a loud bender for three days in a row. It was now late Saturday afternoon and they were still at it. Catcalls, yeehaws and loud music echoed throughout the settlement, disrupting Toni's reading. She had to admire their fortitude, though.

How on earth do they do it? she thought while removing her reading glasses. I'm flattened after just one night of partying; and they've been going since Wednesday.

Toni in reality was grateful for the distraction; alone in her room and with Dina off on a tutoring assignment. She was beginning to become a tad bored. Frustrated in her attempts to get inside the laboratories and basically confined to the schoolroom and her bungalow, Toni was wishing she could play a larger role in the community's development, but the hierarchy seemed reluctant to let her expand beyond the teaching arena. Even her pleas for new books seemed to be falling on deaf ears. Toni thought hard about her situation for a moment and realized she really was in an enviable position; free to come and go she pleased. She could always go back to living outside the community's walls if she desired to do so, but then she remembered the dreaded microchip and shuddered. She decided she would take a little boredom over being implanted any day of the week. Perhaps she would put in a formal request for further aptitude testing to see if she could participate more.

"I wish everything here wasn't so by the book and regimental," she griped to herself out loud.

"Shrrreeeee shreeeeew ..." She heard a loud wolf whistle and looked out the window toward the rowdy bikers. She couldn't really see them from her vantage point, as they were too far away. An inquisitive one, Toni was dying to investigate. *I wonder what they're whistling at. They sure do seem to be having more fun than I am.*

She pondered taking a stroll over to their camp, just to take a peek, then quickly chided herself for being nosy. A half an hour passed with Toni pacing the floors. Unable to concentrate on her work, she finally caved to her craving for distraction. She decided it might be interesting to see what the bikers were all about. *After all I'm free to come and go as I like*, she argued to herself, *I can go see what all the fuss is about, then I can make a full report to Dina when I get back. I'll just observe from a distance so they don't see me.*

Toni mentally prepared herself to make the first venture outside the community walls since her and Dina's arrival over six months ago. She put on hiking boots, jeans, a black T-shirt and a blue jean jacket in an effort not to stand out too much. She then made her way over to the guard gates. She told the guards she was going for a hike in the woods, they made her fill out a brief questionnaire, and she had to sign for the pass. Lastly, they logged her time out, advised her to be careful and discharged her. Relieved to be free, she stepped outside the community gates and looked around.

She did not head toward the woods. She instead walked a few hundred yards directly toward the bikers' shoddy camp. She was quite appalled at what greeted her once she arrived. A rancid odor permeated throughout; trash and litter everywhere, sharply contrasting with the pristine environment she had become accustomed to. She gingerly stepped over and around several bikers who were passed out on the rocky turf, careful not to rouse them from their peaceful slumber. She walked by a biker crouched on the ground shitting by a bush, and she jumped back in alarm. He laughed when he saw her horrified expression and continued laughing as she fled in the opposite direction. She moved quicker now, following the sounds of rough voices and rock music until she reached an ideal cluster of bushes that would shield her from being spotted by the intimidating bunch. There she stooped discreetly and set upon spying on the bikers gathered en masse. Not wanting to be caught, she remained hidden behind the bushes, stealthily watching from a safe distance.

She observed the grungy bikers; some dancing, some wandering about in a foggy daze, some eating and others simply plopped down in the slushy, melting snow. She soon realized they weren't nearly as interesting as they had seemed from afar, and after growing weary of her spying, she became anxious to go home. She turned about, looking for the best way back to her bungalow, but something caught her attention. She spotted off to her right a bunch of Harley-Davidson motorcycles all lined up in a row. She strolled over and walked alongside the cycles, touching their seats and running her fingers across their gas tanks, observing the glossy paint below.

"I wouldn't touch those if I were you!" Toni heard a booming voice behind her. She turned her head and caught a glimpse of a gruff man with a leather vest and a braided beard walking toward her. She didn't wait around to make conversation. She quickly took off running down toward a brook at the bottom of the hill. Hurriedly, she hopped on rocks attempting to cross the creek but, upon stepping on a slippery one, lost her footing and fell splashing into the frigid water, landing squarely on her rump. Panting, she sat in the brook looking behind to make certain she had not been followed.

"Holy shit, that's cold!" she stood wailing out loud. "And now my ass is just totally soaked." She groaned looking behind at her wet pants. *I need to go home. This was a bad idea.* She was now disoriented. She wasn't sure if she had come in from the north side to her right or the south side to her left. She climbed back to the top of the craggy hill to look for landmarks and spotted the compound's fence, but she couldn't see the entrance gate. She knew she wasn't far so she wasn't nervous, but she didn't want to go back the way she had come in for fear of a confrontation with the biker. She saw several paths that looked like good alternatives and set off in the direction that seemed the best bet.

In her hunt for the best path, she came upon some kind of used motor part. She picked it up and looked it over. Guessing it to be a small piston, she stuck it in her pocket, disgusted at the litterbug who tossed it aside. Soon she came across a similar one and then another and another. Dozens of used motor parts of all different sorts littered the ground, forming a trail. She followed the parts trail until she came upon a burly giant of a man lying on his back working on the underside belt of a Harley-Davidson motorcycle. She stepped up the gigantic monster, who was so engrossed in his work that he didn't notice her standing there.

"Ahem, pardon me," began Toni. "Are you the one throwing all this garbage around?"

"Huh?" grunted the humongous stranger.

"You down there," said Toni dangling a gear case cover. "Does this belong to you?" She dangled the part over the giant's prostrate body. Glick went to sit up and banged his head on the tailpipe.

"Oh, I'm so sorry." Toni kneeled down on to her knees. "Are you all right?"

"Yeah, yeah, I'm fine," said Glick rubbing the bump on his head. "So what was it you wanted?"

"Oh, I was just wondering if all these parts belong to you," said Toni, handing the cover to Glick.

"I guess so." He looked the part over, and then tossed it over his shoulder.

"Well, you could at least put them all in a pile so they can be disposed of correctly," chided Toni as she stood and picked up the discarded cover.

"Go right on ahead, little lady, make yourself at home.

"I'll do just that," said Toni, gathering all the little motorcycle parts in sight. She put them all into a tidy stack and went back and sat down next to the gigantic stranger who, for some reason, was not so intimidating to her.

Glick sat up and scratched his greasy head. "I haven't seen you before."

"I haven't seen you before, either," teased Toni with a smile.

"No shit. Where'd you come from?"

"Down the creek, round the holler and up the bend."

"Huh?"

"Just kidding. I came from inside the compound."

"Really!!?" brightened Glick. "I was once told I could go inside, but I fucked that all up. What's it like in there?"

"Well, there's plenty of work to do, but it still gets kind of mundane; and it's so quiet at night you could hear a pin drop. No TV, nothing going on at all. It sounds like you guys are having a much better time."

"Ha! Oh yeah, *sure* we are."

"How did you get here?" she asked. "Why are you outside the walls?"

"We're all supposed to be getting inside once our applications are approved. Like I said, I would have been inside already, but I brought all these other people with me, so now I have to stay out here with them. It shouldn't be too much longer. I hope." Glick stood up and extended his gigantic calloused hand. "I almost forgot my manners name's Glick," he said with a grin.

"Hi, Glick, nice to meet you." Toni regarded Glick's black fingernails and scarred knuckles. She reluctantly shook his hand.

"Oh, man, look at you. You're soaked!" Glick exclaimed. He removed his leather jacket and draped it over Toni's shoulders. "You gotta be freezing to death. You wanna stand over by the fire?"

"Fire?"

"Yeah, over by our teepee. We always have a nice one going."

"Would it be around all those other, uh, people?" Toni wasn't anxious to be introduced to a bunch of new "friends," especially ones so depraved.

"People? Oh, you mean the rest of them guys." Glick read the look on Toni's face. "They won't bother you none. We can go around to the back and avoid 'em if you want."

"That would be ... very nice, thank you," said Toni, wondering what she was getting herself into. She followed Glick over the thawing turf and felled trees, far away from the rowdy bikers until they reached the teepee. There she saw a redheaded, freckled girl holding a sleeping baby. *That must be his wife ... or maybe his daughter.* Toni reached the fire and turned her frozen backside to the welcome warm flames. "Oh god," she groaned. "I'm so cold."

"Hey Amy, you got some extra pants you could lend this gal for me? What did you say your name was again?"

"It's Toni, and thank you, Amy. I really appreciate it."

"Oh yeah, no problem at all." Amy went inside the teepee and retrieved a pair of cargo pants for Toni.

"OK, no one look," Toni said as she went behind the teepee to change. She squeezed her frame into the too-small pants and came out from behind smiling.

"Thank you so much, Amy," she said as she hung her wet pants over a tree branch.

"Where'd you meet your friend?" asked Amy.

"She just showed up at my feet," laughed Glick. "She came from inside the compound."

"Really, how's she like it there?"

"I can talk, you know," Toni smiled.

"Oops, sorry," said Amy, turning to Toni. "Do they have any cigarettes in there?"

"I'm not sure," Toni said with pursed lips. "I haven't noticed. Perhaps you could grow your own tobacco?"

"We may have to at the rate we're going," replied Amy dryly. "Any word from your preacher, Glick?"

"No, haven't heard a thing."

Just then Jimbo exited the teepee wearing nothing but a towel and a blanket draped over his shoulders. Toni averted her eyes.

"I thought I heard someone new out here," he said in a sleepy voice. He kissed Amy on the top of her head and picked up the baby. "Who's this?"

"This is Tony," responded Glick. "Say, isn't that a guy's name?" he asked turning to Toni.

"Um, yes, I suppose it is." She didn't feel up to explaining.

"It's a girl's name, too, you dumb ass," said Jimbo. "Italian, right?" He asked, turning to Toni.

"Yes," she replied, "but there's some Jewish in me, too, on my mother's side."

"Where did she come from?"

"Brooklyn."

"No, not your mother," said Jimbo, turning to Toni. "You. Where'd *you* come from? How did you get here?"

"Oh, I came from the compound. I took a walk and thought I'd brush up on my voyeurism."

Both men looked at each other blankly.

"Voyeurism is like spying," Amy explained to the two illiterate chums.

It's getting a little crowded around here, thought Glick. "Want to go for a walk Toni?"

"Yeah, sure," said Toni, standing up. "It was nice meeting you," she waved to Jimbo and Amy as Glick took her arm and pulled her away. "Perhaps I'll see you another time."

The pair quickly exited the campgrounds with Toni following Glick's lead. "I'll show you my special place," he said with a wink.

"Ooh, don't I feel special?"

Yeah you're special all right, thought Glick, admiring her bust. He took a large stick from the ground and handed it to her. "This'll make a good walking stick for you," he said. "You might need it."

"OK, thanks. Is it far? I'm not much of a hiker."

"Naw, just down the creek, round the holler and up the bend."

"OK funny guy."

Glick and Toni walked for two hours until the narrow creek widened into a fast river, the most beautiful river Toni had ever seen – desolate and remote, wild and wonderful. She gazed in wonder at the beauty of the place. A screech owl perched high in a tree observed the pair from its lofty abode while salmon swam freely near the banks below. Toni, now warm from her hike, felt compelled to jump in the freezing water; instead, she lay on the banks and splashed water all over her face and neck. "Do you think it's safe to drink?" she asked Glick.

"Yeah, I've been drinking it. I ain't died yet."

"Ain't!?? Is that a word?"

"Excuse me, madam. I haven't died yet."

"Much better, sir." Toni cupped her hands and drank from the crystal clear, sparkling water. It tasted fresh and clean. "Is this the special place you were talking about?"

"Naw it's still up the way a little."

"I can't walk much further, Glick – my feet are sore. I'm not used to all this."

"Do you have any cheese to go with that whine my dear?"

"This had better be good."

"It's not bad, beats sitting around doing nothing."

Twenty minutes later, they reached the flat rock. The perfect place for jumping; a short climb to the top, a steep drop and a 16-foot-deep pool of water to land in.

"I can't believe it!" Toni exclaimed. "It looks just like something out of a postcard."

"Go ahead, jump in."

"Oh no, I couldn't. I don't have a bathing suit."

"Never stopped me," said Glick as he stripped off his clothes and climbed to the top. She averted her eyes as Glick did a swan dive off the ledge, landing smoothly in the water below.

"Damn that's cold," he swore as he came bubbling to the surface. "Come on, jump in," he grinned at Toni while treading water from below.

"No, no thanks." She wondered if some dirt had washed off Glick.

"I promise I won't look."

"It looks cold." A chunk of ice floated by.

"It is."

Toni *was* feeling rather warm, the hike had raised her temperature considerably, and she was still thirsty, too. The water looked so refreshing and inviting.

"You have to promise to turn around and not look at me," said Toni.

"Oh yeah, I promise!!!" Glick crossed his fingers.

Toni removed all her clothing except for her underwear and climbed the steep precipice. "OK, turn around now," she yelled down to Glick. He turned and covered his eyes. He felt a big splash and heard cursing when she returned to the surface.

"Oh my god, that's freezing!! What have you done to me?!"

"Har, you know you love it," Glick laughed as he splashed water on Toni's face.

"No, I hate it, and I hate you!" she splashed back.

Glick looked downcast. "Really? You hate me?"

"No, I'm just kidding" she swam to Glick. "I don't."

"Oh, good." He splashed water in her face again.

"I'm out of here," said Toni, climbing out of the water onto the rocky shore. Glick tried to get a look at her boobs, but she slipped out of his sight and changed into her clothes before he had the chance. He wanted to lie naked on the rock to dry off again but knew it would be disrespectful. He shook the water off his frame like a dog and dried himself with his shirt. Then he put the damp clothing back on, bummed out that their brief swim hadn't turned more amorous. He and Toni sat on the big flat rock taking in the midday sun and admiring the view.

"It really is beautiful" Toni said, relishing the landscape.

"It'll be spring soon," said Glick pointing out tiny green slivers of budding flowers just emerging from the trees, signs of renewed life. "Look, there's more flowers just starting to come up on the ground, too. The snows are almost totally melted now. This place will be just amazing soon."

"I can't wait to see it," Toni said wistfully. "I never get to see the seasons in Florida."

"You come from Florida!? Glick said excitedly. "I come from Florida too!"

"Really? What part?"

"Daytona. How about you?"

"Jacksonville. Oh my God, we're practically neighbors! Oh, I just love it there. The beach is my life; walking on the shore, boating, fishing."

"Seagulls eating your lunch," remarked Glick, "then shitting on your head; hurricanes; mosquitoes … "

"I'm going to miss Florida," she said longingly, with a sudden pang of regret.

"Yeah, me, too. All my friends are there."

"How about your family? Are they there, too?"

"Yeah, but I really I haven't had anything to do with them in over 15 years. They're a bunch of assholes." Toni thought better than to press the subject.

"What do all these tattoos mean?" She ran her fingers lightly over the cascade of images covering Glick's right forearm. "Some of these are just beautiful." She then frowned upon further examination. "Some of them aren't."

Glick flexed his bicep and began explaining each tattoo in detail, where they came from and the circumstances that led to them being imprinted upon his body for the rest of his life.

"This one was my first." He rolled up his left pant leg and pointed to a crude outline of what appeared to be a dog … or maybe a cow? "That's Ol' Missy, the best dog I ever had. She died when I was 13. I put this tattoo on all by myself in her honor."

"You put a tattoo on yourself when you were just 13!??" Toni gasped, thinking about her own young son. "What did your mother say about that?" Glick didn't respond.

"This one's a drawing of the sailboat I bought from my uncle Jerry," Glick said, lifting up his shirt. He pointed behind his shoulder. Toni looked, and saw that a panorama covered a large portion of his massive backside; a sailboat with a blazing sunset in the background, an island off in the distance. Beneath the island was an array of underwater sea monsters, whales and exotic water gods. "Jerry said he'd sailed around the world in that boat. That was just a crock."

"Let me see more," said Toni. "What's over here?" She pushed back his right sleeve and observed two dragons in a standoff position, fire issuing from their mouths.

"Here," said Glick, ecstatic that someone had taken an interest in his handiwork, "let me take this off so you can get a closer look."

He removed his shirt altogether, and Toni scrutinized the exhibition of panthers, goblins, wings, stars, insects, death heads, symbols and verbiage all melding together in an outlandish splash of color. Other markings were emblems that simply made no sense to her at all.

"What does this 1% tattoo mean?"

"Long story."

"Oh? What does this mean here?" Toni asked, pointing to a date inscribed on his right shoulder.

"That's the club logo and the date that I was admitted, and here's the date when I left."

"Were you in an outlaw biker gang?"

"It's called a club, little lady. Not a gang."

"But you left? You're not a part of them anymore?"

"Nope. Not anymore, baby. I'm a lone rider now, have been for a long time."

"What made you decide to go?"

"It just didn't work out."

"Really? Tell me why."

Glick was slightly irritated with the barrage of questions but answered Toni civilly. "Well, I have to tell you it was mostly the politics; all the rules, all the factions. It takes a huge commitment, gotta be dedicated, got to have good attendance, got to pay dues. You got to stick together like glue. Hell, even if I just wanted to run out for a pack of smokes, the whole club had to go along, too. It really went against the whole reason I became a biker to begin with, the freedom. The club takes precedence over everything. You can't have an outside life; and to be perfectly honest, I just didn't obey all the rules. I got one too many black marks, and I was out!"

"What kind of black marks?" Toni asked.

"Jeez, woman, you ever stop with the questions? First off, I was friends with some guy from another club. They didn't like that - territorial dogs, you know? I didn't always pay the monthly dues, but they were always hitting me up for the stupidest crap. I missed a couple of runs. That's a big no-no. Then finally I had to fuck up some brother in the club, that's when they'd had enough of my shit."

"What did you do to him?"

"You don't want to know. Trust me, little lady, sometimes the less you know the better off you are. But I gotta tell you, I'm one bad apple. Some people might say I'm a perfect asshole," he replied in his deep rumbling voice.

"Well, I don't think you're an asshole," she said, facing him, "you've been a perfect gentleman." Glick flushed and looked longingly into her eyes like a love-struck puppy. He quickly turned his head in embarrassment.

"Do you miss the club life?"

"Sometimes, mostly I miss the protection being in a big group gives you. Cars run you off the road on purpose all the time. They don't try that shit when you're running with a pack, let me tell you. I get fucked with by the cops all the time, too. I look like I'm part of some outlaw gang to them, but I'm all by myself so I'm easy game. They usually don't fuck with you when you're in a big group, either."

"Those people that you're with now – that's a big group, and you seem to be their leader. Are you? Is that your new gang? ...oops I mean club."

"Them? Oh, hell no! That's just a bunch of leftovers and hang-on's from back when the cabbage patch was a demolition derby and a racetrack. No, baby cakes, I don't claim them, can't wait to be rid of them all, actually. I wish I could just get back to my trailer and forget this whole mess ever happened."

"Me, too. I miss my boy terribly."

"Got kids, huh?" asked Glick, somewhat disappointed. "A husband, too?"

"No, not anymore. He left me for a real bimbo. If you don't mind, I'd rather not talk about him."

"That sounds good to me," said Glick, brightening. "How many kids you got?"

"One boy, and the proper grammar is "how many kids do you have?'"

"That's what I said. How many kids you got?"

Toni rolled her eyes. "How about you? Any children? Wives?"

"Naw, I'm a free bird; like it that way. You *do* look like my first wife, though."

"Really? How many have you had?"

"None."

Toni smiled. "Freedom, yes," she said, gazing off into the distant mountains. "It's very important to me also. I left everything I had, everything and everyone I loved because I wanted to be free, I *had* to be free." She continued: "I imagine the biker life would give you the liberty you crave. I suppose I can see why you became a biker. Perhaps you and I are not so different." Glick nodded his head in agreement. He was admiring Toni more and more by the minute.

She continued her questioning. "How old were you when you knew you wanted to be a biker?"

"Well, I always knew I was different, even when I was just a little kid. My mom said I was a daredevil. I was into doing tricks with my bike, jumping off bridges. Crazy shit. I hated school. I was always in fights even though I wasn't looking for them. I just didn't fit in. Being so big didn't help either. Everyone thought I was older than I was, so I got singled out a lot. I had a real hard time with my first few jobs. I always wound up kicking the boss's ass. That got me thrown in jail a few times." Toni frowned at this information.

"Look, I told you I'm a bad apple. I've grown up a lot, though. I don't go around stomping people anymore, least not too much, anyway. But I always loved motorcycles; I had me a 250 rice burner when I was 15. I saved up my money from mowing lawns and washing cars. I saved and saved till I got my first Harley at 18, happiest day of my life. I was 19 when I joined the club. At the time it was the best thing that ever happened to me; gave me the first real family I ever had. Those brothers don't just watch your back. They really do love you like you're a real blood brother. Them early years were good years. I was in it for almost 12 years before I'd finally had enough. Or they'd had enough of me."

Glick's tummy rumbled. "Damn! Woman, I've got to get some food in me. I'm 'bout starvin', all this talk about apples."

"Oh, I know." Toni lazily stretched out on the flat rock, putting her feet on Glick's lap, luring him into a potential foot rub. He didn't take the bait.

"Let's go eat."

"All right, all right," she said, taking Glick's hand as she stood up. "You have any more excitement to show me once we get back?"

"Come to think of it, I do. Have you ever ridden on the back of a hog?"

"I can't say I have."

"Well, you are in for one fine treat, little lady," Glick patted her ass and visualized Toni wearing a denim jacket with a patch that read "Property of Glick" displayed prominently on her back. He let out a little snort.

"What's so funny?"

"You don't want to know," he said, smiling.

Glick and Toni resumed the long hike back to the camp, and the sun was high overhead when they arrived. Most of the bikers were sprawled on blankets eating, reading or sleeping. Toni observed that some of the shabby bunch were pacing back and forth like caged tigers. Boredom appeared to be setting in for the inhabitants of the biker camp as well as the retreat where Toni resided.

"Hey baby ..." A biker with black teeth leered at Toni as she and Glick approached camp. Glick glared angrily in response; the greasy miscreant shrunk back and resumed eating his hot dog.

Glick and Toni strolled past the moonshine still. "Glick, you ready for a hit off this?" One of the moonshiners offered up a tin cup filled to the rim.

"Maybe later. We're going for a ride right now."

"It might be gone by time you get back. How 'bout a little nip for your gal there?"

"I said no thanks," growled Glick. He put his arm around Toni and pulled her in close.

"Jest trying to be friendly."

"Yeah, sure." Glick looked down at Toni. "Listen, I don't want you talking to any of these dirtbags if I'm not around. You got that?"

Toni grimaced slightly. "I don't think you need to worry, Glick," she said, looking about at the filthy environment. "I probably won't be around too much anyway."

Glick wasn't sure he liked the sound of that remark so he ignored it. The two soon approached the area where the vehicles were parked and walked over to the string of Harleys on copious display. Glick approached his own beauty and placed his hand on the black leather seat. "What do you think?" he asked proudly.

"I saw this one earlier," she replied flatly.

She's playing hard to get, Glick thought to himself. "Hop on, baby, let's go for a thrill ride."

"I thought you wanted to eat something?"

"Naw," said Glick, who was sick of hot dogs and anxious to get Toni away from the other wolves at the camp. "I got something better in mind. Hop on."

Toni regarded the bike and reluctantly maneuvered herself around to step up; she had a hard time getting on.

"Here, chicky, put your foot on this pedal here," Glick coached. "No, the other foot. Good job, you're on. Here, you'll need this." He handed Toni the German-style half helmet, complete with spike. The headgear swallowed her impish head. Glick fired up the wicked-sounding machine and Toni cringed with anticipation. They took off, fishtailing in a blaze of dust and hit the open road.

"What do you think?" Glick hollered over the loud pipes to the terrified woman seated behind him.

"Uh, great."

"Better hold on tighter." Glick hit the gas hard, and they were immediately going 90 mph. The cold wind hit Toni in the face, and tears began spilling from her eyes. She looked down and saw the road screaming past only inches from her feet, adrenaline coursing throughout her body.

"I don't usually go on joyrides like this," Glick bellowed loudly over his shoulder. "Gas is too hard to come by. But for you, little lady, I'll make an exception." Toni couldn't hear a word of what he was saying between the roar of the engine and her own heartbeat booming in her ears.

"Slow down!!" she cried, pounding on his thigh with her closed fist, but he hit the throttle once again, pushing it to 100 mph before finally down-throttling to an acceptable 35 mph. Relieved, Toni breathed easy and loosened her grip.

They cruised joyfully with the smooth, winding road guiding them around amazing mountain scenery. Toni noticed tiny flowers and soft green grasses peeping up through the ground, waking from a long winter slumber. She shortly became acclimated to the rumbling motorcycle and found herself relaxing and enjoying the ride in spite of herself. The early spring air was still quite chilly, and she snuggled tightly against the enormous backside of the gnarly biker, inhaling the scent of old leather and motor grease. Somewhere between the vibrations of the growling motorcycle and the long absence of male attention, Toni soon found herself moved in a mysterious way. *Could this vulgar Philistine actually be turning me on? It must surely have been way too long.*

An hour of riding passed and Glick pulled up into the nearest little town. He again down-throttled to a slow patter through its quaint town square. Like in most small towns, there were the usual post office, hardware store, police department, city hall and a church all on the same main street.

"I've been here a few times," he remarked to Toni, who was more than ready to get off and do some leg stretching and sightseeing. "I actually know some of these fine people," he said, eying a diner that he and Jimbo had terrorized a few weeks earlier. *I wonder how they'd like another visit from ol' Glick.* He pulled in front of the unsuspecting diner and killed the engine. The two stepped got off, and Toni did a few toe touches. Glick called out to Toni.

"Hey, come over here for a sec," he extended his hand. "I want you to wait right here outside this restaurant for a minute, OK? I'm going to go in and get us something."

Toni waited for about ten minutes, and Glick came out smiling broadly with two Styrofoam containers in a plastic to-go bag.

"Wow! Is that food?"

"Yep," said Glick, walking toward the sidewalk.

"But you don't have any way to pay for it. Right?"

"Yeah, that's true."

"Should I ask the obvious question? Why did they give you that food?"

"Oh, they love me in there. We're best friends."

"Really?" said Toni innocently. "That's marvelous that you have people you can turn to when you need help. It's a shame that we have to get to that point, of course. They must truly sympathize with your beliefs."

"Yep, they got sympathy, all right." Glick led the way down a flagstone sidewalk under a canopy of old shade trees.

"Come over here," he pointed to a picnic table seated next to a crumbling fountain. "This looks like a great spot." They sat at the table eagerly anticipating opening the fragrant boxed meal.

"Oh, it smells delicious," said Toni, pulling out plastic forks and napkins. They opened the boxes to behold mounds of spaghetti each with two giant meatballs perched on top. Garlic rolls and a small green salad completed the meal.

"Oh, Glick, this is sooo good," said Toni with a mouthful of the tender pasta. "How did you know I was craving Italian?"

"Took one look at you. Ha!"

Toni flicked a piece of onion off her fork at Glick in response. "Goofball."

"Oh damn, that *is* good," mumbled Glick in between two gigantic bites. He had his whole meal finished before Toni had even taken her first bite of garlic roll.

"Good heavens, you're finished already?"

"Yep, just what the doctor ordered." Glick burped out loud.

"This is just like Lady and the Tramp," mused Toni. "We have the spaghetti handouts, I'm the lady and you're definitely the tramp."

"Yep, all that's missing is the spaghetti kiss."

"That could be forthcoming," said Toni, scooting a little closer.

"Huh?"

"That could happen soon," she explained.

"Oh yeah?" Glick wrapped his massive arm around Toni's waist, pulling her closer. He lifted her chin and stroked her hair with his calloused hands, looking deep with longing into her eyes. Not to overwhelm her, he gently brushed his lips over her mouth. She returned fervently, pressing against his masculine body. He wrapped both arms tightly and gave her a deep, lingering kiss so surprisingly smooth it seemed to have neither a beginning nor an end. The two melded together effortlessly as though they were made for this.

Glick's hands worked their way over the arc of Toni's hips. He greedily kissed her neck and moved his hands to cover the curves of her breast; he squeezed gently. Toni moaned low and ran her fingers through the thick hair at the base of his muscular neck, pulling him in even tighter. Never ceasing the heated embrace, he lay her down on her back and bore down his full weight on top of her.

"Ooh, yucky." They heard small a voice beside them. A little girl holding a pink balloon was just a few feet away and staring intently at the smoldering couple.

"Oh, my God," yelped Toni. "I forgot where I was."

"Oops, me, too," said Glick, shamefaced as the little girl's mother retrieved her daughter, scowling all the while at the would-be lovers.

"Let's get out of here," said Glick, tugging on Toni's shirt.

"But I've barely touched my food."

"Oh all right, finish up. I have something in mind for you."

"I'll bet you do. I'd really love to see some more of town if that's OK. It's not like we don't have all the time in the world, Glick, and I haven't been out of the compound once since I arrived."

"Why not?"

"Where to go? They're certainly not handing out gas coupons. Our car has sat there for months untouched. I'd feel guilty taking off anyway; there always seems to be so much work to do, too. There's constant building and adding on. There always seems to be a lot of action ... but honestly, I feel left out of most of it. I really wish I played a larger role in the community's development. I want to be a little more in the loop. I'm just restless, I guess. Am I making any sense?" Glick just gazed at her.

"I see I'm being perfectly clear."

"No, no, you make sense. I just got one thing on my mind right now."

"Typical male."

"No, I get it," Glick responded in an effort to be polite. "You want to do more. Let me tell you, I'd like to get my hands of some of that work they've got going on. You wouldn't believe what it's like just hanging around all day long. Try to picture being stranded outside the walls just waiting to get in. Ha! They ain't never ever gonna let us in," he said, shaking his head. "I know it."

"Whoa, I hadn't realized. That must really be difficult for you; for all of you."

"Baby, you don't even know how much we been through. But this is great compared to where we was before. Hell, we just survived a whole winter ...in tents!! Don't you worry 'bout us, we'll be OK."

"Mmmm," replied Toni finishing off her styro food. She stood and looked around. "I want to go look at that shop over there."

"OK, little lady," he said, standing up and taking her arm to begin heading in that direction. "You got it. Let's go."

"Glick, aren't you forgetting something?"

"What?"

"The food mess." She shook off his grip, gathering the used containers and napkins. "We need to put it away."

"Oh, yeah." Glick stood and watched while Toni deposited the whole mess in a nearby garbage can. "My gracious, you really are quite the litterbug, aren't you?" Glick responded by clearing his throat and extending his arm for their stroll up the avenue.

The two had a lovely afternoon picking flowers, peeking inside store windows, petting puppies. They tried on hats and shoes that they had no intention of buying and generally killed time. Glick gawked covetously at Toni's rear end at every opportunity, anxiously anticipating the moment he could finally get her alone.

"C'mon, sugar, let's get going." He attempted to prod Toni from a conversation she was having with a woman pushing a baby in a stroller.

"Hold on, I'll just be a sec. Ooooh, he's just the sweetest little thing," she cooed to the tiny newborn. "Don't you just love babies, Glick?"

"Yeah, he's a cute little tyke. C'mon, it's gonna be dark soon. We need to hit the road."

"Oh, all right. Bye, bye, little baby," she said, blowing kisses and waving.

"You're the only baby I'm interested in," said Glick looking down at Toni as they headed toward the diner where the Harley resided. "If I could rearrange the alphabet, I'd put U and I together."

Toni giggled as he helped her to the seat, and soon they were off again. The late-afternoon air was even colder now, and Toni wished she had brought along an extra jacket. I wonder if they're worried about me at the compound. I've been gone all day long. The cold was quickly becoming unbearable. "Glick, I'm dying back here," she said through chattering teeth. "We need to stop and give me a chance to warm up." He pulled over to the side of the road, removed his prized leather jacket and draped it over her shoulders.

"Here you go, little lady."

"Oh Glick, you'll freeze to death."

"Not me, baby. I'm made of tough stuff."

By the time they arrived at the camp, Glick was fairly blue. He pulled the Harley right up to the teepee where a nice, tall fire was blazing away. He hastily removed himself from the bike and headed straight to the flames, hovering in their midst for a good 20 minutes before finally beginning to thaw.

"You guys were gone a long time. Where'd you go?" Amy smiled while handing Glick and Toni two steaming cups of hot sweet tea.

"Oh it was fabulous. We went to this charming little town about an hour away, and we had this great lunch, and we went sightseeing, we had so much fun," responded Toni excitedly, like a child.

"That must be Clarksville. Yeah, it's pretty cool there. I wish Jimbo would take me out sightseeing."

"Hey, times are tough," countered Jimbo. "You know we can't just come and go like the old days. You better get used to the stationary life, too," he said, turning to Toni. "Can't be wasting gas like that."

He then turned and began scolding Glick. "I'll bet you didn't even come back with anything, did you? Wasted a whole tank of gas out there being Romeo and didn't come back with a damn thing."

"Oh, shut up, spoilsport. I gotta get some fun once in a while."

Toni was confused. She turned to Glick. "What did he expect you to bring back?"

"Nothin'," he replied grumpily. "C'mon, sugar butt, let's go in the teepee where it's nice and warm."

Toni regarded the situation and decided it might be better to decline. "Uh, no, I think I need to get back home before they start to worry about me. They probably already are."

"What?! Don't you want to get all warm and snuggly with big bad Glick? We'll make like fabric softener and snuggle." He wrapped his bear arms around Toni's waist and picked her up off the ground. He covered her face with little pecking kisses, and Toni felt her resolve fading away, like the last slivers of sun setting over the horizon. He turned her athwart and carried her sideways over the threshold into the warm teepee where the flickering flames from the fire outside gave a great red glow on the inside.

He lay her down on a mountain of woolly blankets and placed his gigantic hand under the back of her head. He buried his furry face into the folds of her neck while his free hand roamed gratuitously over the contours of her body, down her thighs and back up again, over her breast and up to her face. He stroked and tugged her shiny brown hair.

"You sure have beautiful hair."

"Yes, now please quit pulling it."

"You sure have nice clothes."

"Yes, now please quit pulling them off."

"You know you love it, woman."

It was true, she had to admit it. The woolly blankets and the woolly, gruff man were causing her to feel rather woolly in the head. Toni wasn't sure she could constrain herself or if she even wanted to. She arched her back against the blankets and wrapped her legs tightly around Glick's waist, pulling his weighty body closer. She ran her hands over his broad shoulders and opened her mouth to receive his long, luscious kisses. Her hands moved over his chest and down; lingering lightly over his belt buckle, she sensed the ardent heat that lay just beneath. "This things hurting me," she breathed into his ear.

Glick sat up on his knees and removed his shirt, revealing his muscled torso, sweat glistening over the tattoos. He undid his belt buckle and slowly pulled the belt off, and he lay back down on top of her again. He began moving his face over her shirt; reaching around her backside, he fumbled about trying to unhook her bra when, suddenly, he heard a sound. He lifted his head to be sure, and yes, it was true … voices, calling out her name.

"Toni? Toni are you here?"

"No fucking way. I can't be hearing this," he groaned.

"Hearing what?" Toni spoke with her eyes closed.

"Quick, hide!! Under here, under this blanket."

"Hide? Why, what's going on?" and then she heard it, too. "Toni … Toni, are you here?"

"Oops, I guess they're trying to find me." Toni peeked outside the teepee, and she saw a small search party walking around camp with flashlights, calling out her name. She felt flattered and a tad embarrassed at the same time.

"Oh, Glick, what am I going to do? I can't let them find me here like this."

"I'm telling you, hide!" he said, lifting the blanket. Toni scooted under the blankets until only her eyes showed.

"Um, excuse me." Glick saw Amy's familiar silhouette outside the teepee's thin fabric wall. "I think there's someone here looking for your friend."

"Shit! Leave us alone, Amy, we're busy," Glick whispered out loud.

"No, Glick," said Toni, crawling out from under the blanket. She stood and began straightening her clothes. "I need to go."

"No, baby, c'mon, we were just getting started," Glick whined.

"Another time." She kissed the top of his head, straightened her clothes and then she was gone.

Glick seethed inside the teepee. He heard the search party greet Toni with much relief in their voices. He picked up a woman's voice he didn't recognize:

"Toni, thank God, you scared me to death. You didn't leave a note or anything! What were you thinking, Toni? You could have given me a heart attack, Toni, don't ever do that again, Toni!" On and on until the voices slowly faded away into the distance.

Glick threw his pillow and then emerged from the teepee, disgusted beyond words. He sat on a stump. "Fuck, I need a cigarette."

"You're S.O.L. there, ole buddy," Jimbo sympathized.

Glick stood and began walking. "I'll be at the still. If anyone wants me, you know where to get me." Glick spent a while trying to numb the exasperation, but he shortly realized that the moonshine really wasn't helping much and the banal conversations with the ignorant still rats weren't exactly comforting, either. He returned to the teepee and waited expectantly for several hours inside, hoping she might return, before finally drifting off into a restless sleep.

Chapter 23

Missing You

Toni Vickery awoke to a beautiful Sunday morning, the birds were chirping and Dina Patterson had already brewed them a nice pot of mint tea. Toni was getting used to the beverage now. At first she revolted, preferring her favorite Starbucks coffee, but there was none to be found at the compound. Apparently, the people stocking the food distribution center didn't drink coffee and preferred herb tea. Now, everyone had tea, take it or leave it. *It really isn't so bad once you get used to it,* Toni thought as she poured herself a nice tall cup.

She sat on her cot and rubbed her eyes. Dina was looking at her inquisitively, but the two did not speak. An uncomfortable silence hung in the air. Dina finally spoke. "I suppose you have some sort of explanation for yesterday?"

"Not really," Toni replied absently while looking out the window. "I'm not sure what happened. I was bored so I went for a walk. I ran into some nice people. It got late. I'm sorry."

"Nice people, eh? Well, I certainly hope you don't plan on ever doing that again. You had everyone so worried about you." Truth be told, Toni was already planning her next outing, and a visit to the interesting brute she had met the day before would surely be a part of it.

"There was nothing to worry about, honestly," Toni replied with a twinkle in her eye, giving her best attempt at charm. "I was in good hands."

"Good hands?! Toni, do you have any idea what those bikers could have done to you? They could have kidnapped you! They could have raped and tortured you. Oh my god, you might never have been heard from again."

"Please, knock it off already," Toni retorted angrily. "You shouldn't make judgments about people without ever having once met them! You know, Dina," she said, her voice softening, "you might enjoy getting out and seeing a little of the outside yourself, and I'm sure you'd get a kick out of the bikers. Yes, they're a little rough around the edges, but they're people, too, and they are not out to hurt me or anyone else."

"You have got to be kidding."

"I'm not. In fact, I have every intention of going back there again. The next time the urge hits, I'm going. Maybe even today, it's Sunday and I don't have to work. I think that would be the perfect diversion."

Dina stood up. "Toni, quit being naïve. Those people are far too dangerous for a young woman to be venturing near, especially by yourself! I'm telling you, if you go anywhere near them, I'll call Pastor Bloom on you. I'll call John Reese, too, and Brandenburg and anyone else I can think of."

"Go ahead."

"Oh my God, you are so stubborn sometimes," Dina cried out exasperatedly.

"It's OK, I'm telling you. Don't worry about me so much. I'm a big girl now, mommy."

"Please, Toni." Dina sounded panic-stricken. "You need to let me know if and when you plan on going there again. Please let me go with you, I don't want you going there alone."

"Really, you will? That's great!" Toni burst, delighted to have a companion on her next excursion. "You're going to be pleasantly surprised, trust me."

"I'm sure. You aren't really going today, are you? I just don't think I'm up for all that right now, not after last night."

"No," Toni replied, placing her clasped hands behind her head. "I was just being defiant. Besides, you know I can't go running off out of here on Sunday; there's too much going on. But, the next time the urge strikes, be prepared!"

Sundays were a big day at the Hidden Oaks Village. Church services started very early and continued well into the afternoon. Lunch was usually held in the community cafeteria, where thousands could gather en masse at the rows of fold-up tables and eat a family-style meal. Though Pastor Bloom wasn't the principal minister, he would usually say a few words about following God's word and keeping his laws to those present at mealtime and then say grace. After lunch, the entire congregation would assemble in a spacious field, weather permitting. An open invitation was extended to anyone in the assembly who wanted to speak to step up to the proscenium. A microphone was placed in their hands, and each would describe how God had touched them personally in some way. Many people would accept the invitation. It was an inspirational time for everyone there. Some of the stories were truly miraculous.

After the speakers were finished, the congregation was holding hands and finishing with prayer. Deep in the middle of their benediction, a jet plane could be heard approaching from a far range, coming closer and closer. It was soon upon them. Swooping in low, it buzzed the compound, breaking the sound barrier and producing a large sonic boom just overhead. Everyone jumped at the reverberating shock. Toni yelped and jerked back. Looking up, she gazed into the sky and saw two black jet planes ascending straight up into the clouds until out of sight. She scanned the heavens looking at their lingering contrails trying to follow their movements, and then she spotted them. Plunging furiously, they again rolled toward the compound spiraling down on their descent until they were upon their quarry, producing yet another ear-splitting sonic boom. The congregation scattered, running under trees or to their cabins. Church services were over for the day.

The rest of the week progressed quietly; very little was mentioned about the incident that had happened the prior Sunday, with the inhabitants of Hidden Village assuming that it was a mere chance occurrence as no further intrusions from the skies were to be seen. The denizens resumed their daily routines, doing whatever their vocation happened to be – building, farming, logging or, in Toni's case, teaching. A peaceful repose settled in and with it the usual latent boredom. Even the rowdy bikers had settled down and weren't making their characteristic cacophony.

It didn't take Toni long before her thoughts began drifting toward the biker camp and the rugged man for whom she held that odd attraction. She began to yearn daily to step outside the compound's walls and make a break for their camp but threw off her craving as a silly obsession that would soon pass.

Several weeks went by, and Toni's interest had not subsided in the least. She lay awake at night pondering what they were up to. Consumed with interest, she simply had to get over there and check on the people she had met. *I wonder how they're doing? There's that cute redheaded girl with all the babies. Amy, I think her name was, and the skinny man, her husband Jacko, such a sweet family.* Toni tried not to think about Glick, but it was impossible. He had his hooks in her, plus she fancied another bike ride. *I wonder what he's doing right now. I wonder if he ever thinks of me.*

Glick *was* thinking about Toni. He hadn't stopped since they were forcefully parted. He had attempted to scale the compound's walls a couple of different times but either promptly received an electric shock or he was caught and sent away by vigilant guards. He even would have given a crack at pole vaulting if he had a pole for it. He lay awake, his thoughts haunted by visions of the playful young woman with those eyes like deep limpid pools. *God, I'd love to see her again,* he thought while lying under his blanket in the teepee. He pulled his beard in anguish. *I wonder if I can make a catapult.*

Toni rustled Dina from a deep sleep. "What the ...?" Dina blurted as she shot up. "Oh, it's you Toni, you scared me. What's up?"

"I've been thinking."

"Well, don't hurt yourself," she responded groggily while rubbing her eyes.

"Shut up, smarty, I'm bored."

"You wake me up in the middle of the night to tell me you're bored?!" You're supposed to be bored. It's 3 a.m.!!"

"I need to get out for some fresh air."

"You're in the middle of the woods. How much fresher can the air get?" Dina rolled over and covered her head with her blanket.

"I want to go for a walk, and I want you to go with me."

"Unh uh, I have to work in the morning."

"C'mon."

"No."

"How about later?"

Dina sat up. "Toni, what's this all about? You're wanting to go see those bikers again, aren't you?"

"Maybe."

"Yeah, I figured as much." Dina exhaled through her lips. "I just don't understand you at all. Why in the hell would you want to go there? You must have a death wish."

"No, I don't think so," said Toni.

"OK, OK, I promised I'd go with you the next time you went, and I'm going to keep my promise. But if you think I'm doing it right this minute, you have rocks in your head. We can go this Saturday when its daylight out and I don't have to work. I certainly do hope this gets it out of your system."

"Sounds good, thanks." Toni rolled over and fell right to sleep. Dina, however, was now wide awake and fretting over the decision she had just made.

"Thanks a lot, Toni," she mumbled as she tossed and turned for two more hours before falling off.

Saturday morning arrived, and Toni was nowhere to be found when Dina awoke. She searched the bathrooms and the grounds before discovering her in the community kitchen making sausage and eggs for a group of pre-teens.

"I didn't know you could cook," Dina said while approaching her from behind.

"Sometimes I do. But honestly, I have to tell you, it breaks my heart because it makes me think about my son. I used to make him breakfast, too … once in a while."

Dina looked down at the dried out sausage and the dark scrambled eggs. She suppressed an attack of nausea. "Looks great."

"Liar, you know what it looks like."

"How is the application process going for Joey?"

"Mitch still hasn't responded to the request. I think he's doing it just to torture me."

"That asshole. That's just so typical of him."

"I know," said Toni, her eyes swelling with tears. "This next one will be the fourth request. I'm going to go get him myself and bring him here if he doesn't respond to this one."

Hoo boy, thought Dina, *here we go.*

"Um hmm, I've already figured out how I'm going to do it, too." Toni spoke while spooning the charred food onto paper plates. "I'm going to hitchhike to Jacksonville, and then I'm going to get mom to help me; she won't let me down. I'm going to wait until Mitch drops him at school and grab him just before he goes inside."

"Oh, that sounds great, very practical."

"Thank you," Toni replied while placing the plates in front of the grateful group of kids.

"Why don't you just get your parents to drive here and pick you up instead of hitchhiking?"

"I've asked her. She said it's too far to drive. But when I'm right in front of her, face to face, she won't be able to just hang up."

"What? Your mother is hanging up on you?"

Toni sighed. "Mom just doesn't seem the same anymore. Every time I talk to her, she seems so distant." Toni sat and sipped on a cup of hot herb tea. "I can't keep asking to use Reese's phone all the time, either. It's starting to get embarrassing."

"Maybe she just wants Joey to be closer to her, not 2,000 miles away?"

"Yes, I suppose that would make sense."

"But still you'd think she would side with you instead of your ex. I would expect she'd want Joey to be with you, you're her daughter."

"Thanks, Dina." A small tear slipped down Toni's cheek. Dina took her hand and gave it a tight squeeze.

"It'll be all right, honey. We'll get him here eventually. Right now we need to think of something to cheer you up."

"Yes, I already know what I want to do," Toni smiled. "Today's Saturday, remember?"

"Remember what?" Dina feigned innocence.

"Today we're going for a walk. Remember? The one you promised you'd go on with me. We're going to go see Gli... the bikers' camp."

"Oh, how very exciting," Dina answered sarcastically. "And when are we doing this?"

"How about after breakfast? Toni asked. "I'll make you my special sausage and eggs!"

"Uh, no thanks. I'll make my own.

Chapter *24*

Desperate

Toni Vickery and Dina Patterson enjoyed a quiet Saturday morning. Toni wished there was a traditional newspaper that she could read, but the only news to be had was that which the community produced off their own printing press. It was a whole three pages long. There were a couple of televisions in the recently built recreation center that could play DVD movies, but the rec center was so crowded and there was so much bickering over which movies to watch that the two women usually tried to avoid going there. At least they were adding to the activities. The new center had ping-pong, card games, bumper pool and some old, outdated video games. It was just enough to keep the citizens satisfied and remember their old lives before they were forcefully uprooted. If you were looking to relax and watch a movie, however, one was better off just staying at home.

The morning slipped into the early afternoon, and after their chores were 100 percent completed, the women readied themselves for their adventure that lie ahead, just outside the compound's walls. Toni put on her hiking boots and a dark T-shirt and sweater. *I wish I had a leather jacket,* she thought to herself. *It might help reduce potential stares.* The two checked out at the guard gate, and they were soon outside the community's walls. Toni grabbed Dina's hand and led the way with large strides. Soon they came upon piles of garbage and a foul odor, they knew they had arrived.

Dina looked about. "You know, Toni, if you're looking to go hiking, there's plenty of room right inside the gates. Isn't there like thousands of acres here?"

"Yeah, but there isn't this kind of amusement."

The girls soon had their first sighting of a real genuine native – a man with a sunken chest and pot belly, wearing nothing but a bandana. He was sitting on a fold-up chair next to his tent, playing a harmonica.

"Very amusing. Like I was saying, Toni, I'll go hiking anytime with you inside the compound where it's nice and safe." Toni wasn't listening. She was looking for someone in particular and couldn't spot him, but she knew he was there. She pursed her lips and tried to recall where his teepee was located.

"I think we need to go this way," she said, pulling Dina's arm. "Yes, this looks like it, here it is!" She spotted a familiar cluster of trees, and sure enough, nestled in between was the illustrious teepee, in all its radiant glory. Toni skipped up to the front and stuck her head inside. There was no one there.

"Drats."

"Looking for someone?" Dina asked.

"They're around here somewhere. They can't be too far."

"Who?"

"Just some people, let's go over here." The two women wandered around the camp awhile, trying not to look too conspicuous and avoiding some of the more menacing-looking dwellers. They passed over some women doing their laundry in the river with a washboard.

"Good grief," commented Dina, "just like the Dark Ages."

"Or maybe like the pioneer days," Toni agreed as they passed a group of people stirring a big pot of soup over an open fire. Soon, a group of small children ran up to the two women. A little girl with a dirty face tugged on Toni's sweater.

"My name's Autumn," she said.

"Really?" Toni bent down and shook her sticky hand. "Nice to meet you."

"Why are you here?" she asked in a tiny voice.

"We're looking for some friends. Do you know Amy?" Toni received a blank look.

"Do you know the twins Pablo and Petra?"

"Yes!" said the sticky girl, very excited. "I know Petra; she's my friend. But Pablo, he's a yucky boy," she frowned.

"Where are they?"

"Over here." She tugged Toni's shirt, and Dina followed in an obligatory fashion. Soon they were upon Amy, sitting in a group of other women talking. The twins were at their feet, kicking a ball back and forth.

"Amy! Hi!" Toni came up and gave Amy a little hug.

"Wow, Toni! I thought you disappeared on us." She turned to the group of unkempt women. "This is Toni. She's a visitor from inside the compound." The women nodded and murmured their welcome. "I don't know your friend, though."

"I'm Dina. Hello." Dina offered an uneasy wave.

"So what brings you here today?" Amy asked.

"Just out for a stroll."

"Oh, yeah? Glick's over by the river with Jimbo in case you're interested."

"He is?"

"Uh-huh," Amy said as she turned to pick up the ball that one of the twins had kicked in her direction. "They've been fishing all this week; they're actually even catching some this time." She turned back to Toni, but she was already gone.

"Now, where did she go?" Amy muttered.

"Over here!" Toni held Dina's hand as she led her toward the river. "I know where the river is. I fell in not long ago and almost froze my ass off."

They approached and saw Jimbo first. He was sitting on a cinder block with his pole in the water. Glick was nowhere to be seen. Toni drew near and greeted Jimbo, who had a hard time recalling who she was.

"I know I've met you before," he struggled, "but I can't … "

"I'm Toni, remember? I spent a day over here a few weeks ago. Glick and I went for a long ride into town."

"Oh, yeah," Jimbo smiled and nodded. "Sorry 'bout that. Glick's over there." He pointed in the direction of a discarded pile of building materials.

The girls turned to look, and yes, they could see a prostrate man with his legs pointing toward them; all one could see was his huge bare feet. They walked over, and Dina beheld a gigantic gorilla of a man lying on what appeared to be a homemade weight bench. Glick had taken a sheet of plywood and rested it on top of two stacks of cinder blocks. For weights he was using a two-by-four with four cinder blocks balanced on each side. He puffed and pushed on the homemade weights, not noticing the two women as they approached.

"Glick!!" Toni ran up to him with her arms outstretched.

"Huh?" Glick lost his concentration, and the cinder blocks went sliding to the side. One fell and hit him right between the eyes; the rest slid in the opposite direction and dropped on his groin.

"Aaaaagh!" Glick reeled in pain, and then he opened his eyes. "Toni?? Toni!!!" Glick jumped to his feet and wrapped his arms around Toni 'til she thought her eyes would pop. He tossed her up into the air like a rag doll, catching her in his big bear arms.

"Oh, baby, I didn't think I would ever see you again." He squeezed her tightly and showered her face with kisses. "C'mon, sugar, let's go over to the teepee, we got some catching up to do."

"Hold on, hold on a minute! Glick, I'd like you to meet someone. This is my best friend, Dina."

"Friend? Where? Oh." Glick finally noticed the woman standing next to his beloved Toni.

"Hi there, Dina," he said with a big loopy grin. "Hey, you must be in the wrong place lady, the Miss Universe contest is over *that* way."

"You big kidder," Toni slapped him on the chest. "Can you please put me down now?"

"Oh, yeah, sure." He let her down slowly and stood close by in case she wandered too far off. "You're going to stay a while, right?"

"I think we have the time," she replied. "What do you say, Dina?"

Dina just stood open-mouthed, dumbfounded. "Uh," she answered.

"My, what an interesting weight set you've designed," Toni stood and looked down at the pile of building blocks.

"Got to stay in shape for my baby." Glick thumped his chest. "Wish I had some real ones."

"There's a nice gym inside the compound. I haven't used it yet, though." Toni looked down at her feet.

"Well, I'll show you how to use these ones someday. Top-of-the-line equipment here. Say, can I get anything for you girls? You need something to drink or eat? We have some really great hot dogs."

"No, thanks," Toni replied cheerfully. "We ate not that long ago, but I wouldn't mind trying a little of that whiskey those men were offering us the other day. Do you still have some of that left?"

"It's moonshine, white lightning, little lady ... not whiskey, and yes, I'm sure there's plenty. Them drunks always seem to have some on hand."

"How's that sound, Dina? We haven't cut loose in a while."

"Uh, moonshine? I don't ..."

"She's ready. Lead the way."

Glick led the girls to the still, and sure enough, there was the usual crowd gathered about, talking and passing the time. He spoke in a low voice "I think these boys drink from the minute they wake up; then they go take a long nap, then they wake up and do it all over again. What a life."

"Yeah, really," Toni agreed.

"Howdy, folks," yellow man and his companions greeted the three as they approached. "What brings you here?"

Toni spoke. "We want to try some of that moonshine."

"How much cash you got...?

Yellow man received a blank stare.

Just kiddin'; don't do no good anyway. We do need to make a new batch, though, plus we're running out of yeast," yellow man said as he poured a tin cup full and handed it to Toni. He poured the remaining into a glass jar and handed it to Glick.

"I think I can squeeze one more for your gal friend here," he nodded toward Dina, "if she don't mind sharing."

"Oh, no thanks, I'm on the wagon."

"Wagon? Which wagon's that? Ha, I'm on the wagon to hell."

Toni giggled and poured half her cup into a discarded glass jar on the ground. "Here, let me see yours, Glick." She took a little from his and poured it into the third, which she handed to Dina. "Here you go, like it or not." She returned Glick's glass and assessed the situation. "I think we all have equal amounts now. Let's drink."

Glick raised his glass and made a toast. "To Toni, the most beautiful woman in the world. If beauty were time, you'd be an eternity."

Dina gagged, but not on the moonshine. She looked warily into her glass jar, observed the rainbow swirls floating on top, took a whiff and, while the others drank, she tossed the concoction over her left shoulder.

"Ah, delicious," she smiled.

"Delicious?" Toni choked, "that's the worst shit I've ever tasted in my life. Water, quick! Give me water!" She waved her arms in desperation at yellow man, who produced a jug of water.

"I'm on fire! Help me!"

"Oh, you'll be all right," said yellow man, "jest give it a minute." The others in the group howled at Toni as she hopped in a circle clutching her throat.

"That's not funny! My God, what's wrong with you people?"

"You seem to be the one with the problem, kiddo," they countered between fits of laughter. "Your friend here, she seems all right; must not be as delicate and fragile as you."

Dina, flush with embarrassment, stifled a snicker. She pretended to tie her shoe so everyone would quit looking at her.

"We need to get going now," Glick announced. "Thanks for the snort, boys, we'll see you around." He put one knee on the ground and told Toni to hop on. She climbed onto his back like a child and waved goodbye to the moonshiners. Glick piggybacked her over to the teepee while Dina trudged along, not far behind.

Glick handed Toni a warm soda and sat on a stump watching while she drank the entire can. He offered one to Dina, who declined. Amy soon approached with her two toddlers and another woman. They spread a towel on the ground and sat. She addressed Dina. "Hey, if you see Cassandra, can you please let her know that we could really use some more soap? Toilet paper would be nice, too."

"I'll see what I can do," Dina replied. "Do you know how they used to make soap in the old-fashioned days?"

"No, how?" Everyone faced Dina to hear this one.

"They mixed animal fat and ashes together."

"Ooh, gross. That sounds like it would just make you dirtier."

"No, it actually lathers up and takes all the dirt right off. Amazing, huh? I guess one day they had a big pig roast and someone decided to scoop up all that ash and pig fat and go bathe with it."

"I suppose we could do that if worse comes to worst," Amy said, looking at Glick.

"So Cassandra's been supplying you with toiletries?"

"Yes, they've been very kind. God, I hope they keep it up. I'm not sure how we'd make our own toilet paper."

"Leaves work good for me," Glick laughed.

Toni spread another towel. She and Dina sat down next to Amy and her friend. Glick came crawling on the ground 'til he was upon Toni and pounced. Growling, he tickled her with his furry face sending her backward until she faced the sky.

"Get off me," she giggled while pushing him away. The other women looked at each other with bewildered looks.

"You two need a room?" asked Amy.

"Yeah, that's just what we need," Glick sat up, grinning.

"Oh stop," Toni flirted coyly.

Dina, who had had just about enough, stood up. "Toni, I think it's time we head back home now."

"What!?" Glick groaned. "You just got here!"

"I know, honey" Toni said, smoothing back his hair. "I'll be back soon, I promise. This was just a quick visit to let you meet my friend."

"You *won't* be back!" Glick crossed his arms and pouted like a preschooler.

"Hoo, boy." Dina rolled her eyes. "Well, it was very nice meeting all of you. I wish you all the best; and I'll be sure to speak to Cassandra on your behalf. Are we ready, Toni?"

"Yes." Toni stood. "I'll see you guys later. Bye, bye," and once again she was gone.

Glick watched dejectedly as she and Dina walked back in the direction of the compound. "I ain't never gonna get me some of that," he frowned.

"Oh, get over it," Amy spat. "Don't you think she's a little out of your league?"

"What do you know?" he retorted. "Women love me! What's not to love?" he asked, flexing both arms.

"Well, your smell, for one thing. I hope they come through with that soap."

"Hrmph" Glick snorted.

Dina and Toni strolled along the banks of the river a short while before heading back into the confines of the sanctuary compound. Dina was greatly relieved once they reached the guard gates and were safely inside. "Thank God we made it back in one piece," she said, crossing herself.

"Oh, come on, I told you they were harmless."

"Hmm, I don't think you realize just how vulnerable you are out there, Toni. I really hope you don't plan on going back."

"Maybe. We'll see."

"Well, I guess I'm going to have to find a chaperone for you, because I certainly have no interest in going."

"But you have to admit, it was a little exciting."

"Yes it was, and little dangerous also."

"What did you think of Glick?"

Dina shook her head. "I don't even know what to say about *that.*"

"Come on; tell me, what did you think?"

"Are you kidding me? You couldn't possibly be interested in that, that *thing*! Are you?!"

"I don't know ... I think he's kind of cute."

"Cute?"

"Yeah, like a big grizzly bear."

"Grisly is the word for it all right. You must be desperate."

Toni contemplated this a moment, *maybe I am desperate.*

Chapter 25

A Meeting with the Chairman

Onions and bananas. Marlene Carson stood in line at the grocery store and went over her grocery list one final time. "Damn," she said out loud as she craned her head looking for the missing items. She had forgotten to swing by the produce section and had no idea where it was located. Marlene hadn't been to a grocery store in more than 15 years, delegating such menial work to private assistants or the household help. Now that she was officially out of a job, she might now have to get used to this sort of thing. *This feels like such a phenomenal waste of time,* she thought. *Just last week, I was head of polity, writing bills and setting standards on the Senate floor-reduced to cleaning my own toilet.* The now-familiar agony of the memory of last week's voting debacle came flooding back into her mind.

If those bastards think they're going to get away with this plebiscite rig, they have another think coming. She took out her smart phone and made an additional note about due process and another possible legal avenue to pursue. She had already spoken to several of her Supreme Court justice friends about both a recount of the referendum and a reversal of the microchip directive, but they had little to offer by way of comfort. There were few options to pursue, and they were expensive. Additionally, her time was running out.

She stood at the back of the long line at the checkout. After a few moments, she left her cart and walked to the front; she spoke directly to the cashier. "Pardon me, Miss. How much longer will this take?"

"Shouldn't be but a few more minutes, ma'am," the cashier sniggered. Two women ahead of Marlene gave her evil stares as she walked back to her cart and resumed waiting. "Pardon me," she asked the man ahead of her, "where is the produce section?"

"Over there," he pointed in a general direction.

"OK, I'll be right back. Watch my cart, OK?" Marlene sprinted toward the location the man had pointed to and found the produce section. She quickly snatched up a bag of onions and two bananas. Hmmm grapes sound good, and she grabbed some of those, too. She returned to find her cart askew in the middle of the aisle and the man she asked to watch it walking out the door with his own cart. Three women had taken her place behind him.

"I need to speak to the manager," she waved to the cashier.

"Yes, ma'am. I'll be sure and page him for you just as soon as I can get to it," she replied absently while checking out her other customers.

Marlene's turn came quicker than she thought it would, and she was soon at the front. While waiting for her items to be bagged, she spent a few moments observing the brand new method of payment and the new equipment used. She read an announcement that was taped to the checkout counter. It read as follows:

Re: WCR I.C. Chips:

To all of our valued customers,

Please be aware that effective October 1st, cash, checks, debit and credit cards will no longer be accepted at our stores. The embedded WCR microchip will be the only acceptable method of payment. Thank you for your courteous compliance.

The Management

Marlene shook her head. *I'm going to have to see what I can do to get around this.* After a few moments' deep thought she concluded, *I'm going to need to get in to see the heads of WCR.* She went to her phone to call Kimberly her assistant, and remembered that she was no longer on payroll. "Damn, I hate doing research," she mumbled. She then dialed another number, the cellphone of the former chairman of the now-defunct branch of the New York Federal Reserve Branch Bank, Dale Whitenburger.

"Dale, its Marlene."

"Marlene, my dear, how are you? Terribly sorry to hear about the election results."

"Thank you, Dale, it came as a real shock."

"I can imagine. This never would have happened in a different economic environment."

"Yes, of course, and I'm sorry to hear about what happened to you at the Fed as well. I think we both have a lot to talk about, don't we?"

"We could certainly trade war stories, yes."

"Dale, I'm wondering if you could give me some information regarding possible contacts at WCR."

"I'm under confidentiality, Marlene. I can't give names. But perhaps we could meet in person. Are you in Ohio now?"

"Yes."

"I can have a plane pick you up near Columbus Regional; at Corpo-Jet Aviation. Do you know where it is?

"Yes."

"Good, what day would work for you?"

"Hmmm, today is Wednesday. I think Friday would work."

"OK, I think that will work for me as well. I'll have someone call you by Thursday morning with a time. See you soon, dear, and chin up."

"Thanks, Dale, this means a great deal to me."

Marlene loaded her two bags of groceries and went home. She continued making phone calls the rest of the afternoon, connecting with old contacts and former allies trying to gather information and formulate a plan. She discovered that many of her peers were in a similar situation. Some of the most powerful men and women in the country would all soon be subject to the same law, and all were scrambling for intelligence in order to stave off mandatory chipping for themselves and their loved ones. Very little was offered in the way of comfort, and Marlene finally wrapped up her day of calls, frustrated and angry that she couldn't find anyone more informed than herself or anyone to offer assistance. She resigned herself to wait until her meeting with Dale on Friday so that she could get some good advice.

Marlene awoke at 6:30 Friday morning. Her suitcase had already been packed the night before, and she was rested and ready for her flight to New York. She took a taxi to the Corpo-Jet airport and waited in the lobby for the pilot to make contact with her. While waiting, she picked up a fashion magazine and flipped through its glossy pages, looking at the latest styles and gossip. As she was doing so, she came upon a full-page display ad for the World Central Reserve and its charitable foundation. The ad touted the foundation's generous contributions to society, feeding the hungry and providing housing and health care for the underprivileged. It also promoted the foundation as the defender of lost children, citing their projected number of saved lives that micro-chipping would enable and all the criminals that would be put behind bars as their crimes would soon be discovered. She studied the advertisement carefully that closed with the caption:

"Your WCR, Listening, Caring, Sharing."

Marlene blinked at the advertisement when she heard her name paged over the loudspeaker. "Marlene Carson, please come to the front desk."

She went to the front and saw her designated pilot standing in the reception area, looking at his watch. "Ms. Carson," he began as she approached. "It's a real pleasure to meet you. Are you ready?" he asked as he picked up her suitcase.

"Yes, thank you."

"Then let's roll."

A lineman took the pair in a golf cart to where the plane was being fueled and dropped them off. Marlene waited patiently while the pilot underwent the exhaustive preflight checklist, and soon he led her on board the Avanti P-180 Turboprop that would carry them to Downtown Skyport, a private airport near Manhattan. The plane's interior held about six comfortably, but today Marlene would be its only passenger. In less than two hours, they landed at the Skyport and a private car was waiting to take Marlene to her meeting with Dale Whitenburger, one of the most influential men in the United States. She took her seat in the back and was soon delivered to his penthouse suite in upper Manhattan. The driver parked at the fore of the building and carried her bags past the doorman, escorting her directly to the front of Whitenburger's door. He rang the bell and ran his wrist over the scanner, gave Marlene a quick bow, and quickly withdrew back to his car.

A young Argentinean woman answered the door. "Señor Whitenburger será aqui en un momento," she explained. "Pase, por favor!"

Marlene nodded and set her bags on the gleaming parquet floor, walking to the 18-foot-high main window overlooking the Hudson and East Rivers, taking in the spectacular panoramic view.

"It's really something, isn't it?" She heard Dale's familiar voice behind her. She turned and greeted her host with a clasping handshake.

"Yes, it really is. How long have you been here, Dale?"

"Almost five years now," he smiled. "If you would have stayed in touch, you would know that."

Marlene gave a nervous laugh. "I'm sorry, Dale. I've been working more hours than any other senator that I know of. Or I used to, I should say. And you? Are you currently employed?"

"One might say so," he replied stiffly, "in a consultant capacity until other arrangements are finalized. Can I offer you a drink, Marlene?" He strolled to the liquor cabinet.

"No, thank you. Coffee would be nice, though."

Consuela appeared from nowhere. "Café para la dama," Whitenburger ordered while putting a single ice cube into his highball glass.

"Si, Señora. Con leche y azúcar?"

"No. Negro."

Consuela disappeared to retrieve the coffee, and the two resumed their conversation.

"I don't have a lot of time, Dale, so I'm going to get right to the point. I'm hoping you or perhaps some of your contacts can help me. It won't be long now before the microchip mandate kicks in, and I'm looking to avoid it. I know this can be done, and if there's anyone out there that knows what I can do or who to talk to, it would be you."

"Maybe. Maybe not," Dale shook his head.

She frowned at his remark. "How did this happen, Dale? How did we ever get to this point? How could our government allow this?"

"It's complicated, Marlene," Whitenburger said while pouring a small amount of bourbon into his glass. "Where would you like to begin? Perhaps we should first discuss how you were ousted from your shoo-in position in the Senate?"

Marlene looked tense. "I've made an observation that is very revealing; many of my incumbent colleagues in similar positions as mine also lost their seats. These are senators and congressmen who had absolutely no fear whatsoever of losing the vote. Some of them were running against total unknowns and still lost. This is completely unheard of. I don't know how these votes were tallied, but it appears plain to me that they were fixed."

"Well, look at the timing, Marlene: The microchip vote came about just weeks prior to the election. Do you think that was a coincidence? It let them know without uncertainty

239

which members of the House and Senate would be voting with them and which ones would not. It's only too easy to adjust electronic voting machines to record the ballots any way that one sees fit. Hell, they not only own the corporations manufacturing the machines, but they also own the network the data is transmitted over. They simply took a count of the preliminary results, then expelled those members that refused to vote favorably to the docket and replaced them with members more amiable to the agenda."

"This is exactly what I'm talking about. I just never dreamed it would happen on this level. I wonder when the last time we had a free election in this country was."

"It's been many, many years, my dear."

Consuela returned with a cup of steaming black coffee for Marlene. She took the cup without looking at the servant. "This collapse of all the financial markets, I thought it was the Fed's job to prevent this from happening. The New York branch was the nucleus of the world's economic systems. What happened?"

Whitenburger defended his position. "The Fed has always enjoyed a very high level of credibility as an inflation fighter and maintaining price stability in the U.S., and we always did a spectacular job. In the world of central banks, none was held in higher esteem or enjoyed greater successes than the U.S. Federal Reserve system.

"We've always strived to maintain the stability of all financial systems throughout the U.S., striking a balance between private banking interest and centralized responsibility of government. We supervised and regulated banking institutions, protecting the credit rights of consumers. We facilitated the exchange of payments among regions and responded to local liquidity needs. It's because of our Federal Reserve that the United States has always had such a strong standing in the world economy. It's not always been easy, managing the nation's money supply. There is a delicate balance that must be maintained in order to achieve maximum employment, stable prices and moderate long-term interest rates. Our U.S. Federal Reserve Banks have always been the envy of the world in regard to their effectiveness.

"Where our problems started was first with the Chinese and the OPEC nations. Everyone knows that China owned the vast majority of our debt prior to the collapse, but what most don't know is that European interest actually shared controlling interest in China's central bank.

"The European central bankers first replaced gold as the primary means of international trade between governments and central banks, replacing it with a global system controlled by the International Monetary Fund. To replace the old dollar-dominated system, the IMF created a system of 'Special Drawing Rights' based on a basket of international currencies linked together and homogenized under a single unit, the dollar being the international reserve currency and the rest of the bulk including the yen, the euro and British pound sterling, with a sprinkling of other minor currencies in the mix.

"They released daily conversion and exchange tables for SDRs and greatly circulated them, distributing the SDR's to emerging markets and needy nations as foreign aid - all off the books and at the expense of the American taxpayer; even though most of the IMF's funding comes from the U.S.

"The tide turned sharply when a series of credit downgrades were issues for countries with immense debt-to-GDP ratios and an inability to prove their creditworthiness. Greece, Ireland, Portugal, Spain and Italy; they all fell like dominoes. And then the U.S. lost its AAA rating. Since we were so heavily in debt and we were deemed a credit risk; even then, even though, we had not yet defaulted on a single interest payment on our national debt.

"To compound the problem, relations with Saudi Arabia declined and the oil-producing countries began accepting other currencies rather than dollars. Thus ending the petrodollar system put in place by President Nixon in 1971 dictating that all global oil transactions would be conducted only in US dollars.

"China and other nations began to drop their holdings of U.S. dollars because they were devaluing rapidly. They exchanged those dollars for Special Drawing Rights instead of directly converting them into another standard currency, like euros or yuan. This strategy slowly elevated the SDR as a type of "world reserve currency" and allowed it to replace the dollar entirely. And all the while, the IMF got to play the hero. Special Drawing Rights soon enough became the de facto reserve unit without officially overthrowing the dollar or any other world currency.

"The U.S. Treasury, faced with the precipice of having its own dollars dumped by international central banks, jumped at the chance to support conversion to the Special Drawing Rights to lessen the damage. In fact, the U.S. had no choice but to support the SDR and the IMF otherwise, we faced full collapse. The only support then holding up our financial system was our membership in the SDR basket. We became dependent. The IMF gained total centralized control over our economy and the end result was all currencies becoming tied to and completely reliant on the Special Drawing Rights.

"Next they added the Chinese Yuan to the basket and displaced the U.S dollar as the premier world reserve currency. This was the first step toward the massive devaluing of the dollar.

"What the IMF did was create an environment in which any country that did not participate in SDR exchange was left in the dust by every country that did. They conjured an artificial economic matrix, where traditional laws of supply and demand no longer applied – a manipulated evolution of finance. They became the power determining the value of every currency on the planet.

"However, SDRs did have some serious limitations. Since the values of individual SDRs are closely tied to the various national currencies, anything affecting those currencies will affect SDRs as well. Because the SDR is not a currency, it needs to be converted eventually to a national currency for trade in foreign exchange markets, making them cumbersome to use.

"So the answer was the adoption of a true global currency administered by a global central bank. The Global Central Bank created two very short-lived global currencies, the Bancor and the Amero.

"In order for the Bancor and Amero to be adopted by fiat as common currencies like the Euro, they circulated alongside other national currencies. The most pathetic part was most Americans barely noticed the transition of the global economy into IMF hands, because physical dollars still remained. We might have felt the heartache of a devaluing monetary system, and an extremely weakened economy, but its true impact was obscured for a time from those who were unaware.

"About the same time, a big blow to private enterprise came when the G-20 created a Financial Stability Board to regulate all financial institutions, instruments, markets and private firms worldwide. They set standards on pay and compensation, enforcing its idea of corporate social responsibility. So now we had a new global regulator supervising any institution capable of creating systemic risk. Our federal appointees from that point forward no longer set policy; these decisions were now made internationally. Whitenburger sat down on a brown leather sofa.

Marlene spoke up. "This has been progressing for a long time, then?"

"Yes, slowly but surely.

"How did we lose our creditworthiness?"

"Simple. Print money. Print, print, print. Our high point of true federal debt exceeded $218 trillion. You can't even imagine such a staggering sum. The U.S. continued to raise its credit debt limit without slowing down the spending; we continued to have credit rating downgrades to the point where we finally defaulted. Once we defaulted on the interest on our loans, that's when our currency collapsed. The world would no longer accept our dollar and it became essentially worthless overnight. This sent the world markets into a state of panic, and crucial hedge funds dropped their currency positions in favor of gold. It was all a free fall from that point forward. All the major currencies in the entire world collapsed, and all at the same time. The FDIC failed, then the IMF declared force majeure and that was that. The WCR was the result. One world bank to step in and save the day, stabilize the markets and bring consumer confidence back."

"Are you working for the WCR now, Dale? Or may I encroach on the subject?"

"I can only reveal enough to you, Marlene, to try and put you in a position that will most benefit you, and this I can only do because we are face-to-face. Yes, I have been promised a position, most of the chairmen and advisory committee members of the thirteen regional Federal Reserve Banks in the U.S. were guaranteed a post within WCR. I'm not certain about their deputies, however."

"How many people is that?"

"About 600 from the U.S. private banking sector, very few. There are also the Japanese and European divisions as well, I could safely say just under 2,000 members from the Fed are to amalgamate with the WCR. There is, of course, the European equivalent of the Fed, the ECB; you also have government-owned reserve banks such as India's, China's and Russia's. With these there may be an additional 3,000 or so, but I can really only make an estimation, no firm figures yet."

"I need to get to the chief people at the WCR. I need their contact information and emails. I need to know how to avoid taking the chip and how much time I have."

"I can't give you this information, Marlene. How many times were invitations extended to you for membership into the CFR, hmm? Three that I know of and many invitations to Trilateral Commission meetings. I know men that clawed and scratched their entire lives just for the privilege of having an article published in Foreign Affairs and they were never accepted. But you were given ample opportunity. All those invitations were ignored, and now you want information to get to our foremost members to try and help you."

"I didn't want there to be a conflict of interest, Dale, if my constituents saw that I was a member of these groups, it could have opened the door for potential backlash."

"Nonsense."

"Neither here nor there. I'm never going to accept a microchip; not for myself nor for the peoples of this country. I'm going to fight it to the end. It doesn't appear that you're willing to help me in my efforts to avoid taking the damn thing, so I suppose I'm on my own. Tell me, Dale, how about yourself? Are you micro-chipped?"

"That's confidential information, Marlene. But I can tell you that there is next to no one in the entire world that won't be within the next few months, even those at the very upper echelon. It's useless to fight it Marlene. I do have good news for you though. I can still get you a seat in the CFR, you can join our ranks and I can absolutely guarantee that your own microchip ID number will entitle you to uncommon privileges and benefits that you will not be able to get without being a member of the inner circle."

"No, thank you. I'm refusing to take one."

"Hrumph, suit yourself. That's a very foolish move on your part."

"Perhaps it is, but it's something I feel strongly about. Surely there must be others out there that feel the same way I do. There must be a place that I can go to speak with those of a similar mind."

"I might recommend that you go to the independent island of Colón, part of Bocas Del Toro Archipelago, off Panama. Some principals of the Libertarian Party have established residence there, started their own country. They long ago refused membership in the IMF, and that will help slow down the enforced mandate, but it's only a matter of time for them, too. Yes, they'll also be smoked out before long." Whitenburger took a taste of the bourbon.

"That's probably true from the looks of it. I thank you for the tip, Dale. It's been very enlightening to say the least."

"You're very welcome. I've always had a soft spot in my heart for you, Marlene." He touched her shoulder gently, and his hand strayed lower down her back until reaching her rear. "I want only the best for you." Marlene quickly took two steps to the side to fend off a potentially awkward situation, but he stepped in, closing the gap between them. He put his arm around her back and grabbed her chin; raising it, he pulled her in closer as he leaned his head to deliver a kiss.

"Dale! Please!" Marlene pulled herself away and took to a far corner of the room.

Whitenburger straightened himself tall and cleared his throat. "Will you be staying for lunch?"

"I'd like to, but I have research to do," she nervously spoke. "I want to get out of this country as soon as I can, before it's too late."

Whitenburger gave a closed-mouth smile, but inside he was thinking that it was already far too late for everyone.

"Very well, then." He again approached Marlene, but this time he simply patted her on the head. "You probably should be going. Give my regards to Carl or whatever his name is. Consuela will show you out." With that, Whitenburger turned on his heel and walked out of the room.

Chapter 26

The Libertarian

Marlene Carson and Dale Whitenburger parted ways, and Marlene made the trip back to Ohio. Once home, she and her husband sat in their backyard swing and went over their dilemma. They concluded that it would be wise to leave the country as soon as possible and perhaps explore the Libertarian option. There were a few other places they had penciled in as possible alternatives as well. They would all be thoroughly explored before the couple settled on the perfect place.

Marlene and her husband took one last look at their beloved property with the sparkling clean pool, fountains and aviaries. The grounds were beautifully manicured, and the butterfly garden was impeccably well-kept. Lush green grass covered the large parcel in the summers, and a hammock was nestled between two fine old trees, their colorful leaves now casting a soft canopy of shade throughout. Marlene shook her head. She had thought she was going to live in this house until her golden years. It had taken her so long to get it just the way she liked, and now they would have to abandon it, just like that. Her husband showed her the research he had been doing in her absence. He produced a list of potential places, some crossed out and others circled in red.

"I took the ones that appeared to have the most independent government systems and put them in this column," he explained to his wife. "Then I separated those places that I deemed undesirable to live in, such as the Middle East or Africa. I came up with a few that look promising."

Marlene took the list and gave it a once-over.

"New Zealand? No, they're on a monarchy system."

"Yes but it's independent of the British monarchy. And they have a long record of actively resisting globalization."

"Tobago?"

"Sure honey, just imagine: beautiful beaches, diving, boating, fishing. It would be paradise. It could be the retirement we've always dreamed of."

"I don't know," Marlene mused. "Isn't that over by Trinidad? If we were to go live in some jungle environment, I'd likely consider going to this place that Dale recommended." Marlene pulled a slip of paper from her pocket.

"Bocas Del Toro. He said the national director for the Libertarian Party had taken residence there, a Mr. Augustus Plimpton. He's established an independent government of sorts."

"Where the hell is that?"

"Panama. This could be it. It will be much easier to get back and forth to the States than going halfway across the world like New Zealand. I'm certain we'll need to come back from time to time. We'll have to do our research first, though, to make sure it's a tolerable area. I hear Panama can be quite dangerous. It's a good thing I'm fluent in Spanish. You may need to brush up on yours."

"It's also good that we don't have excess baggage. Children, grandchildren – we'd never be able to just pack up and go."

"True, true. A blessing in disguise, eh?" She leaned over and kissed Curt on the cheek. He, in turn, rubbed her knee.

"I think this place sounds worth investigating," Curt said, taking the scrap from her fingers. "Hmmm. Bocas Del Toro, 'mouth of the bull.' Sounds like bad breath to me." The two shared a laugh and then stood to go make their arrangements and find the name of the director of the Libertarians.

The following morning, Marlene already had their plane tickets in hand and the suitcases packed. This time, however, they would be flying coach, something the high-powered couple wasn't used to. The American consul for Panama was scheduled to meet with them in his office shortly after they arrived in Panama City. He would provide them a safe escort through the harrowing streets to their destination on the northwest coast of Panama and arrange for a face-to-face introduction to Mr. Plimpton; from there, they would be on their own.

After their arrival in Panama, they took a taxi to their scheduled meeting with the consul in his office at the Consular Section of the U.S. Embassy. They went through the security checks and stepped inside his small office, where only a lone secretary sat working at her computer.

"¿Le puedo ayudar?"

Marlene responded. "Sí, complace, tenemos cita con Sr. Cruz."

"Oh estoy apesadumbrado que Sr. Cruz no está aquí ahora."

"¿Realmente? ¿Cuándo él será detrás?"

"Probablemente no hoy. Mi apesadumbrado."

"Pero teníamos una cita. ¡Vinimos una manera larga!"

The secretary shrugged her shoulders and resumed working on her computer.

"What's going on?" Curt turned to Marlene.

"She says he's not here."

"Where did he go?"

"Who knows?" Marlene reported with a scowl. "She said he probably won't be in today."

"What? Doesn't she know we have an appointment?"

"Yes, yes, I told her. Welcome to Panama, Curt."

"I'm certain we can find this Bocas Del Toro place on our own." Curt emulated a Mexican accent: "We don't need no steeenkeeng Senyor Cruz. We don't need no steeenkeeng consulate." Marlene smiled, but she wasn't so convinced; having the consulate's chaperone from the beginning of their trip would have provided her a great deal of comfort. Kidnappings were rampant in the area, especially of wealthy-looking American tourists.

"We need to go purchase a map and rent a car," she said as they left the consulate. They hailed yet another taxi, which drove them back to the airport's car rental area, and they were soon back on the streets of Panama City in a rather old Chevy, headed to their destination. The two traveled over the bad roads observing the typical extremes between grievous poverty amid copious displays of great wealth so common to South and Central America. Near-naked little brown children were playing stickball in the streets, chickens and livestock blocked their path in several spots, requiring much patience on Curt's part, behind the wheel. He grumbled and complained about the lack of traffic lights when a car almost sideswiped their vehicle, but his frustration quickly turned to fear when he saw that the car did a quick maneuver to block his path and two more cars pulled alongside the first one to finish blocking his route.

"Oh my God," he exclaimed. "Kidnappers!"

"What!?" Marlene lifted her head from the map. "No, Curt," she said in a hushed voice, squinting her eyes "they're not kidnappers; they're the policia." She watched two officers emerge from their unmarked car while the others inside the backup units remained inside their cars.

"The police? What do they want? I wasn't speeding. I haven't done anything wrong."

"Let's see," she said as the two officers made their approach.

"Puedo ver su licencia y registro, por favor?" One of the officers asked Curt. He produced his Ohio driver's license and the papers for the rental car.

"Usted es un camino largo del gringo de casa." The officer laughed.

"What did he say? Curt turned to Marlene.

"He said, 'You're a long way from home, gringo.'"

"Si," Curt turned back to the officer.

"Usted casi atropelló a aquel pequeño muchacho atrás allí, y usted dirigió un signo de parada también." Curt again turned to Marlene.

"He said that you almost ran over a little boy back there when you went through that stop sign."

"What??!! There was no stop sign anywhere, and I came to a complete stop for those little brats who were blocking the road!! You talk to him, Marlene."

"No, Curt." She shook her head "I think it would be best if I don't say a word here."

"Siento." Curt said, looking up at the officer.

"Tsk, tsk, muy mal para usted, gringo, este podría costarle mucho dinero." Curt looked at his wife with querying eyes.

"It's OK," she said, breathing a sigh of relief. "He just wants some money."

"Money? He wants a bribe?"

"I think so."

"How much do you think I should I give him?"

"Try a fifty."

Curt went into his wallet and retrieved a $50 bill. He stuck it in the window between the glass and the door. The officer just looked at it. "I think he wants more," Curt said. He pulled out another fifty and put it next to the other.

"Sí, este podría costarle una cantidad de dinero enorme," the officer said as he took the money and turned it over in his fingers.

"Give him a hundred," Marlene urged.

"But I just did!"

"Come on, hurry up, hand him a Franklin."

Curt grumbled and produced a $100 bill. This time he waved it at the corrupt officer, who snatched it from his fingers and left the two in peace.

"Damn! That made me a nervous wreck," Curt said as he started the car, his hands shaking.

"And costly too. Unbelievable," Marlene said. She also was rattled by the unexpected shakedown. "What do you suppose those mercenaries are going to do when everyone here is microchipped? How are they going to extort the tourist then?"

"I'm sure they'll find a way," Curt remarked sarcastically. "Hey, gringo, I'll take three mangoes and your fine mule there." The two tittered at the thought.

Curt and Marlene drove for some while through mountainous terrain. By the time they reached the northwest coast, they were tired and hungry, and it was also starting to get dark.

"What do you want to eat?" Curt asked. "I don't think I've seen a restaurant the whole time we've been driving."

"There were a couple of places a few hours back, but they looked like places I wouldn't let the dog eat at. Phew, I'm starving. I wish I hadn't been so picky."

"I wouldn't mind trying some mystery meat about now," Curt agreed.

Marlene took out the map once again. "I think were supposed to go to this Bastimentos. It looks like one of the principal communities in the Bocas Del Toro area. I'm sure we can find a restaurant there. We might need to ask directions to the residence of Mr. Plimpton and company."

"How much longer?"

Marlene looked around. "I think we're here now."

"This? This is it? A principal community?"

"Well, just keep driving a little more. We might run into a downtown."

They both had to admit the scenery was nothing short of spectacular. A blazing sunset was just creeping down over the horizon, casting a soft orange light over the thatched roofs of the stilted huts scattered throughout the picturesque landscape. Men were casting nets over the sides of small fishing boats into the turquoise seas, and pelicans were begging for scraps by the boardwalks where women were taking their evening strolls. The temperature was perfect, and the peaceful quiet with no sounds of motors or horns had the two relaxed and in a good mood despite their hunger and unfamiliarity with their surroundings.

Shortly, the pair encroached upon what appeared to be the outskirts of a small village. Houses and businesses painted in chipped pink dotted all together on the same potholed dirt road. They passed a two-story hotel adorned with Christmas lights despite it being late September. An outdoor café and cantina beckoned, but they continued driving anyway in hopes of finding something better up the road. There wasn't. They soon found themselves driving along empty coastline again to a dead end.

"I guess this is the end of the road," Curt stated.

They did a U-turn to get back to the tiny strip of commerce, parked and headed straight for the restaurant. A diminutive man was playing a guitar on the porch of the café as they approached, singing a song of lost love:

"Oh, mi amor, no me he olvidado de ti, tu sonrisa y tu beso que me acechan desde lejos...."

The two entered the small café and were met with uncomfortable stares from the local patrons, but the portly woman who owned the café was warm and cordial. "Por favor, siéntate. ¿Quieres un trago para empezar?"

"Si, cerveza." Curt replied.

"Café para darle las gracias."

The woman returned with beer and coffee and also roasted corn nuts and slices of raw fish marinated in lime juice as an appetizer.

"We didn't order this," Curt remarked with his mouth full.

"I think it's complimentary," Marlene explained.

It turned out there was no menu at the café, whatever they cooked that evening is what you got. Fortunately, it was a delicious meal of chicken stewed with yams and onions in a wonderful red gravy. White rice and black beans completed the meal. When the check arrived, Curt raved about the great price.

"Wow! We could have paid 10 times that much at home! It was really good!"

"I concur," Marlene said as she watched one of the patrons pay for his meal with a swipe of the wrist at the register; not a good sign. She took her phone from her purse and tried typing in the address on the GPS, but it didn't seem to work.

"Must be too far from civilization," she mumbled.

"Think we can find it in the dark?"

"I know we're here. Let's see what we can do before we check into that hotel, hmmm?"

"Sure, that sounds fine. Why don't we take a stroll through the area, work off some of those beans, eh?"

"OK, honey."

Marlene took her purse and the two stepped outside into the balmy, tropical air. The soloist was playing a new, much livelier song, and the streets were starting to fill with people stepping out for an evening of dancing, dining and fun. The couple noticed that some of the residents were dressed in strange costumes and a small group seemed to be walking in a westerly direction. Curious to see where they were going, they trailed behind the covey following the sounds of the faraway drumbeats that floated in the gentle breeze, excitement buzzing in the air.

They joined what was now a crowd of people onto a short ridge and, upon peering down over a valley surrounded by lush jungle; they beheld a native festival in full swing. Tiki torches, paper lanterns and effigies of skeletons surrounded the outskirts of the jubilee. Children in skeleton masks zipped back and forth with shouts of laughter, chasing one other with batons that held small plastic skulls with streamers on their ends. There were giant, colorful paper kites, some flying in the air and some decorating the trees. Groups of families were gathered around eating and drinking at the multitudes of flower-lined tables filled with candles, foods, pastries, liquor, toys and candy. Marlene and Curt slowly approached the gala in awe when a drunken man holding a bottle of tequila stumbled backward into them, almost knocking Marlene over.

Curt was about to give the drunk some help to the ground when a boy of about 13 ran up and pulled the inebriated man by the arm, removing him from the touristas, who were looking mighty out-of-place.

"Afliido a está respectos mon oncle," the boy said.

"No problemo," Curt said, curiously looking at the boy, who was dressed as a demon with red face paint and holding a black whip."Que es está aqui?" Curt asked.

"Don't vous connaissez? Dia de Finados," the boy answered.

"What was that?" Curt turned to Marlene.

"I'm not certain. He's not really speaking Spanish. It's more like a mix of French, Spanish and some island lingo. I think it's like some kind of Day of the Dead celebration, like the ones in Mexico."

The boy pulled out his whip and cracked it in the air. "Regresse, regresse ou lhe enviarei aos diabos." He shook the whip at Curt, who took a few steps back.

"He's dangerous with that thing."

"I'll say."

The two retreated toward the drummers, where a group of women were gathered around singing in their native Afro-Antillean dialect. Couples with shells sewn into their clothing were dancing, their shells clanking in time to the music. There were other musicians as well, clusters of men painted in intense shades of black energetically playing their guitars, flutes and bongos, filling the air with a contagious rhythm. The couple stood and watched the merriment for some time, the music getting louder and louder and the dancing more unbridled with each passing moment as more and more people joined in. Marlene suddenly felt she couldn't resist. She shed her shoes and pulled Curt's arm into the midst of the dancers. Together they danced sweetly, with the pearly white sand in their toes and the stars twinkling overhead.

After a few songs, Curt noticed an American-looking man dancing with a dark woman. He stood out from the others just as much as he and Marlene did.

"Look," Curt nudged Marlene and nodded, "a Yankee."

Marlene glanced over to see what Curt was looking at. She saw the man dancing with a native-looking woman, his plaid shirt, pressed khaki pants and leather belt in sharp contrast to the local attire.

"Think we should talk to him?" Marlene asked.

"All right." Curt adjusted their dancing, shimmying a little closer until they were dancing next to the couple. Suddenly, the song ended, and the man took his woman's arm and turned to walk away.

"Pardon me." Curt tapped the man on his shoulder. He turned and looked.

"Yes?"

"Sorry to bother you. We're not from around here, and you looked like someone who might be able to give us some pointers."

"Oh, sure." He held up his finger. "Hold on a sec." He spoke to the dark woman a moment, and she withdrew to a table of other women.

"I'm all yours." The man turned, smiling at Marlene and Curt.

"My name is Curt Ludington, and this is my wife, Marlene Carson. We're from the United States, Ohio to be exact."

"Elliot Fischer. Good to meet you." They shook hands and the loud music began once again.

"I think we should move before we get trampled," Fischer said. He led them to a small unoccupied table loaded with tropical fruit and a used ashtray.

"Orange?" he offered.

"No thank you. We ate."

"How about a drink? There's this really great one they make with sweet rum and some kind of sesame seed milk. Amazing!"

Marlene looked at Curt. "Sesame seed milk?"

"That sounds good. I'll take one," Curt said.

"Me, too," Marlene added as she dug in her purse for some cash.

"No, please; I've got it. I'll be right back. Don't go away." Fischer disappeared and quickly returned with three drinks served in coconut shells rimmed with sugar.

"It's a local specialty," he said, handing the drinks to Curt and Marlene. "Wait 'til you try it."

The drink was great, with an unusual nutty flavor and hints of cinnamon or maybe nutmeg. Marlene could barely taste the rum.

"I like it!" she said over the blaring music. "It's not too sweet."

"There's another really good one made from fresh coconut juice and pineapple. You'll have to try that one next. So you say you're from Ohio? What part?"

"Columbus," Curt responded, "and D.C. as well. Marlene was the Ohio Senate representative."

"Really? Impressive."

"Former senator. I'm retired now."

"What brings you to this part of the world? Are you vacationing?"

"Actually, no, we're looking for something," Marlene said. "We heard there were some principals from the Libertarian Party that we should meet here; a Mr. Plimpton amongst them."

"Oh yes, Augustus. I know him very well. Quite a few Americans settled here a few years ago. This place was a Mecca of sorts for a while. Most have gone back to the States, though. There's a good chance he might be here tonight. I saw some of his people here earlier, and he certainly loves this sort of thing."

"That would be great," Curt remarked, "better than trying to track him down in the morning."

"It's a small island. There are only about 1,200 families living here; you would have found him quite readily. The office is located in the heart of the Bocas Del Toro city district."

"Do you have a contact number for him?"

"I can do better. If you'll hold on a moment, I'll see if I can't find him for you." Fischer left the couple sitting for a short while before returning.

"You're in luck. He is here, but he's in the bathroom right now. His wife promised to send him over." Marlene and Curt both sat up straight and craned their heads, looking about for the man's arrival. About a half an hour passed while they made small talk with Fischer, and the couple grew tired of waiting. Just as they stood to say their goodbyes, a large, eccentric-looking man in skeleton face paint and wearing a loincloth approached their table.

"Elliot! Hello," the man's big, booming voice reverberated throughout as he greeted Fischer. He clasped the hand of Elliot Fischer and patted him on the shoulder as he turned to face the American couple. "I understand there is someone here who wants to meet me?"

"Yes, Auggie. This is Marlene Carson and her husband Curt. They've come a long way to meet you. All the way from Washington, D.C."

"Ohio, actually," Curt corrected, he noticed Plimpton's fluffy white hair had been braided into a ponytail at the top and decorated with what appeared to be ... fish bones? "It's very nice to meet you."

"How do you do? John Augustus Plimpton at your service. And to what do I owe the pleasure?" He sat down at the drink-covered table.

"We understand that you're one of the principal directors of the Libertarian Party?"

"Oh, yes. Any time the word party is mentioned, I'm sure to go." Marlene and Curt looked at each other with raised eyebrows.

Curt spoke: "Perhaps we could meet with you tomorrow to go over some of the actions that have been taken at home? Marlene is a former U.S. senator. We have quite a lot we would like to go over with you. Would you be available in the morning, say, around 9 or 9:30?"

"Yes certainly – that is, if I'm not out on safari."

"Safari?"

"Yes there's quite an assortment of wildlife here on the island. Why, just the other day I bagged six tigers."

"Tigers? Here in Central America?"

"Oh, yes, I bagged them. I bagged them and bagged them to go away, but they hung around all afternoon." He let out an uproarious laugh. Marlene and Curt smiled in amusement.

"And just this morning, I shot an elephant in my pajamas. How he got into my pajamas, I'll never know." He again laughed with a deep, throaty chortle. The couple couldn't help but laugh with him at the absurdity.

"Well, I must be off." He stood and gave three quick bows. "May your home be safe from tigers and other wild beasts. Elliot, please give them my card, will you?" He turned, straightened his knees and waddled like a penguin back into the dancing crowd.

Marlene watched in amazement as he spun onto the dance floor and blended in with the other dancers. "*That's* the National Director of the Libertarian Party??" she wondered out loud.

"Well, yes," Fischer said. "He really is in rare form tonight, quoting some old Marx Brothers routine, I believe."

"Who's on first," Marlene said.

"That was Abbott and Costello," Curt corrected her.

"Whatever." Marlene was starting to feel impatient. They had come an awfully long way just to meet some kook.

"I don't have one of Auggie's cards on me, but here." Fischer scribbled down an address on a paper napkin. "Come by the office in the morning. I'll be in the one a few doors down, Suite 318. If you need me for anything, feel free to drop in. It was really nice to meet you."

"Thank you, Elliot." Curt stood and shook his hand. "Hopefully we'll be seeing you again soon."

"Good night," he waved and went back to the table of his companions.

Marlene and Curt enjoyed a final dance and checked into the hotel with the Christmas lights. The room was small with wooden floors, no air conditioning and a lumpy bed, but it was clean and the two slept surprisingly well. They were up early to take a predawn walk on the pebbly beach just outside the hotel. There they stopped for a moment to behold the most beautiful sunrise either had ever seen. The sky slowly evolved from dark azure, giving way to shades of deep violet with flushes of pink, and then suddenly, a great burst of golden brilliance lit up the sky, heralding the arrival of the sun. Gulls and sandpipers foraged for life in the sand while multitudes of pastel-hued shells reflected soft light from the sun's rays. Mellow waves rolled smoothly onto the shore, licking their toes while a gentle breeze caressed their face.

It felt so good to be in this beautiful, tranquil place where all of life's concerns could be forgotten. Marlene was sad that she had to leave to go and get ready for the meeting with that odd man they had met the evening before. She and Curt held hands as they walked back to their room to shower and have a bite to eat. Soon they were in their car heading to the downtown district for the meeting with John Augustus Plimpton.

The office was in an old five-story building that had no elevator. The pair walked three flights of stairs to Suite 315 and entered without knocking. There was a small bustle of activity. A few people were shuffling papers and a woman was making a pot of coffee. *Thank God there's air conditioning,* thought Marlene, wiping a bead of sweat from her eyebrow. The temperature outside was already in the high 90s despite being early fall. A short, fat man wearing polyester pants stopped and asked if he could be of assistance.

"Yes, we're here to see Augustus Plimpton," Marlene answered.

"You have an appointment, yes?"

"We do, for 9 a.m. We're a little late."

"Follow me, please."

The man led them to Augustus' office, where he sat talking on the phone facing the outside window. He acknowledged the couple with a nod and gestured for them to sit down while he finished his conversation. Once done, he stood to greet them. "Hello again," booming, he moved from behind his desk and extended his hand.

Marlene was flabbergasted. The man looked nothing like the evening before. He was clean cut and freshly shaved with his thick white hair combed back. He wore a tailored shirt with French cuffs and a striped chalk tie, he smelled of soap and fine cologne; very professional. And now that his white face paint had been washed off Marlene observed his handsome features, a large square face with bushy eyebrows, dimples, twinkling blue eyes and a ruddy complexion. She felt herself flush at his robust good looks and checked her skirt to make sure there was no lingering lint or other defilement before she shook the great man's hand.

"It's good to see you again," he said. "Did you have fun at the Dia de Finados Festival?"

"It was interesting," Marlene replied.

"Yes, a time-honored ritual. Many believe that during the Day of the Dead it's easier for the spirits to visit the living. Our people will go to cemeteries and build private altars with photos of their departed loved ones. The intent, you see, is to encourage visits by their souls. Of course, a lot of them just use it as an excuse to get wild and tipsy."

"We saw plenty of that, too."

"I'm sure. But wasn't it so much fun?"

"Yes," Marlene finally admitted, "we really did have a great time."

Satisfied, Plimpton folded his hands on his desk. "So Mrs. Senator, what brings you here to our humble island? I can only guess it has something to do with the most recent termination of liberties in the U.S.?"

"How did you know?" Marlene smiled.

"We've had more than a few inquiries lately. Most don't bother to make the trip all the way here, though, unless they're quite serious. Thinking of relocating, are you?"

"Perhaps so. We're investigating every possible avenue. So far, this place, despite how beautiful it is in its simplicity.... well, so far I can't say I'd want to live here the rest of my life."

"Understood. How did you come upon us?"

"You were referred to us by Dale Whitenburger."

"Whitenburger, really? Of all people. I'm very surprised. Our very own illustrious chairman of the Federal Reserve recommending a visit to us, the lowly, ineffectual Libertarians."

Marlene spoke. "He gave me a real education on how this all came to pass."

Plimpton snickered. "I'd have liked to have been a fly on the wall during that conversation. What exactly did he have to say?"

"Very little in regards to helping us out in our current predicament; in fact, he really didn't have much to say about anything. He just gave me a general overview on the economics. I can see now how fragile our monetary system has been up until now, and how easy it was to topple. According to Dale, European interests are behind the majority of our current problems."

"Uh-huh. Go on."

"The central banks replaced the dollar with a basket of international currencies when we started increasing the money supply and were deemed a bad credit risk. But we didn't learn our lesson from that. Instead, we continued printing money to the point where we could no longer make even the minimal interest payments on our loans to China.

Once we defaulted, the world would no longer accept our U.S. dollar, sending it into a total collapse. The rest of the world's currencies followed suit, sending every country into a great depression."

"I see. So that's it in a nutshell?"

"From the way it was explained to me, yes."

"And the Federal Reserve was an innocent participant, overshadowed by these larger European forces outside its control?"

"I'm not certain."

"And China held all this debt, yes?"

"That's what he said."

"Hardly. The Fed has always been the largest U.S. creditor. And who do you suppose was responsible for increasing the money supply in the U.S. to begin with?"

"The Fed; in conjunction with the approval of the current administration and the Treasury Department, of course."

"Now, Marlene, you don't really think they needed approval from the administration or the Treasury, do you?"

"That's the way it has always been done, yes."

"According to who?"

"I... I believe so. The Fed works with the U.S. Treasury to set guidelines designed to combat inflation. When they see inflation threatening, they tighten the money supply."

"The average citizen thinks the U.S. Federal Reserve has something to do with the U.S. Treasury when nothing could be further from the truth. You do realize that the Federal Reserve is a privately owned, for-profit corporation, right? In fact, if you check your local telephone book, it isn't even listed in the blue government section. It is correctly listed in the business white pages right next to Federal Express."

"Yes, of course I know they are privately owned."

Plimpton smiled. "Our U.S. Federal Reserve is accountable to no one. It has no budget limitations; and no congressional committee is allowed to supervise its operations – you of all people should know that."

Marlene flushed with embarrassment. "No, that's not true. The House Banking and Currency Committee oversee the Fed, the SEC and the U.S. Treasury."

"Yes, but with no transparency. The Fed has devalued the U.S. dollar by over 95 percent since it was created, and has singlehandedly created the inflation that it claims to suppress. Under this system the U.S. government has accumulated the largest debt in the history of the world. Plimpton stood and looked outside his window.

"Congress really doesn't help a bit. They're ignorant of the inner workings of the central banks. Congress simply accepts them as the final authority on monetary policy, never challenging their actions. Most members of Congress are simply too scared to speak up, and fighting the bankers is a great way to see one's opponent getting heavily funded in the next election." Marlene nodded in agreement.

"Wait a minute," Curt broke in, "did you say they *create* inflation? I'm afraid I don't understand. If that's the case then what would their purpose be? And how do they create inflation?"

Plimpton turned and put his hands flat on the table. "For starters we took our currency off the gold standard. When banks print money that they can't back with gold, then prices go up and the quality of the money goes down. If they don't have to back it with gold, then they can just print as much money as they wish.

"And, what benefit is there in an increase in the money supply? Money can't be eaten or used up in production; its only purpose is to be used as a medium for exchange. Once money has been established in the market, no increases in its supply are *ever* needed. And as we know from simple supply and demand, an increase in the supply of any good lowers its price.

"For all products except money, an increase in its supply is beneficial. If food or oil or computers are cheaper than before, then everyone's standard of living rises. But an increase in the supply of money does nothing but make the currency cheaper;

it lowers its value and dilutes its purchasing power. And that is all it does, period.

"As a matter of fact, as long as the society remains on a pure gold or silver 'standard,' with only small increases as the population grows, the currency will remain roughly stable and prices will gradually fall year after year.

"We've been so conditioned by constant price inflation that the idea of prices falling every year is hard for us to comprehend. And yet that is exactly what has happened over history; prices gradually fell every year from the 1700's on, except during periods of major wars. During those times our government inflated the money supply drastically. This drove up prices, until the wars were over, then prices fell once again."

"Wait a minute," Marlene interrupted. "This goes contrary to everything I've ever been taught about the way central banking works. Are you certain about this?"

"Oh yes, The Fed has been printing money that is backed by next to nothing ever since they were created in 1913, and because so few people understand the process of money and banking, it's a simple matter for them to blame greedy capitalists, speculators or wildly spending consumers for rising prices. This distracts attention from them as the ones responsible for price inflation. And of course, you always get their constant propaganda about the 'all-important credit markets.' I get so sick and tired of constantly hearing about the menace of the tightening credit markets. Hogwash! It's all propaganda. They would have you think that credit is the machine that drives the nation's economy. What really drives a nation's economy is its gross national product, not its supply of credit! Everything is backwards. Who are the only ones that benefit when a country is drowning in debt? The banks! That's who."

"You say the money is backed by nothing," Curt interjected. "Can you please explain what you mean by that?"

"All banking institutions in the United States practice something called 'fractional reserve banking.' This means they do *not* keep an equal amount of capital or gold on hand to back the paper certificates that they issue. In fact the reserve requirements are so low that some smaller banks weren't even required to have a reserve at all.

"If you keep money in a bank, any bank, they get to lend out your deposit amount many times over to further a global Ponzi scheme. We should have never gone off the gold standard, and we should have been issuing U.S Treasury notes instead of Federal Reserve notes. The same goes for the rest of the world, too. Most of the world's major currencies were under the control of their own central bank. The Federal Reserve, which claims its primary purpose is to curtail inflation, is actually the very one that created the inflation. It creates unnecessary, artificial cycles of booms and busts and has been orchestrating these cycles since their inception in 1913. The severe boom-bust cycles that all world economies experience from time to time are not natural economic cycles. These are entirely man-made events created and controlled by central bankers."

"Just how does it create a cycle of boom and bust?" Marlene asked.

They create bubbles that inevitably must burst by expanding credit for two-to four-year cycles, but this sows the seeds of future busts.

Fractional banking works essentially like a coil. When the central bank wishes to create new money, it simply prints some. The Fed then spends this money, usually to buy Treasury bonds or to bail out or buy out failing banks, whatever they wish.

They also loan out this new Fed-created money, re-depositing the money and lending it out over and over again. Plus, they are the first recipients of the newly printed money, giving them further leverage to manipulate markets. As you can see, the banks make a killing – that is, until they have stretched the coil to its maximum.

"Once the economy is flooded with the bank-created money, interest rates begin to drop because there is more money to lend and prices rise. The dollar begins to fall. Money begins to flow out of U.S. Treasury bonds due to lower interest rates. Thus ends the expansionary or 'boom' part of this artificial 'business cycle.

"Once the coil of the economy has been stretched to the maximum, then begins its contraction. The Fed now starts raising interest rates to a point that begins to inhibit borrowing and also inflation," Plimpton continued. "The economic 'bust' part of the cycle begins. Loans dwindle and credit terms tighten, loans become harder to get. Home prices fall, businesses begin to fail, bankruptcies increase. This 'bust' part of the cycle continues, and worsens, until inflation is 'tamed,' prices stabilize, and the dollar rises relative to other currencies. Eventually, the higher interest rates begin to attract foreign money, and the Treasury then is able to borrow what it needs at lower and lower interest rates. Interest rates fall. The artificial cycle then begins anew.

"During the more recent bust periods, when the smaller banks began failing, the larger major banks swallowed up the small banks that fell into trouble. As after all prior bust cycles, they emerged larger and more powerful, and fewer. Wealth was even more concentrated under their control, which they used in the next bust to further this process.

"Taxpayer funded bank bailouts postponed the inevitable, but we still eventually came to the point where there were just a few mega-banks left.

Plimpton continued. "And so now we find ourselves in a new situation where all the world's central banks have been consolidated into one under IMF control, and traditional money has now been replaced with 'credits' in one's account. It's a mechanical system that manipulates the supply of credits available on a worldwide scale. Now, instead of individuals manipulating the currency markets and the money supply, a computer algorithm does it far more efficiently. Isn't technology wonderful?"

Again Marlene sat silent, trying to digest the information that had just been presented to her. "I just wish we had done something about this situation sooner. What could we have done to prevent it?" she asked the Libertarian leader.

"Well, it could have been easily prevented with just three easy moves. One, direct the U.S. Treasury to issue U.S. notes to pay off the national debt; number two, increase the reserve ratio private banks were required to maintain to 100 percent; and lastly, go back to the gold standard. This would have terminated their ability to create money while absorbing the funds created to retire the national debt. Why should the taxpayers be taxed by the U.S. Treasury in order to pay interest and principal on bonds held by a private corporation to begin with? Why should the taxpayers be sweated and looted merely to preserve the accounting fictions of the Fed?

"Each bank would have had to stand on its own merits, responsible for its own actions. There would be no lender of last resort, no taxpayer bailouts. On the contrary, at the first sign of balking at redemption of any of its deposits in gold, any bank would have been forced to close its doors immediately and liquidate its assets on behalf of its depositors. This would have created a banking system hard and sound like the one we had before the Civil War. Instead, we've had millions of Americans watching through decades in helpless frustration as the federal government borrowed the American taxpayer into oblivion, borrowing from private banks the money the government had the authority and duty to issue itself, without debt! They saw to it that no one owned anything but the ability to borrow, to go deeper into debt than their neighbors. Not savings, but credit scores now determined the average American's ability to engage in economic activity such as buying a home or a car. No one, it seems, even dares to breathe a word against such power, concentrated in very few hands.

"I wonder why we felt as though we needed a central bank to begin with," Curt broke in. "It appears they serve no useful function."

"Oh. You've got that right. Our Founding Fathers were very conflicted over the decision to create one. Many had left

England to escape the tyranny that the banks and their monarchy had imposed upon them. Jefferson, Adams, Benjamin Franklin and James Madison, they all saw central banking as an engine for financial manipulation and corruption.

"But still the Federal Reserve Act was railroaded through Congress at 1:30 a.m. on December 23rd, 1913, when most were members on Christmas holiday.

"This move transferred control of the money supply of the United States from the Treasury to the private banking elite. The result has been disastrous for the citizens of the U.S and the rest of the world.

"It's criminal what we allowed to happen. And the power was right there in your hands all along, Marlene," Plimpton said, looking Marlene in the eye. "Congress and the Senate had the power to enact and they still do. They are the ones that allowed this coup to take place, and they haven't dared breathe a word to prevent it, much less take action. It's a sad state of affairs indeed." Plimpton shook his head. "The banks have literally committed a coup against our own government.

"Now it doesn't matter which candidate or political party gets in power because the bankers and their front organizations are in charge of *both* parties. They control all sides of the political spectrum from liberal to conservative. Once they position their candidates to become elected, they can simply sit back and watch. Presidents and political parties are all just pawns in the game, having no bearing whatsoever.

"All our recent Presidents have been controlled; and believe me, they make certain promises in order to be deemed an eligible candidate. There have been, however, a few who, once elected, reneged on their pledges and refused to drive the country into debt, either through unnecessary wars, foreign aid or domestic programs, and these soon found themselves in serious hot water."

"It's hard to fathom that we just sat back and allowed this to happen without so much as a peep," Curt remarked.

"The people can only peep so much when they are looking at survival," Plimpton responded. "As the orchestrated global financial crisis worsened, people all around the world noticed that their money did not cover even the barest necessities – all part of the softening-up process that led to the final hammer blow, which is where we are today. As life became more and more impossible and unbearable, the people were willing to accept the planned changes just to get some financial relief. In fact, if you recall they demanded it! But," Plimpton added, "don't think that this was an all-of-a-sudden thing that came up from nowhere. Oh, no, this process has been progressing unhindered for centuries. The pressing issue of the loss of our liberties and one world government far outweighs the issue of central banking.

"This machine has been working patiently and unhurried over the course of 100 years, slowly and systematically attacking from within the world's greatest superpowers, reducing them slowly to Third World nations. Measures were taken to demoralize and leave the citizenry with a sense of helplessness, driving the dollar down to the point of no value and flooding the borders with immigrants until it was hard to distinguish American cities from their nearby poverty-stricken neighbors. The same goes for Europe and the rest of the world.

"The government has the right to search your home or tap your phone without a warrant and established a satellite-based intelligence network that listens to your phone calls and picks out keywords typed into your computer. Then they censored the Internet, and then came more assaults to our rights. X-ray sensors at airports and even more privacy-invasive technologies, all designed to get you used to the idea of your body being violated; all steps toward acclimating you to a microchip being inserted into your body.

"Then came a ban on all automatic weapons for U.S. citizens through international treaties upheld by the United Nations. Then finally martial law was declared, giving the government the right to use lethal force and to take away all of our guns!

"Are you kidding me? Our guns were the only thing keeping us safe from our own corrupt government! Once they take away your guns, you are completely defenseless! Why do you think our Founding Fathers were so adamant about the right to bear arms? Because they knew that absolute power corrupts absolutely! The authors of the Constitution were very wise men who lived through the tyranny of ruthless, debauched governments. These statesmen laid much good groundwork and put as many safeguards as possible into our U.S. Constitution in order to preserve our rights and freedoms, including the right to bear arms!

"Now, without guns to protect ourselves, a 'one world government' has been able to step in and crush all of humanity. The banking cartels along with the CFR and its minions in government have now gained complete control of this entire world. That has been the ultimate goal all along, you do realize, right? One world government, governed by a small elite, with the remaining population little more than slaves."

Plimpton stood and paced. "Sovereign nations were an enemy to be dealt with accordingly." He hit his open palm with his fist. "The notion of sovereignty was to be pounded out of the mentality of the masses. Well, no worries anymore," he said, throwing his arms up into the air. "There are scarcely any sovereign nations left. We on this little island are one of the few left that haven't succumbed to the pressure to coalesce, and believe me," he lectured, wagging his finger, "we had seen some very ugly threats. But we stand firm" – he shook his fist into the air – "we will not be pressured, bullied or intimidated into submission. We will always remain a sovereign, independent nation!"

Marlene watched as Plimpton became more and more indignant, his face becoming redder by the moment. She wasn't certain whether the man was a pure genius or a ranting maniac.

"My," she remarked, "you certainly are ... passionate about the subject."

"I'm beyond passionate – I'm downright fervent," he yelled, slamming his hand on the table. "The banking cartels have wrecked our savings, distorted our currency and now this shameful microchip."

Plimpton sat in his chair and smiled, calming down. "This sort of talk really gets you nowhere, not at home anyway. I've spent half my life trying to warn the populace about the upcoming disasters that we were facing from our central banking system and all I got for my efforts was to be painted as some kind of crackpot. The press really had it out for me, but then what do you expect? If you had all that money and power, you might consider controlling all of the major mass media yourself," Plimpton smiled.

"Ever notice how, when you change channels at the news hour, you'll get the exact same story on every network, literally within seconds of each other? Even the commercials come on at the same time, usually for some pharmaceutical company. Ho," he chuckled, "they're all owned by the same people. A few fringe publications exist if you know where to look, but as far as turning on the evening news … forget it; you're going to get your daily news brought to you by your friendly neighborhood central bank."

"Holy cow."

"Cow? Now, that's another story," Plimpton laughed.

Marlene looked over at Curt. "Would you mind if we step out for a moment Mr. Plimpton? Just to get a little fresh air."

"No you can't. I'm holding you hostage here from now on. You might just fetch a good ransom."

"Ha!" Marlene shook her head as she stood. *What a character,* she thought while walking toward the door. She and Curt stepped briefly outside the office and into the humidity of the street below.

"Wow," Curt offered as they stood under an awning where a woman was selling fresh conch out of a cart, the only shady spot they could find. "That was really intense."

"I'll say. That man is completely nuts."

"You think so? I believe what he's saying is true, Marlene."

"Don't believe everything you hear, Curt. I've encountered conspiracy theorists before. He's not much different from the rest. He does present a strong case and he is very eloquent, but I'm not convinced it's all true."

Curt looked cross. "I think you're in denial. You don't want to believe."

"Believe. What I believe Curt, is that we need some information that we can actually use. I don't want to live here. Do you? In this banana republic? I'd go as nuts as Plimpton in three months' time."

Curt pondered a moment. "It's not so bad," he mumbled as he watched the locals going about their daily routines – women carrying baskets of laundry on top of their heads while vagrant men stood on corners waiting for something to do. "I'm sure we could be happy just about anywhere as long as were together."

Marlene beamed and turned toward her husband. "You are the *sweetest* man. Where did you come from again?"

"From your fondest dreams." He brushed her hair back and kissed her lightly on the shoulder, and then he nibbled her ear.

"Stop!!" Marlene giggled. "Everyone's looking at us." Curt looked up from his wife's ear. No one had noticed the gringo couple standing on the corner.

"Yeah, we're a real spectacle. Heh, heh."

Marlene looked up toward the window of Plimpton's office. The humidity had the window fogged up, and she couldn't see in. "I think we need to be courteous and go back up now."

"What do you want to do afterward?"

"We should probably just make preparations to go back home. Like I said, I don't want to live here, so there's not much point in staying."

"That's fine with me. I've had enough adventure for the day." He took Marlene's hand and led her down the hall to the office of John Augustus Plimpton. They found him once again in heated debate on the telephone, waving his arms animatedly in the air while arguing with some unseen person about the pitiful state of health care in the Philippines.

"He covers a lot of ground, doesn't he?" Curt whispered to Marlene as they stood waiting for Plimpton to finish his diatribe. It wasn't long before he wrapped up and again addressed his visitors.

"Sorry about that. I have family in Southeast Asia and we sometimes get into the most heated discussions."

"How did you wind up with family there?"

"My youngest daughter married into a Philippine family. Can you imagine?"

Marlene recoiled at the thought but said nothing.

"I also have family and friends in New Zealand, not too far from there; a far more civilized environment."

"I would think so. In fact, we were considering making a trip there."

"Highly recommended. I'm certain you would like it; good altitude, fresh water, pristine, unpolluted. They don't just let anyone in, either. The government is very particular about whom they approve for guest visas, especially now. And you can pretty much forget about applying for citizenship, even you, Ms. Carson. I doubt they will grant any special considerations just because you held a Senate position." Marlene and Curt looked at each other.

"We don't care, as long as we can find somewhere to go without being micro-chipped."

"Yes, good luck with that. Even here, they are making it very difficult on our people. New Zealand is in a similar situation – fighting it, but only time will tell if they eventually capitulate. I don't think they will have the power to hold out indefinitely like we will here. We are smaller and leaner, better enabling us to stave them off forever. We will make it just fine."

"If we go to New Zealand, do you have any contacts there for us?"

"Of course I do." Plimpton rummaged through his desk for a pad and paper. "Let me direct you to Jimmy Osgood, an old friend of mine. He moved his family there over 10 years ago. He comes from the Midwest, like yourselves. I'm not sure how he got permission to stay." Plimpton spoke as he wrote down the number. "Perhaps you can ask him when you see him." He handed the paper to Curt.

"This is great," Curt exclaimed as he held up the scrap between his fingers. "See Mar, I told you New Zealand was the place to be." Marlene just smiled enigmatically like the Mona Lisa.

"Mr. Plimpton, it's been a real pleasure." Curt grasped Plimpton's hand and zealously shook it. "We will stay in touch and let you know what we find."

"You're leaving us already? You didn't stay very long. You really should stay for the annual festival of the Black Christ. It's just around the corner, and of course if you stay until spring, you can get to see Carnaval."

"Oh no," Marlene demurred, "we have a lot of work ahead of us. We really must be going, but it's been so nice meeting you. I hope to speak with you again soon."

"All right, then." Plimpton bowed and twirled his hand with a flourish into the air. "Adios, Mrs. Senator, and you also, Mr. Ludington."

"Thank you again for your hospitality, Mr. Plimpton." Marlene responded.

"Please, call me Augustus."

"Augustus. Thank you."

As the couple headed out the door, Plimpton rang out some final words of encouragement: "Fight the good fight, gentle people. Never give up!"

An hour later, back at the hotel, they called the airport to change their reservations to an early departure and headed back to Ohio the following morning. They spoke enthusiastically about the possibility of a trip to New Zealand in the taxi on the way home.

When Marlene returned to her home office in the afternoon, she had several messages waiting for her on her answering machine. One of them was from a fellow retired senator who now resided in Connecticut. He spoke in excited, hushed tones, and Marlene wasn't sure she understood the message clearly or not. She thought she heard him say that he had interesting information about a settlement out in Utah that she might want to research. It sounded like the sort of place that she was looking for. She picked up the phone and dialed his private line but got the answering machine.

"Hal, it's Marlene. Looks like we're playing a little phone tag. I got your message, and I'd like to ..."

"Hello Marlene," he picked up the phone, "it's Hal. I'm here."

"Hi, Hal. Screening your calls?"

"Don't you?"

"Sometimes, I have to admit I do."

"These days, I'm watching everything very carefully, believe me."

"Yes, I understand totally. So what's this you were talking about? You have an area you think I should scope out?"

"I do. I heard about them about six months ago when Governor McAllen was first refusing to cooperate with the WCR microchip mandate. His was one of a handful of states that were protesting so at the time, so I didn't think too much of it. But as more and more of the dissenting states caved in and McAllen started getting more and more publicity, that's when I really started paying attention to him. Utah eventually wound up being the last to concede. He and I started talking about that time. He's a stubborn one, that McAllen. I didn't think he would ever bend, but like everyone else, he had to. The ramifications of losing all federal support were just too enormous, especially Utah, which receives massive subsidies.

We met in person at a settlement out in the middle of nowhere. This was one week before he signed.

"He told me that his hands were tied on this decision. He had to accept it as required. We've remained in contact ever since. I spoke to him last week to get a status update, and he let me know that he would soon be resigning his office. He just can't take it anymore – all the lies and deceit, rigged votes, you name it. He believes we are being cornered more and more with each passing day. It might actually be a blessing for you Marlene that you no longer have to deal with these politics. It's causing a lot of good appointees to lose heart in the process."

"Tell me about the settlement? Is that the place you're speaking of?"

"Oh, yes, I got off track. It is. He's resigning his public office position and moving there. No micro-chipping."

"Interesting. I wonder if he would like to meet with me. What's the place like? How do they survive?"

"I think I'll let him tell you about it. It's not like anything I've ever seen before, and I'm sure McAllen would like to have you there. Any allies would surely be very beneficial."

"McAllen and I have never been allies in the past. We're from differing political parties, plus he's in the executive branch, whereas you and I were part of the legislative branch. I am aware of his record, however, and I must commend him for his mostly bipartisan stance. He always did vote with his heart and his conscience."

"I imagine the micro-chipping issue is something you both can agree on," he answered.

Marlene smiled. "Probably, yes. Hal, I'd really appreciate it if you could arrange a meeting for us. I don't have McAllen's number."

"Consider it done. I'll get him on the horn and you can make your own arrangements."

"That's fine. Thank you, Hal. This means a lot to me."

Marlene hung up the phone and went to the kitchen, where she found Curt rummaging through the cabinets for a snack. "Guess what?" She came from behind and wrapped her arms around his hips, placing her cheek against his back.

"What?"

"I think I may be on to something where we won't have to leave the U.S."

"Really?" he said, turning to her, "that would be fantastic. Where?"

"Utah."

"Utah?? I've never been there."

"Me neither. Keep your fingers crossed."

"'K." He leaned over and kissed her on the lips.

Marlene's phone was ringing within the hour. Curt followed Marlene to the den so he could eavesdrop on the conversation.

"Marlene Carson, this is Governor Geoffrey McAllen speaking." The line was crackly.

"Governor, thank you so much for contacting me." Marlene held the phone out from her ear so Curt could hear.

"My pleasure. You're looking for some peace and quiet in Utah, I hear?"

"You might say that, yes."

"Good. I'm not sure how much Hal told you, but I am soon to be resigning my post and taking on a whole new life as a citizen in a remote outpost in the middle of the state."

"I heard that, yes."

"Good. There you can really get away from it all, and I mean that literally. Hal tells me you're looking to escape micro-chipping."

"That's it."

"Good. I can help you. You must be sponsored, though. It's a private, by-invitation-only settlement, run by a fringe group of religious non-conformists." Marlene groaned and looked at Curt. "Um, that sounds like some kind of commune."

"Much more organized."

"It's not some cult thing, I hope."

"No, Ms. Carson, it's nothing like that. It may, however, resemble some kind of Mormon settlement to you at first glance."

"Mormons? Oh, yes, there are a lot of them in Utah, aren't there?"

"Absolutely. Does the concept of a Mormon-type lifestyle offend you in any way, Ms. Carson?"

"No, I don't think so." Marlene had never considered the question before. She wondered if she would be required to wear a skirt to her ankles.

"Beautiful. I can have you do a walk-through of the facility as early as this coming Monday. Are you up for it?"

"Am I? Oh, yes." She looked at Curt. He was smiling and holding his thumbs up. "We could go right this minute."

"Good, good, very good. I'd like you to book a flight and e-mail me your itinerary. Fly into the Salt Lake City airport, and we will take a shuttle to the grounds. It will be an all-day commute."

"That's fine. May I take my husband with me?"

"Yes, of course, he's very welcome. Do you have children or other family members you would like to have come, too?"

"No, just Curt and I."

"Good. We'll see you Monday." The two then exchanged e-mail and contact information.

"Thank you, Governor. This is a real honor."

"Yes, it is an honor, and it could turn out to be the best thing for you and Curt, too."

"Thanks again. See you later."

Marlene hung up and turned to her husband. "So what do you think?"

"I think we might be riding a horse and buggy to church," he laughed.

"Good Lord, what have I gotten us into?"

Curt smiled and shook his head. "I'm not sure honey, but we must explore every possibility."

"I know, I know. I just … whew. I guess I don't know."

"Heh." Curt pulled Marlene off her chair by her arm. "C'mon, let's pop a bottle of wine. It may be our last chance. I don't think Mormons drink."

"Oh, no!" she groaned again. "Maybe I *will* go get a microchip."

"Don't you dare," he said as he tickled his wife and chased her into the kitchen.

"I think there's a chilled Pinot Noir in here somewhere," Marlene said as she rummaged through the refrigerator. "Here it is! And here's some of that Danish cheese you like."

The two raised a toast to a new life and new possibilities. They then made love on the living-room couch and napped until dusk.

Chapter 27

The Party Plan

Winthrop Shaw sat at his desk dictating notes to one of his personal secretaries. This was a new girl sent from the agency, and she was exactly as Shaw had ordered. Tall and thin, swarthy with big, beautiful eyes, from Manado, Indonesia, one of his favorite haunts. The diving was nothing short of spectacular there - in Shaw's opinion, the best in the world, even outranking Australia. The girl reminded him of quiet, pleasant times spent there. She batted her eyes now at Shaw as he placed a pen to his thin, pursed lips. He was in deep thought, compiling a mental list of those he would choose to include in the upcoming celebration.

He was in particularly good spirits. It had been a very productive month, and everything was nearing finalization. It was almost time for a grand fete, a glorification of Shaw and his monumental triumphs.

Rothfeller himself had directed Shaw to host the event. "It's time for me to relax and unwind a bit, Shaw," the czar had explained last time they spoke on the phone. Rothfeller had been at his chalet near the Champoluc resort bordering Switzerland and Italy at the time, postponing their usual monthly meeting in Luxembourg for some much-needed rest and repose.

Indeed! thought Shaw when he heard the news, *imagine skiing at his age? With my luck, he'll live to be 150.*

"Shaw, I want you to do the honors and make preparations for a first-rate celebration," the czar instructed. "We will have completed our banking amalgam within the next six weeks, and I want to have an observance ceremony followed by a jovial conviviality."

Shaw balked at first. "With all due respect, sir, that sort of thing really isn't my cup of tea," he remarked dryly. "I think we should find someone else to… "

"You will do as *I* say, Shaw. I think it is time you loosened up a bit yourself. All work no play makes Winthrop a dull boy. It will do you a world of good."

"Very well, then, sir." Shaw hung up the phone quickly before he lost his aplomb. He saw no reason whatsoever that he should be the one to put together such an affair. They had event planners galore that could surely do a better job. Though Shaw never considered himself a social animal, he resigned himself nonetheless to hosting a party that would be considered the highlight of the upcoming season – the place to see and be seen, a commemoration of the final victory establishing the WCR as the world's first and only super-bank and a perfect opportunity to establish a laurel for himself in the process.

Perhaps that is what Rothfeller has had in mind all along, he thought as he compiled his list, *an apotheosis to Shaw. I do deserve it, of course; no one has ever worked harder to further the interests of the Global Union.*

The party was to take place on Shaw's private island in the Saint-Jean-Cap-Ferrat Harbor in the Alps Maritimes of southeast France; his yacht, the Suzerain would be harbored there also, easily accessed within minutes for those wishing a quick retreat from the festivities. The list of attendees would include a virtual "Who's Who" of European aristocracy, the usual array of international billionaires, banking magnates, a few Hollywood starlets and the latest top models from Paris and Milan thrown into the mix for amusement. Shaw would make certain that only the right people would be there, and it would give his spies ample opportunity to eavesdrop on the private conversations of his fellow collaborators. Shaw wanted to know firsthand those who would be plotting against him and who would be in his corner when he took over the czar's position.

"Everything has dual purpose, you see," he remarked to the Indonesian secretary. She smiled sweetly and again batted her lashes at the powerful man seated across from her.

"Be sure to notify security to update the equipment on the Suzerain," he said.

"You want me to take care of, sir?"

"Yes. Call Jacques, head of security, and make sure the cameras and audio surveillance are all up to speed on board. We haven't been out on our Suzerain in a very long time; have we now?" The secretary looked at Shaw blankly. "The estate is fine. We won't need any updating there that I know of."

Now back to the list, Shaw frowned. There were close to 1,800 people on it already, probably enough. "I believe we have finished this task." He handed the list to the secretary. "Send the invitations certified, and make sure the ones that don't RSVP within a week get a phone call."

"Yes, of course, sir." The Indonesian girl took the list and walked respectfully backward out the door.

As it should be, thought Shaw watching her tiptoe, *everyone in this wretched world should show such reverence to their superiors. Well, it's in the works now.* Shaw leaned back on his leather chair. *On the 28th of March we will have his damn party, and then we can get back to the business at hand.*

Chapter *28*

Toni Sneaks a Peek

Toni Vickery had all her gear on. She was dressed in black from head to toe, all the way from the black bandanna on her head to the shoes on her feet. Even her socks were black. She took some eyeliner and smeared it onto a plate. Mixing it with a small amount of water, she dabbed the mixture onto her cheeks and forehead. "There, that should reflect the light," she remarked while looking in the mirror. *Look at me. I look just like a woman setting out to rob a bank.*

She was beside herself with curiosity. She had been planning this night for weeks, and tonight would be the night she would finally find out what was going on inside the laboratories on the far north side of the compound. She had waited patiently for a night that Dina Patterson would be out of their cabin and not underfoot as usual. When she heard that Dina had a gentleman wishing to take her out for the evening, she knew it would be the perfect opportunity.

The minute they left, Toni jumped up and began dressing for the illicit occasion, and now she was ready. She quickly slipped out of the cabin unnoticed. Most of her fellow inhabitants were indoors reading and winding down for the night, so no one saw her. She stealthily made her way to the furthest point to the north of the developed acreage, avoiding the lighted areas, until she reached several huge Quonset huts in a row. Here is where guards kept vigilant watch over the area's "scientific research center," granting only those men and

women with their white coats and badges access to freely
enter. Tonight, Toni would find her way inside.

She stayed in the shadows and observed. She saw only one
guard outside her target hut; usually there were at least two.
He sat in a folded metal chair and appeared to be dozing in
and out of sleep. She watched as his head would groggily drop
to the side and he would shake himself awake.

Perfect, she thought to herself. *As soon as he falls off I'll
make my move.* Just then she saw another guard walking up
the path.

Oops! She stepped back farther into the shadows. *I almost
got caught.*

The guard approached his comrade and began a
conversation. Toni made her way around the back side and
waited until they stepped aside. Once they were in a deep
exchange, she quickly slipped inside the now-unguarded
entrance.

She couldn't believe her luck. I'm in!! she exulted.

She quickly looked about. The room was freezing cold,
with a clinical atmosphere, not to mention a spooky silence.
She looked about and observed that the hut's interior had
been divided into sections with some open areas and some
private, smaller rooms. The hut itself was even larger than she
thought possible from the outside – this one must have been
at least 20,000 square feet. It had a clean, white tile floor, air-
conditioning vents and freshly painted walls. Toni saw a white
coat hanging on the wall next to the entrance and draped it
over her shoulders. Moving quietly, she peered around the
corner to confirm that she was not being seen. She'd expected
to see some sort of medical laboratory. She did indeed see
what appeared to be a laboratory, but it wasn't the kind she
expected. This was more mechanical than medical.

Toni wasn't sure what she was looking at as she
approached a table full of diodes and pneumatic tools. Metal
shavings and resin drippings littered the table while spools of
copper and silver sat in bundles. She observed 3-foot cone-
shaped objects sitting in each corner of the room. She walked
over and touched one, running her hands over its clean,

streamlined shape. She looked around for a power cord or something that would reveal its purpose but found nothing. She wound her way through the room and observed big, shiny metallic boxes lined with cedar wood with benches inside.

Looks like a sauna or something, she thought as she opened a small door on one of the metal boxes. She ducked inside and sat on the cedar bench, tinkering with the many sliding parts that pulled inside and out, revealing more copper wiring and dials. "Very strange," she muttered as she exited the box and looked around some more. She wound her way to an adjacent room and hearing voices she jumped back in fright. She ducked behind a door and watched as two men in white coats holding a conversation about skeet shooting passed by. Ever curious, she crawled out from beneath the desk and followed behind them at a distance, listening for the sounds of their heels on the shiny white floor. The men made their way to another part of the lab that held another guard. Toni watched from around a corner as the men showed their badges for entry. *I guess I won't be going in there.*

She retreated and stopped to peek inside another room. This one appeared more like a typical medical laboratory. Beakers, test tubes, computers and equipment lined the walls. She stepped inside and turned on a light. She reached out to a centrifuge, gave it a little spin and then picked up and started examining a clipboard containing some notes when she remembered the light was on and it probably shouldn't be. She replaced the clipboard and exited the room, turning off the light behind her. *That was interesting* she thought as she walked.

She strolled through the corridor and soon came to a room that was similar to the first, with large spools of copper and other unknown metals taking up a corner of the room and work benches lined with all kinds of apparatus: voltage meters, antennas, an analog oscilloscope and small magnets coiled with wire. Then she noticed a few contraptions of differing shapes and designs that appeared at first glance to be some kind of homemade radios. She picked one up and turned it over in her hand. It weight about 2 pounds and had no discernible speaker that she could see, plus to confuse matters even more, some of the devices had electrical outlets while others had 9-watt tubes connected to them. She set it down, baffled.

I wonder if I could plug something in, she thought as she looked about for a power tool. She spotted an electric drill and plugged it into one with an electrical outlet. She hit the power switch and surprise! The drill fired up. "Whoa!" Startled, she dropped the object along with the drill to the ground and stood looking over them, not sure what to do. She gingerly picked them up and pulled the trigger. Once again the drill fired up and ran for a few seconds before slowly losing power and dying.

Wow, that's very interesting. She turned the device over in her hand and gave it a thorough investigation. *I don't see where the power came from. It seems to be self-contained.*

She walked to an adjacent part of the same room and came to a blackboard covered with complex mathematical formulas. Oh my, look at that. She tried reading some of the formulas, but the high physics were beyond her comprehension. She then examined the different charts, graphs and diagrams that covered the surrounding walls.

She then looked to her left and was completely awestruck with what she saw: a giant doughnut-shaped magnet completely wrapped in copper coil. The doughnut was standing on its side and looked to be about 9 1/2 feet tall. She approached the magnet but was scared to touch it.

Will it zap me? She thought to herself, and then she slowly backed away from the intimidating mass and left the room to explore some more. She walked the corridor until she saw something that caught her eye – another room, this time with a smoked-glass frontage, revealed what appeared to be a sound studio with projectors set up throughout.

I wonder what this does. She entered, turned, locked the door behind her and fumbled in the dark until she found the power button to the projector. It came on and suddenly distributed bright colors throughout the dark room.

"Wow!" said Toni, sitting in a swivel chair in front of a control panel. *What is this?? Such a sophisticated setup; someone must have spent millions building this place.* She started pushing buttons, and sounds began emanating from the walls with each different control – sound effects, everything from high-pitched shrieks to the sounds of rushing water, traffic, birds, animal growls, whale songs and peals of children's laughter.

"Oh, this is so much fun!" she said, laughing out loud ... but then she heard voices coming unexpectedly from outside the locked door. With the sounds of a key turning and unlocking the door, Toni knew she was in trouble.

Damn it, I made too much noise. She hid under the table that held the projector. She saw from her hiding spot two men enter the room and turn on the light. *These guys always travel in pairs, my god.*

"What are you doing in here?!" One of the men quickly spotted Toni and pulled her out from under the table by her leg.

"Oh, nothing, I'm just enjoying the light show."

"You're not supposed to be in here, young lady. It's time to go." The two gentlemen escorted Toni back to where she first snuck in and then shooed her out the door.

"Humph," she grumped while walking back toward her cottage. "I never get to have any fun."

Chapter *29*

Marlene Gets an Education

Marlene Carson and husband Curt Ludington were standing in line at the Columbus International Airport waiting to check their luggage. The lines were extraordinarily long, much more so than Marlene could ever remember. *How bourgeois, flying in public airports two times in a row.* Marlene tapped her foot and drummed her nails on the counter, finally irritating her patient husband.

"Would you please knock that off?" he demanded.

"Knock what off?"

"That tapping you're doing. It's driving me freaking nuts!"

"This tapping?" Marlene exaggerated her foot tapping and nail drumming even louder. Curt walked away and sat in a chair at the far side of the lobby, leaving Marlene to push both their suitcases in the long line. It would be a long day. Already they were both cranky from too little sleep and the anxiety of knowing that their time was running out. It would be a five-hour flight from Columbus to Salt Lake City. The closest airport they could find to their destination, which appeared to be in the middle of nowhere, according to the directions they'd received.

Marlene took out the directions and read them again for the hundredth time. They would have to rent a car and travel at least another four hours in the mountainous terrain. There they were to rendezvous with the now-former governor of Utah, Geoffrey McAllen, in the middle of the state and drive to a place called Hidden Village. McAllen said it was just the kind of place that they were looking for and that they'd be very happy there. There might even be some sort of civic position that Marlene could fill eventually. She was very keen to hear more about their political ideologies, what kind of systems they had already established for themselves and their intentions for the future. The governor had been quite vague on the phone when she had pressed for more information about the place, simply stating that "it has to be seen to be believed." Well, in about 12 hours, they would be seeing for themselves.

The already frazzled couple finally approached the front of the line to check their baggage. Attendants inspected the people in line with hand-held readers separating those with a microchip from those without into separate lines. She noticed that the ones with chips were allowed to pass quickly without too much fuss and those without were detained longer as airport personnel scrutinized them carefully, searching their bags thoroughly and giving each one an exhaustive body search along with an X-ray examination. She read a notification posted on the counter announcing that effective Oct. 1, no one would be issued a ticket unless they first had the required WCR microchip. As she stepped up to be frisked and have her bags searched, looking over her shoulder she witnessed Curt enduring the same brusque treatment. He gave her a weak smile as he held out his arms for the pat-down. Another 10 minutes of questioning, and the two were free to board the airplane. Soon they would be in Salt Lake City, somewhere neither Marlene nor Curt had ever been. Hopefully, it would be their ultimate destination.

Curt put on a pair of eye covers and promptly fell asleep once the plane became airborne. Marlene tried to catnap but could not, so she amused herself for the next five hours reading the in-flight magazine until the plane finally landed. The couple rented yet another car, this time a small Hyundai, and proceeded to their meeting with Gov. McAllen.

As they left the city and drove further into the outskirts, Marlene had a chance to take in the amazing scenery of the

Utah landscape. She was genuinely taken by its rugged beauty, dizzying peaks gently giving way to deep valleys and back again. Passing through several ravines, Marlene pointed out water streaming down the steep, rocky sides, forming tiny waterfalls. Curt nodded but, being unused to the altitude and the dry air, could hardly notice as he continually blew his nose and rubbed his ears. He was also freezing cold and couldn't wait to get out of the car. Suddenly, the Hyundai started shaking and making a familiar thumping noise.

"Oh, no!" Marlene groaned. "We have a flat tire."

"A flat?" Curt sat up straight. "What will we do?"

Marlene pulled over to the side of the road. "I guess we'll just have to change it."

"Change it? What!?"

The two got out assessing the situation. Indeed, it was a flat tire. Marlene stood with her hands on her hips and pursed her lips. "Maybe we should look in the trunk." The two rummaged through the trunk for a spare and some tools.

"Wow. This is it huh?" Curt pulled out a small donut tire. This thing is never going to fit."

"It seems to be all they gave us," Marlene replied as she handed Curt the tiny fold-up jack. "Go ahead and try putting it on."

"Who, me?"

"No, that guy behind you."

"But I've never changed a tire before. I don't know how."

"Now might be a good time to learn."

"I'm not going to do it. Call roadside assistance."

"That will take too long, Curt. We're already an hour behind schedule. Can't you just give it a try?"

"No. I'm not getting my hands all dirty," he said, dropping the jack to the ground. "There's nowhere out here to wash them."

"Don't be such prima donna, Curt! We need to get this done."

"Let someone stop and help us." Curt waved at some passing cars.

"I can't believe this." Marlene snatched the jack off the ground and fumbled to get it open.

"What are you doing?"

"What does it look like I'm doing? I'm changing a tire."

Curt gave Marlene a few pointers. "Maybe you should put it here," he said, pointing to a spot that looked like the appropriate place to put the jack.

"Thanks!" Marlene growled as she forced the jack under the car and put the crank into place. To her amazement, the car began lifting as she turned.

"That was easy. Now what?"

"I think we need to take the old one off now."

"Shouldn't we have done that first?"

"I don't know, damn it." Marlene cursed. "Why aren't *you* doing this?

"'Cause you're better at it."

Marlene lowered the car again to start over.

"Where's the wrench thing?"

"This?" Curt produced a tire iron.

"Hmmm." Marlene put the iron on a lug nut and tried to turn, but the bolt was stuck.

"Here," Curt said, wresting the iron from her. He strained and twisted with all his might, and the nut spun free.

"Good job, honey," Marlene beamed as he loosened the rest. "Now, I think we need to raise the car."

"Okay. Go for it."

Marlene shot Curt an evil look as she again raised the car. She managed to get the tire off and put the new tire on, lowered it and tightened the nuts.

"There," she stood up and clapped the dust off her hands, pleased with herself. "Trained monkeys could have done it."

She leaned to kiss Curt, and he jumped back. "Ack! You're all covered in grime!"

The two were now quite late for their meeting, and the drive took even longer than Marlene had anticipated. They were to meet Gov. McAllen at a Waffle House off Interstate 15 at 3 o'clock, and it was now already 4:45. Marlene kept trying his cellphone, but he must have been out of range because it kept going straight to his voice mail. She prayed he would still be there waiting for them once they arrived. Another 25 minutes and they arrived at the Waffle House, over two hours late. The couple quickly got out, stretched their legs and then rushed inside to use the facilities and try to find their man.

The Waffle House was completely empty inside, except for a fat fellow in the back corner with a grease-stained T-shirt eating a stack of pancakes.

"I don't think that's him," Curt remarked.

"Damn!" Marlene cursed as she again dialed, trying to reach Gov. McAllen. This time, surprise! He answered.

"Hello?"

"Hello, Governor, this is Marlene Carson. I'm so sorry we're late, sir."

"Ah, there you are, Ms. Carson. I'm glad to hear you made it in one piece. I was starting to get concerned."

"We couldn't get ahold of you to tell you we were running late."

"Well, my phone died, so I checked into the Howard Johnson to give it a recharge and rest a bit. You can come meet me here. Just keep heading south on the freeway, and you'll see it off Exit 47. Come on up. I'm in Room 214."

"Yes sir, be there shortly."

"Good, very good."

The two soon were at Room 214 and face-to-face with the former governor of Utah. Introductions were made and politics lightly discussed before they considered their next move. It was now 5:40 p.m. and already dark outside. They now had to make a decision about whether to stay and get an early start driving in the morning or take off right then and there, arriving at their destination sometime in the middle of the night. They decided to go with the first option, so the couple checked into the HoJo for a much-needed interlude before taking off first thing in the morning.

The telephone awakened Marlene from a deep sleep. It was the early wake-up call, 5:15 a.m. The room was pitch black, and she stumbled to the bathroom to take her shower and get ready for the drive. She emerged from her shower refreshed and grateful that they had not tried to drive in the condition they were in last night. She turned on the light. Curt was still sound asleep.

"Wake up, honey pot," she coaxed. Edging her way onto the bed, she lay next to him and nibbled his ear.

"Mmm," Curt smacked his mouth open and closed like a fish gasping for air. "Let me sleep some more."

"No way; get up!" She gave him a nudge with her knee.

"Slave driver," Curt mumbled as he opened his eyes and blinked at the ceiling. He ever so slowly got himself dressed without showering while Marlene made a pot of coffee and looked at the front page of the newspaper. Soon, they were ready to call on Gov. McAllen and get rolling.

They knocked on the governor's door, and he did not answer. They found him in the lobby looking bright-eyed and bushy-tailed, chatting energetically with the waitress.

"There you are!" McAllen stood and shook Curt's hand. "Do you two run late all the time?"

Marlene gave a flimsy smile. "I think we're actually ready this time."

They sat and went over the map while Curt spread cream cheese on a muffin. It would only be about three and half hours from where they were, McAllen assured them. "We'll take Exit 58 and drive about 40 minutes to Navajo Road," he said, outlining their intended path with a pen. "Then we'll go east for about a quarter-mile to Chilimi Way, then head north 12 more miles and we will be there at the gate."

"Are they expecting us?"

"Yes, and they're happy to hear that you're coming. They're looking forward to meeting you. It's very good."

Now there's a real positive man, Marlene thought as they stood to go. Curt took the wheel and followed McAllen closely in the car, not wanting to lose sight of him. They only made one stop at a rest area, and soon they were upon their destination. A property marker, just a tiny sign off the side of Chilimi Way, signaled the approach to Hidden Village. Marlene was awed with the sheer size of the tract as they drove down the dirt road – thousands and thousands of acres, and all fenced in. She could see, off in the distance, towers and formidable buildings giving the place the look of a virtual fortress. Marlene was quite impressed, and she wasn't a woman easily impressed.

As they approached the gate, Marlene's phone rang. It was Gov. McAllen advising them to stay in the car until they passed the security checkpoint. She and Curt watched as the governor approached the guarded compound. Two uniformed guards held machine guns as a third briefly spoke to the governor. McAllen pointed to Curt and Marlene seated in the car behind him. The guard nodded and approached the driver's window. Curt rolled it down and greeted the guard.

"Hello, sir," the guard began. "May I see some form of identification, please?" Curt produced his driver's license, and Marlene readied hers. The guard printed the information on his clipboard, returned Curt's license and walked to the passenger side.

"And you, ma'am, may I see yours?" Marlene handed him her driver's license, and he recorded her information as well. He then returned to the front gate and spoke into a yellow walkie-talkie. The two sat for about 10 minutes, and Marlene took in her immediate surroundings. She observed a couple of school buses and many cars parked outside the main gates, with whole families appearing to be living out of them. Blankets were draped on hoods and people sitting on top, just sitting and waiting.

Squatters, Marlene correctly assumed. She squinted hard to the east and caught a glimpse of something that looked like campers on the far outskirts of the property. Yes, tents and some small campfires ... but just then the guards distracted her. They were unlocking the gates, starting with a series of locks, each more intricate than the last, until the gates were opened wide. Some of the squatters scurried toward the open gates, but the guards quickly brandished their machine guns, and they fearfully retreated. The guards then waved their group through and encouraged them to move quickly. Curt followed closely behind McAllen, driving farther up the dirt road to the main office, where they got out stretching their legs. Finally they were here inside the Hidden Village.

"Here we are!" Gov. McAllen greeted Marlene and Curt as he stepped out of his car. "What do you think?"

"It's amazing!" Marlene gushed while Curt beamed. "How much property is this? It's huge!"

"It's 24,000 acres in a fertile valley. It's full of pristine lakes, rivers, and forests, natural springs, just beautiful," he reported joyously as they walked to the main office. "You haven't even seen it yet. Just wait until you see this entire place! It's good. Very, very good."

They entered the warmth of the office. It was only just noon, but the temperature outside seemed to be already dropping by the minute. Fortunately, the office had a fireplace and there was a toasty fire blazing in the far corner. Marlene rubbed her hands together and stuck them in her pockets as she waited to be greeted by her host. Soon, a tall man with bangs and a brown beard made an appearance followed by a pretty, blonde woman with her hair in a ponytail.

Gov. McAllen made the introduction: "John Reese, Cassandra – this is Marlene and Curt Carson. Marlene is our former U.S. senator out of Ohio."

"Nice to meet you," Reese said, shaking Curt's hand while Cassandra shook Marlene's.

"It's Ludington."

"What?"

"My name. It's Curt Ludington."

"Oh! Terribly sorry, Mr. Ludington!" McAllen laughed. "This is Curt Ludington, everyone." He then turned to Marlene. "Ms. Carson you may think of John Reese and Cassandra as your support team. They will be your primary points of contact and will arrange for your introductions to our directors and board members. In fact, we took the liberty of setting up a meeting for 2 p.m. today for you to meet the key players and the founder of Hidden Village, if that works for you." Marlene nodded.

"Very good. That's only two hours from now. We'll show you around the grounds prior to our meeting, or if you care to rest or freshen up a bit, we understand. We are hoping that you enjoy your stay here and are comfortable."

"I think I would like to see some more of the place. How about you, Curt?" Marlene turned to look, but Curt was already sitting in a chair in front of the fireplace.

"I'd like to sit by the fireplace if that's all right with you."

"Oh, puhleeze," Marlene urged. "Come on we're taking a walk."

"I'm freezing, Mar."

"That's true, it is awfully chilly. I never expected it to be so cold here."

"Utah is very chilly this time of year," Reese replied in a subdued voice, "plus there's a front moving in. The temperature is expected to drop about another 30 degrees within the next 24 hours. I hope you brought some warm jackets."

"A couple, yes."

"You'll need them tonight."

"Good," McAllen interrupted. "Are we all ready?"

"I think so." Marlene looked around at the faces of her hosts. "Come on, Curt." She kissed the top of his head, and he reluctantly rose from the comfortable easy chair.

"Good, let's take a little walk then, shall we?" McAllen extended his elbow and Marlene took his arm. They stepped out into the frosty air with John Reese, Curt and Cassandra following closely behind. The walk wasn't far, only to two waiting golf carts behind the main office.

"Think we can all fit in one?" Reese asked.

"If Marlene sits on my lap, there should be room." McAllen sat and patted his lap. You don't mind, do you, Mr. Carson?"

"Uh, I..."

"I think we should take both carts," Cassandra said emphatically. "Curt and Mrs. Carson, you may ride with me. Mr. Reese will drive Governor McAllen."

"It's Ludington," Curt complained as they took off over a dirt trail that led to the housing structures. They drove alongside a small creek that grew wider, turning into a stream and finally a magnificent river. The stream had water wheels set up at various intervals along its shoals. Burly men were busy working old-fashioned sawmills with the water wheels providing the power.

"We're approaching the compound's housing division now," Reese said. "Obviously, this area is under construction; in fact, the entire compound is a work in progress." They stopped in front of what appeared to be the makings of a large apartment complex or some low-rise condominiums.

"Here is the area we have designated as our housing quadrant," Reese proclaimed while extending his arm. "We have already established housing for over 50,000 people, with planned space for at least another 120,000 in the next year. We have broken ground on 150 of these structures, with 200 two-bedroom units in each. Pretty impressive, eh? The equivalent of a small city! We'll show you the complete set of drawings at the meeting today."

"Sure."

"Please step this way, Ms. Carson." Reese took the lead as they all stepped off the golf carts and strolled toward the construction. "We're supposed to be wearing hardhats. Darn it, I forgot them."

"Careful of construction debris," Cassandra warned over the buzz of an electric saw. "You can pick up nails in your shoes pretty easily."

Marlene and Curt looked about at the busy environment. People were scurrying everywhere carrying lumber and tools. Heavy machinery lifted steel beams into place and cement foundations were being poured. Everywhere, men were laying masonry blocks. Marlene noticed that despite the bustle, it seemed unusually quiet compared to a typical construction site.

"We are under the gun to get more housing units built before the snows arrive, so everyone is really giving their all right now," Cassandra noted. "When you see the temporary housing structures compared to these permanent ones, you will really appreciate their sense of urgency."

Marlene realized what was so unusual – it was the machinery. None of it had a typical roar one would expect to hear out of dump trucks, cranes, front-end loaders and the like, only a whirring sound. She approached an excavator, and John Reese called her back. "Please, Ms. Carson, I wouldn't recommend getting that close. Those machines could be quite dangerous!"

"Why aren't they making noise?" she questioned.

"Oh, that's very observant of you." Cassandra smiled wide. "Most of the machinery has been converted to electric, but we have been experimenting with some that have been retrofitted for natural gas, and our engineers are getting ready to unveil a new prototype that promises to be really transforming."

"Really? That's amazing!" Curt appeared from the rear. "It must have cost a fortune to convert them."

"It was at first, until the process was perfected. A necessary expense, though – soon we will be entirely independent from the oil producers."

"That's quite impressive; and where are your electrical and gas sources?" Marlene questioned. "I saw some wind turbines as we were driving up, but I can't imagine that would be enough to supply this entire facility. How many people did you say you have here?" Reese and Cassandra looked at each other and smiled.

"We run a short pipeline from our landfill for bio-gas, and because this property was once used for coal mining, we have large concentrations of coal-bed methane. It requires extensive processing, however, and is a very potent greenhouse gas, so it's not our favorite method. We far prefer to use cleaner and easier energy."

"Yes," Cassandra added, "oil and natural gas are quite Neanderthal sources in comparison to what is made readily available to use simply from the vacuum; and they have been around since time eternal."

"You mean like the wind turbines?"

"One wind turbine will generate power to 300 units, but the wind turbines are just one of many sources. We have created our own electrical grid on site," Reese reported.

"What other kinds of sources are you talking about?"

"Oh, that's our very own secret sauce," he laughed.

Cassandra interjected, "We work *with* nature's laws instead of the contrarian route that has been the norm for as long as most people can remember."

"Clear as mud, thanks."

"You will see soon enough, Ms. Carson" Reese said. "Like I said, some of the world's finest minds work here. Our intentions are to give you a tour of the labs during your stay here if you're interested."

"Of course I'm interested. Are you kidding? May we go there now?"

"I believe the board wants to meet with you first; then a tour. We can show you some more of the housing for now and your own quarters. To see the entire compound, we should take the utility truck. There are a lot of grounds to cover. It's pretty big."

"OK," Marlene agreed, "but back to my question. How many people are here now?"

"A little over 35,000, and there's more and more people pouring in every day. I guess you saw the crowd waiting outside the fence?"

"Yes, there were quite a few."

"That was nothing. You should see when the buses come, trains of cars full of people following behind those buses. Some days, hundreds arrive, all at once. It gets crazy. Today is relatively quiet."

"You're very blessed to be here, Marlene," McAllen boomed, putting his hand on her shoulder. "You, too, Mr. Carson; not everyone can get in here." Curt shot McAllen an irritated look.

"Yes, that's true" Cassandra added. "There is an application process and everyone is carefully screened, plus you must be sponsored by someone already living within the community. Of course, when we heard about you from Governor McAllen, we were delighted to hear about your interest. We'll make sure you are offered one of the better housing units. Yours will have running water." Cassandra smiled.

"Oh," Marlene said, showing her shock. "There's no running water?"

"Most of the occupied housing is temporary, so no, I'm afraid they don't. But we have community showers and kitchens set up throughout. No need to worry about water, we have a very sophisticated water distribution system here. In fact, everything about Hidden Village is rather advanced."

"Really? It looks rather basic to me."

"Don't be fooled by our outer appearance, Ms. Carson" Reese spoke. "We have some of the finest minds in the country residing and working here, top experts in science and technology. I think you are going to be fairly impressed once you see all the advances made at this humble abode." McAllen nodded in agreement.

"Interesting," Marlene remarked. "You have definitely got my attention. These new units you're building, they will have running water, right?"

"Oh, absolutely, and full electric, everything you would expect from an ordinary housing structure outside the community."

"That's a relief. I think I've seen enough here, and I'm feeling brave enough to go look at our own quarters now, if that's all right."

"Of course, let's head back. They are closer to the main gate."

The group headed back toward the area from where they'd come. Marlene could see that it would be easy to get twisted around until she was familiarized with the place. Everywhere was under construction, and it all looked the same. They drove past an area that appeared to be a rustic commercial type of district; some stands were set up with manned booths of people distributing food. Others were dispensing toiletries, some had what appeared to be homemade furniture they were presenting for sale. Everyone there was hustling to sell their product.

"What, may I ask, do you use as a medium of exchange?" Marlene asked.

"Medium?"

"Yes. Do you have some sort of monetary system? These people that are selling, what are they using as payment for their goods?"

"Oh. Right now we are on a barter-type system," Cassandra answered. "Everyone who participates receives credits for the products or services that they put into the system. Some products or services are worth more credits than others. We have a guideline that we use to keep it fairly simple. As an example, eight hours of roofing work might be good for 200 credits, where a homemade apple pie might be good for 18 or so. Some goods, like paper, aren't being manufactured here yet, so the governing board looks at those items as community property and dispenses them evenly throughout. The community leaders maintain a credit pool for these types of items in order to pay for them, sort of like paying taxes."

"Are you going to move to a paper money system in the future?"

"It's possible," Reese acknowledged. "That would be up to the board to decide. Right now, this system is working very well, so I don't see them looking to change anything in the near future."

"I don't see a barter type of system working here forever," Marlene stated flatly. "You're going to eventually outgrow it."

"You may present your comments and concerns to the board when you meet them, Ms. Carson. It's not up to us to determine policy."

The group first returned to the main entry where Marlene and Curt had parked their car in order to retrieve their baggage and was now drawing near to the temporary housing structures, box-shaped modules that dotted the horizon. As they pulled closer, Marlene saw that they resembled large wooden sheds with plywood walls, cut-out screened windows and shingled roofs. A door to one stood open, revealing a plywood floor.

"Oh, good god!" She exclaimed out loud. "We couldn't possibly stay in one of these."

"We haven't heard anyone else complain," Reese replied. "I'm sure you'll find them comfortable enough."

"Think of it as roughing it," Cassandra smiled, "and remember, they are just temporary."

"Do you live in one of these?"

"Yes," she answered happily. "You and I will be neighbors, in fact. You will have the unit next to ours."

"I don't know," Marlene pondered as she looked at Curt, who simply shrugged his shoulders.

"Ms. Carson, you are receiving a premium unit!" Reese was starting to sound annoyed. "Plus, you won't have to share yours with anyone else. You and your husband are going to have it all to yourselves. Everyone else here has to share with up to five other families per structure. Please try to be grateful for what we are offering you." The group drove in silence until reaching their unit. Reese pulled up to a screeching halt.

"Here it is," Cassandra beamed, "what do you think?" These units didn't seem quite as appalling as the others. They appeared sturdier and a bit more private. The walls had been stuccoed with plaster, and a short, wooden fence surrounded the one designated as theirs.

"All right," Marlene sighed as she lifted herself from the cart. "Let's go and take a look." Reese and Cassandra escorted Marlene and Curt while McAllen remained seated in the cart.

Marlene touched a flower in a planter as she approached her tiny new dwelling. She noticed that this one had real sliding windows and a concrete slab for a foundation, and she felt a tad relieved. Reese unlocked the door and handed her the key.

"Welcome home, Ms. Carson," he said as he opened the door wide.

They stepped inside into the semi-darkness, and Cassandra reached for a light switch. "See," she said as she flipped on the light. "It's not so bad; you even have electricity and everything. A lot of the others don't have that luxury yet."

Indeed, there was electricity, even though the exposed conduit ran along the baseboards and up the bare walls to the sockets and light fixtures – unsightly but effective. Marlene looked about and nodded at the sparse furnishings: two cots, one small dresser, a short round table with a ceramic space heater and two chairs.

"Where's the bathroom?" Curt asked.

"They're about 300 yards away outside; it's a community shower and bathroom."

"You've got to be kidding me."

"No. I'm afraid not," Reese answered.

"But look," Cassandra said, pointing to the far corner, "you do have a sink. Remember I said yours has running water?"

"That's nice. At least I can wash my hands." Curt went to the sink and lathered with a bar of soap. "Couldn't you have at least put in a toilet?"

"You are very welcome to do so. In fact, we encourage it. Everyone here has a responsibility to develop their own housing structure. We expect you to participate as well."

"You want me to build a house?!" Curt came back in indignation. Marlene snickered to herself, thinking of the tire incident.

"We will explain later," Reese said as he rubbed his eyes. He was growing weary of his finicky guests.

"Don't worry," Cassandra offered, "we all pitch in and help. This is a community effort. We don't expect everyone to know how to build a house, but plenty of people here do." Marlene and Curt looked at each other with big eyes.

"Well, do you two think you can find your way around a bit?" Reese asked. "Cassandra and I have a lot of work to do prior to our meeting this afternoon. I'm going to advise you two to maybe get a little rest and acquaint yourselves with the place. We will be back in a couple of hours to bring you to your meeting."

"What about..." Curt began.

"No, we will be fine," Marlene cut in, sensing Reese's exasperation.

"OK, then. We will see you in little bit." They headed for the door, Curt and Marlene following them out.

"See you later." McAllen waved goodbye and Curt and Marlene went back inside. They were now alone in their new quarters.

"Well, honey," Curt opened his arms wide, "what do you think of our new mansion?"

"Wow!! It's far grander than I ever expected possible! Do you think it's a bit ostentatious? I'm not sure I could ever get used to living in such palatial surroundings, not with my humble beginnings."

"Yep," he replied in an affected drawl as he approached the solitary sink and used it as a urinal. "And this here bidet is real fancy."

"Curt, stop that! That is so disgusting I can't believe it!"

"What do you expect, Mar?" he sniffed while zipping up. "Do you think I'm going to go walk three hundred yards every time I want to piss? Bad enough I'm expected to shower with others like at some kind of summer camp. We'd be better off building our own house on our own land and doing this by ourselves."

Marlene examined the droplets of urine and frowned. "At least you could rinse it out," she said as she rinsed out the sink with the chilly water. She observed that there was no knob for hot water.

She sighed. "Do you want to maybe go for a walk and sightsee a bit?"

"No honey, not really. I'm just bushed. All I want to do is take a nap, even if it is on a damn cot." Curt turned on the space heater and stretched out on his narrow bed. "You can go. Tell me if you find anything interesting."

Marlene stepped a few feet outside into the frigid air and quickly retreated back in. Curt might not have such a bad idea after all; sleep through it. She went over and sat on the adjacent cot and thought hard about their situation. This place was abysmal. How on earth would they possibly make it through a freezing winter with just one space heater? Not even an extra set of blankets. She stood and checked the dresser drawer. Empty.

If it weren't for the enticing notion of some major advances in technology contained here, she would have already turned on her heels by now and left. She thought about McAllen's encouraging words, "This place simply has to be seen to be believed." Well, that's for certain. Who would believe that she of all people would ever consider living here, in a one-room shanty that was half the size of their kitchen back at home. *I wonder if there's an interior decorator anywhere on the premises.* She looked over at her prostrate husband snoring softly and tried to guess how long it would take until the real complaining began. Here lays a man used to getting a weekly manicure expected to live in a hovel. She knew it would take less than a week before he started pulling his hair out. *Perhaps we can stay just a little while to see how it turns out? Maybe conditions will improve? There are those new units being built. I'm confident we will get the very best one available once they are completed. I'm going to have to insist on at least three bedrooms, though. Hmmm, and a full dining room, too.*

Marlene harbored a supposition deep in her heart that this really was a place of importance and some good work could be accomplished here. She wasn't certain what her role would be just yet, but if they could just ride it out for a while she felt she could be instrumental in bringing forth a good governing system and making a significant impact on the development of the community. *I hope it doesn't take them too long to get those units finished, or we may never get to see.* She looked about at her tiny room and tried to picture it with some draperies and new furniture; some rugs and a coat of paint might do the trick. Then she shook her head. *No, I think I'll just spend as little time as possible here. Just like my days and nights spent at the office.*

Marlene quieted her mind for a while and relaxed. Soon enough it was time to wake her husband, who was now snoring loudly. It was time for their meeting with the board. She shook her groggy man awake. He got up and splashed some cold water on his face.

"Whoa," he rubbed his eyes. "I was really tired, must have needed that nap. Did you see anything good?"

"No, I just stayed inside and thought about how it's going to be living here."

"Don't make me laugh. This little experiment has already grown tiresome, as far as I'm concerned."

"Let's see what happens Curt. We have to give it some time. In all my years, I've never seen such a futile situation before. All of my contacts and all of the favors that I've curried over the years haven't done me a bit of good. You would think by now that someone would have come through with a solution for us, but not a single, solitary person has in all my contacts. Not even one has offered a better solution than this one right here. McAllen is the only person that even got back to me. I think everyone I know is in the same boat, Curt; from senators to judges to presidents, they are all getting micro-chipped. It's unbelievable."

"It might be worth it to have our old life back. I already miss the dog."

"I know what you mean," Marlene replied softly. She heard footsteps outside the door. Reese and Cassandra had arrived to take them to their scheduled meeting.

"I think it's time, honey." She stood to go and open the door for their escorts.

Chapter *30*

Meeting the Board

Curt and Marlene opened the door expecting to see Reese and Cassandra, but it was Gov. McAllen.

"Oh, hi Governor. We weren't expecting to see you."

"Please call me, Geoff. Mr. Reese asked me to accompany you to the board. He and Cassandra are going to be a little late; something about a group of hooligans outside the gates, who can get a bit aggressive at times."

"Yes," Marlene said as they walked toward the cart. "I saw quite a few people who appeared to be squatters outside the perimeter of the property. What are they doing there?"

"We... well, I should say the board, has been gracious enough to allow some people to stay on the outskirts and camp out while waiting their turn to gain entry. We've even provided some with a few bare essentials like blankets and food to keep them from starving to death and also to help prevent riots, of course."

"Really? That's very kind. I'm actually surprised that they've allowed that."

"We'd hate to see people dying off like flies right at our doorstep. That wouldn't be very Christian, now, would it?" McAllen chortled, his eyes twinkling.

The three crossed the property until they came to the main entrance once again. They drove past the main office and then shot off to the side on a service road that led to a part of the property that they had not yet seen.

"This is our administrative headquarters," McAllen announced as he pulled up to the front of a series of aluminum trailers. "We're going to this one, on the end here." They walked up three wooden steps and entered the trailer. They were greeted by a woman with horn-rimmed glasses sitting behind a desk.

"Hello, Nancy," McAllen greeted her.

"Hi Geoff. You can go ahead in. Everyone was supposed to be here by now, but I guess you heard about those maniacs that tried to push through the front gate?"

"I heard a little bit but no details."

"It's probably just those bikers again. They're always trying something."

"Yes, indeed." McAllen led Marlene and Curt into the boardroom, where three men and a fragile-looking older woman were seated at a particle board fold-up table. McAllen quietly shut the door behind them, and the three men stood to attention while the elder woman remained seated.

"Mr. and Mrs. Carson, I would like for you to meet Peter Keller, the founder of Hidden Village, and his co-founder Eldon Tauer. This is Joel Brandenburg Esquire, and this is Mrs. Giorgetta Lucchesi. We're still waiting on one more, Stephen Bissette. He's tending to a minor disruption at the main gate but should be here momentarily.

"Very nice to meet you." Marlene extended her hand and shook all the board members' hands. "This is my husband, Curt Ludington; he is originally out of Massachusetts."

"Cape Cod." Curt smiled as he shook hands. "It's a pleasure to meet you."

"It's good to meet you as well, sir." Keller turned to Marlene. "We understand that you're the incumbent senator out of Ohio?"

"I was." Marlene replied with pride. "I'm retired now."

"That must have been challenging work for you. We actually tracked your career somewhat prior to your arrival. You have a very impressive voting record. McAllen filled us in on what happened to you in the election."

"Thank you. I always tried to do my best, but I guess that wasn't good enough in the end."

"We certainly understand that feeling, don't we, now?" The other board members nodded in agreement.

"Can we get you anything to drink? Have you had lunch yet?"

"Black coffee would be nice. How about you, Curt?"

"I'm OK."

"I'm afraid we don't have any coffee here, ma'am; it's too expensive to keep on hand. We do have some tea, though."

"That will be fine, thank you." Marlene was a tad disappointed.

Keller extended his hand. "Please have a seat. We have a great deal to discuss." Marlene and Curt each took a fold-up metal chair and sat across from the small group.

"I should just get right to the point. Eldon and I are the founders of Hidden Village." He took out a site map, placed it on the table and drew a rough circle in pencil around the property designated as theirs. The majority of this land has been in my family for over 100 years. Eldon owned the bordering tract to the east. We joined our two parcels together over 20 years ago with the help of some outside contributors, we created this project. We spent most of our free time and all of our summer vacations on site developing the land for practical use with very little outside help. Now, as you can see, Hidden Village is an immense success, and it's something that we can all be proud of."

"It is very impressive," Curt remarked. "What inspired you to do this?"

"I have to give a great deal of credit to my father. He was an evangelistic missionary who traveled the world spreading the word of God in his youth. When he grew older, he became a guest sermonizer for various churches throughout Utah, eventually founding his own church on the very property that we are living on today."

"The church that your father started, is it on the premises still?" Marlene asked.

"In name, yes; the original building was demolished long ago. Until recently, we did not have to live here full-time, but now the dire state of affairs worldwide has required us to do so. We thank God every day for giving us this place and for giving my father the intuition to make it happen.

"My father was a pious man who held strong fundamentalist beliefs. He drove it into my head as a small boy that there would come a time when every man on the Earth would be forced to take a mark, he believed that would be the mark of the Anti-Christ. Part of the conditions of my inheriting this property was that I was to turn it into a safe refuge for anyone who needed asylum in those coming days, if we happened to see it in our lifetime. So that's what I did. I partnered with my neighbor to the east, Mr. Eldon Tauer, whom I knew since childhood. Thankfully he shared the vision and had the foresight and the resolve to help accomplish this great feat. He is the one that raised the money necessary to give us self-sufficiency. Together, we built Hidden Village into what it is today."

"It must have taken a fortune to develop."

"It certainly did," Tauer said. "We have had some huge benefactors contribute to our cause."

"Are they here now?"

"Some, yes. Ironic, is it not? Most, however, were institutional churches. We have taken in many of these congregations already, and more are coming. We have word of 12 congregations arriving this month alone. Sadly, though, so many people have already taken the mark, especially those from the cities where they could not grow their own food and had no hope of becoming self-sufficient, they did not receive word that there was somewhere to go, and now I fear for them it is too late."

"Too late?" Marlene asked while sipping her cup of tea.

"Yes. Once the microchip is placed in the body, the person's resolve to fight off its effects diminishes greatly."

"Its effects? I understand it's merely a data transmitter, nothing more."

The board members looked at each other and shook their heads. "The microchip that they are putting in the public is more than just a data transmitter, much, much more." Marlene and Curt were flabbergasted at this. She started to speak when suddenly the door opened. Stephan Bissette with John Reese quickly entered.

"I'm so sorry I'm late," Bissette panted. "I guess you heard about the attempted riot."

"Riot?" Keller stood. "I thought it was just a small outburst."

"It certainly could have been much worse," Reese answered. "We're going to have to increase the garrison, especially at the front gate. All these homesteaders waiting outside are attempting to become gate-crashers."

"Wonderful. Like we don't have enough on our plates already. Everything is under control now, though, yes?"

"Yes, for now. But don't you think it's time to run them off before something serious happens?" Reese questioned.

"We'll talk about that later, Mr. Reese, thank you. If you don't mind, right now the board is in a meeting. We would like a little privacy, please." Reese politely left the room and closed the door behind him, leaving behind Stephan Bissette, the last board member.

"Now, where were we?" Keller continued as he sat back down.

"I think we should introduce Stephen first," Tauer said.

"Oh, yes," Keller said. "This is Stephen Bissette, our last member of the board. This is Curt Ludington and Marlene Carson. You have already heard about their arrival." Bissette nodded and took a seat. He appeared rattled.

"It's a pleasure to meet you, Mr. Ludington," Bissette shook Curt's hand, "and you, Ms. Carson."

The group sat in the fold-up chairs.

"What have I missed?"

"Curt and Marlene are here to go over the site and potentially make residence here. You know Ms. Carson's history. We feel that they bring a lot to the table, and we would welcome their inclusion into the community."

"Yes, agreed."

"We have created a schedule for you that we will follow over the next couple of days." Tauer produced a sheet of paper, which he passed across the table to Marlene. "We will start with a tour of the housing, agriculture and meat production facilities, to be followed with a tour of the water distribution and electrical systems tomorrow morning and then a tour of the laboratories in the afternoon. If you like what you see, which I'm confident that you will, we will discuss the terms of your tenure here at Hidden Village the following day."

"I'd like to hear more about the effects of the microchip," Curt interjected.

"All in good time, sir; we have a lot to show you first, and it's a great deal to absorb. I can assure you that you will be fully educated on the matter before we close out the schedule."

"So, then," Keller spoke, "are you folks ready?"

The couple nodded.

"Very well, then; please follow me." Keller and Tauer led them to a waiting golf cart, and they veered to the left, toward the agriculture production facility. They briskly drove past fields of freshly harvested corn, wheat and soybeans heading in the direction of an area completely surrounded by greenhouses. Here they stopped and were greeted by Cassandra, who stood outside the cloth door of the greenhouse. "Well, here we are, my esteemed guests," Keller waved at the entrance. "Joel Brandenburg is also here. He is waiting for us inside. It's a little chilly for him today, although it isn't much warmer inside," he laughed. "Step right in."

The small group opened a door that was greenhouse film stapled to wood and entered. There they saw rows of small plantings on 2-foot-tall tables that ran the length of the building. Overhead were lighting fixtures and, scattered about, an array of composters, shade material and exhaust fans. Two men were unpacking irrigation supplies in the far corner while three others were unrolling giant sheets of plastic over the length of the tables to cover the plantings. Brandenburg was crouched by a small table littered with papers, cutting open rolls of plastic film. He stood when he saw the rest of the group enter.

"Hello," he welcomed them. "How are you?"

"We're good, Joel; yourself?"

"A little bit stressed. There is a big storm rolling in tonight, and we have to get all these plants covered up quickly or we will lose all the crops."

"Absolutely," Tauer acknowledged. "We really need to hustle to finish getting our fall crops harvested now. This is going to be an early and quite unwelcome frost."

"Reese was already out this morning gathering up the workers. We're well aware that we are up against time now," Cassandra responded.

"Good, then," Keller spoke as he turned his attention to Curt and Marlene. "Let's give our guests the .10¢ tour. He led them around the greenhouse. "This greenhouse that we are in now is one of 450 of similar size, around 1,200 square feet each. In this particular one, we are growing yellow and green bell peppers." The group walked around a few aisles of the baby peppers and then stood by the table with Brandenburg. "We planted some in the ground also earlier in the season, but they have already been harvested. These ones will do us nicely in the middle of winter."

"Are you using all 400 greenhouses?" Curt asked.

"Not quite yet, we have about 100 that aren't in use just yet. We anticipate being fully to capacity in the next few months. We will need to build some more at the rate we are growing."

"There should be plenty of peppers then," Curt remarked.

"Oh, not just peppers" Cassandra noted. "We have every vegetable that you would find in any well-stocked grocery store and even some that you may not find. The best part, which is something that we are very proud of, is that all of our produce is raised 100% organic, no pesticides and absolutely no genetically modified organisms."

"That's quite impressive," Marlene commented. "I've often wondered how organic farming worked. Are you a specialist in this method?"

"Cassandra is our resident botanist," Keller stated with pride. "She has extensive experience in organic farming methods and has brought us her expertise."

Marlene nodded. "So how *do* you keep the bugs off?"

"Generally we use Beauvaria bassiana fungus, B.T., beneficial nematodes, sulfur, diatomaceous earth and horticulture oils. For specific diseases we used more specialized products; there are so many nontoxic methods available to us that it is just absurd to ever use any poisonous chemicals. For weed control we use corn gluten – it inhibits root formation and is also a good fertilizer.

We add nutrients to our soil to replenish its mineral content, but since we cannot rely on a regular supply of inorganic fertilizers, we have been forced to find alternative sources of nutrients. The alternatives are usually more efficient than the inorganic compounds anyway.

"We try to maintain high humus content in the soil. We plant legumes and velvet bean in rotation with grain crops. These crops are not harvested; rather, they are plowed into the soil while they are still growing. They really help prevent erosion and are wonderful for resupplying the soil with nitrogen. We compost, and we inoculate the soil with microorganisms.

"How are you getting your products if you're not using money? You can't go to the store and barter this stuff.

"Fortunately, we have several years' worth of supplies of most of our favorite treatments. I'm not sure what we will do once we run out, though," Cassandra said, looking sadly at Keller. "I guess we'll have to cross that bridge when we get to it."

"We're hoping that since we have one of the few remaining organic food sources in the United States, we will be able to barter our clean food for supplies," Keller responded.

"Still quite impressive," said Marlene. "Thank you for showing us."

"Oh, it's my pleasure," Cassandra replied. "I believe we may go look at some of our outdoor fields and the orchards now. You can get to see us in action."

"Harvesting, right?"

"Yes, and some other things as well. Will we be showing off our livestock today, Peter?"

"I think so," Keller answered, "if we have time."

The group went outside and walked to the rear of the greenhouse to a pair of waiting golf carts.

"I thought McAllen said he would be joining us here this morning," Tauer remarked to the group as they were sitting down in the cart.

"Yes you're right," Keller observed. "Just as well; we wouldn't have had room for him. We all fit nicely in one cart now." Cassandra squeezed in the middle of Curt and Marlene, who would have loved to disagree. They took a bumpy ride down dirt trails and drove up the top of a tall, grassy hill where the group could look down on the fields.

"We have a medley of grains below us," Keller reported as he extended his arm, "wheat, spelt, rye – which grows particularly well in cold weather – oats and our most abundant and favorite crop, corn. You can see the men harvesting the corn right now." Curt and Marlene looked to see several men driving large, self-propelled harvesters. Again the heavy equipment was eerily quiet. They watched for a few minutes as the men unloaded the corn stalks into the carts attached to tractors, and then they were hauled off to the storage area.

"It's real high-tech." Curt rolled his eyes.

"Oh, no," said Tauer, missing the sarcasm, "this is like cavemen days compared to big agribusiness of today. Most all the small farms have been completely eradicated, and now all that is left remaining is very large multinational farming corporations. They use automated machinery with GPS to steer the machines in a straight row; no one sits in tractors anymore. Computerized systems collect data on tillage, applications, planting, weeds, insect and disease infestations, cultivation and irrigation. Now *that's* high-tech." The group descended down the hill toward the corn harvest.

"Unfortunately," Cassandra noted, "we have to maintain our fields constantly by walking through them and handpicking the crops to prevent cross-contamination with outside GMO crops. Our corn is especially vulnerable. We try to keep it as non-GMO as possible, but it's hard. We really have no control over the bees which cross-pollinate or which way the winds blow."

"Oh? Does it really matter if you have some GMOs in your fields?" Curt asked.

"Good heavens, yes!" she spoke with emphasis. All the men turned to look at Curt.

"I'm not certain that you realize just how grave this is," Keller spoke. "GMOs are absolutely horrible beyond belief."

"What's so horrible, exactly? Growers have been grafting trees and hybridizing seeds for years. Isn't it like selective breeding?"

"No, it's nothing like that at all. In traditional breeding, a farmer may reproduce one kind of cow with another kind for a new class of cow, but it would be impossible to mate a cow with an apple or a duck. Even when species that may seem to be similar reproduce, their offspring are usually infertile. With genetic engineering and gene splicing, scientists can breach species barriers set up by nature. It is now possible for plants and animals to be forcefully designed.

"Scientist have combined the genes of spiders and goats, spliced jellyfish and spinach genes into pigs, fireflies into tobacco, fish genes into tomatoes and strawberries, human genes into sugarcane and rice, even nonliving substances such as chemicals can be mixed artificially into the DNA of foods. The results are plants or animals with odd or disturbing characteristics that would be impossible to obtain through normal processes such as crossbreeding or grafting."

"Have you ever eaten genetically modified food, Mr. Ludington?" Cassandra asked.

"No. I've never eaten them," he smiled broadly.

"On the contrary, you have been eating them, every single day. All of us have. GMOs were slowly introduced into our food supply and now they are everywhere. Although these GMOs are banned by most food manufacturers in Europe and other parts of the world, our own Food and Drug Administration does not require any safety evaluations. Not a single human clinical trial on GMOs has been published.

"Most Americans say they would not eat GMOs if labeled, but the U.S. does not require labeling. GMO's are now present in the vast majority of processed foods in the U.S., and they can have disastrous effects on both animal and human health. GMOs are permanent they cannot be put back. Once they are introduced into the food chain, there is no taking them back, they are forever."

"I still don't see what is so dangerous."

"Once it is explained to you what they are doing and how they are doing it, you will see the problem. With GMOs, food manufacturers take genes from one species and insert them into another to obtain a desired characteristic.

"Because living organisms have natural barriers to protect themselves against the introduction of DNA from a different species, genetic engineers had to find ways to force the DNA from one organism into another. These methods included using viruses or bacteria as vectors to infect the cell, or injecting the DNA with microscopic needles into fertilized eggs, or using electric shocks to create holes in the membrane covering sperm and then forcing the new DNA in through these holes. In the case of food crops, you would think that they would aim for increased nutritional benefits or productivity, but unfortunately the results have no health benefits, only economic benefits to the companies that manufacture them."

"The first mass produced genetically engineered food was soybean. They engineered the plant to make it resistant to a patented herbicide by splicing the chemicals directly into the soybean's DNA structure. The new soybean was now resistant to the herbicide because it was now built into its very DNA structure. The bean crops could then be heavily sprayed to kill surrounding weeds in the field, never damaging the soybean itself, making it easier to pick the crop. This is the *one and only* benefit the splicing provides. But here is the problem, now every time you eat the bean you are also ingesting toxic herbicide. Other pesticides are engineered into crops as well and they cannot be washed off because the pesticide is built into the plants very own DNA."

"Oh, that's just awful."

"It is. In independent studies on rats, more than half the babies from mother rats fed GM soy died within three weeks. Their babies were also smaller and could not reproduce. In addition were some effects on heart, adrenal glands, spleen, blood cells and sperm cells also clear links to non-Hodgkin's lymphoma.

"That's amazing!" Curt exclaimed. "Mar, are you hearing this?" But Marlene was strangely quiet.

"You say the government doesn't require any testing or proof of the safety. Why is that?" Curt looked at Marlene.

"The multinational agriculture industry is largely unregulated in the United States," Cassandra continued. "They're not accountable to anyone since they do not have to label their foods and they are not required to do any safety testing.

"GMOs should be labeled, and if they are not labeled, we should all ask why. U.S. consumers seem strangely unconcerned over what they are eating; not so in Europe and the rest of the world. Countries in Europe, Mexico, most of South America and Asia all have strict bans on GMOs."

Keller spoke: "The United States government itself financed and subsidized the GMO companies and gave its owners the power to control the food seed of entire nations or regions.

"Federal agencies like the FDA and others, which were created to protect consumers, often behave like branch offices of the companies which they are supposed to regulate. It is a fact that many judges and government officials were already prior officers -with large stock positions, in the companies they are supposed to be regulating, or they are rewarded with lucrative jobs at the same companies after they help pass legislation in their favor. The question of relations comes to mind: do our government watchdog entities control these corporations, or is it the other way around? Do they control our government? Laws need to be passed to prevent these conflicts of interest, but the public doesn't seem to take much notice or be too terribly concerned."

The group strolled down the rows of corn while Cassandra took samples with a lateral flow strip test designed to detect the genetically modified protein in a sample.

"We will take these samples to the laboratory this afternoon for testing. We must go through this process every single day. It gets tedious, but we do our very best to keep our crops non-GMO and prevent contamination. We plant later in the season than any neighboring farmers and we clean our equipment daily but this hasn't been enough to stop their unintended spread. The GMO crops infect our non-GMO crops and make them weak."

"How did this start?"

"Oh, now we're getting to the nitty-gritty of this whole mess. Insiders say that the key to this entire problem lies in the fact that the U.S. government allowed corporations to put patents on new seed stock and plant genes; so now these food products are considered to be intellectual property.

"Because all these new GM crops are patented, the farmers are prohibited from planting the seeds in subsequent years, meaning that they must purchase the patented seed every year from the seed company. This brings us to one of the most horrific abuses of genetic patents the world has ever seen. They are called 'Terminator' Seeds, you sow them this year, and that's it. The seeds themselves are sterile.

"Seeds were once forever. After harvest, seeds saved from a successful crop for replanting would be planted for the following year, and so it went on for hundreds of thousands of years. Now, when you go to plant next year's crop, you need to go buy brand-new seeds from the Agri-Giants who have made sure the harvest you obtain cannot be sown again.

"This goes against all the laws of nature! God freely gave us plentiful foods that reproduce abundantly, and look what mankind has done! This is another example of our own arrogance, ignorance and sheer greed when man thinks that he can one-up God in the creation department.

At the rate were going we will soon lose all our bio diversity and we will be all eating utterly synthetic foods."

Cassandra rubbed her fingers over the corn tassel and watched the pollen fly into the air. "We would love to see a ban on open-air GM agriculture. We are fortunate in that we are fairly isolated from other farms. The average farmer cannot live within a 20-mile radius of other crops that have GMO crops.

We are one of several small groups out to protect natural seeds. What we do is go through the seed banks searching for ancient species, and try to grow them again, to reproduce them and put them back in the market."

"I don't understand how our government allowed this to happen," Curt said, shaking his head and looking at Marlene. "What do you know about this, Mar?"

Marlene spoke: "Bills come up every single year in regards to GM foods. Those measures failed."

"Why?"

"Agribusiness lobbyists and their contributions, for one; other reasons are the studies that were presented to the FDA in defense of GM foods."

"Whose studies?" Curt quizzed his wife.

"There are always numerous safety studies presented at the time of the voting, Curt. They show just the opposite of what they are saying here. The studies showed conclusive statistics that support the safety of GM foods and many benefits toward staving off world hunger."

"Studies all put out by the multinational food corporations," Keller added. "No independent studies have ever been allowed to be presented."

"I wouldn't know," Marlene replied.

"Well, *we* know. They send their own safety studies to the FDA, and all's good. This country has lost its scruples. Corporate greed is ruining everything. We are in a moral toilet. Tell me, what do you know about the bill HR 875 that would criminalize organic farming and the backyard farmer?"

"Really, Mr. Keller, I couldn't possibly be expected to remember every bill that crosses the floor."

"What do you know about the Codex Alimentarius?"

"I know a bit. It's a trade commission by the United Nations to control the international trade of potentially harmful food."

"That is correct to an extent. Its initial intentions may have been altruistic, but it has been taken over by corporate interests; and they set trade sanctions that punish any nation if it falls outside the Codex guidelines.

"One of the Codex guidelines is designed to permit only ultra-low doses of vitamins and minerals by prescription only. If enough people do not take action, we can expect to watch nutritional supplement manufacturers and health food stores go out of business. The only player left standing would be Big Pharma.

It's a tragedy, really. God put a healing herb for every ailment that mankind suffers on this planet, but the pharmaceutical industry would seek to make them all illegal and replace them with synthetics. Again, it all boils down to patents, because you cannot put a patent on an herb. The pharmaceutical industry will take, say, an Amazon rain forest herb that is known for its healing qualities, isolate its medicinal compounds and then seek to imitate those compounds in the laboratory. Then they sell it to you under the new manufactured and patented name. Yet at the same time they will lobby non-stop to make the original herb that they copied illegal.

"It isn't just GMO crops we need to worry about. There are commercialized, genetically engineered trees that grow straight and tall in neat, tidy rows but they're fakes. They are non-reproductive; they produce no fruits, nuts or blossoms; and no insects, animals or birds will live in them. They produce trees low in wood fiber that are easy to cut up for pulp in paper production.

"There are also GMO fish, meats and, worse, living transgenic animals of all sorts are being patented right now as we speak. Spider genes spliced into goats, jellyfish genes spliced into cats to produce glow-in-the-dark cats... "

"Spider genes in goats! Why?" Curt interrupted.

"Spider silk may seem fragile, but it actually five times stronger than steel! Spider goats can produce milk in quantity that can be used to make flexible artificial limbs, lightweight bulletproof vests..."

"Wow! That sounds great."

"Sure, until the goats get loose," Cassandra laughed.

"And what about those cats?" Curt asked.

"I'm not sure what purpose they serve," Keller continued. "Can't you see that all of this has the potential to escalate into something quite perverse?"

"I don't know. I think I'd like to see one of those cats."

"Sure, and maybe you'd like to see an ostrich dog, also. Personally, I'd prefer to see all this genetic tinkering left in the hands of God. Do you know that mankind is the next transgenic creature, combining our own human DNA with that of animals and plants? It's the wholesale redesigning of humanity! Do we really want to see this happen?" Keller's eyes were intense and as big as saucers. "I don't know if you fully realize that this macabre technology is here and now and being conducted as we speak. It affects you and everyone you know!"

Marlene cleared her throat and attempted to change the subject. "I think we've seen enough of your agriculture site," she said. "Did you have something else you wished to show us?"

Keller continued to fume. "Did you know that in 2006 legislation was introduced that would prohibit creating human-animal hybrids and the buying, selling and patenting of human embryos? The legislation failed. You should know about this, Senator!! Did you not vote on this matter yourself??"

Marlene stiffened. "I was quite young then and not yet in the Senate, or the House for that matter. I think I would have found that interesting, however."

"Interesting?!! It's a bloody nightmare, and now it's here!!"

Marlene's head was now starting to swim. She rubbed her eyes and again changed the subject. "I'm told we haven't much time for this tour today since we need to prepare for a storm. Do you wish to show us more?"

"We certainly do," Tauer said, taking the helm. "Let's adjourn and give you a tour of our livestock."

"Don't think that this discussion is fully over, Ms. Carson," Keller persisted. "You still have much left to learn. We'll resume this subject later."

"Easy, Peter." Tauer put his hand on his old friend's shoulder.

Keller calmed down, and he and Tauer led the group back to the waiting golf carts. They all squeezed in and took a ride to the livestock pastures.

"I think you will find our animals to be quite impressive, our cattle in particular." Eldon Tauer gabbed freely while driving the cart, attempting to smooth out the mood. They drove toward the livestock area, passing fields of beautiful fruit and nut trees brimming with apples, pears, cherries and plums. Workers were harvesting the fruits into baskets and loading them onto pickup trucks.

"That's a lot o' fruit," Curt remarked.

"Yes, we are quite proud of our orchards," Cassandra spoke. "Again, all of our fruits are organically grown. Did you know that tree fruits are the most heavily sprayed crops in North America?"

"No, I did not."

"Have you ever noticed your fruit tasting bitter?"

"Sometimes."

"Sweet fruits like pears that are sprayed conventionally leave a lingering bitterness behind because the food absorbs the poison throughout. It doesn't just sit on the surface. God didn't put that bitter taste there, people did."

"How many different fruit trees do you have?"

"We have dozens of different varieties. We'll be planting our first grapes this coming season. I'm sure looking forward to seeing that."

"That sounds lovely," Marlene said softly as she watched the captivating pastoral scene pass by. The group was driving in the direction of the livestock when, off in the distance, an interesting structure that Marlene and Curt had never seen before caught her eye. It was a relatively short, only about 12-foot-high, circular structure with a circumference of about 400 feet. The entire structure was covered by a clear geodesic dome.

"Hold on, stop!" Marlene exclaimed. "What is that thing over there?"

"Oh, that's our tilapia farm," Keller answered.

"Tilapia? Now that's intriguing. May we see it?"

"Of course you may. We were going to show you this and the shrimp farm after livestock but we can take a look at it now." They did a U-turn and headed in the direction of the dome. They drew near the structure, which was guarded by a single man seated in a fold-up chair and reading a book.

"Juan, we won't be long," Keller said to the guard while still seated in the golf cart. "We're conducting a tour of the grounds today."

"OK, boss." Juan nodded as he let the cart pass. They came to a stop at a door that led inside the dome to a ramp-type platform that allowed personnel to walk up and work the fish farm and also allowed Marlene and Curt to get a better view.

"This must have cost a fortune to build," Curt exclaimed. The entire site was at least 300 yards. They walked up the ramp to the first tier and looked down into the water. It was teeming with silver fish.

"Very nice," Curt remarked. "The water looks so clean. I always thought the waters from farmed fish were dirty."

"Not ours," Keller replied. "This design assures that we always maintain clean water and don't have to rely upon antibiotics or hormones to preserve the integrity of the fishes' health."

A man approached the group and announced his presence by clearing his throat. "Hey there, Peter," he said. "What's up?"

"Oh hi, Dan, just giving a little tour of the farm. This is Marlene and Curt out of Ohio." Then, to his guests, he beckoned, "Dan is our aquaculture specialist. He essentially runs this farm."

"Nice to meet you," Dan extended his hand warily. He didn't seem very happy to have visitors inside his fish farm.

"Dan, would you mind telling our guest a little about how this facility works?"

"I suppose, as long as they don't put their hands in the water."

Dan stretched out his arm and gestured. "This structure here is a one-of-a-kind, world-class facility. As you can see, we have a lot of adult fish here in the last pond. They are very close to harvest. In fact, we will begin making preparations for harvesting next week."

He led the group across the platform to the second pond. "Here you see that the fish are much smaller; this is our adolescent pond." They walked the perimeter of the pond before he led them to the last area. "This last one is our pupae tank. This is the one that we put the hatchlings into." Curt and Marlene looked into the pupae tank; indeed, the fish were not much bigger than minnows.

Dan led the group down to the bottom and closed a ventilation window on the geodesic dome. "This dome helps maintains a constant temperature, cool in summer and warm in winter. We have an aquaponics facility on the north side of this structure and a much smaller shrimp facility about a half-mile away. We can't grow any shrimp out of there right now, though."

"Too cold?"

"Well, no; actually, we can control the water temperature pretty easily. But they need 12 hours of daylight in order to develop an exoskeleton. This time of year, it just does not work. We have a three-month growing season that we can get one good harvest out of, so we'll enjoy those shrimp when we get them. We grow tilapia and barramundi in those tanks during the off season."

"Shrimp mmm," Curt smiled. "What's for lunch?"

"No shrimp, sir," Cassandra said, "not this time of year."

"We can sure do some tilapia, though," Tauer added. "We still have plenty frozen, and there's going to be another big harvest in just a week or so. I think we should go check out the aquaponics tanks now though. That's my personal favorite."

The group took a short drive on the golf cart north of the tilapia farm to the aquaponics fields. This was an open air series of tanks with produce growing out of holes cut in PVC pipes suspended above and multitudes of fish swimming in the water below. A succession of pumps and filters, 55 gallon drums, drainage beds and bulk containers compassed the structure.

"This is an experiment of ours with aquaponics micro-farming," Keller spoke while giving the introduction. "It's a type of gardening where plants and fish are grown together. The ammonia from the fish waste is transformed into nitrates that provide the nutrients for the plants. The water from the fish tank irrigate the plants and then drains back into the fish tank. We are using 4" PVC pipe as the grow bed.

"The fish waste feeds the plants and the plants keep the tank clean. It's a very delicate ecosystem and we regularly work to maintain the balance between beneficial bacteria, nitrogen and PH levels.

"In these tanks we raise Bluegill which can survive in colder temperatures all the way down to 34° and right now we are ready to harvest our cool temperature crops, beets, carrots, bib lettuce and Swiss chard. Our next crops will be more cold tolerant; cabbages, peas, kale and bok choy. We erect temporary hoop greenhouses in the late fall and take them down later in the year, they can turn into an oven in the summer. Were behind schedule with the houses on these, should have put them up a couple of weeks ago."

"This is really cool," Curt remarked looking into the tank teeming with fish. "They're pretty."

"Thank you." Tauer replied. "We could grow *very* pretty fish such a koi but were far more focused on survival right now and food and water production is our most major challenge in maintaining our independence."

"So how about eating some of these fish?" Curt was still thinking of lunch.

"We could do that. You may change your mind though and want some steak, after you see our livestock," Keller winked; or maybe some chicken or pork. We have some of that, too."

They resumed their trek the over many acres via dirt road until they came upon a pasture of cows grazing in the distance.

"We have 8500 acres devoted to cattle production, with around 4,000 full head cattle."

"Wow."

"It sounds like a lot, but actually for all the people that we are harboring here, it's not very much at all. Of course, we don't eat anywhere near the amount of meat that the typical American has grown accustomed to. We rely much more heavily on fruits and vegetables."

"I may never eat vegetables ever again after that little tour," Curt remarked.

"You have no need to fear any of the food you will find here, Mr. Ludington. It is all as healthy as God intended it to be," Keller assured him as they pulled alongside the fence that contained the herd.

"We are currently preparing for the wintering of the animals. They will need some kind of lean-to or shelter from freezing rain and wind. These bales of wet hay that you see here have higher protein content than dry. We're wrapping them for the coming months; extra salt and minerals should be provided for them as well. The cattle like to eat oats, and we, of course, provide plenty of room and an abundance of grazing grass for them; but we never feed them corn."

"Really? Not even your non-GMO corn?"

"Correct."

"Why is that?"

"Corn isn't natural for cattle to eat. They are designed to eat grass. Grass feeding is an effective way to nourish cows, as grass is their natural food. The end result is a leaner but much healthier, natural beef.

"From a humanitarian perspective, there is yet another advantage to pastured animal products. The animals themselves are not forced to live in confinement. The cruelties of modern factory farming are so severe that you don't have to be a vegetarian or an animal rights activist to find the conditions to be intolerable, and a violation of the human-animal bond." Keller reached for a piece of straw, which he stuck between his lips. "It's a beautiful thing to know you have raised an animal in as benign an environment as you possibly could. It's akin to doing your very best."

"We should show them the rest now," Cassandra said. "There is still a lot left to see, and we still have tons of preparations to make for tonight."

"OK, everybody load up," Keller announced. "Next stop is swine."

The group resumed their trek over the property toward the pig pens, and their arrival was heralded by an overwhelming stench.

"Good God, what is that disgusting smell?" Curt asked.

"I see you haven't spent much time with pigs, Mr. Ludington," Keller laughed.

"No, there aren't that many pig farms in Cape Cod. Thank God."

"They certainly do reek," Marlene added.

"It smells like the dump, maybe worse." Curt held his nose.

"We won't be stopping, then. I don't want to offend your nose," Keller stated as he drove by the pigs and headed toward the poultry pens. Marlene and Curt looked at the hundreds of pigs lolling in the cold mud as they propelled over the rough terrain toward their next destination, sheep.

As they approached, Tauer spoke. "We have about 600 acres devoted to the sheep, not nearly as much as cattle but then sheep aren't as popular as a good steak."

"I love lamb," Curt answered.

"Well, if you had to slaughter one, you might feel differently. They sure are cute when they're little. They're not nearly as cute when they get older and turn into grown sheep, plus they taste pretty darn dreadful when they grow up, too."

"Oh?"

"Yes, it's a very strong flavor," Cassandra chimed in. "We do get a lot of wool from them, though, and milk, too."

"If you look out over the field to the left," Keller pointed, "you will see an adjacent pasture for a few heads of alpaca.

Now, there is some beautiful wool; not very good eating, though."

Marlene saw a shelter for the animals but didn't notice any special provisions being made for the sheep or alpaca. "Aren't you going to prepare something for them for tonight's cold?"

"No, they have plenty of fur to keep them warm. They love the cold, the colder the better. But if you look over to the right of the sheep, you'll see the goats. They aren't nearly as fond of the cold, and yes, we are going to have to close up the openings in their pens for them. Next stop is poultry if you're ready."

They drove to three gigantic barn-looking structures with simple pitched metal roofs. "These are our poultry houses," Keller said. "They currently contain about 160,000 chickens but we will need at least three times as many in the very near future. Want to go in and have a look?"

"I guess so," Curt muttered. "Will it be warm?"

"Warmer than out here," Cassandra laughed.

They got out of the cart and went inside for a look. Inside, there were thousands of chickens roaming loose on wood chip flooring. "Notice the construction," Keller pointed as he spoke over the loud clucking. "The coop has been constructed on top of concrete footings to keep predators from burrowing underneath the coop. We also used strong rafters to support the snow and ice that accumulates in the winter."

"And..." Cassandra added, "to avoid respiratory problems and heat stress, the coop has good cross-ventilation with these two large openings. They close tightly when it's cold. We also have insulated nesting boxes, and plenty of perching space, see? These poultry feeders have been suspended from the rafters, to help keep mice away from the feed. The wood chip flooring acts as compost for the litter produced by the poultry."

Unfortunately, the chickens didn't smell much better than the pigs.

"Oh my," Marlene remarked, crinkling her nose. "I've seen enough. Let's move on, please."

"Ducks, anyone?" Keller looked at Cassandra.

"Yes, ducks are next," she replied.

The group again embarked on a short journey to a nearby small lake. Curt and Marlene could see some ducks lounging beside the still waters and hundreds more bathing in the lake. "This is a man-made lake," Keller mentioned. "We diverted water from a spring on the property and created this beautiful, pristine lake. It is home to our domestic breeds of ducks such as the Pekin and the Rouen drakes, which cannot fly, and there are a few geese as well. In the summer months, we have some gorgeous wild duck visitors, but most of them have flown south already."

"Smart birds, Curt commented.

Cassandra smiled. "You know it. This lake will be frozen solid in a month or so."

"Then what do they do?"

"We have duck houses set up for them, similar to the chicken houses, but they have more free range than the chickens do. We like to rotate the flocks in large pasture areas so they have access to air, bugs and sunshine every day. Our laying duck breeds are the Khaki Campbells and the Rouen mallards, which have been bred for their prolific laying and friendly dispositions, and their eggs are just so good."

"I can't say I've ever had a duck egg," Marlene stated.

"Well, you should try one when you get the chance."

"Something worth mentioning," Tauer said, "is that we try to keep the ducks as far away from the pigs as possible."

"Oh, why is that?"

"Because it's unsanitary. That is how flu viruses get started."

"Huh?"

"Yes. Current thinking is that each year's new flu virus originates in southern China and then spreads around the globe. It's the way they farm out in the villages. They keep the pigs near the house, and they raise the ducks right next to the pigs, so there's a lot of opportunity for close interaction of the three species. First the duck gets the flu, but a human cannot contract a virus from an avian. A human can, however, catch a virus from a pig because humans are more closely related genetically to pigs. So the duck gives the flu virus to the pig. The pig then gives it to the human, then it spreads all over the world."

"Yuck," Curt stuck out his tongue, "all these flu strains we see in the cities are really duck flu?"

"Yep, you got it."

"That's gross."

"A lot about livestock production can be gross sir. That's why we try to maintain as clean and natural an environment as possible for our animals. It benefits us, and it benefits the animals."

"Well, then," he said while glancing at his watch, "that just about concludes our tour of the livestock. What do you say we take a break and have some dinner? You saw our aquaculture facility. Do you like tilapia?"

"Any fish is great with me," Curt brightened. "Too bad it isn't cod, though."

"We love fish, thank you," Marlene added.

"Good, tilapia it is then."

The group sojourned for the moment to take repose in the cafeteria. They chatted amiably and made small talk about family and hometown in an attempt to lighten the mood. The air was turning colder by the minute and the winds were starting to pick up. It felt so good to enter the cafeteria, with its inviting warmth and its enticing aromas.

"I hope they have some kind of soup in the pot," Keller remarked as he strolled into the kitchen. There were several women inside, chopping vegetables and preparing the evening meal. Curt took this as a queue and entered the kitchen area uninvited.

"Mr. Ludington," Keller beckoned, "this is our resident chef, Drusilla Pasco. She was a prodigy like Wolfgang Puck in her former life. Now, she cooks fish soup for us." He laughed heartily.

"No fish soup tonight, Mr. Keller. We have mushroom and barley. How does that sound?"

"Darn, had my heart set on fish," he gave an ironic smile.

"Mushroom sounds great to me," Curt said.

"It goes well with the chicken tarragon and egg noodles that we have as an entrée."

"Wow! This is better than what I get at home," Curt said.

"Please understand, Mr. Ludington," Keller spoke, "it will probably be far more noodles and less meat than you're used to seeing at home. Meat here is considered a luxury. We use it quite sparingly, more like a condiment than a main course. After all, we have thousands of mouths to feed here. It all gets rather expensive."

"And more mouths keep coming every day," added Drusilla.

"Yes, that's true."

"How do they pay for their meals?" Curt asked.

"Initially, we give newcomers some community property credits until they get established here. Then they have a certain time frame to begin creating their own credits in the system. If they fail to meet their obligation to establish their own, then they are shown the door."

"Does that happen often?"

"Every society has its share of freeloaders, but we will not tolerate anyone that doesn't live up to their potential. We simply don't have enough resources to allow it. This isn't a welfare system."

"That sounds like a pretty fair deal to me."

"It certainly is more fair than the treatment one could expect on the outside right now."

Mmm, Curt thought wistfully to his life back at home. He hadn't made a decision in his mind yet as to which was the worse of two evils, staying at home and living with a microchip or living here for the rest of his life in this regimental environment and eating in a… good Lord, no… not a cafeteria. He sighed deeply, knowing that Marlene would never agree to be microchipped in a million years. If life grew too unbearable here, he would have little choice but go back home and spend his remaining days without her. The thought made him thoroughly depressed.

"Can we get a spot of that soup?" Keller asked, eying the pot.

"OK," the chef agreed, spooning the fragrant dish into two bowls. "Just eat it in here so no one sees you. It isn't dinner time yet for another 40 minutes."

"Now, you would think I would get special privileges around here, wouldn't you, Mr. Ludington?" Keller smiled and blew on a spoonful.

"Mmmm ... yeah, sure," Curt mumbled with his mouth full of the piping hot soup.

"I guess you realize that we left Ms. Carson and the rest out in the main dining room?"

"Mmph, I guess we did." The two snickered.

Just then, Marlene poked her head around the corner. "Where are you two? Oh, there you are," she said. "That doesn't look like fish," she said, peering into Curt's bowl.

"No, honey, it's mushroom soup. Try it, it's awesome."

"Mmmm, that's great. Where's the fish?"

"No fish. Tonight it's chicken."

"Oh."

"We're not supposed to be doing this," Curt smiled at Marlene. "But Keller here has special privileges."

The three stepped back into the cafeteria and chatted with the others until the designated hour when they were finally doled out heaping portions of egg noodles topped with a couple of tablespoons of chicken in tarragon sauce, for which they were quite grateful. Then, it was off to bed to spend the night on a lumpy cot that sat on a concrete floor. Curt and Marlene spent a cold night as a large snowstorm rolled in. They huddled together for warmth in one tiny cot, listening to the wind howling outside.

Curt couldn't sleep despite being exhausted. He cursed out loud, wishing he had remembered to ask for some extra blankets, but it was the wee hours now. It would have been a 30-minute walk to the main office if he could even find it in the dark. Then, suddenly he remembered that Cassandra had said they were staying in the unit next to hers.

"Pssst, Marlene, wake up."

"Wha? Wazzit?"

"Honey, go next door and get us some blankets."

"Huh? Next door where? Where am I?" Marlene rubbed her eyes.

"In the bungalow next to ours; Cassandra lives there remember?"

"What time is it?"

"3:30."

"Not a chance. Why don't you just do it yourself?"

"C'mon honey. I'm cold."

"Go do it yourself." Marlene rolled over and shut her eyes.

"Please?"

"No."

Curt reluctantly sat up and put on a pair of slippers. He stepped outside, and the wind nearly swept him off his feet. He returned inside for a pair of boots and negotiated the short walk to the neighboring place where Cassandra lived. He got lucky and found her unit on the first try and returned shortly thereafter with two thin blankets.

"See, honey," he said as he crawled back in bed next to his wife. "I even got an extra one for you." But Marlene had already fallen asleep again and didn't hear a word.

Chapter *31*

Shaw's Big Moment

Winthrop Shaw had his party catered by the best of the best, in a copious display of extravagant taste and elegance to be spoken of for years to come. No expense was spared for the momentous, three-day occasion. Specialists were called in for the lighting and sound and top designers for the decorations. Guest arrived on the helipad off the bow, and each guest was escorted by a crew member and personally greeted by the captain before stepping aboard. Once inside, they indulged in an inordinately plush soiree costing millions in celebrity talent fees alone.

Violinists lined the yacht's stairwells, and a grand fountain showcased a dramatic spectacle of water, music and light thoughtfully interwoven to mesmerize its admirers. A magnificent chandelier adorned the antechamber in colorful splendor. Fine glass and gleaming surfaces emblazoned the ship's interior, its walls accented in scalloped silver leaf with fine art featured predominantly. The Suzerain was as imposing a vessel as was ever built, rival none. It was expertly constructed, down to every last detail. Its electronic system featured computerized navigation that monitored and controlled eight diesel turbine engines that gave her a blazing speed of up to 40 knots. Her cavernous, plush garage housed three 30-foot boats that were used as dinghies, an assortment of jet skis and jet boats and even a private submarine, Shaw's preferred method of arrival. It featured 19 staterooms, a theater, a library, a billiards room, an observatory, an art gallery, a wine cellar, a fully equipped kitchen, a beauty salon, a gymnasium and a basketball court. One could also partake in world-class gaming in the clubhouse, which furnished baccarat, craps, poker and roulette.

The Suzerain's 320 crew members always made sure that the Suzerain was shipshape, polishing her fixtures, faucets and sinks, made of solid silver, daily to a shiny gleam. It an exterior staircase linking the aft portion of each deck with a panoramic lounge opening into a private rooftop sundeck, complete with a genuine grass lawn to cater to the lucky guests' pets.

The bash included themes. On day one, guest partied to an all-white theme. On day two, they experienced a whimsical masquerade, and day three, a red velvet theme with the Brazilian samba played by a 20-piece orchestra spicing up the dance floor. Partygoers enjoyed live concerts in the disco by the latest hot pop stars, who entertained a crowd of nearly 1,800 guests, including foreign dignitaries, heads of state, Middle Eastern oil barons, Saudi princes, Russian tycoons and members of the banking elite.

Attendants lavished attention on each distinguished guest; if a single ash landed in an ashtray, it was immediately disposed of. Dancing, drinking, frivolities and gambling were de rigueur during the day. The evening's entertainment included a cirque act, fashion show and spectacular fireworks display. Guests could escape the hullabaloo by slipping off to sun by one of three Mediterranean-style pools with classic courtyards, receiving a massage in the spa or engaging in skeet shooting off the stern; or they could simply depart in one of the several jet skis that were provided for the guests' pleasure. There they would splash in the cerulean waters of the Côte d' Azur.

Extra accommodations were provided for guests along the coastline of Shaw's own luxurious, secluded island, where they could stroll along the quays or through the private resort's lush gardens scented by lavender bush and lemongrass.

Inside the dining room of the Suzerain, a large ice sculpture of a majestic swan formed a grand centerpiece while 200 waiters attended to the needs of all the partygoers. On the menu were a Devon crab and white truffle half-filled tomato dressed with gold leaf and topped with Beluga caviar and black abalone which served as hors d'oeuvres. Waiters in black tails sailed by efficiently and quietly, whisking away small, half-eaten plates of oysters, chilled Scottish lobster and Kobe beef tartar and foie gras appetizers.

The main courses consisted of veal cheeks with Périgord truffles and for dessert: Crème brûlée with goji berry-infused Riesling jelly. Kopi Luwak cappuccino topped with 24-karat gold dust sprinkles rounded out the meal.

Fine, rare vintage bottles of Louis Roederer flowed freely, and the glass menagerie bar opened to reveal crystal decanters holding single malt designated for Scotch connoisseurs.

Shaw hovered nearby supervising, his watchful eyes gauging the success of the party. He approached his peer, Baron Gavin Astor IV and showed him a secret passageway that led to his own private den. There sat Shaw's faithful assistant, Nelson Thurn, in front of the television. When Thurn saw his superior, he quickly stood to attention.

"Nelson?!" Shaw exclaimed. "Whatever are you doing in here? You should be circulating amongst the guests."

"Apologies, sir. I was getting a bit of a headache. I'm not really much of a drinker, and the music is a bit loud for me."

"Yes, I know what you mean."

"I'll be happy to go, sir." Nelson took a turn to leave and go to his own quarters.

"No, no, Nelson, you may stay. Just take a seat."

"Thank you, sir."

"No, Nelson, not that one – that's mine. Go sit over there." Shaw pointed to an albino eel skin easy chair. "You remember the Baron?" Shaw nodded toward Astor.

"Yes, of course," Nelson replied as he shook the Baron's hand. "It's a pleasure to see you again."

The Baron took off his glasses, wiped them clean and put them back on his nose as he examined Thurn's face. "I really don't remember you at all, young man."

"This is Nelson Thurn," Shaw spoke. "He is my most trusted confidant."

"I see. And where *is* Rothfeller?" Astor asked. "I haven't seen him once all night."

"He's conspicuously absent, I'm afraid," Shaw replied. "A touch of rheumatism, I believe. He never sent word that he wouldn't be making it."

"Pity, I was looking forward to going over projections."

"Yes, it is."

With the czar safely out of his hair, Shaw had some very good ideas about a new direction for the commemoration ceremony. Some changes would be made.

The three conversed in the den until bedtime, which was 4 a.m., and after a restful sleep, they rose at noon to start the revelry all over again. On the third and final night of festivities, an announcement was made for the guests to convene in the main dining room; there, Shaw raised his glass in toast and spoke to those gathered:

"These hundred-year-old bottles of Champagne are from the Heidelstiek vineyard in the Champagne region of France. They took over 90 years to reach their final destination. They were originally shipped to the Russian imperial family in 1914, but a hurricane caused the ship to wreck off the coast of Madagascar, sending this champagne to the bottom of the sea until divers discovered over 200 bottles in 2017. I bought the entire lot, all of them. This evening, I'm sharing this exceptional wine with its extraordinary tale and incredible age with all of you, in celebration of the final amalgamation of nations and the commencement of the new World Central Reserve Bank."

Applause issued from the inebriated crowd, and Shaw continued, "So tonight, my friends, I present a toast and an unveiling of a magnificent piece of sculpture done by the acclaimed artist Jean Philippe Kees." A drum roll resonated in the background, and Shaw extended his arm to present a tall figure draped in a red cloth. When unveiled, it displayed a 20-foot bronze effigy of none other than Shaw himself. A standing ovation of acclaim and exaltation broke from the guests, in honor of Shaw and his triumphant accomplishments. Shaw basked in the glory of the moment and drank his fill from his fluted champagne glass. *How sweet it is indeed.*

The toast was followed by a cannon salute off the stern. Then, the social event of the season drew to a close, and the guests disembarked for their journeys home, to attend polo matches, camel racing, high-stakes betting and other aristocratic pursuits. After the party, Shaw spent several hours reviewing tapes of the private conversations that the guests had amongst themselves. The recording devices had been carefully concealed inside windowpanes, walls and floors. Not a single inch of the Suzerain had been left untouched by the spying hand of Winthrop Shaw.

Chapter *32*

A Tour

Marlene Carson yawned and stretched like a cat. The morning was cold but sunny and amazing. Icicles hung off every tree branch, and 2 inches of snow covered the ground. The torrential winds from the night before had died down to nothing, and the panorama outside couldn't have been more enchanting. She was up shortly after dawn and stepped outside to greet the winter wonderland. It was the first real snow of the year. The sun's rays tinkled between the long drips of ice that hung everywhere, creating a kaleidoscope of color in every direction. The crisp air smelled clean and wonderful. It was truly magical.

"Curt, wake up. You have to see this!"

"Uh-uh. I didn't sleep all night. Leave me be."

"Spoilsport." Marlene quickly got dressed and went outside for a nice walk. *I wonder if I could get used to this place,* she thought as she shuffled along with no particular place to go. She returned after an hour long walk and rousted Curt from his slumber. The two sat on the edge of the bed and discussed the day's events.

"I believe we have a tour of the labs scheduled for today," she muttered while brushing her hair.

"Yeah, that's what I heard. Any idea what time?"

"Should be after breakfast, I would think."

The two spent a relatively unexciting hour waiting for a time to head in when came a knock at the door. It was John Reese, looking ready to escort them to their scheduled day's events.

"Good morning, Mr. Reese," Marlene cordially greeted the tall, bearded man.

"Morning to you, ma'am. Are you both ready?"

"As ready as ever," said Curt.

"OK. Cassandra is already in the cart waiting. If you're hungry, we can swing by the cafeteria and grab some food. Boiled egg, anyone?"

Marlene repulsed at the thought of a boiled egg. "I'm not really hungry. How about you, Curt?"

"No, thanks," Curt replied. "I'd like to get this show on the road."

"OK, then." Reese smiled. "Let's get this show on the road."

The foursome took a frigid ride in the golf cart back to their original meeting point at the aluminum trailers that served as the administrative main office and met up again with Hidden Village founder Peter Keller and co-founder Eldon Tauer. Utah ex-Gov. Geoffrey McAllen was also present and standing by the fire.

Nancy, the woman seated behind the desk with the horn-rimmed glasses, nodded at their arrival and continued with her typing.

"Good morning," Keller said, welcoming Curt and Marlene. "A tad chilly this morning, yes?"

"Oh my God, it's freezing!" Curt bellyached while blowing his warm breath onto his icy fingertips. "I forgot to bring my gloves."

"At least the winds died down. It's actually quite pleasant, I think."

You're nuts, Curt thought, but he only nodded his head and moved across the room closer to the fireplace to where McAllen stood.

"Good to see you again, Mr. Carson." McAllen extended his hand, adding: "My apologies for not attending the tour yesterday. I was quite buried helping to prepare for the storm. Thank goodness it was a brief one. At this time of year, a storm like that could last several days, maybe even weeks."

"It's Ludington."

"Yes, of course," McAllen chuckled.

"And how are you, lovely Senator?" McAllen took Marlene's hand and gave it a kiss. "Did you sleep well?"

"I did, but I don't think Curt slept well at all. We could use a few more blankets, if that's all right," she said, looking at Keller.

"That's not a problem at all," Keller replied. "I wish you'd have spoken up yesterday. I'm so sorry we forgot, but it was quite hectic here yesterday."

"Of course, we understand."

"If you'll kindly step inside the boardroom for a moment," Keller said, "I would like to go over today's agenda." The group stepped inside and shut the door. "Today, we are first going to tour our wastewater facility and then the energy research facility," he said while handing the pair the day's agenda.

"What about the labs?" Curt asked.

"Yes absolutely, the labs will follow. It should be an exciting day for you."

"Even more exciting than chickens?" Curt jibed.

"Or pigs?" Marlene added.

"I sense sarcasm," Keller replied eyeing the pair and nodded toward Reese. "John, can you please get two guest badges to the labs for our visitors?"

They sat a moment and waited while he retrieved the badges. He then nodded toward the door. "Are we ready?"

"Yes, sir. Let's go."

The group traveled by cart. "You already know that we have an above-ground aqueduct system." Keller pointed to the arched structures that ran alongside the chain-link fence as he drove the cart over the bumpy dirt road. "We also have one running underground that you don't see. It distributes water from the mountain springs and wells spread throughout the property right to where we need it. We are in the process of branching the water supply to service our soon-to-be-built wastewater and sewage facility." They pulled up to a partitioned area where the facility was being constructed.

"We have a remarkable supply of good, clean water; but, like every growing community, we will need the type of sewer treatment that we have been accustomed to our entire lives. We can't very well go back to the use of chamber pots in our homes, so, here we are." Keller stopped in front of the construction site. There were excavators and bulldozers hauling off dirt in front of several man-made lagoons and ponds.

"This facility reproduces natural purification processes with artificial, little deep basins. We will fill with them with inert material and aquatic plants after they are completed. Our citizens' homes currently use decentralized aerobic composting toilets with a heavy reliance on fungus and also traditional septic tank systems; but eventually, this facility will be finished and we will have our own natural wastewater plant."

"Very nice." Curt remarked. "Are we getting out?"

"No need, this facility isn't finished yet. We still have to install the inlet and outlet pipes, dig an outlet stream and recirculate it to dilute and oxygenate the wastewater. It will be at least a year before it's ready. But at our energy production research facility, we have plenty to show you."

"That sounds very interesting."

"We think so," Keller mused as he took off down the dirt trail. "We have been very blessed by God. Our property contains many natural resources. We have some oil shale deposits, which we use as a low-grade fuel in our furnaces. It's kind of interesting to watch it burn. It looks just like rocks on fire. We also have an abundance of natural gas. Getting it out of the ground, however, has proven to be very difficult. Natural gas, as it exists underground, is not exactly the same as the natural gas that we have seen coming through the pipelines to our homes and businesses. Natural gas, for home use, is almost entirely methane. When we find our natural gas underground, however, it comes with an assortment of other trace compounds and gases, as well as oil and water, all of which must be removed before use. The other option is to use hydraulic fracturing or 'fracking,' as it's known, to release the gas. We were approached by one of the major energy companies to give them rights to do this on our property a few years ago, but the risk of toxic contamination to our aquifer and the damage to the environment was simply too great. Some things are more valuable than money."

"I see," Marlene said.

"Besides, these backward conventional methods are soon to be a thing of the past. The notion that you have to burn something in order to create energy is quite Neanderthal, to say the least."

"Oh?"

"Oh, yes," Keller replied as they pulled up to another row of Quonset huts on the far north side of the compound that served as the power research facility. "This is our energy production research facility. It is here that we have made our most significant contributions to science and humanity." They disembarked and approached a chain-link security fence. Two guards sat in folded metal chairs playing cards. The group was immediately greeted by the security personnel, and Keller and company were quickly allowed inside.

They navigated the white tile hallways in the cold, clinical atmosphere; Keller was talking all the while.

"We are completely independent of the U.S electrical power grid; in fact, we have created our very own power grid. Here, we are not only re-creating the Tesla technologies that were originally discovered over 100 years ago, but we also are experimenting with some very promising applied sciences utilizing the Earth's own magnetic field as an unlimited power source."

"That sounds very cool," Curt smiled.

"It is more than cool. If we can accomplish what we set out to do, it will be life-changing. McAllen tells me that he has told you a little bit about what goes on here?"

"Actually, he was quite vague in his descriptions. He simply said you had to see it to believe it."

Keller smiled. "Come on, let's go inside."

Keller led the party through a set of swinging doors, and they entered a laboratory, there they were acknowledged by a small group of people working on a project. One of the men from the group approached Keller and the rest.

"This is physicist Michael Fresenius, an esteemed colleague." He introduced Curt and Marlene to the scientist.

"Hello, it's a pleasure to meet you." Marlene and Curt shook his hand.

"Michael, can you explain to our guests what we are doing here?"

"It would be my pleasure," he said softly.

"Here we are working on synergistic magnetic power generators." He took a 12- by 12-inch open-top wooden box off the table and presented it to Curt and Marlene for them to have a look. Inside was a series of small magnets coiled with copper wire with posts and permanent magnets extending in an alternating fashion between each plate. An output coil extended around each of the posts, and input coils extended around portions of the plates.

"The magnetic power generator uses the basic principle of applying the basic magnetic field to generate the electric power," Fresenius explained.

"As we know, the magnet has two poles, which are north and south poles. We alternate pulses between these plates to cause induction current within these output coils. These input and output coils extend around portions of the magnetic core. This permanent magnet is positioned in middle of the magnetic core. It furnishes a magnetic flux line outward into the core material, resulting in a right and a left magnetic path. A driving electrical current through each of the input coils acts as a choke coil, reducing the level of flux from the permanent magnet within the magnet path around which the input coil extends. This generates a voltage spike on the output coil."

He pointed to an attached wattmeter. "As you can see, these simple prototypes we have now provide close to 0.5 watts of power per day each."

"Is that a lot?"

"No, it is actually quite little. We can power small electronic devices such as a drill or a blow dryer but only for a few seconds."

"What good is that?" Curt demanded.

Keller scowled. "I think you're missing the point, Mr. Ludington. These devices defy all our currently established scientific laws. They generate more power than they use." He took the box from Fresenius and replaced it on the table. Fresenius cleared his throat and moved to a far corner of the room, beckoning the rest of the group to follow.

"This one over here is a little different," he said, showing them a much larger object. It was a 6-foot revolving wheel set on its side resembling a Ferris wheel, again with a series of magnets between layers metal plates wrapped in coiled wire.

"This mechanism uses rotating magnets to accomplish the same goal, only more efficiently; magnetic attraction and repulsion provides movement of the engine. It's a thing of beauty: The coils never get hot, and this magnetic field can produce free energy forever. It generates 3.5 times more energy than it uses, it doesn't slow down when more load is added and emits zero radiation."

"Thank you for your time, professor. We will be getting out of your hair now. Let's move along, shall we?" Keller asserted as he led the group outside. They moved to another Quonset hut featuring a garage environment with several cars, tractors and other heavy equipment.

"This is my personal favorite area of research," Keller stated as they walked inside.

"You saw the front-end loaders this morning and how they were equipped with electric power?"

"Yes," Marlene nodded.

"We are working on a project that makes those conventional electric vehicles look like something from the horse-and-buggy years." He stopped in front of a backhoe and a compactor; and then turned to Curt and Marlene.

"See how these pieces of equipment have antennae on the top of their roofs?" He pointed to a 3-foot metal antennae as he spoke.

"Uh-huh. Yes?"

"These are electromagnetic conductors. We are trying to harness radio waves in free space and convert to an electrical current. This electromagnetic conversion has the potential to eventually power all our machinery, including our automobiles."

"With that little antenna there? How is that possible and why isn't everyone using it?" Curt queried.

Keller smiled. "I suppose you know about Nikola Tesla; the inventor of alternating current and also called the 'Father of Electricity'?"

"Yes, of course."

"This is just one of the Tesla technologies that I mentioned earlier, but it's not the antenna that does the work. We are attempting to re-create his original work done back in 1931. In the summer of that year, Tesla took the gasoline engine out of a new Pierce-Arrow touring car and replaced it with an 80-horsepower AC electric motor with no external power source. He also installed a mysterious box on the front seat. The box was 24 inches long, 12 inches wide and 6 inches high. Out of it protruded a 1.8-meter-long antenna and two ¼-inch metal rods. Inside the box were a dozen 70-L-7 vacuum tubes, some wires and assorted resistors. Two wire leads ran from the box to the newly installed AC motor that replaced the gasoline engine.

Getting into the car with the circuit box in the front seat beside him, he pushed the rods in and announced, 'We now have power.' It's reported that using no gasoline whatsoever, Tesla proceeded to drive the car for a week and at speeds of up to 90 miles an hour. The AC motor ran at 1,800 rpm and got fairly hot when operating, requiring a cooling fan. He captured this free energy and was able to drive for hours without ever once having to stop for a recharge. Tesla's electric car was much lighter than a traditional car, there was no battery pack, no gas tank, no exhaust system and no heavy combustion engine. But most importantly, the source of power for his vehicle was available for free. You would never have to recharge this vehicle or pay a penny to do so. The source of power that powered the AC electric motor was scalar electromagnetic waves. When questioned about the origin of its operating power Tesla just answered: 'Ether which permeates everything and is in inexhaustible supply.'

"He could pick it up with just an antenna? That's hard to believe."

"Is it so hard? Once upon a time, we had free radio, free television and free citizens band radio for short-distance radio communications – all picked up with a simple antenna. These are all electromagnetic radio waves. Why would electrical current waves be any different? Now, all of these once-free communications paths are metered, and antenna-based technologies have been curbed. Why? Because they were free.

The multinational energy companies were understandably threatened by this emerging technology that would potentially power the entire world for free, and they launched a campaign to discredit Tesla's new discovery just as they tried to discredit his AC invention in prior years. They painted the genius in the press as a madman dabbling in black magic and openly scoffed at his free-energy car and his other amazing inventions. The sensitive Tesla didn't like the skeptical comments of the press. He removed his mysterious box and returned to his laboratory in New York; the secret of his power source died with him. When Tesla died, the government swooped in immediately and confiscated what writings and papers he had hidden away. So, most of Tesla's secrets, including this one, sadly, were lost to humanity."

"But you think you have discovered it again?"

"We are hopeful, but no, not yet. We know that it exists, and if it exists we can get it back. But we have made tremendous progress in its uncovering. Our prototype design modifies the linear element of Tesla's Patent, to a rotating element, and some additional electronics are employed for stability, power control and correct wave frequency range.

Our scientists at our research facility believe that these waves exist only in the vacuum of empty space. They call them 'electromagnetic longitudinal waves' as opposed to 'transverse' electromagnetic waves – the transverse ones are commonplace. Our cellphones, televisions, microwave ovens, wireless networks and so forth all operate on transverse waves. Scalar waves on the other hand, work by having two oscillations anti-parallel with each other, each originating from opposite charge sources. Rather than modulating in three dimensions, they are modulating in the direction they are going, accordion-like, along the axis of time, the fourth dimension.

"The sad part is that, most likely, the technology to harness this unlimited power source has already been realized and patented by our government and now is just sitting somewhere shelved."

"That's a shame." Curt frowned.

"It is, yes. There are thousands of these discoveries in that grievous state."

Tauer spoke: "When we talk about any type of energy that could possibly upset the existing Establishment's apple cart, you can be guaranteed they are going to do their very best to squash it! Who will make the money if the energy is unmetered? Even our own government steps in. Freely available electromagnetic energy cannot be metered and therefore is un-taxable! Of course, the government wants to charge you a carbon tax but squash any alternative energies as they come up.

"Instead, we focused solely on oil, coal and god awful nuclear power. We could have saved ourselves trillions of dollars on oil, not to mention the pollution. They would rather keep us in a filthy, polluted cesspool than harvest the Earth's own electromagnetic field."

Keller resumed: "We have made better progress with hydrogen fuels and cold fission. Come, we'll show you." The group progressed to another room and walked inside to greet a group of engineers and scientists.

"Here is where our scientists have developed a prototype fuel cell that separates water into oxygen and hydrogen using radio frequencies. We have found that the amount of energy needed to split the water into hydrogen and oxygen is surprisingly small," he explained.

"The bond between the oxygen and hydrogen atoms in water is very strong. The bond needs to be broken, and cold fission does this. The goal is to return water or split the liquid state of water back to its three original atoms. We simply apply a resonant frequency to accomplish this."

"Wow, that's awesome!" Curt declared. "How can I see it work?"

"We're in development plans to build a cold fission reactor to produce hydrogen fuel. If we can get it to work, we will have an abundance of energy, enough to power the entire state with just one small body of water."

"A reactor?" Curt questioned. He raised an eyebrow. "That sounds like a nuke to me."

"No worries. There are no environmental side effects, no carbon emissions, no toxicity and no radiation with burning hydrogen-oxygen fuel; and any water will do the job, even seawater. Conversely, hot fusion research has received billions of dollars of government money for over 70 years, and had yet to put a single watt of energy into the grid."

"Incredible."

"Plus, if they ever *do* get it to work, the radiation levels just don't make it worth it."

Tauer spoke up again: "When are we going to wake up to the facts? Radiation is a killer! Until about 2 billion years ago, there were no life forms on Earth because there was so much radiation on the planet's surface that life was impossible. Gradually, the amount of radiation subsided and an ionosphere formed to protect the surface from cosmic radiation, making it possible for the first life forms. Now, in man's infinite wisdom, we go to using nuclear power, creating radiation that nature first eliminated in order to make life possible. Every time you produce radiation, you produce a product that has a guaranteed half-life, in some cases a half-life of billions of years, and there is no safe way to dispose of it! The radioactive waste that we have stored underground currently will take 250,000 years of intensive care. The reactors leak radioactive waste every year, and then we are exposed to much more dramatic crises such as periodic meltdowns.

"Why are we doing this to ourselves? It is imperative that we get control of this horrible force and eliminate it! We could simply concentrate on simple geothermal energies, wind and solar energies and be in much better shape. Who knows how much different the quality of our lives would be if we weren't exposed to so much pollution from radiation, oil and coal? We have been living so long in such filth that most people think it's normal to feel bad."

Keller nodded in agreement. "This concludes our tour of our energy production research facility." He looked at his watch. "Let's go have some lunch, and then we will tour the microchip labs."

Chapter *33*

Back to the Bad

Toni Vickery looked out at the children in the cafeteria as she spread peanut butter on an organic apple and placed it into her mouth. She was wishing it were a couple of pieces of bread instead, especially the processed, fluffy white kind from her childhood.

Mmmm, Dandy, she thought, *now that bread went perfect with peanut butter.* Bread was in very limited supply at the commune. Good bakers seemed to be a real commodity, and as soon as a loaf was baked it was quickly consumed. The first loaves were always designated for the children. Any leftovers could go to the adults, but it seemed that there never was any left over after the little ones had their fill.

She felt blessed. True, it was a tad unexciting at times, but this place was beautiful beyond her dreams. She had grown accustomed to the regimental lifestyle and was settling in nicely. Her routine consisted of sleeping until 7 a.m., starting classes at 8:15 and instructing the 6- to 8-year-old children. Cute as the dickens, they were a welcome change from the fifth-grade monsters that she was used to teaching back at home.

Home... Toni thought wistfully. It wasn't as though she was terribly longing for home, but there was one issue that kept tugging at her heart – her son Joey. God, how she missed him! The last time she spoke to Mitch was over a month ago, and he had refused to put Joey on the phone, accusing Toni of being an unfit mother who had abandoned her son. How could

Mitch possibly understand her motivations? She had never intended to abandon Joey, not even for a minute. She just had to find a better life for the both of them. But now that she had found the perfect place for them to live in peace, she was being prevented from contact with him.

In her absence, Mitch had taken Toni back to the courts to overturn her full-custody status. With Toni being a no-show the day of the hearing, the court swiftly ruled in his favor and granted Mitch full custody without visitation rights. When she heard the news, she cried for three days, but the worst part was when Mitch informed her that while she was away, he'd had poor Joey micro-chipped!

Oh my poor baby, she wailed inside while Mitch droned on about the latest conditions of their new divorce decree, *Mommy will come back for you and save you.*

It was true. She had a plan brewing in the back of her mind. It would take some careful planning, but she was certain that it would work. She might need a little help and some muscle, and she knew just the person to help her pull it off.

A beautiful Saturday morning in early May arrived. Toni and Dina took the opportunity to do absolutely nothing. They opened the windows of their cottage, propped their front door wide open and relaxed, kicking back in their cots, filing their toenails, sipping herb tea and enjoying the soft breeze.

"This is the life, eh?" Dina remarked.

"Uh-hmm. I'll say."

"Toni," Dina asked, "whatever became of that big ogre you kept sneaking out to see?"

"Who, Glick? I haven't thought of him in weeks," Toni lied. Glick was on her mind constantly. She was hoping to stage an opportunity to accidentally run into him so she could ask him to help her with Joey. The thought of Glick gave her a strange, giddy sensation that she couldn't quite explain.

"Well, thank God you came to your senses. I thought I was going to have to have you quarantined against that atrocity."

"Don't worry. I'm safe and sound right here. *And bored.*

"Please make sure you stay safe and sound. You have a tendency to go chasing after the very things you should be leaving alone, young lady."

"Yes, mommy."

"If the sign says no trespassing, that's the first place you want to go explore."

"Yes, mommy."

"Just *have* to go see why it's no trespassing."

"Yes, mommy."

Dina threw her nail file at Toni, and the two women giggled.

Later that evening, as the sun began to set; Toni was doing dishes and planning a rendezvous with the very person she should be leaving alone. Her intentions were to wait until Dina was fast asleep and then go pay her potential helper a little visit. She had to time it perfectly. There was a new curfew established and she only had a few hours' window to get out and back in again or the guards would not let her back in for the night. She was hoping to see Dina fall off early and suggested some nice chamomile tea to get her drowsy, but Dina wasn't in the mood for tea and wanted to stay up even later than normal, reading her new book. She didn't have to work in the morning and saw no reason to tuck in early. Toni tossed about frustrated in her cot, pretending to be asleep, until the lights finally went out. She lay there quietly for an extra 20 minutes until she began to hear Dina's methodical breathing turn into a slight snore. She knew it was now safe. Toni fumbled about blindly in the dark, donning a pair of jeans, a T-shirt, sneakers and a light jacket before slipping quietly out the door.

Toni didn't have to answer to Dina, really. She just didn't want to have to listen to the inevitable lecturing that she knew would follow if Dina knew she was sneaking out at night, especially if she knew it was to go see the dreaded Glick Monster. *Honestly,* Toni thought to herself; *sometimes it's just like being 15 and living with Mom and Dad. Come to think of it, I used to sneak out my bedroom window back then, too.* She tiptoed outside their cottage, making her way in the dim light to the guard gate at the front of the compound. There she was addressed by two armed sentinels; a third sat in the watchtower above.

"Evening, ma'am," they nodded. "What can we do for you?"

"I'd like to go out for a walk."

"There's 24,000 acres here, ma'am. You can't walk inside?"

"It's just not the same."

"You're free to come and go, ma'am, but it's our job to inform you about the dangers that lie outside these gates."

"I'm already well-informed."

"We are discouraging anyone from leaving except for emergency circumstances. We are starting to get some big problems with crashers at the gate. They may seek to do you harm."

"This is an emergency. *Sort of.*

"A walking emergency?"

"Am I allowed out or not?"

The two guards looked at each other and shrugged. "You're aware of the new curfew, right? You must be back by 10:30 p.m. or you will not be allowed back in for the rest of the evening."

"Yes, I'm aware."

"The gate will remain locked at 10:31. As long as I have an acknowledgment from you on this, please sign here." Toni took the paper and signed her name. The guard tore off the top and handed her the yellow copy. "You will need to present this paper when returning or you will not be allowed back in."

"Okie-dokie." She took the yellow paper, folded it and slipped it into her back jeans pocket.

"Please be careful, ma'am," he stated while unlocking the gate that slid open smoothly on roller wheels. "There are more and more vagrants on the outskirts every day." Sure enough, upon seeing movement, several dark figures on the outside fringes edged closer to the gate. It quickly closed upon them, however.

"Thanks, guys!" Toni waved goodbye. *Freedom!* She looked at her watch. *10:30, that gives me just over one hour to get to Glick's tent, talk him into some help and get back. I hope I can do all that in one hour.*

Toni trotted off in the direction of Glick's camp, which was about a fifth of a mile away. She hurriedly moved past several other small camps that had sprung up since she had last been on the outside. She could see and smell little campfires burning from the new camps that dotted the surroundings as she drew near to the one that held the man she yearned to see. She reached the camp soon enough and meandered through the familiar setting. Not much had changed since she was there in late March. If anything, it just looked dirtier, with small piles of trash sprouting up all over and undernourished, grubby men gathered in clusters. The place reeked of piss, anxiety and desperation. She jogged again now, past the memorable row of unused Harley-Davidsons that she knew would lead to the tent site that Glick shared with that young girl Amy and her boyfriend what's-his-name.

Toni stopped running and cautiously approached from behind what looked like the tent that she recognized as Glick's; and tucked behind a clothesline that held dark clothing flapping in the breeze, she saw the outline of his back. *He's here!* She deftly lurked from the rear and observed his gigantic shape sitting on a log. He was roasting a hot dog on a long stick over an open flame; no one else in sight. She snuck up silently on Glick and gently placed her fingers over his eyes.

"Guess who?" she purred. Glick instantly stood and reared like a bear upon feeling her touch.

"Toni!!!" he dropped the hot dog and swept her up into his hairy arms. Holding her, he spun in circles, making her feel like a little girl. Toni fairly melted into his gargantuan bulk, and she gave his forehead a modest kiss. He held her tight against his chest and swayed from side to side, gasping "Oh! Oh! Oh!"

With Toni still clutched to his waist, he headed straight into the tent, where Amy and Jimbo were curled into balls, sound asleep.

"Hey you two…" he bellowed, "get the fuck out!!"

"What?!! What's going on?" Amy sat up.

"Come on, sister," Glick nudged her with his foot. "I need some privacy."

"Are you friggin' kidding me? I'm trying to get some sleep here!"

"Glick, really, this isn't necessary," Toni said.

"Sure it is," he said as he gently set her down. He picked up Jimbo's sleeping carcass and deposited him gracelessly on the ground outside the tent, and Amy soon followed.

"Hey, fuck you, man!" He heard Jimbo complaining in the open air, but Glick was far too distracted to care. He had the girl of his dreams back and would never let anything stop him ever again. Glick plopped onto the lumpy, makeshift mattress and pulled Toni down on top of him.

"Come here, baby," he growled. "Oh, God, I've missed you." He rolled on top of her small frame and stroked her hair back while looking deep into her eyes. "I didn't think you would come back."

"Well, I…"

He covered her mouth with his and gave her a long, silky kiss; gliding his face over he gently bit her earlobes and dug deep into her neck with his hungry mouth, his scruffy beard lightly scratching her nape. Toni groaned with ecstasy and wrapped her legs around his bulky loins. She placed her hands behind the scruff of his neck and grabbed his thick hair. He peeled off her shirt effortlessly and tore her bra into two pieces with a quick twist. He then greedily stripped off her jeans and feasted his eyes on her naked form. Toni arched her back and allowed Glick to devour her with endless kisses from head to toe.

Ten-thirty came and went, with no thought of returning to the compound. When the dawn's early light peeked through the flaps of the tent, the pair was still nestled in a loving embrace. They hadn't slept a wink all night.

Glick ran his fingers over the curve of her hips and brushed his lips against her damp inner thigh, inhaling her aroma.

Toni sighed. She hadn't been made love to like this her entire life. Who knew this coarse brute could be such a masterful lover? He fondled her breast and wrapped his tongue around her nipple, igniting a feverish passion in her once again. She had never before experienced this kind of carnal desire for anyone. *Is it chemistry? Is it loneliness? What is it?*

She clung to Glick's torso and licked his salty, tattooed shoulder. She knew she would have to leave soon. Or would she? Toni feared she was falling in love with this muscular untamed beast. As for Glick, it was already far too late. He had fallen in love with Toni the minute he laid eyes on her.

"What am I going to do with you?" she asked her new treasure while running her fingers through his long, greasy hair and stroking his unkempt beard.

"I dunno," he replied.

"Just love you, I guess." *When you least expect it, what you least expect.*

"You love me?"

Toni blushed despite herself and whispered, "Yes, I do. I can't help it."

"I love you too, woman, more than anything in the world." He sat up and placed his sturdy hands around Toni's waist, lifting her onto his lap. He pulled her close, crushing her to him and rocked back and forth. "Let's get married."

"I think we would need our own tent."

"Oh, shit!" he exclaimed. "I forgot all about Jimbo." Glick crawled on his knees and peeked outside the tent. Jimbo and Amy were asleep on the hard ground next to their children's tent about 20 feet away.

"Whew!" He fell back onto the mattress. "I think you're right. We would need our own tent."

Toni crept up and lay on top of Glick's bare body. "That was pretty rude of us, wasn't it?" She giggled.

"Oh, piss on it. You know how many times they've kicked me out? Plenty. I've slept on the ground more times than I can count."

"It just made you all the tougher." She teased and tormented Glick first by nibbling his ear and then stroking his enormous frame with both her hands; he grunted with pleasure as he, in turn, explored every crevice of her body with his rough fingertips. Overcome with arousal, he eagerly spun Toni onto her back and in a heated frenzy of aching desire, drove her to heights of passion she never knew existed.

Chapter *34*

Off to the Labs

"I think the best way for you to fully understand all the capabilities of the microchip is to see them for yourself." Hidden Village founder Peter Keller spoke to Curt Ludington and his wife, the former Ohio governor and senator, Marlene Carson, while seated in the cafeteria sipping an after-lunch cup of tea. "Has either of you actually seen one of these devices yet, up close?" he queried.

"No. I haven't. How about you, honey?" Curt asked Marlene.

"No. Neither of us has seen one, outside the body if that's what you mean," she said. "I've seen plenty of people who had theirs inserted already."

"And how did those people appear to you?" co-founder Eldon Tauer asked.

"They seemed like people," she shrugged, "just like normal people."

"Have you ever seen anyone try to take theirs out?"

"No, I can't say I have."

"It's a shocker – quite literally."

"What?" Curt questioned.

"Stop teasing them, Eldon," Keller interjected. "We'll give them a firsthand look now." He stood and headed toward the exit. "Well, are you coming or not?"

"Yes!" Marlene stood now, quite excited. "Where are we going?"

"To the labs." Curt and Marlene looked at each other with expectant smiles.

The group stepped out into the brisk air and returned to the waiting golf cart. They traveled up the dirt road toward yet another new area, a new series of Quonset huts that appeared to be heavily protected. They approached a guarded gate, and when the guards saw it was Keller at the wheel, they opened the gate for them to pass. The men nodded at the guards as they went through into the middle of the huts, where they came to a stop.

Keller turned to Marlene and Curt, who were sitting in the back. "This area houses our microchip research center and our laboratories." They all got out of the cart and walked up to yet another pair of guards; flashing their badges, Keller and Tauer were admitted inside with their guests.

Keller spoke as they entered the clinical environment and walked down the hall. "Every day, as you know, hundreds of people come here to establish new residence. Many of these people have already been microchipped and are here because they either want it taken out or they have been persuaded by family, friends or their church to have it removed. Do you recall we said that once the chip is in, the resolve to remove it diminishes?"

"Yes."

"Well, there is a reason for that." They stopped in front of a set of swinging doors. "The chip is sending signals to the brain telling it that the person is happy and content." Marlene and Curt glanced warily at each other as they stepped inside.

"Here is where we address the issue of the microchip firsthand," Keller gestured toward a few people working, their faces covered with surgical masks. A young man was lying on a gurney covered in paper. He appeared to be nervous.

"Please put these on," Tauer interrupted, handing out five surgical masks. "We need to maintain sterile conditions."

"This really is a very minor procedure," Keller continued, "but we like to give the patient light sedation first, and we must also neutralize the chip prior to its removal. Once that's been done, we simply cut it out, a couple of stitches, and he's good to go."

Marlene and Curt watched in fascination as the team worked quickly, first administering a cocktail injection of fentanyl and diazepam until the young man faded into a light sleep. Then they took a scanner to precisely locate the microchip and sterilized the area with an iodine solution. One technician then picked up a scalpel and made a slight incision just under the groggy youth's skin, exposing the tiny, rice-shaped attachment for all to see.

"See," Keller urged them closer to get a better look, "there it is: a single integrated circuit, often known as a microchip. Because the anti-migration sheath on the implant bonds with subcutaneous tissue, the flesh must be cut away from the implant in order to remove it. Occasionally, the chip does migrate, though. That usually makes it harder for us to remove it.

"Now watch this," he said. The team stealthily attached a tiny probe coil from a portable table to the chip and gave it a quick burst of radio waves, countervailing the electromagnetic signature pattern. They then removed the coil, wheeled the gurney to a large, round machine, positioned the semiconscious man's wrist between two plates, stepped back and let the machine do its work. After a few minutes, the process was complete. They returned him to his original spot and finished the procedure, using a scalpel to delicately cut the chip away from the tissue and then gently plucking the microchip from his wrist with a simple set of large tweezers. Giving him a few stitches, the head technician declared the entire job complete, all in less than 20 minutes.

"That was amazing," Curt raved. "What just happened?"

"A couple of things," Keller said. "First, you'll recall I said that the chip needed to be neutralized in order to dismantle the shock wave capacitor. We accomplished that with a simple radio wave burst with the opposite spectrum. After that, we subjected the chip to a super-strong magnetic field of 4700 MHz, making it impossible for the reader to decode its signal. This machine is very similar to the common magnetic resonance imaging machines that one would find in hospitals and imaging centers, but much stronger and able to pinpoint a tiny area with incredible accuracy."

Tauer spoke up. "The powers that be have long struggled with ways to make these chips withstand strong magnetic fields, such as the types produced by nuclear magnetic resonance spectroscopy or MRIs. They did finally accomplish that feat, but our technology is able to dismantle any and all microchips in existence today, including simple RFID chips."

"What is an RFID chip?"

"The acronym RFID stands for Radio Frequency Identification. The technology was first used by manufacturers to convey information to retailers and keep track of shipping and inventory on their products in the late 1990's. Over the years they developed into tracking humans; and while they have certainly evolved, they are still much less sophisticated than the chips that are inserted into humans today.

"Beginning several decades ago, manufactures began embedding them in ordinary consumer items such as clothing, warehouse pallets and packaging on many items. And like the name says, they just use simple radio waves to transmit the data." Tauer explained, adding ominously that the waves can travel through just about any material.

"RFID chips could be considered the grandfather of today's microchip. They're definitely its predecessor, and if previous generations had recognized the insidious scourge they represented and done something to stop their widespread use, we might not be in the mess we're in today. RFID technology is used in many forms – everyday items that you buy daily, such as shampoo, toilet paper, office supplies, furniture, food, books, tires, medicine bottles, light bulbs, bedding and, of course, electronics. It can be incorporated into fabric fibers, plastics, metals, wires, paper, paint ... almost anything."

"How's that?" Curt asked.

"Because the integrated circuit chips are so tiny - about 1/64th the size of a grain of salt; and each has its own individual identification number." Tauer went to a closet and retrieved several items, which he laid out on top of a table. He held one up to show Curt and Marlene.

"There are two types of RFID tags – passive and active. This one is an active RFID tag, so known because it has more components than just the IC chip. As you can see, it also has an antenna and battery. There are three parts to this kind of tag – the chip, antenna and battery. The antenna takes up the most space, and usually is a level metallic whorl that extends around the chip." He ran his finger around the perimeter of the tag. "The larger the antenna, the greater the range, but for consumer goods on average they run about the size of a small paper clip. Some even have metallic Nano-fiber paint that functions as an antenna that can simply be printed on paper, and some are equipped with biodegradable batteries."

"I've seen these things before," Curt said. "That's just an anti-theft device."

"No," Tauer corrected. "It resembles one but they are very different. This is an RFID tag with its own unique number assigned to it. It uses radio waves such as marine or aircraft communications operate on. Plus it doesn't need a reader because it is an active tag - with its own battery - it can broadcast data with much, much further range than a passive tag."

Tauer set down the active tag, then picked up a sealed petri dish containing a clear liquid. He shook it and held it up to the light for the couple to see. Thousands of dust sized black flecks floated inside. "Inside this are 15,000 IC chips," he said as he passed the dish to Marlene.

"Wow!" Curt exclaimed, "you can barely see them, they are so small."

"Yes, the IC chips are incredibly small and inconspicuous. These chips can store 38-digit numbers using 128-bit ROM. Now that you see just how miniscule the chips are you can understand how easily the tags can be hidden inside almost anything; from the hat on the top your head to your underwear or even the soles of your shoes."

"My shoes?" Curt looked down at his feet. "My underwear?"

"That's right," Tauer answered. "Every time you step within range of an RFID reader, the tags can be detected and their information extracted by anybody who has a reader in that RF range all unbeknownst to you," he explained. "But a passive RFID tag needs an RFID reader in order to transmit information to a database." Tauer placed the dish down and picked up a hand-held device with buttons and a small screen.

"This is a hand-held RFID reader. It would have a range of about six feet to pick up the signal on this little passive tag. When the RFID tag gets within range of the reader, the tags antenna sends its unique identification number. The reader then captures this information and sends it to a data bank for processing. One reader can communicate with multitudes of passive tags."

"And you say that these are used to track people?" Marlene stiffly quizzed Tauer. "Who in their right mind would want to walk around all day pointing a reader with just six foot range?"

"But this handheld reader isn't the only type of reader. Like their tag counterparts, readers have become so small they can also barely be seen. Now they are hidden in store displays, public buildings, woven into carpet, embedded in ceiling tiles, incorporated into shelving, homes, sports arenas, shopping malls, bathrooms and even public spaces like parks with their composite benches, they even put it in flooring to tell where you are walking. They simply place the readers in key locations, and you never know that you have been probed. RFIDs incognito characteristics have enabled it to easily blend into our lives.

Your every move has been tracked for decades by the prying eyes of corporations and governments through the ordinary objects in your possession such as your cell phone, your key fob, your watch, your jewelry, your purse or your wallet; and you likely never had a clue about it. They use the chips to evaluate your status, age, sex, purchasing preferences and more.

"School children's and government uniform providers sew RFID tracking tags into the uniforms to keep an eye on the wearer revealing where they have been and who they have been associating with.

"The U.S Postal Service embeds every U.S. Postage Stamp with an RFID chip and back in the days of cash our own U.S Currency and International banknotes were embedded with RFID chips.

"The Dept. of Transportation has long subsidized RFID technology, going as far as creating an exclusive radio band for surveillance systems that extract information from vehicles as they drive past pole mounted readers. The Federal Highway Administration some years ago required that every car manufactured in the U.S. is microchipped at the factory complete with global positioning satellite receiver that can identify any cars exact location. Automatic Vehicle Identification stations are now placed along the road monitoring your vehicles speed, direction and the date and times that you travelled. Toll booths have them as well. RFID enabled license plates, registrations and inspection stickers also monitor our travels.

"When the U.S. public resisted a National ID card, our government simply RFID chipped our Drivers Licenses and passports, so you really wound up with a National ID card whether you wanted one or not. Big Brothers gone wild.

"Retailers and marketers are of course thrilled. With RFID technology they are able to evaluate a household's income level, habits and purchases. RFID enabled refrigerators might record your eating habits and report to marketers what kind of goods are inside. When it is time to restock, a coupon might be sent in the mail or a targeted commercial may play on TV just for you. Or perhaps your RFID enabled fridge may make a recommendation for you; warning you about expiring milk or even compose a weekly shopping lists for you.

"Medicine cabinets may talk to your insurance company, doctor or government official and report your meds usage. Then there is the matter of the garbage that you throw away every day, RFID readers are placed inside garbage cans and garbage trucks. The marketer collects the data on your trash and then sells it on the open market.

"Have you frequented a drugstore and used a loyalty card that offers you 'rewards' for shopping with them? Well guess what? You just gave them some good information they could use. Health officials track our prescription drug use and attorneys can subpoena your home activity records for use against you in court. Have your health insurance premiums gone through the roof lately? Perhaps your insurance company monitored your consumption of alcohol, junk food and cigarettes and set rates accordingly."

"Hold on a second," Marlene interjected. "It sounds like you are saying that every inanimate object on the planet can have or already does have an RFID chip in it somewhere. How can that be? Wouldn't we run out of identification numbers?"

"One would think so, but guess again. The plan started back in October 1999 with the formation of the MIT Auto ID Center. They came up with the original concept of putting low-cost RFID tags on every manmade object as an addition to the existing bar code numbering system and linking them to data stored in Internet databases. The Auto-ID Center's director, coined the term the 'Internet of Things' a unified network that connects people, things and services.

"To make this work, each object would have to have its very own exclusive identification number; considering the near infinite number of objects on the earth, the numbering system would also have to near infinite potential to match up to each item. A 96-bit code was created, enough to uniquely number 80 thousand trillion, trillion objects. With this system, you could number every single grain of sand, aspirin, animal or person on the planet. An exclusive data file can be created on each item that can store virtually unlimited amounts of information about it. That is how today human micro-chipping works. Also; not only are there huge amounts of data stored in the microchip itself, but the chip transmits to giant databases in the Internet cloud that have the ability to store unlimited amounts of information on you."

Marlene considered this information and remarked, "I can see huge potential for abuse."

"You have no idea. Not just marketers and government agents have access to our information but also criminals. RFID gives thieves a huge advantage to scope out valuables and identify easy marks. They can easily identify what is inside your shopping bag, car or house. More sophisticated criminal activities might include hacking, jamming, sabotage, eavesdropping or even terrorism. There is also a large threat of peeping Toms, perverts and stalkers using RFID to harass and intimidate their victims."

"With all these drawbacks, I am truly amazed that the public accepted it so readily."

"Never underestimate the power of convenience. Arguments in support of RFID include faster checkout, educational benefits, consumer safety, quick access to diagnostic tests and other information, theft prevention, improved planning and forecasting, shaved labor cost and improved productivity; all resulting in greater profits!"

"It was quite a massive jump from chipping bottles of aspirin to human beings." Curt remarked.

"Yes, but slow and steady the course. Once RFID was allowed to slowly infiltrate our lives and began showing up everywhere, it became accepted as the norm. First came RFID-microchipped inanimate objects, then came microchipped pets and livestock, then prisoners, then military and security personnel; then immigrants, then came the voluntary chipping programs, then a national RFID medical device registry tied to healthcare, then schoolchildren in the classroom, then government workers, then newborn babies; and then, finally, as a show of absolute dominance and control, the general public. They slipped RFID in, and once it was there firmly entrenched into society, the people felt powerless to fight against it. Hell, we grew up with it!

"It was a series of small steps designed give us a sense of security while whittling away at our rights and freedoms until one day, we woke up with no freedoms left to fight for. If the generations that preceded ours had the guts to demand liberty, we wouldn't be in the boat we are in today. Now we find ourselves completely and utterly under their control.

"They could just as easily have microchipped only infants and waited for the older, un-microchipped generations to die off; there would have been little protest from the microchipped masses because they'd had it from the time they were born. But no! They wanted to show their complete and total dominance! This was a psychological ploy to show just who has the upper hand! Anyone who refuses to submit to their suppression dies!"

Keller resumed: "The Bible provided ample warnings about these times, when governments begin talking about safety and protection. It cautions us in Thessalonians 5:2 *For yourselves know perfectly that the day of the Lord so cometh as a thief in the night. For when they shall say, peace and safety, then sudden destruction cometh upon them ... and they shall not escape."*

"Yes, thank you." Marlene quipped. "We just had a similar lecture regarding liberties from Augustus Plimpton. I'd really prefer not to go into it again. If Curt and I weren't proponents of freedom and independence, we would not be here today and I would still hold my position in the Senate."

"Understood, Ms. Carson."

"You said earlier that the chip was sending a 'be happy' signal to the brain," Curt interjected. "How is that possible?"

"Through transcranial magnetic stimulation. Inaudible to the human ear, electromagnetic pulsation frequencies target specific brain circuit areas. This is why they want the microchip inserted as close to the brain as possible.

"With electromagnetic frequency brain stimulation, a land-based operator sends coded signals to the brain. They can stimulate your brain and manipulate you, without you ever knowing that you are being controlled. They can produce anxiety, fear, sleep disruptions or emotional manipulations. They could also administer punishment in the event of mass protests by causing painful cramps, ringing in the ears, headaches, loss of vision and loss of motor skills, and so forth.

Marlene cleared her throat. "With all due respect, sir, we admire the work you're doing here, but ... you couldn't possibly expect us to believe that a simple data chip is going to control our moods and our physical well-being. I just find that entirely too preposterous."

"Oh, it's far simpler than you could ever imagine. Our bodies are made up almost entirely of water and electromagnetic charges. This work has been going on for far longer than you realize.

"They originally used Ground Wave Emergency Network towers, an array of radio transceivers operating in the VLF radio band to inundate us with subliminal messages while we slept. Then they expanded to Milstar SCAMP terminals; now they use towers and digital signals operating in the 4-8 Hz frequency. It's called Silent Sound Spread Spectrum.

"The towers create a 360-degree radius of low frequencies, generally in the ranges of 4.26 hertz, 8.33 hertz, 217 hertz and 1.73 KHz."

"Now, of all the ranges on the electromagnetic spectrum they specifically chose these ones. Why do you suppose that is the case?"

"I don't know." Curt said. "Why?"

"Because they operate in the same electroencephalographic frequency as the brain wave state known as theta. Theta is the frequency of 4-8.5 Hz, which is the drowsy minds first stage of sleep.

"This is one of the brain's most powerful states – the one that hypnotists attempt to reach when putting someone into hypnotic induction. When a person is in his theta brain wave state, he is at his most susceptible time to suggestion. It's abundantly easy to control us when we're bathed in an artificial electromagnetic wave. Sound waves are incredibly powerful – quite probably the most powerful force on the planet."

Marlene shook her head. "No, I don't see how this possibly can be."

"Mrs. Carson. We have been researching this for many years. Ours is a highly skilled team of cognitive scientists and medical professionals. including electrophysiologists, nano-technology and genomic experts, neurobiologists and some of the world's leading authorities in synthetic biology, germ line engineering, stem cell research, genetic enhancement, cybernetics and artificial intelligence. We have completed some of the most comprehensive analyses ever done on brain mapping and brain wave therapy determining how the brain processes information.

"What kind of signals are they sending?" Curt asked.

"Oh, it varies from time to time. Usually obedience, duty, submission, powerlessness, forgetfulness, work harder, be practical – that sort of thing. There truly is an ongoing battle for your mind.

"Lately, due to the new introduction of the microchip, they have been sending a strong pleasure signal at 38 Hz, but they can just as easily revert to sending fear or anger at 10.80 Hz or depression at 6.6 Hz. Original thinking is also quite discouraged. I hope by now you're getting an idea of just how easy it is to control an entire society through their thought processes?"

"I get it all too well," Curt replied.

Eldon Tauer stepped forward and interjected. "I think we need to point out that towers aren't really needed at all. They are quite prolific and offer a concentrated and direct line of sight, which is very good for accurately pinpointing targeted individuals or organizations, but there are other ways they can achieve the same results without using them."

"Oh?" Marlene asked.

"Yes, absolutely." Another way is to bounce a high directional signal off the ionosphere. With this they can affect entire cities or a general widespread area, but it's very dangerous."

"Really? And how does one bounce a signal off the ionosphere?"

"Have you ever heard of an ionospheric super heater?" Keller asked.

"An ionospheric super heater? I've never heard of such a thing," Curt proclaimed as he and Marlene took seats on hard plastic chairs.

"Yes, everyone in the world should be made aware of their existence and the dangers that they potentially hold. Have you ever heard of the High Frequency Active Auroral Research Program? Otherwise known as HAARP?"

"No," said Curt.

"Wait a minute." Marlene uttered. "That's in Alaska, right?"

"Yes, it is."

"It's a bunch of radio antennae, right?"

"Transmitters yes, as far as the eye can see, at an Air Force-owned site in Gakona, Alaska. Ionospheric research instruments, they call them. They operate in the high frequency range."

"I'm vaguely familiar with it. They are studying the aurora borealis, from what I understand. So what?"

"Hardly," Keller replied cynically. "That remark illustrates just how uninformed the public is on the matter of ionosphere heaters and gigawatt probes. HAARP is just one of nine of these research facilities set up worldwide, several of which are located in the former Soviet Union. HAARP is the largest of them all.

"HAARP is a military project jointly financed by the U.S. Air Force, the U.S. Navy, and D.A.R.P.A. Its stated purpose is to analyze the ionosphere and enhance technology for radio communications and surveillance purposes such as missile detection. We, however, believe it to be much more than that, and quite possibly the most abhorrent doomsday device the world has ever seen."

Marlene suppressed a snicker that Keller did not miss. He continued on.

"Truth is, Ms. Carson, the government-owned patents related to HAARP mind control, weather modification, information gathering, tectonic earthquake-producing weaponry and natural phenomenon manipulation are a matter of public record and very easily accessible to anyone willing to take the time to do the research, I suggest you do yours.

"HAARP's other uses for the Pentagon include over-the-horizon radar applications, determining the nature of payloads on incoming craft to locate those carrying nuclear warheads, deep space radio surveys, scrambling enemy radar systems, disrupting microwave transmissions of enemy satellites and enemy communications systems, earth-penetrating tomography and, lastly, charging particles in the Earth's geomagnetic field, producing a shield to deflect enemy warheads. That is the good news.

"The bad news is the methodology used to create these effects. HAARP focuses a radio frequency beam of enormous intensity, emitting millions of gigawatts at the Earth's ionosphere, interacting powerfully with the charged particles that exist there. They call it 'exciting' the ionosphere, but what they are doing amounts to *boiling* the Earth's atmosphere. The heating effect of the focused beam not only pushes a plume of a large section of the ionosphere up and outward from Earth but also produces holes and incisions in our delicately balanced ionosphere.

"Our ionosphere works in conjunction with the ozone layer to protect the Earth from the constant bombardment of gamma rays, X-rays and shorter wavelengths of ultraviolet light from space. Without them, our atmosphere would be like that of Mars – no oxygen, no water, no life, nothing.

"HAARP zaps a concentrated beam of focused energy into an extremely delicate molecular configuration similar to a soap bubble-like sphere surrounding the Earth. If you've ever watched a large bubble closely, you will see rainbow-like movement swirling over its surface. Then you see a black spot where the wavelengths of light are so short they can't show the bubble, but it hasn't burst yet. Then a hole forms, and suddenly it pops! Our ionosphere is subject to these types of catalytic reactions. If one small part is altered, a major change could be the result.

"The potential for disaster is obviously here. HAARP could easily do irreparable harm to the Earth's atmosphere, threatening our very existence. Mars once had an atmosphere, and lost it. Our own Earth could eventually heal itself after a nuclear holocaust, but once the Earth's atmosphere is gone, it will never return. The potential for any life on Earth would be nonexistent. This is why we think it is the most serious threat to all life on the planet, and it needs to be stopped!

"We don't need to be punching holes in our atmosphere. It reminds me of a bunch of punk kids trying to wake up a sleeping bear by poking it with a sharp stick. The public needs to call for a moratorium on the use of super-powerful ionosphere heaters until independent scientists and other non-military decision-makers can determine the just what outcome these experiments can have for the planet. The long-term survival of the human race depends upon us retaining our precious atmosphere. Perhaps you can help us, Marlene? You have strong political connections. We need all the help we can get."

"I agree," she nodded. "It sounds like a very serious threat."

As long as Marlene could remember, there had always been some sort of threat to the delicate balances of power. The menace of nuclear war always loomed overhead, with the lives of billions hinging on the mere press of a little red button. *How fragile we are.*

Keller continued. "Electronic weapons, psychotronic weapons, information weapons, high-altitude ultra-low frequency weapons, scalar weapons, plasma weapons, electromagnetic weapons, sonic and ultrasonic weapons, laser weapons, chemical, biological and environmental weapons, climate weapons, tectonic weapons, nuclear weapons! When are we going to say enough is enough?? Do we really need this?"

Marlene thought about this a moment. "Mr. Keller, we must have a strong military to ..."

Keller interrupted: "If we are all up to our necks in a vat of gasoline, do you feel any safer because you have two matches and I only have one?"

"May I please finish my sentence, Mr. Keller? We simply must safeguard ourselves from fanatical cultures that would seek to destroy our country. There are entire societies out there that hate everything to do with the West and would stop at nothing to see us wiped off the planet.

"You think we really need to protect ourselves from a fringe group of obsessed primitives?" Keller retorted. "Where on the news are they showing the faces of the denizens that only want to live in peace? Do they show harmonious foreign families living out their day-to-day lives? Merchants, professionals, scientists, farmers – do we see any of these? No. They don't want you to think of them as human beings like ourselves. They only want you to think of them as 'the enemy.' It keeps the war machine in perpetual motion. Here we go again ... Korea, Vietnam, Iraq, Afghanistan, Iran, China, Russia, Pakistan ... do we see a pattern here? Give the people a group to hate, and they'll give you their all.

"Once we realize we are all one human unit and refuse to participate in government-sponsored war and hatred, we will remove ourselves from the shackles of fear of destruction from a nonexistent enemy!"

Marlene rubbed her eyes. "This theoretical discussion is giving me a headache, Mr. Keller. Can we move on to more practical subject matter, please?"

"Boys will be boys, and they want to play with their toys."

"Mr. Keller, please! I'm not sure just what kind of clout you think I have, but I can assure you there isn't a whole lot I can do regarding our government's military applications and the state of affairs on this planet. I am just one person! I can certainly sympathize with your cause, however. If everyone were like you, we would be living in a utopian world."

"We need to raise the consciousness of this planet."

"Yes, I agree, we do."

"Will you propose legislation to shut down the ionosphere heaters?"

"I'm no longer in office, Mr. Keller, but I will certainly put the word out. I agree the public needs to be made aware of them. I give you my word: I will talk to some very powerful people about it."

"That is fine, Ms. Carson. Thank you." Keller seemed satisfied.

"You may call me Marlene."

"And please, call me Peter."

"And you may call me Ludington," Curt tossed in. The group laughed.

Marlene sat quiet a moment. "The public has absolutely no idea that their thoughts are being artificially manipulated. This is truly an outrage."

"I'm afraid it goes deeper Ms. Carson," Keller said.

"Oh?" Marlene wasn't sure she was prepared to hear exactly what was deeper.

"Each of us has a unique bioelectrical resonance frequency in the brain, just as we have unique fingerprints. These chips are contributing to your own unique resonance disappearing and being replaced with a global collective intelligence system or a 'hive mind' where everyone has the exact same brain wave pattern and thinks the same thoughts and shares the same information with each other, on a global scale!"

"What?"

"Yes. They call it 'machine integration enhancement.' They use predictive programming to create a global collective intelligence system that will merge our biological bodies with machine intelligence – not just free-standing machines but nano-robots built into our bodies, making our brains machine-readable and interfaced with artificial neural networks."

"That sounds creepy," Marlene observed.

"You think so? We do, too," Keller affirmed. "But don't think that the technology isn't without its pluses. The non-biological portion of our intelligence can be billions of times more powerful than unaided human intelligence. Select groups can be enhanced with brain computer interfaces and trained to be more creative and vastly more intelligent. They can share thoughts and information freely without having to study the subject matter, expand memory and sharpen concentration."

"So that is a *good* thing?" Marlene asked inquisitively.

"Remember, I said *select* groups can be enhanced with brain prostheses? For these groups, it places a new means of control in the hands of totalitarian, transhumanist regimes."

"For those outside the select groups, however," Tauer interjected "it is not so pretty."

"True," Keller continued, "but imagine if your body never had to sleep or exercise, had millions of times more thinking power and energy, could photosynthesize its own food, heal wounds immediately, not feel pain or could live to be thousands of years old ... living super-minds, immensely more powerful than ordinary human beings. Super soldiers with super vision, hearing and strength, super rulers vastly more intelligent ..."

"Where on earth are we going to put all these people?"

"Only the very super elite and wealthy will have access to the good benefits; the rest, I'm afraid, will be destined for short, meaningless lives of servitude. With the patenting of these new life forms, groups can be segregated and controlled by patent holders of specific genes related to the genetic makeup of certain groupings of people. They could then withhold medicines or other life-supporting systems designed solely for that genetic group."

"That is the ultimate goal, you realize, don't you?" Tauer jumped in. "Transhuman eugenics – a ruling class with eternal youth, beauty and enhanced human capabilities and a slave class of non-thinking automatons living essentially in work camps.

He added. "An ideal slave class would be able to work 20 hours per day without rest, and they would be sterile, with no need to care for children. They would be even-tempered and docile, expressing a limited range of emotions. They no longer would struggle, love, aspire, make difficult moral choices, have families or show any other of the characteristics that give us human dignity because, for one thing, they do not know that they are being dehumanized. And worse, they would not care even if they did know – happy little slaves in a happy trance."

"Oh that's horrendous!" Marlene shook her head.

These are the poor bastards that will have their thoughts and minds controlled." Tauer stated, crossing his arms.

"Through the microchip?"

"Yes, through the microchip and synthetic biology. Just as computer code is written to create software, genetic code is now written to create life forms and augment civilization."

"This is amazing!" Curt exclaimed. "And terrible."

"I'm afraid it gets much, much worse, Mr. Ludington" Keller declared. Curt and Marlene looked at each other with dread.

"The merging of human biological matter with nano-sized transistors and germ line alterations have created living, implantable machines that influence and control brain and nerve cell function. These are actual DNA robot molecules 100,000 times smaller than the diameter of a human hair. They can migrate, turn, replicate and even create tiny products of their own on a nano-scale assembly line within your body."

The couple were left speechless at this bit of news.

"It's true." Keller pulled a tiny, rice-shaped implantable chip out of his top pocket and held it up for all to see. "The microchips are not only transmitters but bioengineered constructs that fuse man's original genome with synthetic DNA that initiates intracellular changes, not only in somatic body cells but also in germ line cells such as ova and sperm. The former alters the recipient only; the latter alters the recipient's descendants as well."

Curt gasped. "How does it work?" he asked warily.

"You recall our discussion about the use of viruses as vectors to transmit and insert animal and plant genes from one species to another, creating new DNA in foods and the dangers associated with such?"

"Yes."

"It's the same principle. The elitist class with their staff of genetic mad scientists has utilized microbiological nano-vectors to accomplish their genetic splicing. The vectors provide the means of transport and integration. Think of these vectors as biological trucks that carry genetic building materials and workers to your body's cells. Such trucks could be a microsyringe, a bacterium or a virus particle. Any entity that can carry genetic information and then gain entry into the cell is a potential vector. Viruses, for example, can be stripped of certain innate genes that might harm the cell. Not only does this supposedly render the viral delivery truck 'harmless,' it also clears out space for cargo.

"Once inside the cell, the workers take over. Some of these 'workers' are nano-robots that cut human genes at specific sites, while others integrate, or load, the 'cargo' into appropriate reading frames. Once the payload is stored in the cells' nuclear stacks, the new genes can be translated, copied and read to produce altered or brand new, alien polymers and proteins. They move along a track comprising stitched-together strands of DNA's double-helix molecule. By using strands that correspond to sequences in the track, the robot can be made to walk, turn left, up or down. The robot's 'body' is a common protein called streptavidin. Attached to it are three 'legs' of single-strand enzymatic DNA, which binds to, and then cuts, a particular sequence of DNA. The fourth leg is a strand that anchors the robot to the starting point.

"After the robot is released from its start site by a trigger strand, it follows the track by binding to and then cutting the DNA strands. Once the strand is cut, the leg starts reaching for the next matching stretch of DNA in the track. In this way, the spider is guided down the path set by the researchers. Eventually, the robot encounters a patch of DNA to which it can bind but which it cannot cut. At that point, it is immobilized.

"The resulting cell is no longer purely human. Muscle cells may grow larger and more efficient; retina cells may enable the enhanced human to see farther distances or to see infrared or ultraviolet light. Hybrid ears may now sense a wider range of sounds; taste buds harbor a greater range of receptors. If a brain cell, the new genetic instructions could produce an altered neurotransmitter that reduces or even eliminates the need for sleep. If a hybridized skin cell, it may now glow, or perhaps form scales rather than hair or claws rather than fingernails."

"Oh, nonsense!!" Marlene erupted. She turned to her husband Curt and shot him a painful look.

"Hold on, honey," he put his hand on her back. "I'd like to hear them out."

Eldon Tauer cleared his throat and spoke. "Government-sanctioned scientists originally began creating new forms of life by inserting artificial genetic material into cells that were then able to split and duplicate, creating the world's first synthetic genome. Genetic restructuring and tissue engineering are directly modifying the organic brain that God created us with, remanufacturing man with animals, plants and other synthetic life forms."

"Is this that business with the glow-in-the-dark cats?" Curt asked.

"Yes," Keller replied. "Recombinant DNA technology, germ line engineering and transgenic technologies are altering our species by transferring one set of genes to another, creating new biology not found in nature. Germ line genetic engineering has the power to truly reassemble the very nature of humanity into post-human by altering an embryo's cell structure. This extends to all succeeding generations, reworking the physical nature of mankind with no hope of reversal. Soon, the human species will no longer be recognizable as itself."

"They have been trying to accomplish this for decades. We have already been subjected to bioengineered attacks through spraying programs that dispense conductive, self - replicating, nano-fiber filaments that do not exist in nature. But they couldn't trick the body's immune system to keep it from attacking the fibers. As soon as any foreign object slips into the human body, our immune system kicks into high gear.

"Everything that is native to a body is essentially key-coded with a biological pass that tells any immune response that it's OK to be there. If something inside isn't properly coded, then a rapid kill response is launched which then attacks the surface of unrecognized cells with a variety of binding proteins.

"This natural response is something that took many years to overcome. They have now discovered how the biochemistry of the interactions between nano-particles and our tissues functions, and use this to allow the nano-bots to stay operative while surfing in the bloodstream."

Curt and Marlene sat silent for a moment. "*Why* are they doing this?"

"This is the greatest deception of all by Satan; the corruption of God's most perfect creation - man, and turn him into something completely unrecognizable, something akin to the devil himself. This is why God is so vehemently opposed to the mark of the beast and will not allow anyone who takes it to enter into his holy kingdom. The bible clearly states it is forbidden to do so.

Marlene shook her head and mumbled something.

"What's that, honey?" Curt touched her arm.

"I think I need a little break, Curt. Can we get a spot of that tea, please, Peter?"

"Of course, Marlene." Peter gestured to one of the lab assistants. "Would you please get Ms. Carson a cup of tea and bring it to the main office? Anything for you, Ludington?"

"Uhm. A Tanqueray and tonic, extra lime."

"Tea for Mr. Ludington also, please."

"Black tea, please," Marlene said. "No cream or sugar. We're going back to the office now?"

"I think it's time," Keller replied sympathetically noting Marlene's exhausted appearance.

"I suppose one can know too much," Curt said while walking outside to the waiting cart.

"Yes, but we must be as wise as serpents and as gentle as lambs at all times, always keeping our eyes and ears open. The day of the Lord is upon us."

"It would appear so." Marlene agreed.

The group drove in silence back to the main office, where Curt resumed his favorite position by the fireplace. Soon the lab assistant arrived with lukewarm cups of black tea for Marlene and Curt. He placed his on the mantle, where it remained untouched. Keller and Tauer retired to the makeshift boardroom, and Marlene sat in a recliner comfortably for some time, undisturbed, quietly sipping her tea and contemplating the events of the day. Finally, she looked up at her husband and spoke.

"Curt. We have to do something." He sat on the arm of the recliner and held her hand, put his other arm around her and kissed her forehead.

"I know," he said softly.

The couple rose and knocked on the boardroom door. They entered without waiting for a reply. Keller, Taylor and Gov. McAllen, Pastor Bloom and Joel Brandenburg were seated at the fold-up table and chairs. They welcomed them in.

"We're very close to making a decision," Marlene announced as she and Curt unfolded a pair of chairs and sat down with the rest. "I think we are going to stay."

"Oh that's wonderful," Keller beamed. "I thought you might, given the circumstances."

"Is there anything we can do to help? Is there anything that can be done to offset the effects of the chip?"

"We are trying enormously hard, not just to offset them but render the DNA nanobots inert. Once you are fully settled in, we will open up to you some more information about our sabotage efforts," Keller promised her. "We have friends on the inside who have infiltrated the ranks of the enemy and work inside their own labs. They are doing the best they can, but it is very difficult. Our adversary has grown extremely powerful."

"I've been thinking about what was said in regards to those bioengineered DNA nanobots."

"Yes?"

"Why haven't we seen any mutations in the general public from them?"

"That's a very good observation, Marlene. Not all vectors deliver their payload immediately, and the foremost virus vector that they are using operates on a time delay. It's a cytomegalovirus, and it is a common infective agent that was already present in the cells of most humans today. This CMV vector 'sleeps' in our system, so to speak, until the catalyst that readies it for activation arrives."

"Which would be what?"

"It could be from a buildup of particular proteins or molecules introduced into the food chain or the water supply Keller speculated. "It could be any number of things. Remember, they have segregated the populace into particular groupings based upon genetics, intellect and predispositions. They are not using the same vectors for everyone. Some are receiving benefits and others are receiving detriments. Some are getting delayed vectors, some control groups aren't getting any vectors, and some are getting instantaneous vectors.

Many physical changes you will not see on the outside at all. With all the changes going on inside, it's all one great big experiment, but there is one common denominator throughout ... "

"What?"

"Everyone receives a chip. No matter what their station in life, everyone gets one, from the president to the trash man."

"So we can expect to start seeing changes then?" Marlene asked.

"Oh, there are already many intracellular changes going on inside, Marlene. We just don't see them on the outside yet."

Marlene blanched, and her hand jumped to her mouth in reflex. "What kind of changes will we see?" she asked.

"Now there's one for you. Our own scientists are trying to crack the genomic sequences as we speak. But I can tell you this: We are starting to find many variations of different genome chains in the various chips, some animal, some plant, some synthetic, some are unknown."

"Oh my God!"

"We periodically send operatives out into the public to observe and take notes of any evident alterations."

"What are their findings?"

"Some groups are starting to display behavioral changes. There seems to be mounting intensification of anti-China sentiment right now in the general public, clearly a programmed response and a precursor to a possible conflict in the near future – but not too dramatic, not yet."

"What can we do?"

"An educational campaign would be helpful. This is why people of influence like you are very welcome here, Ms. Carson – indispensable, really. Knowledge is the light that they would keep from you. It is knowledge that empowers."

"I wonder, would anyone listen? Is it too late?"

"Even if a handful of society's DNA were to remain unsoiled, it would be a tremendous victory for humanity. The last semblance of what we once were, created in God's image, uncorrupted."

"This isn't Gods way," Pastor Bloom added. "God's intentions for us are a world where all resources are free and life is easy, but we are the ones who have chosen to make it difficult on ourselves. We have chosen to go our own way, and we have been deceived into believing that we have no other options – that we must put up with present-day rulers and leaders who are completely devoid of conscience, that we must forever live in a world where killing and suffering continue unabated. But this is simply not true! Believe me, the last thing these devils want is for us to realize just how powerful we really are.

"We pray earnestly for a world where our leaders are true leaders, worthy of their position; where our teachers prepare others to respect all of life; and where people everywhere have taken a stand, firm and strong, for the highest good of all humanity. A world where soldiers and fighters are a thing of the past because everyone has finally seen that fighting and violence have never given them the results they were looking for."

Curt and Marlene gazed at each other and held hands. Marlene felt turned inside out. "What do you say, Curt?"

"I say it's time."

"We would like to establish permanent residence here, Mr. Keller," he said. "We'll need a few days to go back home and collect our belongings. We'll return within the week."

"Congratulations, Curt." Keller leaned over the table and shook Curt's hand while McAllen patted him on the back. "And thank you, Marlene." He shook her hand vigorously. "We are very excited to have you here."

"Thank you for having us," she replied. "I know we haven't been the most pleasant people you've ever worked with."

"Quite all right," Eldon Tauer spoke up. "The end result is worth it. We must all stick together."

"And we intend to do just that," Curt replied.

Chapter 35

A Meeting with the Czar

Winthrop Shaw sat in the courtyard of the Küssnacht Castle in Dresden, Germany, which now served as one of Rothfeller's private offices.

The nerve, Shaw fumed to himself, *making me wait while he fritters away time with a common treasury secretary. We already have everything we need from them. I see no need to further waste time.*

Shaw had already been kept waiting long enough and he stood to leave, but then discretion returned and he sat back down again. When one is called for an audience with the Czar of the Global Union, you don't just get up and leave because it takes too long. To do so would have been an affront and an unspeakable breach of code. So Shaw continued to wait until he was finally called forth to pay his respects to the aging ruler. Once he was in, he greeted the czar warmly with a handshake and a tight smile.

"It's good to see you, Shaw," the czar greeted him. "I must apologize for not attending the celebration on the Suzerain. The arthritis in my hip had me bedridden for three days."

"You're feeling well now, though?" *The damn party was your idea.*

"Oh yes, much better. I've been getting injections of stem cells directly into the joints. It's a painful procedure, but the results are quite dramatic. You should try it."

"I will have to look into that."

"Don't ever get old, Winthrop. It stinks."

"I would imagine so."

Shaw knew that the czar recently had been participating in a progerin suppression project at the Defense Advanced Research Project Agency's Restorative Biomedical Technologies Division, in studies designed to enhance human lifespan through genetic manipulation. The research was already five to 10 years ahead of what most of the elite would ever see, and as far as the proletariat was concerned, they would never have a whisper of a chance of participating. Shaw wondered just how much upgrading Rothfeller had taken already. No matter. The old man was still miles behind Shaw, who had five specialized laboratories devoted full-time entirely to his own trials.

"And even though I feel as fit as a fiddle," Rothfeller continued, "I must still prepare for the inevitable; you Shaw, are destined to carry the torch. You are the driving force that will prevail in these upcoming years and herald our victorious conclusion." Shaw smiled. He was truly proud of what he had achieved so far, and there were even greater achievements to come, ones that this feeble relic could never hope to comprehend.

"Have a seat, Shaw. I have something I'd like to tell you." Shaw took a Klaussner chair and leaned back.

"Cigar?" Rothfeller offered his box, and Shaw took one from the top. He cut off the end and pulled a lighter from his pocket. "Light one for me as well," the czar commanded.

Shaw did as he was told and passed the cigar back to Rothfeller, who put the aromatic Ramon Havana to his wrinkled white lips and licked around its edges. Shaw looked on with distaste.

"I want you to know," Rothfeller croaked, "that I have finalized the paperwork and designated you my primary beneficiary."

"Thank you, sir! Shaw beamed. "I don't quite know wha ..."

"Silence!" Rothfeller shrieked in his frail voice. "Despite the fact that you are not my direct descendant, I have chosen you to be the scion that will inherit the seat of czar upon my demise. You will be the one in charge of all arms of the New World Order, and its officers will report to you directly. I am having a file prepared for you that will give you the information on how to access the accounts along with the passwords, also a directive on how I expect to see my wishes carried out after my passing. I anticipate the file to be finished this week, and then I'm going to hand it all over to you."

Shaw sat silent.

"Winthrop, you may speak now. What do you think?"

"I'm quite pleased, of course."

"Of course," the czar nodded. "I want you to meet me in Brussels next week at the Château du Cloudenberg. I will give you the file then and only in person. This information is too valuable to trust with anyone else. And I want you to be certain that you have heightened security on your trip home from Brussels." Rothfeller tapped his ash into a Tiffany crystal ashtray.

"Very well, I'll make certain."

"Winthrop, I want you to know that you are like a son to me. I have the utmost confidence in your abilities to govern, and I am certain that I have made the right choice."

"Thank you sir. It's an honor and a privilege. Oh, and sir, if I may request one small indulgence?"

"Hmm? Yes?"

"Since you were unable to attend the ceremony, may I have the favor of entertaining you in my own Brussels château instead? I will have Stephano prepare you your favorite cassoulet."

Rothfeller pondered this a moment. "You *do* know the way to my heart, Shaw. I've been thinking of that dish of late, and no one prepares it better. Yes, I will come to yours, and will send notification when I am ready."

Shaw stamped out his cigar and stood up. "Will there be anything else?"

"No Shaw, you are dismissed."

"Good day, then. I will see you next week." Shaw straightened his tie and left.

Chapter *36*

A Real Scare

Glick and Toni Vickery emerged from the tent after several more hours. Amy, Jimbo and the kids were up and cooking some breakfast – hot dogs with tater tots.

"Mmm, healthy," Toni remarked while looking over the frying pan.

"Well, good morning to you, too," Amy said without looking up.

"We haven't seen you around in a long time," Jimbo said. "Where have you been?"

"Not far," she answered, looking up at Glick, who had a shiny new, gratified look on his face.

"It got damn cold last night without a blanket," Amy griped. "Give us a little warning next time, will you?" The bags under her eyes proclaimed her fitful evening.

"Sorry about that," Glick frowned.

"I don't suppose you have something a little lighter to eat than those hot dogs, do you?" Toni asked. "Like maybe some yogurt or something?"

"Yeah, right." Amy laughed as she rolled her red-rimmed eyes. "Every family out here's been eating like this for months now, it seems. If I eat another one, I might hurl."

"It's better than starving to death like we were before, though," Jimbo added.

"Yeah, I'll say," Glick agreed. He popped a whole dog into his mouth and gobbled it up.

"Frankly, I'm worried, guys," Amy continued. "I haven't seen Cassandra in over three weeks now. She used to come by every day and bring us something. The last time she came by, all she brought was some stupid seeds. Kept rambling on about how great they were. I suppose she thinks we're going to start growing green beans or something. We're out of toilet paper, meat, everything."

Toni felt ashamed, both because of her thoughtless question and also the mention of family. The whole purpose of coming out here was to talk to Glick about retrieving Joey, and she hadn't even mentioned his name once the whole night long.

"Glick," Toni asked, "may I talk to you in private for a moment?"

"Sure thing, sugar butt, let's go for a walk." Glick snatched another hot dog off the grill and stuffed it in his pocket. He put his arm around Toni's waist, and they strolled off toward the creek. Once they reached its banks, Glick sprang over a few of the large, flat stones and extended his arm to Toni for some needed assistance. Together they hopscotched through the creek until they found a nice scenic spot, where Toni asked Glick to sit down with her.

"What's on your mind, baby cakes?" Glick pulled the lint-covered hot dog out of his pocket and offered it to Toni. She made a face and shook her head, so he stuffed it into his mouth.

"Glick, dear," she spoke up timidly, "I have a little plight."

Uh-oh, he thought, *here it comes.*

"Do you remember when I told you about my little boy Joey?"

Glick only vaguely remembered but answered, "Uhm-hmm, sure I do."

"I need to go get him. Do you think you could help me?"

Glick beamed. "Hell, yeah, I will!!" *Anything for you.*

"Oh, that's so awesome!" she exclaimed. "We should leave right away. Do you really think you could get me all the way to Florida to get him? Really?"

The actuality of the situation suddenly hit Glick between the eyes. *Holy shit!! Florida?! It took me forever to get from there to here the first time! Oh fuck, what about gas? How am I going to do this?*

"Yeah, baby, it'll be a piece of cake."

"Oh, Glick, you're the best!!" She threw her arms around his neck and gave him the biggest, best hug she had to give. He countered by humping her leg. "Hey, pussycat," he patted the flat rock. "This looks like a great spot to get it on."

"No time for that now. We have prep work to do! I have to get packed. I have to get ready! Can we leave today?"

"Uh, I guess so," he answered, somewhat bewildered. A road trip wasn't really high on his wish list at the moment. "I have some things I'll need to do, too." *Food, gas, clothes*, he compiled a mental list. *Where the hell am I going to put this kid? I hope he's not too big.*

"We can take your motorcycle. It'll be fun! I'm going to go back to the compound and get ready," she said excitedly. "I should be back in under an hour."

"I'm gonna miss you. Don't go getting lost on me."

"Don't worry, silly." Toni glowed with happiness. "I promise I'll be back."

"Don't forget to grab some food. You guys have more than we do, I bet."

"Absolutely."

"And you'll need your toothbrush."

"Of course."

"And a roll of toilet paper."

"OK."

"Toni," Glick paused for a moment "you sure you're up for this? It's a long ride. It won't be comfortable. Your ass will start to hurt after about 500 miles. I don't know if you can take it."

"I'll be fine."

"All right, then," he sighed. "Let's go." Glick led the way back to camp and saw Toni off. Then he sat down for a moment to collect his thoughts.

Phew, this sucks. I wonder if I could get some help from Preach. Glick hadn't heard from Pastor Bloom in so long, he wondered if the minister had totally forgotten about him. He thought long and hard about the best way to handle it and decided not to blow a chance with Preach unless it was an emergency. *No, I can handle this without anyone. I'm going to need to take a look at the bike and make sure she's roadworthy. Then go steal some gas, grab some provisions and hit the road. Shit.*

Glick walked over to the black, dangerous-looking Harley with the grinning skulls, wiped some dust off her gas tank and gave a tire a kick. "You ready for a nice long trip?" he asked the waiting bike, *I'm not.*

He took a walk to the trash heap that contained the old sidecar that they had used to get from the cabbage patch. He dug through piles of refuse to get to the sidecar, which was all the way at the bottom. He pursed his lips. Upon closer examination, the thing had totally crumbled, rusted to pieces, and the axle was broken. *I guess we won't be using this.* He shook his head.

He went back to his Harley, gave her a good once-over and then ran her up to the closest gas station, which was still 12 miles away. He normally avoided this particular station because they had come to recognize Glick as a thief long ago. It had been months, however, and it was a special circumstance, so he took his chances once again, lingering at the edge of the station until he saw the perfect mark, a graying man wearing high-water pants and driving a Buick; there were no other customers in sight. *Babe in the woods.*

He waited until the senior had swiped his wrist, and just before he inserted the nozzle into his own Buick, Glick pulled up next to him and laid claim to the gas for himself. Then he was off in a snap, leaving no trace of his crime. He returned just as quickly and sat patiently, waiting for Toni's return.

Toni approached the guard gate. She waved her yellow paper and knocked on the door to be allowed reentry. The guard who was sitting in the watchtower disappeared momentarily, she assumed to let her in. Even though it was now daylight, the strays that lived on the borders of the compound were making her extremely nervous. They stealthily slinked up on her; one was carrying a wooden post that he swung menacingly, others were brandishing knives, and some swung chains into the air. She had no idea it was getting so scary out here.

"Hurry!" She yelled while pounding on the gate, "They're coming!" The group formed a wide circle around her with more joining in. They started moving in close to her, nearer and nearer, but still no sign of the guard.

"Please hurry!!" she screamed frantically now. The clot was almost upon her. Still nothing.

Unable to wait any longer, Toni panicked and took off running back in the direction from which she had come. Shocked and terrified, she blindly ran and ran until she again reached the bikers' camp. Only then did she look behind her to see if she had been followed, but no one was there. "Whew," she breathed a sigh of relief. Her heart was beating out of her chest. "That was nuts!"

Still rattled, she moved aimlessly in the direction of her boyfriend's campsite. As she approached, Glick could tell right away something was wrong.

"You OK?" he asked. "You're white as a ghost."

"I'm OK, honey, but I have a little problem. I couldn't get back in."

"Oh no! They wouldn't let you in? Why?"

"I'm not sure. I think they just couldn't get to me in time. Oh, Glick, it was just awful!" She placed her cheek against his stomach. "There were dreadful people all around the gate, they had knives and they would have killed me I think. I had to run. I ran back as fast as I could."

"Whoa." Glick was dumbfounded. Not knowing what to say, he tried to comfort her to the best of his awkward abilities. "It's OK, babe." He pinched her cheek. "We won't need anything except each other. I can get us everything we need on the road."

"OK," she replied with some relief, but her lower lip was still trembling. He gave it a tiny kiss and patted her butt. "I filled her up about an hour ago, so if you're ready, I think we can ride." Toni nodded, and very shortly they were packed up and on the road, with just one change of clothes, an extra helmet, a few cans of Vienna sausages, four cans of beans and each other.

Back at the compound, Dina was freaking out. When she had awakened in the middle of the night, Toni wasn't in her cot, nor was she there the next morning. Now it was almost noon, and Dina still had no idea where she was. She told herself to be calm, and she began walking about asking her neighbors whether anyone had seen her, no one had. Distraught, she finally consulted the guards at the compound's entrance, and they disclosed the events of the prior evening and that morning. Dina was baffled. What on earth was Toni thinking?

"I have to go get her," she declared to the main guard. "I'm going to go talk to Mr. Brandenburg, and he'll have some people help me."

"Oh, no, ma'am, you can't. We have a situation on our hands right now, and under order of the board of directors we are not allowing anyone else to enter or leave until we have it under control."

"Well, what if you never get it under control?"

"I'm confident we will have it resolved very shortly, ma'am." The truth was that even the guard wasn't certain they could quell the growing mob at the entrance, not without resorting to violence. "I'm afraid there is nothing we can do about Toni right now. I'm terribly sorry."

"Oh, my God!" Dina cried. She didn't know whether to be angry, disappointed or terrified.

"That damn Toni!" she mumbled as she stomped off toward home. *Always getting in trouble. I'm going to quit bailing her out one of these days.* Dina knew just where Toni was, and boy, she was going to get an earful when Dina saw her again, *if* she ever saw her again. Tears welled up in her eyes as she tried to put her best friend out of her mind and get on with her Sunday. It was, after all, a gorgeous day.

Chapter *37*

On the Road

Toni and Glick were on the road and passing through the city of Jacksonville, Florida, toward her son Joey's and his father's house in Jacksonville Beach, only 15 minutes away.

"I'm so excited!" Toni squeezed Glick's backside. The trip had been grueling, dangerous and far more tiring than she could have ever dreamed possible. The bike was loud and obnoxious, and the vibrations that she once found so pleasurable had now numbed her body from head to toe. She was hungry, exhausted, grimy and cranky, plus the beans that she had consumed last night were making her fart. It was also hot, much hotter than she had been used to in the north. Wetness clung to the air and a sweltry wind blew in her face. The sizzling asphalt swam in the tropical heat. She couldn't wait to get off and stretch.

"Glick, we need to pull over and freshen up a little before we get there." It was time to game-plan a little; the whole ride, they had not once discussed what they would do once they got there. Would they just knock on the door? Would they wait for Joey to come outside? Would they try to pick him up around the school? Everyone knew Toni there; it might be easy. But then she thought about that, and no, there would be too many questions to answer. They pulled over at a nearby gas station. It was time to refill anyway.

They both stretched and stepped inside. Toni went to the bathroom and filled their canteen. She cupped water over her weary face and dabbed herself with soap, then she applied some lipstick and smoothed out her hair. They had forgotten to bring a comb. She frowned in the mirror; thinking she looked a hag. Glick waited until she was back outside and rounded the corner before he did his usual shove and fill. They had their routine down pat. Toni would wait around the corner until he was done, and then she would hop on the back of the black Harley once the coast was clear. She hated every minute of it. Once they were back on the road, he looked for a private place to pull over again and shared the pretzels he had just shoplifted. Together, they sat on the pavement in the shade of a building that housed an upholstery shop and chatted about what to do next.

"Good thing we did this trip when we did," he grumbled, noticing his soon-to-be expired tag. "Damn tag gonna expire this month. Don't know what I'm gonna to do after that."

"We'll be stuck." Toni's eyes clouded dark. She was worried what the future would hold for her and Joey, will we ever get back into the Hidden Village community? *What if I can't? What if I have to live in Glick's tent from now on? Would Joey really be better off then? Oh Lord!*

Glick, too, was having his own set of worries. As much as he loved Toni, he hadn't expected to have an 11-year-old kid hanging around cramping his style. *It might be kind of fun to have a boy, though.* He could teach him mechanics and how to fish. *Will he call me dad, I wonder?*

Break was over; now it was time to do the deed. "You ready?" he asked while helping her to her feet.

"I guess so. Let's check it out." The plan was to do a drive-by and see if there were any cars in the driveway. Joey should be home from school by now, and Mitch wouldn't get home until after 6. Jeanette was the wild card. If her car was there, they would have to hang around until an opportunity struck, and God only knew how long that would take. The drive was only minutes away and soon the black Harley was slowly puttering through the well-groomed neighborhood, its two riders standing out like sore thumbs.

"There it is on the left, 2803. It's the gray house with white trim. Pull up." Toni's heart was bursting with apprehension and grieving. This was the house that she and Mitch once shared. Joey had been born here, and now this was where he lived with his new mother, Mitch's new wife.

"I don't see any cars. Looks good, let's stop." The couple pulled in, and the Harley dripped oil onto the spacious and spotless driveway.

"You had better wait here." Toni said, "I'll be right back." She took off to the side of the house and peered into Joey's window. She couldn't see anything, so she went around back and let herself inside the gate. She could hear voices and splashing in the pool. She edged around the corner of the house and peeked to see. There he was – her precious son on the dive board!

"Watch this one!" he told a friend, a boy his own age, as he did a double forward spring with a big splash at the end.

Toni approached the side of the blue water, and as Joey came up for air, she was standing there with the biggest smile on her face.

"Mom?" Joey blinked.

"Yes, son, it's me."

"What are you doing here?"

Toni just stood there smiling while Joey got out of the pool and towel-dried his face and arms.

"Uh, this is Joshua," he pointed to his friend. "Josh, this is my Mom."

"Hi, Mom," Joshua waved.

Toni couldn't contain herself. She enveloped her arms around Joey and gave him a long, heartfelt hug. The tears were now rolling down her face.

"I've missed you so bad," she sniffled while kissing his cheek. "You don't know."

"Me, too," Joey said. He wiped the offending moisture off his cheek. "What happened to you, Mom? We've been worried."

"I've tried to talk to you, honestly, so many times. Mitch wouldn't let me."

"They said you went crazy."

"No, no, it's not true," she said, looking at Joey with pleading eyes. "Joey, I've come for you. I live in the most wonderful place now, it's a safe place and everyone there is going to love you just as much as I do."

"Huh?"

"I'm going to need you to get packed. You can't carry too much; only what is absolutely necessary. Can you do this for me now?"

"What?"

"Joey, we don't have much time. I need you to get inside and just get a few items to wear and maybe your phone and a couple of toys. Do you want me to help you?"

"No."

"OK. I'd like to come inside and make a sandwich or something while you get ready. Come on." Toni took his hand and began pulling him inside.

"No, I mean, I don't want to go." He pulled his arm back.

"Oh Joey, you don't know what you're saying. It isn't safe here. You have to come with me."

"What's not safe ... the pool? Why do I have to come with you?"

"Just listen to me. You don't understand. You must come!"

"No way! I like it here. I have friends, and I like my school. I'm not going! You can't make me."

Toni had halfway anticipated this. She gazed at her beautiful Joey standing there with his hands on his hips, looking and sounding just like Mitch; he had grown so much. She started to cry again, and her head was spinning. She sat on a tastefully cushioned lounge chair and rested her face in her hands, heartbroken.

"Don't cry, Mom. I love you." Joey placed his hand on her head. "I just don't want to go anywhere. It's not fair for you to keep trying to move me around."

Toni thought about Glick out front and wondered if they could drag Joey out by force. It would be for his own good; he would be mad at her and maybe even hate her for a while, but then he would realize, eventually.

"Mom, you OK?"

"Yes, I'm fine." Snail trails of tears stained her face. She stood and straightened herself. "I'm going."

Joey would never understand, no matter what. And she couldn't bear taking him from his enjoyable, happy life. She would return home, empty-handed and empty-hearted. She turned to walk back, and Glick was standing at the fence with a pitiful look on his face, he had witnessed the whole incident. Toni ran sorrowfully into his arms, and together they walked back to the Harley and took off in a noxious cloud of smoke.

The two rode in silence for a very long time. It was a sad ride back to Utah. They were hungry, and Glick struggled to keep a good attitude for Toni's sake, but it was difficult under the circumstances. They pushed themselves to the limits to hurry and get back, driving through the day and evening for more than 30 hours straight. Even though Toni took frequent catnaps on the back of the bike, she was still delirious from exhaustion and kept urging Glick to pull over, *anywhere,* even on the side of the road to get some much-needed rest, but he refused to stop. She squirmed and flexed her back, resting her head on the back of the sissy bar, and hummed old television theme songs in an attempt to break the monotony. She observed that a certain hawk in the sky seemed to have been following them for many miles. He playfully dipped and swooped, cutting out of sight behind the orange canyons, only to reappear a few minutes later.

"Hey, check it out," Glick pointed his weary head toward a sign for I-15. "We're almost there." They could finally get off Interstate 70 now.

"Glick," Toni shouted over the loud pipes, "I know that we are almost there, but this is ridiculous – we both need sleep. Please pull over."

"Look around you, woman. There's nothing here but desert. We're better off to keep going. We'll be close to Provo real soon. We'll pull over there, I promise."

Toni groaned. Provo was still 130 miles away, and Glick was now weaving all over the desolate road. She wanted to jump off and run, but like he said, it was desert all around. All she could do was hold on tight and pray. She felt her heavy eyes grow droopier and droopier, she struggled to keep them open but couldn't. She begins to nod off, going to a soft, misty place, when a large friendly bird swoops down and plucks her from her seat, lifting her high into the air. Then she becomes the bird. Opening her mouth, a cak-cak-cak sound comes out as she flies higher and higher into the clouds, the blue sky spinning out of control.

A blinding pain in her right shoulder woke her from her pleasant daydream to the shocking horror of the realization that she was now freely rolling across the hot pavement.

"Oh, my God, no!!!" The bike skewed out of control. Glick must have dozed off, and now he was trapped on his right side under the Harley as it skidded off the road and into the dirt embankment. Toni lifted her head and watched as he kept sliding with the bike on top of him, until finally disappearing over the lip of the ridge below.

"Oh shit! Oh shit! Oh shit!" She got to her knees and cringed with pain. The road had shredded her jeans to ribbons, and the flesh underneath peeked out, bloodied and slashed. She had no thought of her own pain as the adrenalin began pumping through her veins. She hobbled over the ridge in a crush of hysteria and came to Glick, who lay helpless, trapped under the weight of the half-ton Harley. She ran to his side and began lifting, straining with all her might. She was able to lift the Harley about 6 inches, giving Glick a hint of wiggle room, but he still remained caught under the heavy machine.

"Oh man, I'm fucked," he groaned before passing out.

Chapter *38*

Meet the Locals

Toni maintained a vigil by Glick's side, occasionally trying to lift the monster motorcycle up from its position, but now that the adrenalin had worn off, she couldn't budge it even an inch, especially with her shoulder in the shape it was in. She was in excruciating pain. And after looking herself over, she thought that she surely had a dislocated shoulder, or worse, and her right ankle was swelling up so badly that she feared it must be broken. She needed water but couldn't get underneath to the saddle bag that was holding their canteen. Glick never once stirred. She removed his helmet and examined his head. She didn't see anything obvious, but she knew that didn't mean much.

Again, she dragged herself to the road and waited for a car to come by. She had seen only one in the past hour and even though she had stood in the middle of the road to wave him down, the bastard had just swerved around her and kept going. Now the late afternoon sun was turning amber, illuminating the sky with a tawny glow. Evening would soon fall, and they would be left to the mercies of the night. She scanned the horizon looking for some kind of miracle. If she could walk, she might consider hoofing it to the next town, but with her ankle in this condition, not a chance. She lay down on the side of the road and, resting her head on a rock, she prayed.

Something made her open her eyes, and when she did she thought she spotted the dark outline of a figure on a distant cliff staring at her. She turned and it was gone. She shook her head and peered closely. There it was again! The same dark figure in the distance, looking in her direction! She waved and shouted for help.

"Hey! Hey! Over here! We need help!! Please help us!" She stood and, forgetting her ankle, jumped into the air waving and shouting, "Hey! Hey!" But like a phantom, it was gone. She attempted to run toward the apparition, but her leg buckled and she fell to her knees. "Please help us," she spoke softly now.

Twilight turned to darkness, and Toni stayed close to Glick for protection, both hers and his. He had briefly opened his eyes and mumbled something earlier, and she had tried to keep him awake, but he had just as quickly fallen off again. She dreaded that he could possibly die out here if someone didn't help them soon.

Eerie sounds of the nighttime held shadows that crossed over the plain, and she shrunk in fear. Glowing eyes in the murk spied and stalked, an owl hooted, a coyote howled. Toni jumped nervously, her eyes darting in and out. Would this nightmare ever end? She grabbed Glick's hand and squeezed it tightly. *Don't die on me honey, I need you. Please don't leave me.*

Somehow, she must have managed a little sleep, for the sky was now turning pink, the first hint of daylight's blush peeking over the panoramic vista of canyons. Toni fluttered her eyes open and looked around trying to remember where she was. When it occurred to her, the knot in her stomach clinched. She turned to appraise Glick, who was still out cold. She checked his temperature and pulse; would he sleep forever? Thirst consumed her. She knew that if they didn't drink soon, they would both die from dehydration; the precious canteen resting in the saddlebag, so close, yet so far. She peeled back her jeans to look at her raw leg and grimaced when she saw the damage done. This, too, was bad, and her ankle was now an angry purple-and-black.

What am I going to do? She rose to go to the road and wait for cars when she thought she saw something.

It was the same figure from last night, this time much closer and standing in the gorge. He was dark and wearing a fringed suede vest over his bare chest with blue jeans. Feathers dangled loosely from his braided hair. He was striking to behold, wild and sleek. He turned and, as quickly as he had surfaced, was gone again, disappearing into the craggy rock face of the gorge.

Again, Toni waved and yelled for assistance, but only her own mocking voice answered her as it echoed throughout the canyon. "Help! Help!"

She heard Glick moan, and she quickly came to his side. "Wa's going on?" he rasped with a thick tongue. "Oh," he groaned, "this bike, off me."

"I've been trying to all night, honey. It's too heavy." No response from Glick. He went out cold again.

"Glick, honey, wake up!" She shook his shoulder. "Glick? *Damnit."*

She sat by his side and pondered her situation. *We have to get out of here. Hardly anyone passes on this road. When I do hear cars go by, I'm over here with you and can't get to them. I'd better stick by the road. I'll stay by the road all day if I have to.*

She stood to go back to the asphalt when she saw the Indian again. This time, he had four others with him and they were approaching. Some wore flannels and others pearl-button shirts with bandannas, boots and large eagle feathers in their cowboy hats.

"Oh, thank God," Toni cried as she tried to hobble closer.

"Hello? My name is Toni. Hello, how do you do? This is Glick. He's hurt very badly, and he won't wake up. Can you help us, please? Hello?"

The Indians did not answer. They moved quickly however, and lifted the bike off of Glick and hovered over his prostrate form.

"Oh, thank you so much," she gushed. "I thought we might die out here. Thank goodness you showed up." She went to the saddlebag and quenched her thirst with the canteen, polishing it off, she wiped her mouth with her sleeve. "Whew, I've never been so thirsty in my whole life."

The first Indian offered her an additional bottle of spring water, which she declined, indicating that they should that give it to Glick instead. He crouched low and dabbed a little inside the comatose biker's closed lips. Two of the Indians took off in the direction they'd originally come from.

"Hey! Where are you going??" Toni hollered. Again, they did not reply, only silently departing to be swallowed up into the nooks of the ravine.

"Strange," she stood with hands on hips, "don't you guys speak English?"

"Of course we do," the first Indian replied.

"Oh?" She raised her eyebrows. "Why didn't you say so?"

"You didn't ask."

"OK." Toni was too relieved to really care. "Where did your friends go?"

"To the truck."

"I see," she nodded her head. Toni could clearly appreciate that her new comrades weren't big on conversation, so when they arrived with their pickup, she spoke as little as possible. After allowing them to lift Glick onto a gurney and carefully place him in the back, she climbed inside the crowded cab with them as they drove off the main road toward a new destination. Strangers in a strange land.

Never a dull moment, Toni thought to herself as they pulled into the reservation. It was like something from a postcard; little half-naked brown children ran free around the huts and teepees that were set up across the divide. Farther away, dozens of tumbledown shacks and old trailers sprinkled the sides of the jagged mountains.

The land had been cleared. Old women in colorful skirts gathered hay to bring to their stables; others were weaving baskets and sewing. Toni noticed a woman hunched over a boiling pot adding root vegetables when a young girl walked by with an earbud in her ear listening to music – a unique mixture of old and new. Boys played soccer, their dirty faces grim with determination. Some old men gathered together in the shade playing checkers.

They drove the pickup right up to the front of a teepee and quickly lifted Glick out and carried him on the gurney to a teepee with an old, leathery woman sitting in front smoking a long pipe. The men and the old woman had a brief dialog in their native tongue, and she pointed for the men to bring Glick to a thatch wigwam behind her. Then she led the men inside. Toni trailed closely behind but was stopped at the entrance and told she wasn't allowed in. Feeling displaced, she stood outside looking at the closed door, wondering what to do.

Some time passed and the grizzled, primitive woman came outside and went to her teepee. She returned shortly with a girl of about 14 carrying a basket and a pot of herbs steeping in hot water. Toni attempted to peer inside and examine its contents, but the old woman gave her a dirty look and brushed her aside as she entered the wigwam. More time passed, with several people in and out, but Toni was never allowed in. By now she was eaten alive with curiosity and tried to pry for information but was met with deaf ears. She peeked inside and observed a dark, smoky room; its rich walls were painted with images of animals and strange symbols and ornately decorated with circular feather arrangements, masks and hanging gourds. A small fire burned in a recess surrounded by weapons: spears, tomahawks and arrows. Shelves held an assortment of pottery bowls, jars and shells, and a low table bore dried cactus, matches, large leaves and plants, a rattle and large black feathers.

Toni saw Glick laid out on a blanket on top of a long table. The old woman was doing something to his feet and humming a tune when she heard a voice behind her.

"The table will transform into a flying horse in the spirit world ..." It was the young girl who was assisting the shaman speaking. "She has already thrown her baton to find the right spirit to bring your man back from the shadow land, but she will need help."

"We had an accident," Toni replied. "I think he may have a concussion."

"His wound is deep. He is in the land of clouds and shadows."

"Is anything broken?"

"Tonight, medicine woman will do sacred dance and bring life to his body. She will bring others to help. This evil is strong. She will need much help."

"Shhh," the medicine woman spat on the floor and waved them off. The girl adjourned to her teepee with Toni by her side. She was invited in. Toni was surprised at how clean, airy and bright it was inside. A futon was covered with woven blankets and comfortable, plump cushions were strewn about. Toni took a seat on the floor and looked up at the open tip of the teepee. *I wonder why they live in these things.*

"Because there is power in the shape of the teepee," the girl spoke as if reading Toni's mind. "There is no power in a square, such as you whites live in."

Toni studied the girl's face "I've never been on a reservation before. This is really amazing. What's your name?"

"Kuwanlalenta. You may call me Ku. The medicine woman is Hausis. She is much older than she looks."

"She looks pretty darn old to me."

"She was here when the land was full and blessed. When the land is happy, the people are happy."

"I suppose so."

"And you are called?"

"Toni."

"Toni. What does your name mean?"

Toni dwells on this a moment. "It means teacher."

"I don't think so. I think you need new name. I will call you Mochni. It means bird that flies to the unknown place."

"Toni works better for me, if you don't mind. I don't think I could get used to being called Mochni."

"Mochni is your spirit name. You may call yourself what you wish, but I know you are Mochni, inside here," the girl said, pointing to her chest.

Toni sat quietly a moment and considered this new information. "I'd like to see more of the reservation later, if I may."

"Yes, that would be a good thing for you and maybe good for our people. I have not seen a white on this land before. But I must go, though. I must fetch help for Hausis. You may come with me."

"Where are you going?"

"To our neighbors, the Goshukes; they live in the Oquirrh Mountains in the east and in the Steptoe Mountains. They are small in numbers, like us. There is a spirit talker there, a very powerful healer."

Toni regarded her ankle and shoulder. "I think I should stay. My ankle is killing me. I'm not really up for travel."

"You are hurt. The spirit talker will help you, too."

"That would be very nice. Do you have an Ace bandage in the meantime, so I can wrap my foot?"

"I can get you something." Ku left for a few moments and returned with a poultice, some leaves and twine. She applied the poultice to the road rash, wrapped her wound in leaves and tied it securely with the twine.

"This will make the swell go down. You may rest here in this place. I will return. There will be a great medicine circle at tonight's moon."

That evening, when the moon was high in the sky, a powerful medicine man arrived. He had two boys in tow about the same age as Ku and carrying duffel bags to assist him. He assessed Glick's condition by waving his hands over and walking in circles around him while Hausis and Ku prepared

an elixir of fresh barks and roots taken from the earthen jars
sitting on the shelves of the medicine hut.

The helpers went to work beating drums and dancing
around Glick while the spirit talker passed the wooden bowl
and drank its thick, fluid mixture. He sat on a rug on the floor
next to the unresponsive biker and chanted ancient verse.
Raising his arms, he quivered and shook as he moved into a
deep, trancelike state. The spirit talker rose and paced the
floor. Holding his head in agony, he cried to the heavens and
fell to his knees as the potion pushed further into his
bloodstream. He rolled into a ball and became very quiet as he
began his gradual descent into the shadow world. He then
rose to his feet and began a strange dance around Glick's
prostrate body.

Hausis took smoking embers from the fire and held them
in a flat dish over Glick. The medicine man took a raven's wing
and waved the smoke over the biker's supine form. The
moving vapors bit by bit took the distinct shape of a wolf and
then formed an owl before dissipating into a fine mist. The
medicine man now knew what shape he must take to guide
the spirit wolf to help him. He called for a piece of fresh raw
meat, which Ku brought to him. He waved it over the smoke
and blew on it for several minutes; he held the bloody steak
high over his head and chanted songs before tossing it into a
corner. He then took a colorful blanket woven with cryptic
patterns and draped it over Glick's body. Ku sewed the
blankets shut into a cocoon with a large needle and braided
coil.

For over an hour the medicine man danced, his arms
flapping like a bird while he trilled incantations. He shook a
crude rattle over the silhouette that lay under the blanket and
motioned for his helpers to retrieve a knife from the duffel
bag, he used the knife to cut the coil and pulled the blanket
back off of Glick's face; the biker began fluttering his eyes. The
shaman then pulled the blanket completely off of his subject
and lifted Glick into a sitting position while Hausis and Ku
supported him up from the back. He took Glick's arms, pulled

them out in front of him and shook them, he lifted and bent his legs at the knees and patted his back. Glick slowly came to.

"Wha'? Wha'?" he wheezed. "W'as this? Where am I?"

Hausis made the universal gesture for quiet, "shhhh," and hurriedly exited the room. Once outside, she brushed off her body with her hands and splashed water on her arms and face while Toni watched from her post outside the door. The old woman looked exhausted.

"I heard something. Did I hear Glick?" Toni quizzed. No answer came from Hausis, but Ku stepped outside and smiled at her.

"I did hear him, didn't I?" She stood excitedly and went to enter the forbidden hut but was halted by Ku.

"No no. Mustn't now; must rest."

Toni stomped her foot and stuck out her lower lip like a child. "Bullshit!" she replied. Inside, the spirit talker was purifying himself as well while his assistants offered Glick small sips of water.

"What's going on?" Glick grumbled. "Where's Toni?"

"I'm out here! Out front!" She tried to pry her way in but was again held back. Glick stood and gave the spirit talker's minuscule helpers a little push out of the way while he sought out the location of his lady love. She beat him to it, however, and despite her ankle she finally eluded Ku, forcing her way inside. The two lovers met in the middle of the dark hut, heedlessly folding themselves into each other's arms. He held her to him for the longest time.

"Oh Glick, I was so worried!" He responded by trying to pick her up, but what usually came so easily was now too great a task. He buckled and stumbled.

"No! No! No! Must sit!" Hausis had reentered the wigwam and was now fussing over Glick like a mother hen. It is the first time Toni had heard the old woman speak English since her arrival. "You sit here. You sit now."

Glick obediently found the spot on the blanketed floor that Hausis directed him to. He at first sat, but then quickly lay down horizontally again. He looked around and focused up at the rafters to the ceiling of the wigwam, trying to remember how it was that he had arrived to such a peculiar place. *I don't remember a thing.*

"Toni, baby," he gestured for her to sit down next to him. She sat at his feet, too frightened to lie next to him the way she wanted to. "What happened?" he asked. The concern on her face had him worried.

"We crashed, Glick; around 4 p.m. yesterday. I think you must have fallen asleep."

"Crashed? Are you OK, baby?"

"I'm fine. My ankle might be broken, but I'm OK."

"Let me see that ankle. Oh, shit, that don't look too good."

"You were trapped under the Harley, honey. I tried to get it off of you, but I couldn't lift it. I've been worried sick about you. I thought you might die."

"Yeah," he gulped, "it's about 600 pounds. But nothing can kill me, toots – they've all tried." He closed his droopy eyelids for a moment and sighed. "Have I been out this whole time?" He looked about the inside of the dim wigwam, at the curious markings on the walls and the strange trappings held inside. "What *is* this place?"

"These people saved us, honey. We owe them our lives. You had a very serious head injury." Glick felt his head and winced, realizing what she said was true. He watched the natives scurry about, putting items back on shelves and tidying up. Rolling to his side, he rested his head on his arm.

"Thanks for being there, Toni. You're one of a kind."

"You're one of a kind, too, you maniac." She kissed him lightly and sat up. "Hey, Ku, you missed a spot over here," she said, pointing to the smoldering remnants of a charred piece of gray ash in the corner on the floor. It was the steak, consumed to mere burnt embers.

Glick looked at her ankle and stood up. "If that thing is broken, we need to get you to a doctor right away."

"It doesn't hurt nearly as bad as it was earlier. Ku wrapped it in these leaves, and it seems to be much better."

"We shouldn't take any chances, though." Glick's head spun. He braced himself against a wall.

"You should not be on your feet." Ku came to his side. The medicine man who had not yet spoken also came to Glick's side, and together they directed him back to the table and lay him down. The spirit talker held up three fingers and uttered, "Three days."

"Three days what?"

"Three days, then better. You stay."

"I can't stay here three days. Toni needs help."

"We will help her," Ku replied. "Hausis says is not broken, just twisted."

"How can she tell? She never even looked at it," Toni asked.

"Hausis knows. She tossed the baton for you. You will stay in my teepee. Your man must stay with the other men folk. Three days."

Toni and Glick looked at each other and sighed. "Three days."

The spirit talker gibbered to Ku in their native tongue for a moment and pointed to his out-turned palm. Ku turned and faced the couple. "He will want his pay."

"Pay?" Glick questioned.

"Yes, he expects payment."

"Good luck with that, Hoss. I'm broke."

"His name is Tuketu, not Hoss."

"Tuketu." the spirit talker smiled and pointed to his hairless chest.

"How would he like to be paid?" Toni asked. "We haven't used cash for some time now."

"Tobacco is good. Tobacco has power."

"Man after my own heart," Glick countered. "Will a pack of Camels do?"

"Camels, yes," Tuketu smiled and nodded.

"Sure, soon as I can."

"I am surprised that Tuketu agreed to come see you," Ku spoke up. "He doesn't come for everyone, especially a white.

The spirits must have spoken loudly to Tuketu for him to come."

"We are very lucky to be alive," Toni agreed. "Don't you think so, honey?" But Glick was already sleeping again; snoring softly, he dreamed of wolves running free in the desert.

Chapter *39*

A Confrontation at the Gates

As promised, the Indians provided well for Toni over the three-day period, tending meticulously to her injured foot and shoulder, and she was soon on her feet. Glick recovered nicely as well and spent a great amount of time with Tuketu before the spirit talker left for his own tribe over the Oquirrh Mountains and to the east. Tuketu took an unexpected liking to Glick and spoke to him for many hours about the ways of the tribal shaman. He told Glick about how he came to be a spirit talker and how his father before him was a spirit talker. He spoke of the shamanizing journey ritual that he undertook as a young man, which brought him to the brink of death and allowed him to emerge as the tribe's holy man who communicates with the underworld. He taught Glick about spirit animals, even revealing his own spirit animal: the jaguar. He divulged that he would sometimes take on the form of a rooster when he journeyed to the unknown. The rooster would shield him from wandering evil spirits by making him invisible; the evil spirits would only see a worthless rooster spirit and leave him alone.

Tuketu spoke to Glick about dreams, signs and omens and showed him songs and dances that were recovered after they were lost for many years while it was illegal to practice their own culture. He instructed Glick on how to construct a shaman's drum by stretching an animal skin over a bent wooden hoop and how to make a proper pipe, a most sacred instrument. He taught Glick about the importance of proper diet, fasting, silent meditation and, of course, smoking.

He told Glick a story of long, long ago; when out of the sky came the Anunnaki. "They came down from the heavens to the Earth to take our gold and the light of the sun. They told the people that they were gods and we should worship them. But we refused to worship them, and this caused a great anger in them. They removed the earth's shady brume and for the first time we felt the flame of the sun. They taught us language and claimed it a better way to communicate; but in truth they did this because the mouth could lie but the mind cannot. So now we spoke with the mouth and no longer the mind. They taught each tribe a different language, and so we as one people became divided. They taught us everything, how to destroy the forests to make houses to live in. They claimed they had liberated us and made us civilized, but they had in truth made us slaves – slaves to our wants. Man became a greedy race now, hoarding wealth and waging war with his brothers.

"We used to be a spiritual, strong people. Our spirit powers were great then; the Anunnaki came from the heavens and divided us and enslaved us. This is how we came to be like this. The Anunnaki never left the Earth, they took our daughters and wives and made them full with their children. They told us that the children that they would bear would be our kings and chiefs to rule over us, because they now had 'royal' blood in them."

Tuketu told Glick that "the Indian people were once the keepers of the sound. Our drums matched the heartbeat of the great mother keeping the Earth in balance and we drew strength from the Earth. But they moved us away from our sacred places and put us in lands that had no power; our drum songs then had no power. Our sounds could not reach into the heavens. The Earth once played her harmonious song, but we have lost the music."

When it was time to see the spirit talker off, Glick felt as though he had been chosen somehow for great things – a feeling he had never had before in his entire life. He promised to bring Tuketu the tobacco that he owed him as soon as he was able, owing him a large debt of gratitude. He was sorry to go.

Toni also had time to learn the ways of the first American people, and Ku made an ample teacher. She discovered that some of the men in the tribe worked far outside the reservation as ranch hands and firefighters. Children now went to school on the reservation rather than being bused to Indian boarding schools such as in years past; and the women mostly sewed beaded purses and jewelry, were doll makers and casino workers.

"Are your people microchipped?" Toni asked Ku on an evening walk after dinner.

"I have heard of this thing. Yes, some of them are, the men that work off the reservation and the women that work in the casinos all had to do this. I do not have this strange thing in me."

"That's good; don't do it. What about the rest?"

"There have been many talks with the elders. It is something that is a divide amongst my people. We have had visits from the government men. They were friendly at the beginning, but they are not so friendly anymore."

"Oh?"

"We had to tell them that we are our own nation; we are not subject to their laws. They did not like to hear this."

"I can imagine they wouldn't. What did they say?"

"They said that they would be back." Ku sighed.

"I would expect that. You should make preparations."

"I will tell the elders that you think so."

"Why don't you have your own casino?" Toni asked Ku as they strolled past their own tiny bingo parlor.

"We do not want this. The whites are crazy. They are the last thing we want to see here. We live by the old ways. Many other reservations live like the modern people and have all their kinds of possessions: phones, Internet, dishwasher, satellite TV. Our families spend time together, not sitting in front of TV; that is not our way. Medicine, education, Social Security and other things that they think are supposed to be provided by the government, these things we take care of ourselves. Everybody gets what they need. We are self-sufficient, without the government's help."

"But you live in such dire poverty." Toni observed boys playing ball in cargo pants, moccasins and bandannas. "One casino could make you very rich. I've heard about how much the casinos earn for the Indians."

"The casinos make the elders rich, but not the tribal people. We have seen many tribes broken over this."

"I see."

"We prefer a simple life. It is hard sometimes, yes, but I love it. I once drove into a big city; it was very far away. Everyone seemed so rushed there. It made me very sad. I never went back to that place again. To live in a city would make me lonesome for the stars and the trees and the land."

The evening of the third day arrived, and the tribe had a potluck dinner and a powwow to commemorate the new friendship that they had developed with Toni and Glick. Beans, squash, fresh bison and greens were on the menu, and the two feasted to their hearts' content before leaving first thing in the morning, Soon they were back on the desolate road and headed toward Hidden Village.

Only two hours on the road and they were almost home. It was a good thing, because the Harley was starting to run rough, missing and occasionally stalling. As they drove up the dirt road that led to the entrance gate at Hidden Village, they noticed that there was an even greater multitude at its threshold than before. These were not happy people. They clamored at the walls, their dire exasperation, radiating anger, screaming and turmoil contrasted sharply with the harmonious and gentle culture that the pair had just left.

The garrison was increased at the gate and the guards brandished their arms, freely waving their machine guns from their tower post at the swarm in anticipation of the clash to come. Several people were attempting to climb the electric fence, and others were dragging logs from the nearby woods to function as battering rams. Soon there would be an uprising, and inside, the inhabitants of Hidden Village were powerless to defend themselves.

There was only one road in and no way to avoid the bitter mob. Glick and Toni drove ahead slowly and cautiously, and then, the Harley backfired just before sputtering and stalling out. The horde turned and looked at them and began to charge. Waving sticks and throwing rocks, they swiftly advanced upon on the couple in a full-scale attack.

"Glick, do something quick!!" Toni screamed. He kick-started the antique hog to get her going again and blew past the would-be assailants, heading toward his own sweet encampment not so far from the front gate. Relieved to be back at his tent but still on guard, Glick quickly dismounted and looked for his partner Jimbo. He found him by the stream fishing; he hurriedly rushed over to him.

"Hey, man. There's a problem at the main gate."

"Yeah, we know. They've been at it a while. Welcome home, by the way."

"You know about what's going on at the gate?"

"Yep."

"Why haven't you offered to help?"

"What for? I'm not looking to get my head busted."

"Look, Jim," Glick spun him around, "if Hidden Village goes down, then *we* go down. No electricity, no food, no help, nothing. Were damn lucky we haven't been attacked."

"Nothing here's worth taking, man."

"This ain't gonna get it! I want to see every man in this camp at my tent in 15 minutes. No later. No excuses! We're going to help Preach and the rest of them people. Now go get everyone rounded up."

"*Your* tent?" Jimbo mumbled as he reluctantly set forth to collect the vagabond crew. Glick also scrambled to round up all the help he could muster, and soon the entire cabbage patch gang was gathered together at the tent to listen to the voice of their unlikely leader.

"Listen up, you all," Glick announced to the disheveled scrounges. "There's a riot going on at the front gate to Hidden Village, and we have to help them! If we don't, there won't be any more help from them 'cause they won't be there! Now, they've been real good to us so far, and they deserve our help; so get your guns and knives and weapons and let's go kick some ass!!"

"Yeeeeaaaahh!!!" A roar of glee went up from the clan as they ran off to gather their arsenal. In next to no time they were astride their hogs and en route to the front gate. They arrived not a minute too soon, for the mob had convened and were in the middle of battering their way inside with a fallen log. The exasperated guards fired warning shots up into the sky, but it was to no avail; driven by hunger and abandon, the mass ignored their warnings and continued bashing at the front and at the chain-link electric fence that contained the unsuspecting citizens inside.

The loud sound of dozens of Harleys soon distracted their attention, and the cabbage patch gang was upon them in a flash: knives, chains, fists and guns were utilized in a bloody brawl that lasted all of five minutes. The riot was soon over. Its remaining participants scattered with the wind, leaving only Glick and the rest of the cabbage patch gang behind to gloat over their easy victory.

"Oh, man, that was fun!!" T-Bone and Raunch slapped high fives. "I needed to get it out, man – been cooped up too long!"

The buzz of excitement that hummed throughout the bunch was quickly dampened, however, when Glick assessed the damage that had been done to his comrades. Bodies lay strewn about on the ground. One in particular caught his attention.

"Shut up, bitches!" he yelped. "Jimbo's down!"

Jimbo lay on the ground in a puddle holding his side. He'd been stabbed between the ribs and his left ear had been cut off, he was profusely losing blood.

"Help!" Glick cried to the guards who had witnessed the battle. "Open up!! My buddy's gonna die!!" The sentries promptly opened the gate for Glick, who hauled the lanky

Jimbo over his shoulder. Once inside, he was welcomed briefly by the board of directors, who gathered around grimly taking measure of the injury. Cassandra soon pulled up on an ATV with Pastor Bloom in the passenger seat.

"Hurry, Richard," Bloom said, "get him inside. We'll rush him to the medical unit."

"Hold on, buddy," Glick whispered to his old friend as they took bumps on the gravel path that led to the Quonset hut that functioned as the medical unit. Jimbo looked up at Glick with shell-shocked eyes, he was fading fast. They scrambled inside, and Jimbo was soon on the operating table; the on-staff doctors did the best they could with limited medical equipment and no anesthesia, while an anxious Glick paced outside. He was soon joined by a familiar face, his beloved Toni who came rushing into the waiting area along with Pastor Bloom.

"Toni, baby." Glick put his arm around her waist and nodded to Pastor Bloom. "Preach," he said with somber eyes, "I've never asked this before in my life: Please say a prayer for him. Please."

"Of course, son. We should pray together; when two or more are gathered together in the name of Christ, he is present in that very room." Glick and Toni nodded and held their heads low while Pastor Bloom appealed to God.

"Jesus, we come to you humbly as your servants. We pray in your holy name to preserve the life of our dear friend and companion Jim. Please look upon him with your favor and send your angels of healing to watch over him and protect him in his time of need. Thank you, oh, gracious Lord. Amen."

"He's in God's hands now, Richard." Bloom comforted Glick with a pat on the shoulder. The doctor then came out of the swinging doors, took off his glasses and rubbed his eye.

"Will he be OK, Doc?" Glick asked.

"I think so. He certainly was a bleeder, and we only have frozen and dried plasma here, no real supplies of blood to speak of, so he will be weak for some time. Just a fraction of an inch in either direction, and his liver or his lung could have been punctured; then we would have been in big trouble. Your friend is very lucky."

Toni and Glick looked at each other. *So are we.*

"If he needs some blood," Glick volunteered, "you can count on me." The doctor gave a half-smile in acknowledgment.

"We may have to take you up on that," he answered.

"Well, Richard," Bloom said, "this is your first time inside Hidden Village. What do you think?"

"It's pretty cool. Can I stay?"

Bloom softly laughed. "Maybe. Perhaps we can put in a word for you at the board. Now, how is it that you and Toni came to be so ... close?"

Glick squeezed Toni and pulled her in tight and, with a big loopy grin, declared, "Preach, we want you to marry us. We're in love."

"Oh! This comes as quite a surprise." Bloom raised his eyebrows. "Does anyone else know about this? Toni, you know you have been sorely missed here. We had a full search party out looking for you for over a week at their own peril." Toni looked down at her feet as Bloom continued. "And your students were left without any substitute. No notice, no courtesy on your part. We have been very worried."

"It wasn't my fault," she pleaded. "I went for a walk, and I couldn't get back in. Glick helped me, Pastor; without him I might have been killed. I'm very sorry."

"You'll have to explain yourself before the board if they are to consider Richard's application for entry."

"Entry?"

"I don't suppose we can keep a husband and wife separated, now, can we?" Bloom smiled.

Glick and Toni also smiled wide. "You mean that, Preach? You think I have a chance?"

"Regardless of what they decide, this is a happy announcement and a good day for a wedding. If you two are going to have relations with one another, then you must be married right away. Meet me at the main office in an hour, and we will talk to the board. Maybe the help you gave us today will help sway their decision."

"Sounds great, Preach." The pair and Bloom parted ways, and Toni turned to Glick and gave him a big hug.

"I love you, honey, but I have just one question."

"What's that?"

"Who's Richard?"

The wedding was held the following morning on the Hidden Village grounds with Jimbo, stitched up and lying on a stretcher, as best man and a resentful Dina as bridesmaid fuming in the background. None of the other Cabbage Patch gang members were allowed inside for the ceremony, and the board still had yet to make its decision regarding Glick's entry. They finally made their judgment around 4:00 that afternoon.

A great celebration followed, and the happy pair were made official members of Hidden Village. Glick was honored for the gallant effort he made in fending off the insurgents at the door and given a full tour of the facilities. In return, he cleaned himself up, shaving off his scratchy beard, trimming his fingernails and shampooing his freshly cut hair. Toni hardly recognized the man.

He filled out paperwork for his position as mechanic and made all his other necessary living arrangements. Only Glick was allowed in, however; the rest of the Cabbage Patch gang, including Jimbo, were excluded. This made Glick mournful for his friends, but he vowed that he would take care of them to the best of his abilities, bringing them food and supplies for as long as he could. Everything was perfect except for one small thing: the living quarters situation and Dina. Neither party had anticipated this change of events. The current dwelling arrangement a tad awkward.

Glick gave Toni a slight nudge and nodded in the direction of Dina, who was putting on her dressing gown that evening at bedtime.

"Hey, uh, Dina," Toni voiced gently, "you know tonight's our wedding night. This is kind of like our ... uh, you know, our honeymoon. You know?"

"I hope you don't think I'm going to be sharing a room with the two of you on your precious honeymoon," she snipped in reply. "Where are you going to stay?"

"It's just for a little while, Dina, we'll start putting up a wall tomorrow. Right, honey?"

"Yeah, sure. First thing tomorrow."

"But what about tonight? What do you suggest we do about right now?" Dina whined. *I can't believe I'm living with biker trash.*

"You think you could bunk at Cassandra's or maybe Mrs. Dawson's? It's just for tonight."

"Humph." Dina draped herself in a blanket and stomped out the door without another word. Toni went to go after her, but Glick held her fast.

"She'll be OK, babe. I'll start building a unit that's just for her. It won't take too long."

"Oh that would be great, honey. You can do that?"

"I can do anything, sugar," Glick thumped his chest. "I wish I had a little help from a friend, though. I see how these people here look at me, like they're just barely tolerating me. I could sure use Jimbo right now."

"He could be down for quite a while."

"Looks like I'll be babysitting him for a change. That is if he lets me, he's seriously pissed off at me right now."

"Oh?"

"Yeah, he called me a poser yesterday." He briefly mused, but then changed the subject. "What are we talking about these people for? We have important business to attend to." He lifted Toni off her cot and carried her outside like a baby in his arms; then he turned around and went back inside.

"What are you doing?"

"I'm carrying you across the threshold. Har."

Chapter *40*

Intrigue

Winthrop Shaw prepared for a splendid evening of entertaining the Czar of the Global Union, Devon Rothfeller, at the Château de Themes, Shaw's own magnificent alcázar in Brussels. He had made special preparations for the czar by stocking up and making certain that all of his preferred items were served. The two were seated at Shaw's 30-foot mahogany Palladian table in his regal dining room, the czar feeding sumptuously compared with Shaw, who picked tidily at his plate. Cassoulet de pigeon was far from his favorite. Shaw pushed the food about from one end of his plate to the other while the czar made idle talk in an attempt at friendly discourse. The two retired to the den shortly thereafter for cigars and brandy and to speak of the pending business at hand.

"Winthrop," the czar spoke, "you have been a most valuable asset to the furthering of the Global Union, and after all of your hard work and contributions, I believe it is only fair that I present this to you now." Rothfeller handed Shaw a sealed manila envelope, which Shaw graciously accepted.

"Go ahead," Rothfeller assured him, "you may open it and look inside." Shaw gingerly opened the envelope with shaking hands; inside were several sets of keys and a stack of papers about an inch thick.

"In here, son, are the files that I spoke of last week in Dresden; here you'll find all the combinations, pass codes and access to the accounts ... also a copy of my last will and testament. It's already been recorded with our attorneys in Luxembourg. They have all the transcripts. It's all in the file." Shaw took the papers and gave them a quick review; everything seemed to be in order.

"I'm going into semi-retirement, Winthrop. This is why I'm handing you access to the pass codes now. I am growing tired."

"A well-deserved respite, sir." Shaw poured cognac into two snifters and presented one to the czar.

"It certainly is. I have accomplished a great deal in my lifetime; some things I am very proud of," Rothfeller gazed deeply into the crystal goblet as he twirled its fluid amber contents, "and some other things I'm not necessarily so proud of."

He held the goblet into the air with his pale, thin hand. "Here's to your bright future, Winthrop, and all the promise it holds." The two autocratic rulers drained their snifters, and Shaw promptly stood to pour another.

"Where is my cigar, Winthrop?"

"Oh yes, of course, coming right up. A Ramon or a Cohiba Behike?"

"The Ramon."

"Of course; your favorite."

"I'm meeting with the Earl of Strathmore's widow for tea and crumpets in the morning," Rothfeller spoke, "so I shouldn't make this a late night."

"I thought you regarded the Bowes as dull," Shaw replied as he lit two cigars. He sat in a cushy leather chair, put his feet up on the ottoman and passed the Ramon over to Rothfeller. The czar ignored Shaw's remark.

"My intentions are very clear in the documents, Winthrop; and I expect them to be carried out to the letter. Specifically in regards to the underground bunkers, I want you to see to it that the evidence is destroyed afterward."

"Yes, yes." Shaw's eyes glinted in the dark den. He pulled on his cigar and closely observed the czar's mannerisms. "I have every intention of fulfilling all your wishes." He smiled with a reptilian sly smirk. *You wish.*

"Good, then. As long as we're all on the same page, we'll all be like one happy family."

Ugh.

"And as far as the widow goes," Rothfeller spoke, changing the subject, "I don't recall ever mentioning that I considered the Bowes dull. In fact, I've always held Margaret in rather high esteem." He took a long, deep draw on his cigar. "I remember the first time I ever laid eyes on her. We were scarcely older than 18, just children, really. Even back then I knew she was special." Rothfeller coughed.

You doddering fool. What on earth are you talking about?

"Winthrop, it's getting a little warm in here," the czar choked on his words. "Would you kindly turn the fan on?"

"Certainly." Shaw strolled leisurely to the wall and turned on the ceiling fan.

Suddenly, the czar fell off his chair and wrapped his hands around his neck. "Aaaaagh," he gasped. "Help! Oh, god, no ..." he desperately tugged and pulled at his collar, futilely looking for relief from the burning furnace raging in his closing throat. Shaw merely stood and watched with delight.

"Heeellp meeee ... " the czar wheezed, and Shaw stepped closer.

"Are you wondering why you're feeling so hot under the collar, my dear czar?" Shaw walked around in circles over Rothfeller's writhing body. "Well, let me enlighten you. It's a little tiny poison pellet about 3 millimeters in diameter. It was embedded deep into the Ramon that I gave you, so you wouldn't have felt its effects until about midway through.

"Nonetheless, the pellet contains 140 milligrams of nicotine; that's the equivalent of about 90 cigarettes, by the way, enough to kill two or three healthy teenage boys." Shaw crowed with glee. "Pretty darn clever, if I must say so myself. The pellet is designed to volatize under the heat from a cigarette or, in your particular case, a Ramon cigar. Perhaps you should have chosen the Cohiba after all," Shaw laughed.

"Yes, I had a dickens of a time getting that cigar manufacturer to hand-roll a special cigar just for you." Shaw sat in his cushy chair and rested his chin in his palm as he watched the czar squirming in torment on the floor. "Do you know I had to fly all the way into Cuba to get that job done? Damn hot there. I don't recommend the place at all.

"The beauty of all this," he continued, "is that when they do your autopsy, they are going to find a fairly large amount of nicotine, that is, if they are smart enough to consider looking for it." Rothfeller's chalky white skin began turning a shade of blue.

"...And after examining your lungs, they will come to the conclusion that you must have been a heavy smoker. And that's *all* that they will find, nothing more. They will most likely attribute your death to your ripe old age." Shaw stood glowering over the gasping czar, whose body began to pitch and flutter.

"Are you quite done with this business of dying yet? I have matters to attend to! Hurry up about it already." He walked to the bookshelf and picked up a concealed antique red rotary telephone that was hidden inside. He dialed 202, and his butler answered.

"Aldrich, I need you to call a paramedic. It seems Mr. Rothfeller is having a heart attack."

Chapter *41*

T.J.

The days grew longer, the sunlight turned honeyed golden, and pollen twinkled all around; summer again. Glick and Toni were now finally settled into a tranquil routine, and their ardor grew stronger every day. Glick, unaccustomed to much affection in his hard life, took to his new environment with gusto and an anxious-to-please attitude, but lurking deep within the crevices of his psyche he harbored inner doubt and a fear that all his newfound joy could be taken away from him without a moment's notice. He was on a probationary period and would be for the next eight months, so he knew that he had better not screw this one up. He vowed to be a problem to no one but himself.

He had taken the required aptitude test, and it came up as expected; Glick had a gift for mechanics and logistics and was entered into an apprenticeship program for an academic training on engines, a certification that he had never formally earned. He spent many hours to earn his degree and was even introduced to an education on the conversion of gasoline engines to electric, hydrogen and other fuel cells. He busied himself for countless hours tinkering and converting old vehicles and attempted to expand his knowledge repertoire by studying voltammetry, current cycling and impedance spectroscopy, though most of the scientific studies were far over his head. He built Dina her own prefabricated housing unit and spent his remaining time volunteering to help build private units for those who could not help themselves.

It was during this time that Glick came to know a certain elderly woman. It turned out that she was one of the older people in Hidden Village, but she was still as spry and feisty as anyone he had ever met. Glick felt a spot for her and her little great-grandson in his heart right away; their names were T.J. and Emma Jackson.

Little T.J. was a student of Toni's and was a source of joy to Glick. He would come around his mechanic shop after his studies and hang out for a exactly a half-hour each day before Emma would come and retrieve him. T.J. was smart as a whip and cute as a button. He always had a good story to tell, and if he didn't have an interesting story, he would just make something up. The kid had an incredible imagination. He was also inquisitive and wanted to learn how to tinker with engines the way Glick did.

Emma was wary of the frightening biker and would never leave T.J. alone with him at first, but she soon warmed to him, realizing he wasn't nearly as scary as he looked. Plus, it turned out that Glick was extremely accommodating. He helped her not only get her own tiny house built, but he also helped her with fixes when things broke down, which they inevitably did. In return, Emma showed Toni how to tend to her own garden and taught her some much-needed cooking skills. The two ladies began a friendly rapport that lasted throughout the remainder of their lives.

On one sweltering Wednesday afternoon in August, T.J. came calling on his favorite person, Big Glick.

"Hey Big G, what's happening?" T.J. slapped Glick a high five.

"Not much, small fry." Glick turned back to his wrench and applied torque to a crankshaft.

"You gonna come watch me pitch in the game tomorrow?"

"Sure thing, runt," Glick grunted as the loosened the bolt. He absently glanced at T.J. and thought it a good thing that the boy had taken up baseball as a sport; way too small for football, they'd tromp on him. He thought the boy seemed rather small for an 8-year-old. If he had to guess, he'd say the little guy looked around 6 or maybe even 5. He put his hand to his chin as he gave T.J. a quick once-over. *If that kid wasn't black, I'd swear he's looking pale.*

"How you feeling, squirt?"

"A little tired." T.J. sat down. "Got any water?"

"Yep." Glick handed him a jug, and the boy tried a few sips but then complained that his throat hurt.

"I think you might be coming down with a bug, kiddo. You'd better get home and get a little rest. You got a big day tomorrow, pitching in your first game and all."

"OK, G man," T.J. mumbled. "Don't forget about the game. It starts at 4:30."

"Naw, I wouldn't miss it for nothing. Go on, go get some sleep now." Glick ushered T.J. out the door. He really wasn't in the mood for entertaining kids that afternoon and was grateful for a reprieve from T.J., who sometimes drove him nuts.

The following afternoon, T.J. didn't show up for his usual visit. Glick attributed it to the game and the boy preparing for his big moment, but when he sat in the bleachers at 4:30, he noticed a different boy on the pitcher's mound. T.J. was nowhere in sight. He strolled over and struck up a conversation with the coach.

"Hey Tom, what's up? Why isn't T.J. pitching?"

"He didn't show up today, Glick. His grandma sent word that he's sick."

"Oh yeah, when I saw him yesterday I thought he was looking a little peaked."

"Mmm," Tom nodded but quickly turned his attention elsewhere. "Run!! Run!!" A base hit had the coach distracted, so Glick slipped away unnoticed. No reason to stick around unless his little buddy was in the game.

The next day, T.J. missed his habitual social call as well, and Glick grew concerned. That evening after dinner, he and Toni went to Emma's and knocked on the door, but there was no answer. This also was out of the ordinary. Emma rarely left. As they were walking away, her neighbor Rita stuck her head out the door.

"If you're looking for Emma, she's at the infirmary."

"Oh?" Toni asked. "Why?"

"T.J.'s been running a high fever, they've had him on an IV for the past two days; he was so dehydrated."

"Poor kid." Glick scratched his beard. "We should go see him."

Glick and Toni paid their visit to the clinic and sat in the waiting room until finally being admitted into the area where Emma sat vigilantly at the bedside of her great-grandson. When they saw them, they knew his condition must be serious from the look on Emma's face. Toni approached the haggard-looking matriarch and took her hand.

"What happened, Emma?"

"He done come down sick on Tuesday night, say his throat hurt. He ran a fever so high I couldn't get it down; not with ice or nothin'. He had a seizure right in front of me, and I gots him over here as quick as I could. Ain't nothin' helping, though. Tylenol ain't touching this one. They got him on antibiotics right now but ... " Emma's voice cracked. "I'm scared for him. I ain't never seen a fever this high even in a little one. He was 106 last we looked."

"Oh my Lord, 106!"

"An that's down, he was 107.2 when I brought him in." Emma felt her great-grandson's forehead and stroked his hair. T.J was unresponsive to her touch.

Toni's brow furrowed. "He could get brain damage with a fever that high and for so long."

"Oh yes, I already knows this."

"What can they do for him?" Glick asked.

"They testing now for osteomyelitis 'cause his legs all swelled up. They did a test on meningitis and appendicitis already; come back negative. I don't know what's wrong with him. They don't know, either."

"We have to do something!" Toni exclaimed.

"He's in God's hands now." Emma kissed her baby's cheek while holding a cold compress to his head. Glick and Toni stayed on for several hours. A concerned nurse came in periodically, checked T.J.'s vitals and chatted with Emma. Feeling they could do no more, the anxious couple went home. On the way, they discussed the situation.

"I didn't see the doctor come in once, Glick. Do you think he cares?"

"Yeah, sugar, I'm sure he does, but they're covering a lot of people. The nurse was on it."

"Emma is a retired nurse, too, honey."

"Yeah, she'll tend to him. He'll be OK."

That evening, Glick was awakened by Toni. "What is it?" he grumbled as she turned on the light.

"Honey, wake up. It's T.J. I think he's dying."

"Oh shit. He's worse, huh?"

"He's having convulsions." Her moist eyes were welling with tears. "His fever is higher, too."

He sat up and leaned against the pillow. "C'mere, you." He pulled Toni close. "When did you find out?"

"I couldn't sleep, so I went back to the infirmary. He started convulsing; it totally freaked me out. I heard the doctors talking to Emma; they don't think he'll make it through the night."

"Damnit," he frowned. "I really like that kid." He stood up, got dressed and he and Toni went to talk to Emma further and perhaps even pay their last respects. The prognosis was grim. T.J. had a series of seizures over the evening. The doctors now knew that he had an acute streptococcus bacterial infection that had led to streptococcal toxic shock syndrome, a life-threatening condition. The particular strain appeared to have developed a resistance to penicillin, tetracycline and clindamycin. Toni held Emma's hand and did her best to comfort her.

"He's going to be OK, Emma. They have antibiotics in him. They'll take hold."

"Listen, I'm a nurse and I can tell you without the proper meds, this boy gonna die. We need something this bug ain't immune to; they done used up all they have here. My poor baby got every kind of antibiotic in him already." Toni looked toward her husband, who was in heated discourse with the doctor; he returned with an angry countenance.

"He's asking us to go, sugar. He says we're not immediate family and we shouldn't be in here. He says he doesn't know how we got bedside to begin with."

"We have to go, Emma," Toni squeezed her hand hard, "but we'll be back."

"Yeah, we sure will," Glick spoke, "and if I brought someone to help, would that be OK with you? Do you want to meet him?"

"Eh? What you mean?"

"I know of a doctor that's ... well, he's, uh, uhm."

Toni finished for Glick. "Let's just say he's unconventional; unconventional but highly effective."

"I'd do anything to save my baby. I don't care about no details. Just get your doctor in here to help him."

"I'm not sure he'd be allowed inside, Emma," Glick replied. "You may have to work that from your side, but I promise I'll do my best." He glanced back at the doctor, and he and Toni made a hasty retreat.

"You're going to go see that witch doctor? You really think he can help?"

"He's a medicine man, baby, not a witch doctor, and all I can say is I hope so."

"Do you think you can find him?"

"I'll do my best." And with a kiss goodbye, he was soon back on the leather seat of his beloved hog; off to the Oquirrh Mountain range to search for the holy man Tuketu.

Glick had been gone for over six hours, and his wife Toni was growing concerned. Pastor Bloom was called in to deliver last rites to T.J., who was expected to die at any moment, but the plucky boy hung in there, even if only by a thread.

She hung around the waiting area of the infirmary pacing and worrying. *Seems all I ever do is sit and wait anymore*, she thought to herself when unexpectedly she heard an excited buzzing in the room. Glick had returned, and he had with him a reverent guest, but they were stuck waiting outside the gated walls of Hidden Village.

John Reese accompanied Peter Keller and Eldon Tauer into the waiting area, and Emma and Toni came forth to participate in an agitated dispute about what to do with this native healing person that Glick was trying to get inside.

Pastor Bloom was vehemently opposed to allowing some possibly possessed spellbinder inside their Christian compound. The doctor was coldly aloof, stating that it was pure nonsense and if conventional medicine could not save this boy then nothing could, while Keller and Tauer protested that no one was allowed to be let inside the compound without following the established protocol of a new application, a full review and final approval by the board of directors. Emma and Toni passionately pleaded their case, but it seemed that they were stuck in a deadlock.

The argument ensued for a good 20 minutes when sudden tragedy struck. A nurse burst through and announced that T.J. was coding. The doctor wasted no more valuable time arguing with the two crazy women; he rushed inside and quickly began to administer CPR and used a portable defibrillator in an attempt to bring T.J. back to life. His quick response and efforts were rewarded: T.J.'s heart began beating. The tenacious little boy had cheated death.

A half-hour passed and the doctor came outside into the waiting area. "He's stable for the moment, but he isn't out of the woods yet. We need a miracle."

Toni cried at this news. Just outside the walls there was a miracle man waiting, and these unyielding bastards wouldn't allow him in.

"Please," she begged, "I know Tuketu can help him! He saved Glick's life. I know he can do it again."

"I'm sorry, Toni," Pastor Bloom put his hand on her shoulder. "I'm afraid you really don't understand the nature of shamanism and the means that the medicine men use to get the healing that they desire."

"Oh?" Toni looked at the pastor with imploring eyes.

"Yes Toni, these natives use spirits to help them get what they want. It goes contrary to everything we believe in here at Hidden Village."

"Does it matter as long as the end result is what we ask for?"

"Yes it does matter, very much. These spirits may be willing to help you, but it is not necessarily a good thing. Usually they're demons."

"Demons? Why would a demon help anyone?"

"They will grant you all sorts of favors, my dear girl. You may want to save a life, but is it worth the risk of losing a soul?" Keller and Tauer nodded their heads in agreement. Toni remained silent at this new information.

"Jesus has the authority to heal T.J., and we will all gather together and pray for him right now." Pastor Bloom, Toni, Emma, Reese, Keller and Tauer all held hands and stood in a circle. Together they prayed to Jesus to save little T.J.'s life.

Several hours passed while Glick and Tuketu remained outside the walls of Hidden Village waiting – waiting and wondering. A guard finally opened the gate and addressed Glick, allowing him to come inside, but not Tuketu.

"Wait here, Tuketu." Glick held up a finger. "I'll be right back!" He quickly headed to the infirmary and found the group in the designated waiting area. Toni rushed up to her husband and gave him a hug.

"Honey, it's been brutal," she reported. "T.J. flat-lined, but he's OK for the moment. I think he might make it."

"I'm happy to hear that, doll, but why won't they let Tuketu in? I spent so much time getting him and he came all this way. He sure didn't have to."

"It's a long story, hon. I'll tell you later."

"Can I see the little guy?"

"I think we can sneak a peek," Toni said. The two stuck their heads inside the door. The nurse, upon seeing them, stepped over to confer with them.

"He's doing well," she announced. "His fever is starting to break."

"Really? Oh, that's fantastic." Emma, who was sitting bedside with her baby boy, gave them a big smile and an OK sign.

"Can we come in?"

"Not with Doctor Williams on the loose, not a good idea," the nurse countered. "I'll let you know as soon as possible if he continues doing well."

"Thank you, nurse."

Toni and Glick went back to the waiting room and sat for a moment. "I can't leave Tuketu sitting outside all day, babes. I gotta go get him back to his tribe."

"I understand. I'll be here waiting for you." She kissed him on the cheek and sent him off once again. Glick stepped outside the guarded gates of Hidden Village and called out to Tuketu, but he was nowhere to be found.

"Tuketu!!" he called out. "Tuketu, where are you?" He got on his hog and took off down the long dirt road but saw nothing. The spirit talker had vanished, like a wisp of smoke.

Glick anxiously traced back his route looking for Tuketu all the while, but he did not see him anywhere. It was now very late, and he regretfully made his way in the dark back to the Oquirrh Mountain range, home of the Goshuke tribe, dreading the task ahead of telling the elders that he had lost their holy man. But when he arrived, surprise! Tuketu was already there in front of his teepee with his long feathered pipe in his hand, waiting for Glick's arrival.

"How? How did you get here ahead of me?" Glick asked incredulously.

"Jaguar spirit guided me."

"But how did you get here so fast?"

"I rode on jaguar spirit's back."

"You rode on ...? I don't get it."

"There are some things you will never comprehend, white man," Tuketu smiled. "You shouldn't bother to try."

Days passed, and little T.J. made a slow, steady recovery. Toni and Glick came by to visit as often as they were allowed. Each day, Glick would bring T.J. handcrafted toys that sat untouched on the table next to the boy's bed. Toni would bring cookies and other treats that she had baked herself. These, too, remained untouched. After a week, however, when they made their usual after-work call, the couple was surprised to find T.J. sitting upright in his bed surrounded by the miniature cars, motorcycles and figurines that Glick had welded in his shop.

"Vroom, vroom, crash!" T.J. rammed a toy car into a small carved glider that Glick had whittled from balsa wood. "I got him, G man. That one's 15 points," the boy exclaimed when he saw Glick standing in the doorway.

'You get em, tiger." Glick grinned from ear to ear upon seeing T.J. playing happily after so much time spent in a languid state. "You should be getting out pretty soon now, I'd think." He looked over to Emma, who never once in the entire 16-day period had left T.J.'s side.

"They sayin' another day or two; maybe less. I sure be happy when this is all over."

"You hear that, squirt? Just a couple more days and you can go home.'

"Yay!!"

"He getting his appetite back, too. He's been eating everything in sight."

"I'm hungry right now, Grammy," he proclaimed, and the group laughed.

Smiling, Toni sat on the edge of T.J.'s bed and took his hand. "So, you liked my cookies?" she asked.

"Uh," he suddenly got a confused look on his face and crinkled his nose. "Is *that* what those were?"

Chapter *42*
The New Czar

Winthrop Shaw sat in a high-backed, red leather chair and addressed his cabinet members and generals. He had already instituted many changes since inheriting the role of czar, and even bigger changes were in store. *To think that my silly predecessor wanted to focus solely on underground bunkers. Ha. With my plan, we'll never have to step foot in one of those miserable hellholes and still accomplish all we need.*

He turned to his reliable assistant, Nelson Thurn, and the two held a quiet private conversation. All that the other powerful men in the room could hear, were their hushed whispers. Nelson now had an expanded role in the affairs of the new Global Union to be carried out by Shaw and was now considered to be his right-hand man. First and foremost was an immediate escalation of the long-established timeline that had been instituted by the previous czar. Nelson, true to form, kept his opinions to himself, never questioning the wisdom of the choices made by the chief commander as he stealthily traveled the world delegating Shaw's shocking new orders to the Global Assembly. All of Shaw's plans were now moving forward at lightning speed, and the newly appointed czar could not have been more pleased.

The industrial nations' populations were proceeding as scheduled but there was the untidy matter of some indigenous tribes in Africa, the Amazon, South Asia and Australia left to deal with, but these, too, were being addressed. *Yes, the noose is closing on even those blowtorch-blowing, aborigine, bush-dwelling headhunters.* Shaw laughed inside with glee. Soon there wouldn't be a single person anywhere on the entire planet whose mind was not held 100 percent under his control.

"Gentlemen," he turned to his cabinet, "I have called you here today to give you a briefing on what to anticipate and acquaint you with the newly established conventions in Asia," he spoke as he unrolled a map of China. "The Asia Pacific Economic Cooperation has been slow to react to China's recent insurrection. And since China is already becoming a bit troublesome for us, I am going to nip this situation in the bud before it becomes an embarrassment." He addressed his generals: "See to it that reinforcements are brought in here at Sinuiju, North Korea; also here in the mainland at Hohhot and Taiyuan. These troops will be on put on standby." He turned to his admiral, "An additional armada will flank here at Qingdao.

"We will stage a revolt here in Tianjin. The strategy is to make it appear that these forces are rebels and not WCR squadrons. After five days, we will bring in our private militia and have them swarm Beijing. Now our WCR naval forces will finally have a chance to exercise their new aircraft carriers and stealth submarines. Our anti-ship missiles will render the China navy totally obsolete in a matter of days. The capitol in Beijing will fall shortly thereafter." Shaw put his clasped hands behind his head. "Hu Jintao needs to be reminded that globalization was largely developed and instigated by the Western nations, especially the U.S. and Europe. The benefits, however, have largely accrued to India, East Asia and China. If he thinks just because they were once a world superpower that they can take on the WCR singlehandedly, then he will be shortly obliged to adopt a different viewpoint."

After the meeting was over, Shaw dismissed all in attendance except for Thurn. He sat across the table from his right-hand man, and together they went over a series of graphs, charts and atlases. Shaw circled with a felt-tip marker some key areas of interest to him.

"Thurn," Shaw lit a cigar and leaned back in his chair, "you were given orders to have those inbreds in Brazil and Australia taken care of by June 1st, and I see to this point it has been a miserable failure. What's happening? Why haven't you concluded this simple task by now?"

"It's been NAFTA, sir. Rousef is holding us up in Brazil. They aren't allowing the troops into the Iquitos. The area is under protected rainforest conservation laws. The problem in Australia is ..."

"WHO'S IN CHARGE HERE!!!??" Shaw furiously pounded his fist on the table. "Do I have to take care of this matter myself?!"

Thurn looked at his shoes and mumbled an apology to the czar.

"Very well, Nelson, I'll tell you what," Shaw calmly directed. "I'll deal with Rousef directly; and you will go to his majesty and remind him that the bicameral Parliament of Australia no longer exists. We have a *new* form of government now. Any noncooperation on his part will be regarded as an act of treason and will be dealt with in a most severe fashion. Do you think you can handle this?"

"Yes, absolutely, sir."

"Don't disappoint me, Thurn, or there will be grave consequences."

"Yes, sir."

"I want you to meet me for a follow-up briefing around the 15th of this month. Have Selena check my calendar and let me know where I'm scheduled to be then. I believe I'm to be in London around that date, meet me at my Kensington Square office and we'll go over your report then. And Nelson, I will expect results."

"Yes, sir, you will have them."

The 15th was near. Shaw had spent the last two days in Brazil subjugating its president into obedience. The troops would now be fully allowed to storm through the delicate Iquitos region, set up military bases in preparation of forcefully inoculating its indigenous people with the new required microchip. Shaw flew directly to London from Brazil on his private jet, feeling the satisfaction of another job well done.

No more Mr. Nice Guy, he thought to himself while looking over the most recent white paper sent from his biological weapons lab. *The bygone days of gentle persuasion are over. Just wait until the world sees my next big move.*

When he arrived, he was immediately picked up by chauffeured limousine and driven through the slick streets of London. A light evening's drizzle pattering on the car's windshield soothed his agitated mood until he was delivered to his Kensington Square office. It was after hours, and the staff was gone for the day. His first call would be to Nelson Thurn to receive his report on Australia. He'd make the mandatory administration calls to a few other key operatives and then, finally, home for a nice long bath.

As Shaw entered the dark hallway, he saw a light on in his office quarters. *Strange.* Shaw didn't recall leaving a light on. His biometric door entry systems identified Shaw by his own physiological profile using face recognition, palm print, hand geometry and iris recognition. It would be next to impossible to break into his any of his private chambers. He shrugged it off and sat at his desk. Everything was exactly as he left it when last in London.

He picked up the phone and dialed Nelson Thurn, who was already on standby and waiting for his call.

"Hello, Thurn."

"Hello, sir."

"I have arrived in London. It's been a long flight and I would like to get home as soon as possible. How soon can you be here?"

"I can be there in less than 10 minutes, sir."

"Hurry up." Shaw hung up the phone. *He'd better have good news or else.*

Nelson arrived in 10 minutes flat. He sat across from the czar and presented him with a jump drive. Its contents included a copy of a Memorandum of Understanding that was signed by both his majesty the King of England and Australia's prime minister, witnessed by Thurn; a gentle reminder to the monarchs that they were subject to the conditions set forth by the WCR and the Global Union, including its right to compulsory acquisition, even of the aborigine territories. Shaw quickly scanned the document while rubbing his hands together.

"Excellent," he smiled broadly and ran his tongue over his teeth upon seeing the signatures. Australia would no longer be of concern.

"That's what I like most about you, Thurn, no surprises." Shaw treated Nelson to a rare bit of praise. "Yes, well done. I can assure you that you will be rewarded for this, and for your loyalty."

"Thank you, sir."

"Loyalty is everything to me, Nelson. You will see in the upcoming months how much bounty is in store for those who are most loyal to me, and how I will punish those who are not."

He stood and walked to his bar. "We should celebrate. How about a little taste of this Le Voyage de Delamain cognac, hmm?" He pulled a leather box off the shelf of the glass bar and placed it in front of them on the desk. "This one is over 200 years old." He removed the crystal decanter from its box, pulled the cork and inhaled the rich aroma of coffee with subtle hints of spice. "Get me two snifters from the rack," he said, pointing in the direction of the glasses. Nelson retrieved the snifters and placed them in front of Shaw.

"Oh, and those cigars also, next to the cabinet. No, there on the left. That's it."

Nelson sat and handed Shaw the cigar box.

Shaw pushed the box back across the desk. "Light one for me."

"Yes, sir." Nelson clipped off the end of a Havana, lit it and passed it over to Shaw.

"You may have one as well, Nelson. No need to be shy."

"Thank you, sir," Nelson enthusiastically replied. He clipped an end and enjoyed the fragrant smoke with his superior.

"I'm grooming you for a position of great power, Thurn, probably more powerful than you could ever imagine." Shaw spoke as he poured two shots into the snifters. "If you play your cards right, it is very possible that you could someday even inherit the mantle of czar."

"Czar? Me? I'm quite flabbergasted."

"No need to be, Nelson." Shaw removed his shoes and stretched his arms out like a lion. "You're my top man, and you know the workings of the inner sanctum almost as much as myself. Yes, in 30 or 40 years from now, you may just make a fine czar indeed. Of course, we are both still quite young yet, and with the advances we've made in life extension, it's possible that I may live to be several hundred years old. Undoubtedly, I would say we have a great deal to look forward to. So let's drink a toast, shall we?" Shaw lifted his glass. "Here's to a very, very long life."

"To long life," Nelson smiled and put the snifter to his lips.

"Now, we must discuss something of grave importance," Shaw said as he set his empty glass down. "You recall at our last cabinet session, we had a brief discussion about China and our lead out engagement of mercenaries?"

"Yes."

"There has been a slight change of plans. We are not going to use the guerillas; instead we are going to shock them with the element of surprise ..." Shaw made a slight grimace; his stomach was starting to churn and he suddenly had a strong urge to evacuate. *Must be the Brazilian food.*

"If you'll excuse me a moment," he stood, "I must use the lavatory."

"Certainly, sir."

Shaw took two steps and quickly keeled over, retching profusely. He stabilized himself against an alabaster pillar.

"Whatever is the matter, sir?"

"Sick, oh," Shaw began urinating and defecating at the same time. He vomited blood and bile over his marble floor and then fell over and bashed his head against his trompe l'oeil painted wall. He was dead in less than 10 seconds.

Nelson walked over to the cadaver and gave it a kicking nudge to roll it onto its back. Shaw's vacant, bulging eyes were open wide in shock; the tongue on the inside of his yawning mouth, a curious shade of purple-black.

Nelson smiled at the morbid-looking corpse. He reached inside his coat jacket and retrieved a plastic vial; inside was a nasty-looking spider. He tapped the spider out, setting it loose on Shaw's neck, and poked it with the tip of a Montblanc fountain pen. As expected, the spider stung the already expired ruler's dead body, injecting even more of the same deadly poison than he already had inside his system.

"Good work, Phoneutia," Nelson said calmly as he crushed the spider with the diamond-tipped cap of the pen, leaving its remains in the creases of Shaw's neck. He then sat cross-legged down on the floor next to Shaw and placed his chin in his palm, contemplating his handiwork.

"How are you feeling these days, sir?" He put his hand on Shaw's jaw and forced his mouth open and closed to mimic speech.

"I feel great, thanks! I might live to be 200 or maybe even 300 years old at this rate."

"But what about this ugly bite you have on your neck here?" He fixed his face just inches away from Shaw's corpse.

"Oh, it's nothing," Shaw jawed under Nelsons hand, "just a little inconvenience. I'll be as good as new in no time."

"Really? You're not looking so good."

Tired of the macabre game, Nelson removed his hand from the deposed ruler's face and sneered. "I guess you're not nearly as smart as you thought you were ... sir. You somehow managed to pick up the world's most deadly spider; the Brazilian wandering spider. However did you manage to do that? I wonder. I know how!" He snapped his fingers. "It must have been on your trip to Brazil."

He took his still-full glass of cognac, poured it back into the bottle, washed both snifters clean and hung them back on the rack. "But I *do* wonder how that particular spider's poison got into your favorite brandy."

Nelson Thurn sat in Shaw's chair, put his feet up on the ivory-inlaid desk and nonchalantly finished smoking his cigar. He rooted through the drawers for any items of significance but found nothing notable, certainly nothing more than what he already had. After many long months of constant surveillance, computer hacks and wiretapping, Nelson had everything he needed to take over the czar's position immediately. No one else was as equipped to do the job. No one else had been given access to the systems; no one else had been given such extensive knowledge as to the plans and motivations of Winthrop Shaw, and no one within his inner circle was more trusted than his confidant Nelson Thurn. There would be a quick ushering-in of the new guard, and Nelson Thurn would be at its head. He would lead the New World Order into uncharted territories that even the likes of Winthrop Shaw could never have foreseen.

"You had no idea." He stood ominously over the deceased Shaw.

"Ah … this mortal coil. Do you really think that it's impressive to live to 300? How about living tens of thousands of years? What if I, Nelson Thurn, were to *never* die!?

"You could have had this, too, but you were too damn stubborn and stupid to see the potential just sitting right there at your fingertips. We can make ourselves immune to almost any human disease. And poison? Ha!" Thurn picked up the bottle of cognac and danced in a circle around Shaw's body. "What is poison when you have the strength of hundreds of men?" Nelson placed the bottle back on the desk and sat on Shaw's shins, facing his deceased predecessor.

"What if we weren't fully human, hmmm? I'm not. I've already altered my own DNA, giving myself superhuman abilities. I specially handpicked the characteristics I desired from different species; I do believe I'm already feeling the effects.

"And my dear Mr. Shaw ... you should see the wonderful creations we're working on in *my* laboratories: centaurs, minotaurs, mermaids, a hydra, why we've even created a pegasus; well, almost. Usually they die at birth, but we're close. Very, very close. Soon I'll have an entire stable filled with my unique, not quite human, pets. How do you like that?

"And I have plans to use this. Oh, yes, I most certainly do intend to use it. Not just on myself either, oh no. The next generation to receive their chip will have some very *special* attributes given to them. I do believe that these useless eaters already resemble cattle or perhaps sheep. Docility, I think, suits them quite well.

"How perfectly appropriate ... how perfectly ... beastly." The devils inside Thurn stirred.

"And now, I must say my adieu." Thurn picked up Shaw's cold, stiff hand and kissed it. "Fare thee well, oh beloved shitbag. I won't be missing you one bit."

And with that, Nelson Thurn made his exit, taking the tainted bottle of cognac with him on his way out.

Chapter *43*

It's All So Perfect

Tim Conner stood in the long line at the auto-parts store when he heard a voice behind him.

"Tim? Tim Conner? Hey buddy, how have you been?"

Tim slowly turned to see his old city co-worker Farney standing directly behind him holding a used CV axle.

"Oh hey, Farney, good to see you."

"Yeah same here. What are you doing for work these days? I heard you quit the city, but then we never heard back from you again."

"I tried my own business for a while, but it failed. I took another city job in Rockville."

"Wow, that's a long drive. Do you like it there?"

"Same ol'. I quit Fairfax just short of qualifying for my pension and had to start a whole new one, unfortunately."

"That's a real shame. Hey, you're lucky you got one at all. There's not too many pensions out there anymore."

"Yep just 30 more years to go. What will that make me what, 75 years old? I can't wait."

"Holy moley."

"Yeah, that's what the wife says, too."

"I heard your wife made you quit Fairfax because she didn't want you to have a microchip."

"That's right."

"How did that turn out?"

"We couldn't make it. It was impossible to live without one."

"So you have one now."

"Uh-huh. The whole family does. I never could figure out what her problem was with it anyway. It's perfectly fine as far as I'm concerned."

"Yeah, women." Farley shook his head. "So how is she doing? Good?"

"Oh she's just fine."

"And the kids?"

"Mmmm, yes, fine."

Tim answered the questions politely with a flat smile. He wasn't really all that interested in the conversation, nor was he paying much attention to what Farney was saying. He was far more focused on the pleasurable sensations that were coursing through his body. The feelings vaguely reminded him of something, but he couldn't quite remember what.

It was difficult to remember much of anything these past few months. The pleasant hum in his head drowned out much of those old bad memories and feelings, leaving behind the sweetest lull that he could get lost in forever.

He gazed vacuously at Farney while watching his mouth move, his droning words filling the empty air around them.

Tim thought to himself, *life is finally perfect.*

References

1. Boettke, Peter J.; Peter T. Leeson (2003). "The Austrian School of Economics 1950-200". Warren Samuels, Jeff E. Biddle, and Tim B. Davis. *A Companion to the History of Economic Thought*. Blackwell Publishing. pp. 446–452. (qtd. Ludwig von Mises Institute)

2. Woods, Jr., Thomas (2007). "22: Did Capitalism Cause the Great Depression?". *33 Questions about American History You're Not Supposed to Ask*. New York: Crown Forum. pp. 174–179. (qtd. Ludwig von Mises Institute)

3. (qtd. Friedman, Milton. "The Monetary Studies of the National Bureau, 44th Annual Report". *The Optimal Quantity of Money and Other Essays*. Chicago: Aldine. pp. 261–284.

4. Friedman, Milton. "The 'Plucking Model' of Business Fluctuations Revisited". *Economic Inquiry*. 171–177.

5. Krugman, Paul (1998-12-04). "The Hangover Theory". Slate. http://www.slate.com/id/9593. Retrieved on 2008-06-20. (qtd. Ludwig von Mises Institute)

6. Laider D. (1999). *Fabricating the Keynesian Revolution*. Cambridge University Press. (qtd. in Rothbard, Murray "The Case Against the Fed")

7. Rothbard, Murray America's Great Depression

8. Ludwig von Mises, Part III, Part IV Theory of Money and Credit,

9. Rothbard, Murray The Mystery of Banking, 1983

10. Ludwig von Mises, Theory of Money and Credit, , Part II

11. Ludwig von Mises, Human Action, p.572

12. Thorsten Polleit, Manipulating the Interest Rate: a Recipe for Disaster, 13 December 2007 (qtd. Ludwig von Mises Institute)

13. Skousen, Mark (2001). *The Making of Modern Economics*. M.E. Sharpe. p. 284. (qtd. Ludwig von Mises Institute)

14. White, William (April 2006) (PDF). *Is price stability enough?*. Bank for International Settlements.

http://www.bis.org/publ/work205.pdf (qtd. Ludwig von Mises Institute)

15. Laidler, D. *The price level, relative prices and economic stability: aspects of the interwar debate*, p. 11. *Bank of International Settlements* discussion paper. (qtd. Ludwig von Mises Institute)

16. Eckstein, Otto; Allen Sinai (1990). "1. The Mechanisms of the Business Cycle in the Postwar Period". in Robert J. Gordon. *The American Business Cycle: Continuity and Change*. University of Chicago Press. (qtd. Ludwig von Mises Institute)

17. Walsh, Carl E. (May 14, 1999). "Changes in the Business Cycle". *FRBSF Economic Letter*. Federal Reserve Bank of San Francisco (qtd. Ludwig von Mises Institute)

18. Federal Reserve Bank of New York "How the Fed is Audited" newyorkfed.org/aboutthefed/fedpoint/fed35.html

19. Sanders, Bernie U.S. Senator for Vermont July 21, 2011 "The Fed Audit" sanders.senate.gov/newsroom/news/?id=9e2a4ea8-6e73-4be2-a753-62060dcbb3c3

20. Congressman Paul, Ron "Audit the Federal Reserve" ronpaul.com/on-the-issues/audit-the-federal-reserve-fed-hr-459-s202/

21. Rothbard, Murray "The Case Against the Fed" 1994 pgs. 21, 145

22. Carmack, Patrick SJ Producer of "The Money Masters"

23. Smith, Brandon WHAT'S NEXT: Doing The Global Currency Shuffle- 21st Century Wire.com

24. Ross, Gaylon Robert Sr. "Who's Who of the Elite"

25. Elliot, TS "The Hollow Men"

26. The Money Masters: How International Bankers Gained Control of America - commentary by Peter Myers, June 7, 2003; update March 17, 2010 www.mailstar.net

27. Engdahl, F.W. (2007). Seeds of Destruction (qtd. Ludwig von Mises Institute)

28. Institute for Responsible Technology
www.responsibletechnology.org

29. Rogers, Sherry Dr. May 2001 issue of TOTAL WELLNESS, The World's Most Vicious MACC Attack

30. Smith, Jeffery Doctors Warn: Avoid Genetically Modified Foods- May 30. 2009 newswithviews.com

31. Codex Alimentarius (World Food Code) Summarized in 7 Points healthfreedomusa.org

32. Study of GMO fed rats
http://www.biolsci.org/v05p0706.htm#headingA11-

33. Griffen, Andy Corn and Isolation Published September 28, 2009

34. Godoy, Julio Privatization Making Seeds Themselves Infertile ipsnews.net

35. Forbidden Gates: Tom and Nita Horn, Defender Press

36. Meet the Nano Spiders, Source: www.dailymail.co.uk

37. Scalar Field Theory retrieved from
http://en.wikipedia.org/wiki/Scalar_feild_therory

38. Begich, Nick Dr. M.D. Angels Don't Play this HAARP: Advances In Tesla Technology U. S. Government's Ground-Based "Star Wars" Weapon: Frequency Active Auroral Research Program

39. Smith, Brendan Article "6 Steps by the IMF for a One-World Currency." www.alt-market.com

40. Morgan, Bill Article "Scalar Energy - A Completely New World Is Possible"

41. Morgan, Bill "Scalar Wars -The Brave New World of Scalar Electromagnetics"
http://prahlad.org/pub/bearden/scalar_wars.htm

42. Miller, Iona Article
http://virtualphysics.50megs.com/about_1.html

Recommended Reading:

1. Dr. Joel Lubar http://www.eegfeedback.org/joelbio.html

2. The weeds of destruction". The Economist.
http://www.economist.com/finance/displaystory.cfm?story_i
d=E1_GRSRVJS.

3. Stagman, M. Phd. (2006). GMO Disease Epidemics: Bt-cotton
Fiber Disease.

4. Articles Link Between Morgellon's Disease and GMOs
Retrieved from portland.indymedia.org
http://www.globalresearch.ca/index.php?context=va&aid=8
464

5. GMO and Morgellons Articles by Barbara H. Peterson

6. Millions Against Monsanto organicconsumers.org

7. American Academy of Environmental Medicine (AAEM)

8. Ermakova, Irina "Genetically modified soy leads to the
decrease of weight and high mortality of rat pups of the first
generation. Preliminary studies," *Ecosinform* 1 (2006)

9. Ermakova, Irena "Experimental Evidence of GMO Hazards,"
Presentation at Scientists for a GM Free Europe, EU Parliament,
Brussels, June 12, 2007

10. L. Vecchio et al, "Ultrastructural Analysis of Testes from Mice
Fed on Genetically Modified Soybean," *European Journal of
Histochemistry* 48, no. 4 (Oct–Dec 2004)

11. Oliveri et al., "Temporary Depression of Transcription in
Mouse Pre-implantion Embryos from Mice Fed on Genetically
Modified Soybean," *48th Symposium of the Society for
Histochemistry, Lake Maggiore (Italy), September 7–10, 2006*

12. Alberta Velimirov and Claudia Binter, "Biological effects of
transgenic maize NK603xMON810 fed in long term
reproduction studies in mice" Forschungsberichte der Sektion
IV, Band 3/2008

13. A. Dutton, H. Klein, J. Romeis, and F. Bigler, "Uptake of Bt-toxin
by herbivores feeding on transgenic maize and consequences
for the predator *Chrysoperia carnea*," *Ecological Entomology*
27 (2002): 441–7; and J. Romeis, A. Dutton, and F. Bigler,
"*Bacillus thuringiensis* toxin (Cry1Ab) has no direct effect on
larvae of the green lacewing *Chrysoperla carnea* (Stephens)

(Neuroptera: Chrysopidae)," *Journal of Insect Physiology* 50, no. 2-3 (2004): 175-183

14. Washington State Department of Health, "Report of health surveillance activities: Asian gypsy moth control program," (Olympia, WA: Washington State Dept. of Health, 1993).

15. M. Green, et al., "Public health implications of the microbial pesticide *Bacillus thuringiensis*: An epidemiological study, Oregon, 1985-86," *Amer. J. Public Health* 80, no. 7 (1990)

16. Ashish Gupta et. al., "Impact of Bt Cotton on Farmers' Health (in Barwani and Dhar District of Madhya Pradesh)," *Investigation Report*, Oct-Dec 2005.

17. Burns, Tim M. "13-Week Dietary Subchronic Comparison Study with MON 863 Corn in Rats Preceded by a 1-Week Baseline Food Consumption Determination with PMI Certified Rodent Diet #5002," December 17, 2002 http://www.monsanto.com/monsanto/content/sci_tech/prod_safety/fullratstudy.pdf

18. Finamore, Alberto et al, "Intestinal and Peripheral Immune Response to MON810 Maize Ingestion in Weaning and Old Mice," *J. Agric. Food Chem.*, 2008, 56 (23), pp 11533-11539, November 14, 2008

19. See L Zolla, et al, "Proteomics as a complementary tool for identifying unintended side effects occurring in transgenic maize seeds as a result of genetic modifications," J Proteome Res. 2008 May;7(5):1850-61; Hye-Yung Yum, Soo-Young Lee, Kyung-Eun Lee, Myung-Hyun Sohn, Kyu-Earn Kim, "Genetically Modified and Wild Soybeans: An immunologic comparison," *Allergy and Asthma Proceedings* 26, no. 3 (May–June 2005): 210-216(7); and Gendel, "The use of amino acid sequence alignments to assess potential allergenicity of proteins used in genetically modified foods," *Advances in Food and Nutrition Research* 42 (1998)

20. Pusztai and S. Bardocz, "GMO in animal nutrition: potential benefits and risks," Chapter 17, *Biology of Nutrition in Growing Animals*, R. Mosenthin, J. Zentek and T. Zebrowska (Eds.) Elsevier, October 2005

21. Hye-Yung Yum, Soo-Young Lee, Kyung-Eun Lee, Myung-Hyun Sohn, Kyu-Earn Kim, "Genetically Modified and Wild Soybeans: An immunologic comparison," *Allergy and Asthma Proceedings* 26, no. 3 (May–June 2005): 210-216(7).

22. "Mortality in Sheep Flocks after Grazing on *Bt* Cotton Fields— Warangal District, Andhra Pradesh" *Report of the Preliminary Assessment,* April 2006, http://www.gmwatch.org/archive2.asp

23. Jeffrey M. Smith, *Genetic Roulette: The Documented Health Risks of Genetically Engineered Foods,* Yes! Books, Fairfield, IA USA 2007

24. Arpad Pusztai, "Can Science Give Us the Tools for Recognizing Possible Health Risks for GM Food?" *Nutrition and Health* 16 (2002): 73–84.

25. Stéphane Foucart, "Controversy Surrounds a GMO," *Le Monde,* 14 December 2004; referencing, Tim M. Burns, "13-Week Dietary Subchronic Comparison Study with MON Corn in Rats Preceded by a 1-Week Baseline Food Consumption Determination with PMI Certified Rodent Diet #5002," December 17, 2002 http://www.monsanto.com/monsanto/content/sci_tech /prod_safety/fullratstudy.pdf

26. Netherwood et al, "Assessing the survival of transgenic plant DNA in the human gastrointestinal tract," *Nature Biotechnology* 22 (2004)

27. Domingo, Jose "Toxicity Studies of Genetically Modified Plants : A Review of the Published Literature," Critical reviews in food science and nutrition, 2007, vol. 47, n°8, pp. 721-733

28. Hall, Angela "Suzuki warns against hastily accepting GMOs", The Leader-Post (Canada), 26 April 2005.

29. Anne Paez, Kathryn et al, "Rising Out-Of-Pocket Spending For Chronic Conditions: A Ten-Year Trend," *Health Affairs,* 28, no. 1 (2009): 15-25

30. Minton, Barbara Sunday, April 13, 2008 citizen journalist

31. World Health Organization. 2002 Foods derived from modern technology: 20 questions on genetically modified foods. Available from: http://www.who.int/foodsafety/publications/biotech/20ques tions/en/index.html

32. Smith, JM. Genetic Roulette. Fairfield: Yes Books.2007. p.10

33. Freese W, Schubert D. Safety testing and regulation of genetically engineered foods. Biotechnology and Genetic Engineering Reviews. Nov 2004. 21.

34. Society of Toxicology. The safety of genetically modified foods produced through biotechnology. Toxicol. Sci. 2003; 71:2-8

35. Hill, AB. The environment and disease: association or causation? Proceeding of the Royal Society of Medicine 1965; 58:295-300.

36. Finamore A, Roselli M, Britti S, et al. Intestinal and peripheral immune response to MON 810 maize ingestion in weaning and old mice. J Agric. Food Chem. 2008; 56(23):11533-11539.

37. Malatesta M, Boraldi F, Annovi G, et al. A long-term study on female mice fed on a genetically modified soybean:effects on liver ageing. Histochem Cell Biol. 2

38. Velimirov A, Binter C, Zentek J. Biological effects of transgenic maize NK603xMON810 fed in long term reproduction studies in mice. Report-Federal Ministry of Health, Family and Youth. 2008.

39. Ewen S, Pustzai A. Effects of diets containing genetically modified potatoes expressing Galanthus nivalis lectin on rat small intestine.Lancet. 354:1353-1354

40. Kilic A, Aday M. A three generational study with genetically modified Bt corn in rats: biochemical and histopathological investigation. Food Chem. Toxicol. 2008; 46(3):1164-1170.

41. Kroghsbo S, Madsen C, Poulsen M, et al. Immunotoxicological studies of genetically modified rice expression PHA-E lectin or Bt toxin in Wistar rats. Toxicology. 2008

42. Gurain-Sherman,D. 2009. Failure to yield: evaluating the performance of genetically engineered crops. Cambridge (MA): Union of Concerned Scientists.

43. Lofstedt R. The precautionary principle: risk, regulation and politics. Merton College, Oxford. 2002.

44. GMO Disease Epidemics: Bt-cotton Fiber Disease", Myron Stagman, Ph.D.

45. www.GeneticRoulettemovie.com

46. William Engdahl engdahl.oilgeopolitics.net

47. Health Scandal - Monsanto's GMO Perversion of Food http://www.newswithviews.com/Richards/byron189.htm

48. What About Grass Fed Beef ? foodrevolution.org April 18 2002 Implantable RFID chips Human Branding antichips.com

49. Smith, James RFID Clothing Tags Would not be Private Labels
    Article on the future use of RFID tags on retail items including
    clothing. Published: 3/21/2008

50. Garreau, Joel Radical Evolution 2005
    Prof. Fukuyama, Francis "Our Posthuman Future:
    Consequences of the biotechnology Revolution" 2002

51. pesn.com

52. http://www.takepart.com/foodinc/film

53. Russo, Enzo and Cove, David Genetic Engineering: Dreams and
    Nightmares 1995

54. cheniere.org Tom Bearden website

55. DARPA article wired.com/dangerroom/2010/02/pentagon-
    looks-to-breed-immortal-synthetic-organisms-molecular-kill-
    switch-included/

56. darpa.mil

57. Van Kranenburg, Rob Article: The Sensing Planet -Why The
    Internet Of Things Is The Biggest Next Big Thing

58. Report: http://www.smart-systems-
    integration.org/public/internet-of-things

59. autoidlabs.org

About the Author

Chey Barnes' expertise is in the Telecom and Streaming Media Communications Industries, where she wrote several technical white papers. She is Cisco certified and held N.A.S.D. Series 7 & 13 Licenses. Chey has lived in South Florida the majority of her life; she is an accomplished artist, gardener and chef. Her hobbies include boating and sports. She is the mother of two girls.

Chey volunteers her time at Feeding America and Feeding South Florida food distribution centers. She is an active member at South Palm Church, where she is a participant in the Video Production Team, Baptism Team and Good Samaritan Growth Group. Follow at www.cheybarnes.com

www.ingramcontent.com/pod-product-compliance
Lightning Source LLC
Chambersburg PA
CBHW071340020726
47502CB00001B/182